Praise for
THE BODY ON THE FLOOR OF THE ROTUNDA

"There is a 'Montana Way' in everything Jim Moore does. This book is an example of his dedication to a good story under the Big Sky. The novel is written well and deserves to be read by everyone who loves our great state." —***Neil J. Lynch*, Former Majority Leader, Montana State Senate**

"Jim Moore's The Body On The Floor Of The Rotunda is Montana storytelling at its best. The scenes of the legislature in session are so real they could only have been written by someone who lived them. I could hear the click of heels on marble floors and feel a crackle in the air.

"The plotting is brisk, and the characters are deftly drawn. Aficionados of courtroom drama will especially appreciate Moore's tense portrayal of a criminal trial. The courtroom dialogue is razor sharp and whip smart. As often happens in a close case, the fortunes of the defendant rise and fall with each witness. Moore's trial scenes are the real deal, and he captures the stress and excitement of trial as few writers can.

"Don't pick up this book expecting to go to bed early."
—*Judge William Russell McElyea*

"In this fast-moving murder mystery charged with political intrigue, Jim Moore draws on his background as a Bozeman attorney and Montana State Senate Minority Leader. Set against the backdrop of the capitol building in Helena, Moore's story gives insight into state politics and the maneuvering of politicians—with deception occurring at the highest levels. Love and lust drive the action that ends with a dramatic courtroom scene. This novel captivates right to the end.
—*Kathleen Mohn*, **Founder of Speak and Write, a corporate training firm**

Praise for THE BODY ON THE FLOOR OF THE ROTUNDA, continued

"Anyone who likes a good 'who done it' will love the latest from Jim Moore. I thought I had it figured out and had several great surprises at the end. The intertwining of the legislative process, cross party politics, unscrupulous politicians, a murder and a senator/attorney/rancher who helps the damsel in distress makes for a great story. All that with a twist of Montana passion! You couldn't ask for more in an intriguing weekend read." —*Cindy Younkin,* **Attorney and former Majority Whip, Montana House of Representatives**

Praise for Jim Moore's Ride the Jawbone:

"When you read Jim Moore's *Ride the Jawbone*, you have to constantly remind yourself that it's fiction and you haven't slipped into Montana in 1902—One heck of a read."
—Craig Johnson, author of *The Cold Dish* and the *Longmire* series.

"Mystery! Romance! A look back at some early Montana times! And the good news is that author Moore promises more to come about the Bruce family." —Sue Hart, Professor, MSU, Billings

"Lovers of Montana history and a good yarn will find much to enjoy in the debut of Jim Moore, who puts his love of his state and his legal background to good use in introducing T.C. Bruce and the Bruce family to readers. A rippling read." —Craig Lancaster, author of **600 Hours of Edward** and *The Summer Son*

A woman's murder in turn-of-the-century rural Montana; a crazy suspect; a newly-minted lawyer's first case. These are the elements of a drama remarkable for its authenticity. Mr. Moore's attention to telling detail and historical accuracy effortlessly carry the reader into that long-gone world." —Richard S. Wheeler, winner of the **Golden Spur Award** and author of more than fifty novels.

"Brilliantly using his vast knowledge of law and Montana history, master storyteller Jim Moore plunges the reader into a world of mystery and moral dilemma. Realistic, intriguing, captivating." — Lauri Olsen, author, **Cold Moon Honor** and **Whispers on the Wind**

"The Jawbone railroad binds a community of small towns and ranches populated by quirky people, while a young man is torn between following his father's footsteps into ranching and starting his law practice, his mother's dream. A novel of memorable characters, among them the Jawbone railroad, in an odd corner of Montana history." — Carol Buchanan, author of **God's Lightning Bolt** & **Gold Under Ice**

"Rich in detail, Jim Moore's novel enlightens readers about the day-to-day labors, cowhands, horses and equipment involved in ranching in 1902 and the habits and mores of people struggling to exist in the small towns strewn along the rails of the Jawbone. Interspersed in this history are a fascinating murder trial and the young untried attorney who defends a seemingly indefensible accused. We root for this young protagonist and smile a little at how easily he is distracted by attractive young ladies." —Joan Bochmann, author of *Absaroka, From War to Wyoming*

Praise for Jim Moore's Election Day:

Jim Moore is a retired lawyer, a former Montana State Senate Minority Leader, a former director of the Montana Stockgrowers Association, and a Trustee of the Museum of the Rockies. He is not unlike his protagonist in this new novel, Bobby Hobaugh, and despite that or because of it *Election Day* is an excellent story.

The book is timely in that we are on the verge of another nasty general election for our next president. Mr. Moore looks inside the dark machinations of the candidates who will do anything to win with the buying and selling of votes that taint our political landscape. We all recognize the open arrogance and greed that transpires in Washington, as it does in this book, and the elections go on and the laws are made to the benefit of the highest bidder.

But Moore also taps into a sense of government service for the greater good through the emergence of Bobby Hobaugh — a throwback to an ideal of an older time. His plainspoken, common sense demeanor is a stark contrast to the other two purely political animals at the center of this mystery novel.

Yes, mystery novel. It is a political thriller based on the premise that three days before the election the challenging vice-presidential candidate is accidentally killed by a truck crash in Billings. Hobaugh is called upon by circumstance to fill the gap temporarily, to finish the scheduled appearances of the deceased. His presidential candidate wins, then promptly dies of exhaustion from the trying campaign. Now what? The president-elect is dead without a vice president elect. How does the U.S. Constitution address this eventuality?

I have not given away too much here, as this is just the beginning premise of the book. The real ride and surprises come toward the end when Moore's story gains speed and runs towards yet another election day with its astounding victory of common sense, only to be rammed into political chaos again by the dark side of power. Moore has given us a very entertaining novel. Probing the arcane procedures that our Constitution has established to keep government viable, and giving us an old-time, trustworthy public servant in Bobby Hobaugh who "may be a nobody to you, but he's somebody in Montana." —Montana Quarterly, Summer, 2012

Jim Moore's **Election Day** is not only a clever civics lesson, but also a high-stakes thriller in which an unlikely band of political operatives struggles to keep the presidency out of the hands of a madman. —Ben O'Connell, Montana native and Washington, DC, political journalist

The unimaginable becomes inevitable in this riveting thriller by Montana cowboy legislator and lawyer Jim Moore, who takes the reader on a thrill-ride of unexpected and sometimes blood-chilling "what if" situations, arriving at a fantastic conclusion actually possible within the legalistic intricacies of the American election and Presidential succession process. —Bob Brown, former Montana Senator and Secretary of State.

Jim Moore knows the law, and he knows politics, and he's brought both to bear in this crackerjack of a read. —Craig Lancaster, author of **600 Hours of Edward** and **The Summer Son**

Political suspense, constitutional crises, murder, mayhem and romance -- Jim Moore's book has it all. The bonus is that the whole crazy plot revolves around a decent, no-nonsense Montana cowboy. —Ed Kemmick, Reporter and columnist for the Billings Gazette and author of **The Big Sky, By and By**

ELECTION DAY is an entertaining story told by a gifted story teller—also an exceptional gentleman, lawyer, rancher, and Montana senator who could have found himself in the shoes of Bobby Hobaugh. It is a "must read" for political wonks wondering when the flaws of our presidential election system are going to catch up with us, students trying to stretch their minds about the oddness and origins of the electoral college, and anyone who enjoys a good mystery entwining interesting characters, politics turned on its head, and a surprise ending – all in a way that could honestly happen in real life. —Dorothy Bradley, former Montana legislator

As a former Chief of Staff for a U.S. Senator during the tumultuous 2000 Presidential Election that the U.S. Supreme Court ultimately resolved in Bush v. Gore, I did not believe the circumstances of an election could provide more drama or interest. But then I read **Election Day**. What a story! Jim Moore spins a fascinating tale based on facts that could actually happen and would make any other election contest seem like a bore. — Will Brooke, attorney

Jim Moore, in his recent writing of ELECTION DAY, has provided the public with an important lesson in provisions of the United States Constitution governing succession to the office of President of the United States in certain circumstances.

In addition to an important lesson about the United States Constitution, the book, from the first to the last chapter, holds the reader's attention to the story of political intrigue, evil political maneuvering, and murder.

Author Jim Moore's ability to create such a literary work can be understood when the depth of his real life experience as a successful Montana rancher, member of and leader in the Montana State Senate, member of the State Bar of Montana, practicing lawyer, and most recently an author of obvious ability and skill. —J.A. Turnage, Former Chief Justice, Montana Supreme Court (retired)

The Body on the Floor of the Rotunda

Jim Moore

Raven Publishing, Inc.
Norris, MT

The Body on the Floor of the Rotunda

Copyright © 2013 Jim Moore

Cover design by Craig Lancaster

ISBN: 976-1-987849-14-6

Published by
Raven Publishing, Inc
PO Box 2866
Norris, MT 59745
Info@ravenpublishing.net   www.ravenpublishing.net

All rights reserved. Except for inclusion of brief quotations in a review, no part of this book may be reproduced or transmitted in any form or by any means, electronic or mechanical, including photocopying, recording, or any information storage and retrieval system, without permission in writing from the publisher.

This novel is a work of fiction. Names, characters, places, and events are the product of the author's imagination or are used fictitiously. Any similarity to any person, place, or event is coincidental.

Library of Congress Cataloging-in-Publication Data

Moore, Jim, 1927-
  The body on the floor of the rotunda / Jim Moore.
    pages cm
  ISBN 978-1-937849-14-6 (pbk. edition : alk. paper) --
ISBN 978-1-937849-15-3 (hardcover edition : alk. paper)
-- ISBN 978-1-937849-16-0 (electronic edition)
  1. Legislators--Montana--Fiction. 2. Murder--Investigation--Fiction. 3. Political fiction. I. Title.
  PS3613.O5626B84 2013
  813'.6--dc23
                              2013015346

Dedicated

to Kay

with thanks for tolerating my legislative activities

and

to the fond memory of my dear friend, Judge Joe Gary, who read every manuscript I wrote and declared this book to be the best.

1

She froze as she saw a body falling from the fourth floor balcony of the rotunda. Instinct pulled her back into the darkness of the west gallery. The sickening sound of the body's impact on the unyielding tile floor echoed through the vast expanse of the capitol building. The witness wrapped her arms around her chest to control the trembling, then peered carefully out into the dismal gloom of the rotunda. A single shaft of light shone on the crumpled figure of a woman—on a thigh so white as to be nearly translucent.

Letting out a stifled sob, she ran toward the governor's suite.

2

In the dreary hotel room that he called home during Montana's ninety-day biennial legislative session, tall and lean Lynn Bruce stood at the bathroom mirror running an electric shaver over his face. With his thoughts focused on legislative matters, the announcement on the radio did not register for a moment. The senator from Musselshell County pulled the plug on the razor and stepped out of the bathroom as the newscaster said, "To repeat our top story, a woman's dead body was found early this morning on the floor of the rotunda of the capitol building. We have received an unconfirmed report that the body is that of Gloria Angel, chief aide to Governor Albert Shewey. We will interrupt our regular broadcast to bring you more information as it becomes available."

The senator stood immobile, his shaver still in hand. A picture of Gloria Angel as he had last seen her at one of Helena's innumerable social functions filled his mind. She had been standing among a group of admiring men, each one vying for her attention. Most were old enough to be her father, if not her grandfather. With one hip slung slightly to the side, she easily balanced a plate in one hand and a wine glass in the other. Everyone laughed as she delivered the punch line of some story about the president of the United States. Her dark eyes shone as she smiled. Her long, shining hair of deepest brown framed a comely face. Her petite, curvaceous body added to her charm.

She moved with confidence and grace. Standing alone at the side of the room, Senator Bruce had chuckled at the disappointed faces when the governor had led her away.

"God!" He muttered. "I hope they're wrong and it isn't Gloria."

The senator finished his morning ablutions and dragged a dark brown sport jacket with leather elbow patches from its hanger. He shrugged into the jacket, turned for a last glance in the mirror, and straightened his tan and yellow tie. Finally, he pulled on a heavy topcoat, buttoned it to his chin, and stepped out into the bitter winter air. With the collar pulled up against an icy gale, he tramped across the parking lot to the restaurant, dodging bits of wind-driven debris.

The waitress served the scrambled eggs, bacon, and toast that constituted his daily breakfast. She muttered, "Did you hear? They have someone dead at the capitol." The senator nodded and gave her his usual warm smile. As he gathered the utensils to attack the repast, sounds made by others in the room crowded into his consciousness. It was a place where legislators, lobbyists, and other hangers-on gathered to eat and exchange the latest capitol rumors. The murmurings of those close at hand carried excited speculation about the cause of the woman's death and gossip that one would only hear in a community mired in politics. Senator Bruce hurried to finish his meal. She may have had faults but Gloria Angel deserved better than the scandalous gibberish he was hearing.

Repeated reports about the woman found on the rotunda floor, interspersed with commercials, blared from the radio of Senator Bruce's Ford Expedition as he drove through a light, wind-driven snowfall toward the capitol. None of the reports elaborated on the information provided in the first report he'd heard.

14   Jim Moore

After pulling into his reserved parking spot, the senator strode through the blowing snow toward the south entrance to the Montana capitol. He found a youthful policeman standing at ease just inside the double doors. The officer, sober-faced, said, "Sorry, sir, the rotunda's closed to everybody but law enforcement personnel. You can't use the grand staircase to get to the third floor." Then he pointed to the elevator.

Bruce stopped at the band of yellow tape that blocked the way out onto the floor of the rotunda. City policemen and sheriff's deputies milled about. Yellow tape outlined the form of a body on the tile floor. The senator turned to the elevator and made the short trip to the third floor where the chambers of the Senate and House of Representatives were located. More yellow tape ran from pillar to pillar around and behind the Centennial Bell that overlooked the rotunda floor.

A policeman discouraged anyone from ducking under the tape. He acknowledged the legislator with a curt nod, "Good morning, Senator Bruce."

The senator smiled and responded, "Good morning, officer," and moved toward the doors to the old Supreme Court chamber.

He was surprised to notice Audrey Welter, the diminutive, attractive, and always-gracious senator from Missoula, leaning over the balcony railing beyond the yellow tape. Although her attention had been focused on the scene below, she turned at the sound of his footsteps and said, "Good morning, Stretch. Here at your usual early hour, I see." She glanced back over the railing and added, "But today isn't usual, is it?" Her face, framed by short, slate-gray hair, didn't show its customary glowing smile.

Lynn Bruce, known to one and all as "Stretch" nodded, smiled, and teased, "My favorite Democrat is also here early." Then he turned beside her to look down at the crime scene with its bustling activity and yards of yellow tape. He stepped back from the railing, turned to his Senate colleague and agreed, "No, Audrey. There is nothing usual about the start of this day. The radio said it was Gloria Angel, the governor's right hand lady. What could have happened?" Stretch put his hand on the wooden railing as though to measure its height and integrity, shook his head, and continued, "This railing should be high enough to keep someone from accidentally falling over, especially someone as small as Gloria Angel."

With a frown Senator Welter mumbled, "Who knows?" Then she reached out to put her hand on the arm of his topcoat. At five feet five inches in height, Senator Welter's head barely reached Bruce's shoulder. She tilted her face upward. "I've been waiting for you, Stretch. Come along for a minute. We need to talk." She led him to a tiny, seldom-used office adjacent to the old Supreme Court chamber. Audrey opened the door, stood aside to let Bruce enter, and locked the door behind them. She sat in a chair at the desk and took a deep breath.

Stretch Bruce shrugged out of his winter coat. Eyebrows raised, he asked, "What's up?" Then he grinned, "We're not in here so you can put a move on me, are we?"

Senator Welter didn't smile when she shook her head. "In your dreams, Stretch." She waved him to a chair and gave a wan smile. "I wish it were that easy." Audrey Welter looked down at her hands, clasped tightly on her lap. She took a deep breath, then spoke in a rush. "I want to hire you to represent me."

"Represent you? Represent you for what?"

"I want you to be my lawyer," she said. "I think I'm going to need one."

"Why in the world would you need a lawyer? Did you get a speeding ticket?"

Senator Welter took a handkerchief from her handbag and began to slowly twist the cloth. "Stretch, that woman didn't accidentally fall over the rail onto the rotunda floor. That just couldn't happen. Someone must have pushed her."

"That may be, but what does it have to do with you?"

Audrey walked away from her companion and stood with her back to him. After a long moment, she turned to look at the lanky man still seated, all the while twisting the handkerchief. "This is what it may have to do with me." She took a deep breath. "I was here at the capitol late last night to talk with Gloria Angel. She left my office about ten o'clock. It's possible that I'm the last one to have seen her—except for the person who pushed her over that railing."

"What makes you so sure that's what happened?"

"Aw, for goodness sake, Stretch. It had to be that way. She didn't just fall. The railing is too high. You said that yourself."

"Okay. I agree. It's possible she simply fell, but not likely." With his eyebrows raised, he asked, "Why is that a concern of yours? You didn't push her, did you?"

"No, of course not. But when the sheriff learns she was with me late in the evening, he may start to make some assumptions." She blew out a big breath and was silent for a moment. "That's why I need a lawyer."

"You think the county attorney might charge you with a crime, maybe deliberate homicide?" he shook his head. "That's ridiculous."

"I hope nothing like that happens, but I need to be ready. How about it? Will you represent me if I need a lawyer?"

Senator Bruce got up, and, with his arm outstretched as he leaned against the wall, looked down at her. "I think you're worrying about something that is unlikely to happen. Gloria Angel wasn't a large woman, but it would take someone bigger and stronger than you to manhandle her. What do you weigh, anyway? A little over one hundred pounds? No one will believe you could have pushed her over that railing, even if you tried."

Audrey's face brightened as she grinned. "Stretch, it's bad enough to ask a woman her age but never, never ask how much she weighs."

"Okay. Don't tell me." Stretch straightened and rubbed the back of his neck. "Anyway, if you're ever charged with a serious crime, you need a better lawyer than I am. And it should be someone here in Helena who specializes in criminal law—or maybe an attorney from Missoula, one you already know."

"No, I want you."

"Why me, for God's sake! I'm just a sagebrush lawyer from Roundup, Montana."

Audrey stepped around him and returned to sit in the chair behind the desk. "Stretch, two or three years ago you successfully defended a young man accused of killing an entire family, a family liked by everyone in your town. It was big news. And you got him off. That took a lot of ability and a heck of a lot of courage, considering the sentiment in your community at the time." She smiled a quick smile as she went on. "The papers said the citizens wanted to hang you when the verdict came in, since they couldn't hang the defendant."

Bruce returned to his chair. "That's right. Lots of people were upset. And that's understandable. The members of the family who were killed were greatly respected. Anyway, not long after the verdict, a drifter was arrested for burglary in Billings and confessed to the killing, so people forgot how mad they were at me."

"I remember that too. The confession came just before you filed for re-election to the Senate. And because of the confession, the populace changed its collective mind and decided you were a hero for saving an innocent youngster." Audrey grinned and added, "And no one ran against you."

"My good luck." Bruce stretched out his long legs, leaned back, and clasped his hands behind his head. "Tell me, Audrey. Why would anyone even think you'd want to kill Gloria Angel?"

Senator Welter leaned forward. "You know I'm divorced, don't you?"

Stretch nodded.

A bitter expression settled over her face, and she spoke quietly. "That woman was the cause of the divorce. You've seen Gloria. She's drop-dead beautiful." She pursed her lips. "I guess that's not the best way to describe her today." She continued to wring the handkerchief. "When she chose to, she could be as warm and charming as anyone you ever knew. She was young, at least fifteen years younger than I am."

She raised her eyes to look directly at Senator Bruce. Stretch could tell it was difficult for her to speak of Gloria. "When my husband, Howard, got involved in the governor's election campaign three years ago, I was delighted. I know you Republicans think Shewey's the worst thing that ever happened in Montana, but I was sure he'd be a great governor, and I wanted him to win. Well, Howard began to spend more and more time on Shewey's campaign activities. I hardly noticed because I was doing my own campaigning. I was running for my second term in the state Senate and had tough opposition."

Stretch nodded. "And both you and Shewey were elected."

"Yes, we were both elected. But right after Election Day Howard announced that he wanted a divorce. He was going to marry Gloria Angel."

"That's a hell of a note!"

"I was devastated, as you might guess. And I was angry—so angry that I said some foolish things to a faculty member that I thought was my friend. I said on one occasion that I could kill her." She stopped, then added, "No, it's worse than that. In my anger, I said it too many times. In the end, though, I just told Howard to get the hell out of my life. And he did."

"But he didn't marry Gloria Angel."

"No, of course not. He was just someone she used for entertainment when they were together during the campaign. Frankly, I think she's had her eye on Shewey, even though he's married. Anyway, as soon as the election was over, Gloria spent all her time in the governor's wing of the capitol, leaving poor Howard moping around the university campus like a brokenhearted teenager."

"Audrey, that was what, three years ago? Even if anyone believed you then, they wouldn't think you could still be angry enough to commit murder after all this time."

"I wish that were true, but it isn't. Howard and I are both on the faculty at the University of Montana. That's a hellhole of malicious gossip. Howard likes to blame me for our breakup, and he's jealous of the success I've had as a legislator. He has friends who would call the Lewis and Clark County Attorney today if they already haven't done so. They'll make it sound as though I've just been waiting to get even, and finally got the chance."

"You're exaggerating."

"I wish I were. You live in a quiet little town in eastern Montana where everyone knows everybody, and they all like and help one another. A university campus is filled with some very competitive but insecure people. Too many of them feel that if they can bring another person down it will further their own standing in that closed community. It's something outsiders can't really understand."

"Audrey, no county attorney is going to base an accusation of homicide on the gossip of someone's associates. It isn't worth your worry."

"I hope so. But just the same, I want to have legal help

waiting in the wings if things go wrong." She leaned toward him again. "How about it? Will you help me?"

Bruce responded with a question of his own. "If you hate Gloria Angel, what were you doing with her late last night here in the capitol?"

Audrey rotated her head slowly from side to side. "It's all so innocent. As you know, the Republican majority in Congress has plans to open the Rocky Mountain front to petroleum exploration. I think that would be a terrible tragedy. So I wrote to the governor to suggest some things that might be used to put a stop to it, things he might pass along to the congressional delegation. He called yesterday, said he didn't have time to see me personally, and asked if I would share my ideas with Gloria Angel."

"Didn't he know that would be awkward for you?'

"I don't know. Sometimes Albert Shewey is just plain obtuse when it comes to the feelings of other people. But, no, he probably doesn't know of the problems I have with that woman. Anyway, what could I do? I told him I'd see her after the end of the legislative session yesterday. He said she and some other staff members were to attend a dinner with him and would be busy until nine o'clock. Could I meet her after nine?"

"Not asking much of you, was he?"

"I guess a governor thinks he's busier than state senators who only meet for three months every two years," she said with a wry grin. "I told him to send her up to my office. Well, I was there at nine o'clock. She showed up about nine thirty."

"It must have been a tense meeting."

"She's never acknowledged that she broke up my marriage. Perhaps she doesn't even realize she did. She was cordial, and I kept my cool. We only talked about environmental concerns and ideas for protecting the Rocky Mountain front from desecration."

"You know my feelings are diametrically opposed to yours on that issue?"

Audrey dismissed his comment with a wave of her hand. "Stretch, we differ on everything having to do with the environment." She pushed on. "Gloria left after half an hour, saying that another one of the governor's aides would pick her up. I signed some letters to constituents and then walked out of my office. But that isn't the reason we're having this discussion. We're here because I need a lawyer. What about it? Can I put you on a retainer?"

"Oh hell, Audrey, there's no need for a retainer. You know I'll help any way I can. You and I are as far apart philosophically as two people can be, but I've thought of you as a friend since we got acquainted during the first legislative session we served together. I'll tell you what I'll do. I'll talk to the county attorney, Hefty Hogan. We were law school classmates, so I've known him for a long time. Maybe I can find out what he and the sheriff are thinking." After a pause, he added, "It's a cinch the pressure will be on them from the governor's office—demands that they find out what happened to Gloria Angel before the sun sets tonight. I'll bet Al Shewey has been all over 'em already."

"No doubt." She touched his hand. "Thanks, Stretch. I hope I never need your services, but if I do, it's nice to know I can call on you." She stood to unlock the door, then turned with a wide smile. "But this doesn't mean you'll get my vote on your bills to trash the environment. Remember, I'm still the tree hugger from Missoula. That doesn't change."

"I wouldn't want it to change. Our arguments are too much fun."

Stretch and Audrey found the railing around the balcony lined with curious onlookers, gawking at the activity on the rotunda floor. When they reached the yellow tape near the

Centennial Bell, Audrey smiled, nodded, then turned toward the Senate chamber. Stretch watched as she walked away, admiring the grace of her movement.

In Montana, ordinary senators don't have private offices. Each one shares space with one or two others in rooms that are tucked away somewhere in the vast capitol. The exceptions are the leaders of the two political parties. Down a long hallway from the balcony to the rear of the old Supreme Court chamber are offices that were once used by members of the court. The president of the Senate, the Senate majority leader, and the Senate majority whip now occupied the larger of the offices at that location. Democrat Audrey Welter was majority whip. The smaller office occupied by Republican Stretch Bruce, as minority leader, was farther along and on the other side of the hallway. At its end, the hallway led to rooms used for committee meetings and space for legislative staff.

Stretch, head down in thought, ambled down the dim hallway toward his office. Pat Shea, likable Irishman and Senate majority leader, came striding toward Stretch from the other direction. Shea's freckled face lacked its usual smile as he nodded a greeting. "It's official. The body is that of Gloria Angel." He shoved his hands in his pockets. "We can't just ignore her death. We have to do something. Harry McCullum and I've just discussed the possible cancellation of the floor session and all the committee meetings for the day." Harry McCullum was the president of the Senate. Shea paused a second. "Or maybe we shouldn't. What do you think?"

Stretch pondered for a moment. "I don't know that it will do much good to cancel. The woman's already dead, and from the look of things out there..." he gestured with his thumb toward the rotunda, "everyone's already arrived, ready to go. We all feel some need to acknowledge the tragedy. How about holding the committee meetings as scheduled and then have a prayer reading and a moment of silence before we begin the afternoon's floor session?"

Shea nodded. "That's good. Harry and I had about concluded the same thing. I'll alert the chaplain. Maybe Harry, you, and I can say a few words after the prayer is finished. That'll show we're not calloused. Then we can go ahead with the day's work." He stood quietly in thought. "A lot of us will go to her funeral service. We'll have to cancel a day's session then."

Stretch didn't respond for a moment, reflecting on the wasteful death of such a beautiful and talented person. Finally he observed, "I'm sure there'll be a good turnout for her services, no matter when or where they're held. Your suggestion sounds good to me. Let's do it. What's the House going to do?"

"Damned if I know." Shea shook his head. "You ask the Speaker. He's your guy."

Stretch grinned. "Ah c'mon, Pat. He's not that hard to get along with. But I'll let him know what you've got in mind."

Stretch turned back and started the long walk around the rotunda balcony toward the House of Representatives and the office of Larry Sloan. The Republicans had a majority in the House and Sloan was the Speaker. He was a persuasive but arrogant man who ran the House of Representatives like a personal fiefdom. The animosity between Sloan and the Democratic leaders in the Senate was extreme. Stretch Bruce, who liked to seek solutions to legislative differences, disliked Sloan's confrontational attitude. But, as Shea said, he and the Speaker were both Republicans. It seemed to be his continuing duty to smooth over differences between the parties and between the two houses of the legislature. But even Sloan shouldn't make a partisan thing of the death of Gloria Angel, despite the fact that she worked for a Democratic governor.

3

Lewis and Clark County Sheriff Brent Mendenhall, gray-haired, six feet tall with a paunch and bandy legs, rubbed his hand along his jawbone as he looked around the rotunda. At last he turned to the Helena chief of police, standing by his side. "I wish we could get all these folks out of here until we've had a chance to go over the entire building."

The chief, erect in his blue uniform, agreed. "That would be great, but we can't do it. There are just too many people. And for some of 'em it just isn't practical to be away from their offices. We can't throw the governor out. And the legislators think they're even more important than the governor."

"Of course we can't evacuate the building. And it's too late anyway. People are scattered all over the place. If there was anything that would help us determine why that woman went over the railing, it's probably gone or contaminated by now."

The chief hoisted the gun belt at his waist to a more comfortable position. "My men will keep everyone out of the rotunda. And we'll keep everyone out of the area on the balcony above the place where the body was found. We can do that much."

"What about the victim's office?"

"One of your deputies secured it first thing." The chief paused a moment before he said, "Someone may have been in there even before my men arrived."

"What makes you think so?"

"The deputy told me her office was neat as a pin. But one of the drawers in a cabinet was partially open, kind of like someone had been snooping and left in a hurry."

"Who would have been in that area ahead of us?"

The Chief squirmed a bit before he answered. "Gloria Angel's office is part of the governor's complex. The governor, or one of his people, could have gotten in there before word of her death was out. It would have been difficult but not impossible for anyone else, I suppose. Anyway, we got here as soon as we could after the capitol security detail contacted us. We called it in to your office. Your deputy—Kramer, I believe his name is—got here first and sealed her office right away."

The sheriff gazed down the gallery toward the governor's suite. "Interesting. That may require some digging into the governor's activities."

The chief nodded and looked upward at the place where the body apparently came over the rail. "This looks like an accident, but if it's something worse, then it's your jurisdiction. Your people can handle the investigation, including dealing with the governor. My folks will cooperate." He turned again to the sheriff and added, "And I suppose you'll want to be certain that Ms. Angel's home is sealed."

Sheriff Mendenhall looked at his companion. "When you said something worse, are you thinking homicide?"

"Could be. But probably not. Anyway, we'll do our best to keep this area secure. The rest is up to you. I'm going back to the station, but my chief deputy will be here to coordinate with you. If you need anything from us, just ask him." The chief walked away.

The sheriff called after him, "Thanks, Chief. If we need more help, I'll let you know." After another look around the vast rotunda, he walked toward two of his detectives and asked,

"Well, what do you think happened here? Did she fall or was she pushed?"

"There's no way to tell." One man pointed to the balcony directly above the outline of the body on the floor. "I went up there to look around, first thing, before all these people arrived. There wasn't anything out of the ordinary, at least in the area in front of the doors to the old Supreme Court chamber. She must have tipped over the rail on one side or the other of the Centennial Bell. I gave that general area a quick going over and found nothing that would indicate a struggle."

The other detective chimed in. "If there was any evidence around here and we ain't got it now, we ain't gonna get it. Too many people everywhere, and it'll just get worse as the day goes along."

The Sheriff rubbed his jaw in thought—a habit he didn't even realize he had. "The city police will keep the rotunda secure and do the best they can with the balcony area by the bell. They'll direct the legislators and everyone else to stay away from those locations." Looking around at those gawking from behind the yellow tape, he added, "At least the onlookers can be kept out of that much of the building. I'll send a couple of deputies to Gloria Angel's home to secure it. The rest of the crew may as well go back to their usual duties. You two spend as much time as you feel is necessary going over things here. You better interview the security people who were on duty throughout the night as well as all the night watchmen that patrolled the building. Get statements from each one of 'em. And find out who else has been in the building since business ended yesterday evening." The sheriff thought a moment. "It's possible she was whacked somewhere in the building and then dumped over the rail. Doesn't make sense but could've happened. If so, there may be blood some place that's nowhere near that railing. The watchman found the body a little after midnight. See if you can find out why that woman was in here at that hour. What was she doing? Give Gloria Angel's office another good going-over. If someone got in there ahead of us, we better find out who it was and what they were after."

The ten o'clock Senate Judiciary Committee meeting was delayed while everyone in the hearing room stared at the small television set showing the governor. He stood beside the long table in the governor's conference room and spoke without notes. Albert Shewey, still ruggedly handsome at sixty-two years of age, had a body that was six feet of hard muscle. The bright light reflected off his forehead. He spoke with obvious emotion. "It appears that Gloria Angel accidentally fell from the rotunda balcony, and that the fall caused her death. I've been asked why she was in the capitol in the middle of the night, and I just don't know." He stopped, his feelings evident in the way he swallowed before continuing. "Gloria Angel has been one of my most trusted assistants. She is irreplaceable." He paused. "I've called and expressed my sympathy to her parents who live near Sidney." He closed his eyes briefly. "We should be able to confirm the cause of her death soon. At that time, I may have more to offer. Thank you all for watching. And please keep Gloria Angel and her family in your thoughts and prayers."

With the television set turned off, the committee room filled with conversation, most of it conjecture regarding the relationship between the governor and Gloria Angel. There seemed to be a consensus that the relationship was both ongoing and romantic. At last the chairman banged his gavel, and the Judiciary Committee meeting got under way.

Whenever a question arose in another legislative committee about the legal effect of a pending bill, the usual suggestion was,

"Let's send it over to the folks in Judiciary and let them take a look." As a consequence, that committee processed more material than any other. This day the committee members plowed their way through discussion, argument, and votes on a dozen bills. When the meeting was mercifully over, Stretch Bruce decided to skip the State Administration Committee meeting and drive to the Lewis and Clark County courthouse. The county attorney's office was on the main floor.

County Attorney "Hefty" Hogan got his nickname early in life because of his size. He wasn't fat. He was just big—six feet four inches in height with broad shoulders and a well-proportioned body. Despite his lack of hair—he was completely bald but for a monk's tonsorial fringe above his ears—the man was handsome in a rugged way and always dressed to complement his appearance. Today he wore a dark blue, tailored suit with an ivory colored shirt accented by a perfectly knotted, patterned tie of scarlet hue. Hefty leaned back in his chair with his feet up on the corner of his desk and looked across at his visitor. The corner was the only place on the desk's surface that wasn't covered. Shelves bearing the Montana Codes and various treatises on criminal law lined one sidewall. The other wall was covered with framed degrees, licenses to practice, plaques for service with various organizations, and pictures of the county attorney with a number of dignitaries—including ones with Governor Albert Shewey and Attorney General Henry Sawyer.

"So far we don't know a hell of a lot." Hefty's voice was deep and mellow. "If it was something other than an accident, there aren't any immediate suspects, although the security people said a transient was caught in the building at 2:30 this morning, a couple of hours after the body was found. They took him to police headquarters for questioning. He probably sneaked into the building in the late afternoon and hid out so he'd have a warm place to spend the night. Damn cold sleeping under an overpass when the temperature is five below. Anyway, they don't think he's the one who pitched that woman over the railing—if she was pitched." Hogan stopped his monologue to take a breath. "We've had the usual crank calls, including one from some nut in Missoula who says Gloria Angel was killed by your fellow senator, Audrey Welter, the lady you're always quarreling with about the environment." He dropped his feet to the floor. "As you can guess, our good Governor Albert Shewey wants us to solve the mystery before noon today. One of the governor's aide suggested we should get the feds involved. All we need is the FBI snooping around, interfering, and causing problems. And the attorney general called to offer assistance—as if he had any to give. We're waiting for the coroner's report on the cause of death."

Stretch had remained standing as he listened. "The cause of death should be evident. The fall from the balcony to the floor of the rotunda must have killed her."

"It would seem so, but we want to know for sure."

"Isn't it possible she just leaned too far over the railing and fell? Maybe she'd been drinking."

"Sure, it's possible, but no one thinks it's likely."

"So you think someone did her in?"

"Hell, I don't know. As I said, we still don't have much. Sheriff Mendenhall and his deputies are working with the Helena chief of police to gather whatever evidence might turn up."

"But no suspects?"

"Not yet. The watchman found her body at about midnight during one of his routine walks around the building. That's only been a few hours ago. Give us time, Stretch. We'll learn a lot in the next day or so." Hefty leaned forward with his elbows on his desk. "Why are you so interested anyway?"

"Just curious, like everyone else, I guess." Stretch reached for the doorknob, then turned to add, "Let me know what develops, will you? Lawyer to lawyer."

"Sure, Stretch." As the county attorney rose from his chair, a sly smile came over his face. "Maybe you can do me favor in the future. As you know, the attorney general can't run for that office again because of term limits, so the office will be open at the next election."

"I know that, Hefty. The AG plans to run for governor. Apparently he thinks he can beat Shewey, if Shewey runs for governor again and not for the U. S. Senate. And it's no secret that you have your eye on the attorney general's job."

"Well, I'm still just thinking about it." He stood with his hands in his pockets. "If I do decide to make the race, your help in those counties out east of the mountains would be appreciated."

"I have to see who else might want the Republican nomination. Maybe I'll go for it myself." Seeing a look of disappointment fall over Hogan's face, he quickly added, "Oh hell, Hefty, I'm only kidding. I wouldn't be attorney general for any amount of money." Stretch took his hand off the doorknob and turned back to face the large man. "The truth is, it's been known by the Republican Party regulars for a long time that you plan to run. The likelihood is that no one will run against you in the primary."

"Well, you're never sure until the filing deadline passes."

"That's true." Stretch grinned. "If Gloria Angel was murdered, you'd better find the one who did it right away. And, when you find him, you'd better convict him. The killing, if it was a killing, will be on the front page of all the newspapers in this state everyday, day after day, from now until a jury brings in a guilty verdict. This case can make or break your ambition to be AG."

Hefty's eyes dropped to the carpet as he rubbed a hand across his bald head. "I guess you're right about that." He looked back up at the senator, hand reaching out "Well, Stretch, the capitol is your bailiwick, and it's always a hothouse of rumors. If you hear anything of importance, you know where to find me."

Bruce briefly grasped the man's hand. "Have you thought to look into the life of Gloria Angel? If she was killed, her past activities might lead to the one who did it."

"You're right. And it's on my list of things to discuss with the sheriff."

Outside on the sidewalk, Stretch Bruce muttered to himself, "It's always the same in this damn town. Politics governs everything." As he tramped through the cold across the parking lot, his thoughts turned to Hefty's remark about capitol rumors. He thought of the things Audrey Welter told him in confidence and muttered quietly, "Audrey hasn't anything to worry about. What evidence could there be to tie her to that woman's fall? All she has to do is tell the truth. When they look into Gloria Angel's past life, they'll find out about her relationship with Audrey's husband. It might be a good idea for her to go to the sheriff voluntarily and tell her story." Stretch hoisted himself into the seat of the Expedition. "But probably not. If by chance she ends up as a criminal defendant, it would be a mistake to give the law enforcement folks anything beforehand. I'd better discuss the whole notion with her." Talking to himself, he realized, had become a bad habit. Probably a result of living alone. When he looked at his watch, it was way past time for lunch.

The Montana Club, a six story stone structure located on Lawrence Street just off Last Chance Gulch, is a place where businessmen, as well as some legislators, often go for a noon meal. When Stretch wandered through the door, Senate President Harvey McCullum waved him to the table he was sharing with two of their colleagues, one a Democrat like McCullum, the other a Republican. Stretch shook hands all around before taking the remaining chair. After he was seated, the conversation, quite naturally, had to do with the woman whose body was found on the rotunda floor. What was she doing in the building in the middle of the night? Who could have dumped her over the railing? What had the police learned? What was the motive? That question led to gossip about the activities and lifestyle of Gloria Angel, most of it malicious, and, Stretch guessed, most of it pure fabrication.

"My guess is that she's pregnant." This from George Newton, the Republican.

"Nah, but she and Shewey were probably getting it on. They both have that kind of reputation." That offered by Louis Wilson, the Democrat.

The Senate president looked from one to another, then confided, "I got a call this morning from a reporter wanting to know if there was anything to the rumor that Gloria was mixed up in some kind of criminal activity. I tried to find out where he got that idea, but he wouldn't tell me." He was quiet for a second, then added, "I told him there was nothing to it, of course. Don't you wonder how those things get started?"

"Maybe there is something to it." Newton said. "That transient they found in the capitol this morning could have been a professional who offed her."

Stretch decided Senator Newton had read too many cheap murder novels. Picking at his meal, he remained quiet as the chatter droned along. Tuning out the conversation, he contemplated just how little he could say about the matter under discussion at this table, or anywhere else. While he never thought of himself as a gossip, he still enjoyed the banter that was part of life in the legislature. Now, however, because of his agreement to represent Audrey Welter, he would have to be the most silent politician in Helena—at least when his fellows at the capitol wanted to discuss Governor Shewey's assistant.

After lunch—and the gossip at an end—the four members of the Senate walked toward the doorway, exchanging greetings with those seated at tables as they passed. The afternoon legislative floor session would begin at two o'clock.

To reach the Senate parking area, Stretch turned off Broadway and drove along the street that passed in front of the capitol. As was often his custom, he traveled slowly in order to gaze at the great structure in its entirety. It was a magnificent view—a view too often ignored by those who toiled in the building's bowels.

Completed in 1902, the design of the building has been described as a Montana version of the American Renaissance architectural movement. Viewed from above, it lies in the form of an elongated letter T, with a spacious central section to which two shorter wings are attached at right angles. Constructed of sandstone, the building is four stories in height, with a dome above. It stretches broadly behind a vast expanse of grass, in wintertime often covered with a dusting of snow. The tall imposing dome, sheathed in copper, towers over the center of the building. Atop the dome, Lady Liberty, resembling the Statue of Liberty, holds a torch and shield and is deemed to be lighting the way and protecting the populace.

A broad concrete walkway leads from the street past a statue of onetime acting governor, Thomas Meagher, seated heroically on his horse. An expansive staircase leads to the large doors that open directly onto the second floor rotunda. It is seldom used. The common way into the capitol from the north is through doors under the staircase. Those doors lead to the ground floor.

When viewing the edifice, Stretch felt his responsibility as a legislator. It provided a solid sense of permanence, of the need to act properly for the lasting benefit of the people of the state.

Stretch parked in the lot on the south side of the building and hustled through the double doorways, his mind on the matters to be debated in the Senate floor session. Ambrose Swan, elderly dean of the capitol reporters and a man respected by every lawmaker, was wearing his usual rumpled suit when he stepped from the pressroom. He winked at Senator Bruce who was passing by on his way to the doors of the Senate. "Do you suppose that the governor and the attorney general may be thinking the same thoughts today?" His voice was gravelly, probably from years of puffing cigarettes.

Stretch paused with a puzzled look on his face. "Why should they be thinking the same thoughts? They don't seem to be able to agree on anything."

Swan grinned. "No, that's not exactly right. Once in while they agree." He turned back toward the door to the pressroom and said over his shoulder, "Sometime I'll tell you of one thing about which they may agree right now." He stepped through the door and out of sight, leaving Stretch wondering what he was missing.

That evening Senator Audrey Welter, dressed in pajamas and a warm robe, lounged with her legs tucked beneath her in a comfortable chair in the apartment she rented during legislative sessions. Her eyes strayed from the packet of bills she was holding to the television and back again, without really seeing either of them. Her mind was on the occurrences of the day and especially on her impulsive decision to confide in Stretch Bruce. The minute she heard of the death of Gloria Angel, Audrey realized that her late evening discussion with the woman could present a problem, a legal problem. It was an instantaneous leap of her mind from that realization to the conclusion that Senator Bruce was the lawyer she wanted at her side if any legal difficulty did arise.

The Body on the Floor of the Rotunda 35

Now, with time to reflect, she pondered that decision. What had led her to act on impulse when she was not impulsive by nature? Despite their party and philosophical differences, she knew that Senator Bruce always strove to further the best interests of the people of the state and never in a purely partisan manner. He was tall and gangly and could hardly be called handsome although he was nice-looking. Stretch always conducted himself as a gentleman—a kindly, considerate gentleman. Now she wondered if that characteristic was the thing that swayed her mind. After all, she really had no clear way to measure his ability as a lawyer. But she trusted him. In the end and after mulling over the matter in her mind for a long time, she concluded that trust was the most important thing.

Her mind turned to her former husband. Howard had been in Helena the day before—the day when Gloria Angel died. She happened to look up to the gallery that surrounded the Senate chamber to find him standing near the rail and staring down at her. As her eyes reached his face, he immediately looked away, turned abruptly, and strode from the chamber. With a jolt, she wondered if his presence in town and the death of Gloria Angel could be related. Audrey quickly put that notion from her mind as too outlandish to contemplate. Her former husband would never have the toughness required for such an act. He was a thinker, not a doer.

With that as her last thought about the day's events, she forcefully turned her attention to her own legislative bill that was scheduled for floor debate the next day—the bill that would prohibit the state from issuing a permit to drill an exploratory gas well on a section of land owned by the State of Montana lying along the Rocky Mountain Front. The 640-acre section and an adjacent privately owned section were isolated and surrounded by federal land upon which the prohibition was already in place.

The Rocky Mountain Front was a pristine area that everyone in the environmental community agreed had to be protected from the desecration that gas exploration and production would create.

4

Senator Audrey Welter's environmental bill was one of the most important to come before the Senate for floor debate the following day, and all the members were at full alert when she rose to present her argument for its passage. The arguments, both for and against mineral development, had been made and heard by the members of the Senate in past sessions, so Audrey faced a daunting task. That she was able to capture the senators' attention sparked admiration in Stretch's mind. But when she completed her presentation and placed the microphone in its holder, he was soon on his feet. "Will Senator Welter yield?"

"I yield."

"Senator, isn't it true that geologists project that several million dollars in state revenue might be generated if gas wells are successfully drilled on the state section in question?"

"Yes, Senator, that's been said."

"And isn't it also true that the adjacent privately owned land has potential to produce even more tax revenue from wells drilled on that land?"

"That's what we've all heard."

"And we are told that the best prospects for success lie in drilling on the state section and that there will be no exploration of the private land unless it is combined for exploration purposes with the state section. Isn't that right?"

"Senator Bruce, that's what we are told. It may or may not be true."

"Knowledgeable petroleum engineers tell us that is so, don't they?"

"Yes, Senator, but they're not always right. You know that. You live in a county with lots of oil and gas wells. Not every well drilled is a producer, is it?"

"No, Senator, not every well is a producer. But you would agree, wouldn't you, that the only way to know for certain is to poke the hole in the ground?"

"The problem, Senator, is that in the process of poking the hole in the ground, we all too often do irreparable harm to the environment. I've been to your county. And I've seen the waste and destruction that has occurred when petroleum extraction is allowed to go forward unchecked. Some of the messes that have been left behind are pretty horrible, aren't they?"

Stretch had to grin and admit, "You're certainly right about that. Some of them need a lot of cleaning up. But the messes came from wells drilled at another time, at a time before oil men became aware of their societal obligation to refrain from leaving well sites in such condition. And as you know, we now impose strict reclamation requirements on all those who are in the petroleum production business. You didn't see any catastrophes at the new well sites in my county, did you?"

"But such catastrophes still occur, sir. And we cannot run that kind of risk along the Rocky Mountain Front."

"Even if it means that our schools will have to go without the millions of dollars of money that the completion of successful wells on the state section would provide?"

Exasperation crept into Audrey's voice. "Senator Bruce, you know perfectly well that my background is in education. I do not take lightly an accusation that I'm uninterested in providing adequate funds for the operation of our schools, from kindergarten through the universities. But we have to make choices, and our choice should not be to desecrate one of the last best places in North America on the outside chance that it would generate some unknown amount of money. If that area is ruined, it will be ruined forever."

Stretch smiled across the room in her direction. "Thank you, Senator." He glanced around the chamber. "Members of the Senate, those of you who are not in your first term have heard this debate before, and I suspect most of you have long since made up your minds about the way you will vote. But please bear in mind the importance of our school system. And remember that all the money from the lease and rental of the lands owned by the State of Montana go into the state's educational funds. We need to lease the mineral rights to this state's section. We need to lease those rights to a reputable petroleum exploration company under strict requirements for the protection of the environment. And we need to allow that company to drill an exploratory well so we can learn whether or not the gas is there. To do otherwise is to abdicate our obligation to provide properly for the education of the children of the state." He paused to cast his glance at each senator. "I have the greatest respect for the senator from Missoula. She believes as firmly in her position as I do in mine. But in this instance I'm confident my position is the better one for us to take. Please vote 'no' on the motion that this bill do pass."

When the votes were tallied, Senator Welter's bill passed. Every Democrat and four Republicans voted for it.

It was mid-afternoon when Stretch and Audrey entered a small room at the offices of the Montana Environmental Council. Stretch knew that the Council was one of the many "Green" organizations that had Audrey's ear. In his note to her he suggested they meet there rather than in his office or hers.

When they were seated across from one another at a small table, Stretch said, "Congratulations, once again. Your presentation was superb. You had them eating out of your hand."

"Not so, Stretch. The senators just understand that Montana's wonderful environment is its greatest asset and we must preserve it at all costs."

"Even if we have to forgo a potential source of significant revenue for our schools?"

"Listen, Senator, we aren't going to debate it again in this room. You lost and I won. It's over."

"Your bill still has to get through the House, you know."

Audrey grimaced. "I know. And your guy, Larry Sloan, is determined to kill it." Her face brightened. "But as you know, some Republicans in the Senate saw the light. There's still hope that enough of them in the House will do the same."

Stretch grinned and said, "I almost hope you're right... but not quite." He sobered and leaned forward. "I went to see Hefty Hogan. He told me he'd received the call you anticipated. Someone from Missoula told him to check you out."

"Check me out? In what sense?"

"You can guess what the caller might have said, 'Audrey Welter may know something.' That kind of remark. Hefty blew it off as of no consequence."

"That's somewhat comforting. What else did you learn from our esteemed county attorney?"

"They don't know if it was an accident or something else. He said it was only a few hours since the body was discovered, and they were just beginning their investigation. They caught a transient in the capitol sometime after the watchman found the body. The sheriff apparently thinks the guy just wandered in during the day to find a warm place for the night. They took him in for questioning, just to be thorough."

"What else did you find out?"

"Nothing more from Hefty. I ate lunch with some of our colleagues, and they have a whole bunch of squirrelly ideas about Gloria—that she's pregnant, that Shewey's the father and had her bumped off, that she was mixed up with the Mafia—those kinds of things."

"The usual baseless capitol rumors."

"Yup, that's it." Stretch leaned forward. "Hefty will learn soon enough that Gloria met with you last night."

"No one but you knows."

"Al Shewey knows. He asked you to meet with her. And he'll tell them the first time they talk to him."

Her face twisted into a scowl. "You're right. He'll tell them so he can point a finger at someone besides himself."

Stretch straightened up. "That's an interesting thought."

"What is?"

"Shewey pointing a finger at someone else. Do you think he's involved somehow?"

"No, of course not. He wouldn't risk either his reputation or his desire to be a United States senator by doing something as stupid as that."

"You're probably right. When she left your office last night, where did she go? Did she meet Shewey?"

"I don't know where she went. I saw her out the door and then turned back to my desk to sign the letters. I just assumed she was going to one of the main doors and that the governor or someone else would pick her up."

"Didn't she bring her own car?"

"No. She mentioned that another of the governor's aides gave her a ride from the dinner meeting. Something she said, but I don't remember exactly what it was, made me think she expected Shewey himself to come for her."

"Did she mention a time when he would be there?"

"No, but after we talked for a while she started looking at her watch. At about ten o'clock she got up from her chair to let me know we were finished. That told me she was expecting someone at about that time."

"I wonder if Al Shewey came into the building to meet her. Maybe the sheriff has checked. We can ask Hefty."

Audrey shifted uneasily in her chair. "Should I should go to the county with my story? Just tell him that Gloria was in my office. And tell him I don't know anything more than that?" She waited for Stretch to answer. When he remained silent, she added, "Or would it be better to wait until he asks?"

"I've been thinking about it. Generally defense lawyers don't want their clients to say any more to the authorities than law requires. But you haven't been accused of anything, and I don't believe you will be. Perhaps it would be wise to make it plain that you have nothing to hide and to do it right away. That should satisfy the law enforcement folks and, if they finally decide Gloria Angel was murdered, they'll concentrate their efforts somewhere else."

"You'll go with me, won't you? I don't want to do it alone."

"Of course. I'll break the ice by telling Hefty I advised you to make the visit."

"Okay. When do we do it?"

"How about right now? I'll call Hefty and set it up."

Hefty rose from his chair and stepped quickly toward Audrey and asked, "May I take your coat, Senator?" His behavior brought the word "fawn" to Stretch's mind.

Audrey's answer was courteous, "Thank you, Mr. Hogan. The coat is fine. And it's kind of you to see us on short notice."

"Always at the service of members of the Senate, ma'am. To

what do we owe the honor?"

Stretch answered for her. "Senator Welter is here to tell you that she met with Gloria Angel night before last and to explain the circumstances of the meeting. I suggested she bring it to you before someone else does, some person who might distort the report and get you thinking there was something sinister involved. You need to hear it straight."

Hefty's eyebrows went up. "Well, I appreciate that." Turning again to Audrey, he asked, "So, Senator, what happened?"

Audrey was composed as she responded. "The day before they found her body, the governor asked Gloria to visit with me about some environmental legislation in which we both had an interest. The only time she could come to my office was after an evening dinner meeting. She didn't get there until about nine thirty. We talked for approximately half an hour and she left. That's all there is to it."

"Well, that certainly doesn't sound sinister." He leaned forward. "What else can you tell me that might have to do with the late Gloria Angel?"

"Nothing about the way she died." She leaned slightly forward to look directly into the eyes of the large man. "What have you learned about her death? Do you know if it was an accident? Or was it something else?"

"We haven't learned much since Stretch was here yesterday. The transient wasn't any help." Hefty rubbed his open hand across his bald head. "Was it an accident? We don't know yet. Could it have been an accident? Maybe, but not likely. We'll know more after we get the autopsy report."

Stretch interrupted. "Assuming it wasn't an accident, who are you focused on as suspects?"

"Ah hell, Stretch. We haven't any idea who might be a suspect. I'm waiting for the autopsy."

"What does the sheriff think? He's the one closest to the investigation."

"Brent Mendenhall and his deputies are busy checking things up at the capitol. They're going over the entire rotunda area, looking for anything that might be of interest. And they're questioning the security people to learn who was in the building. They're talking with any others who might know about the activities of Gloria Angel that evening. Sheriff Mendenhall's supposed to talk with Governor Shewey this afternoon. The governor may be able to provide some helpful information."

The mention of the governor brought to Stretch's mind the comment made by Ambrose Swan, the newsman, that the governor and the attorney general might be thinking the same thoughts. "Is the governor a suspect? Would he have any reason to want her out of the way?"

"I'm not going to speculate about that. I'm just going along until the sheriff brings me something to sink my teeth into." He stopped and blinked his eyes at Stretch as though he had just realized the possible significance of the lawyer's presence. "By the way, why are you here? Did Senator Welter need you to hold her hand?"

Stretch looked toward Senator Welter with a smile and then turned back to Hogan. "Audrey's a friend. When she mentioned Gloria Angel was at her office, I suggested she should share that information with you. She just asked me to come along. I'm a lawyer, after all, and she said she would be more comfortable if I were here."

"Are you representing her?'

"Representing her for what?" Stretch shook his head. "C'mon, Hefty. She's a friend."

"I thought you two were mortal enemies. That's the way it appears in the newspapers. You're always fighting about some damn thing having to do with the environment."

"That's right. We don't agree on a lot of legislative matters. That doesn't mean I don't respect and admire her. Like I said, we're friends."

Audrey stood. "As Senator Bruce said, Mr. Hogan, we're friends. And if you don't have any further need for us, we'll get back to the capitol. I have a late committee meeting."

The two men rose from their chairs. Hefty Hogan led them to the door and smiled as he grasped Audrey's hand with both of his. "Thank you for telling me of your visit with the deceased Gloria Angel. It saves a lot of time. If I need to visit with you some more, may I call?"

Senator Welter withdrew her hand. "If that need should arise, please call Senator Bruce."

Stretch reached for the county attorney's hand. "Call me whether you need to talk with Audrey or not. Let me know what you learn about the death of Governor Shewey's lovely assistant. I'm curious as all get out."

Hefty nodded slowly before he responded. "I'll try to keep you informed. But remember, a whole bunch of people feel the same way you do—the governor, the attorney general, even the Speaker of the House. I can't just keep on calling everyone to report. I'd never get anything done."

"Understood. And thanks, friend. Just keep me in the loop without putting yourself to a lot of trouble. By the way, does the night watchman's log tell if Shewey was in the capitol building late last night?"

Hefty Hogan scowled. "I don't know. We'll be checking that out along with everything else." He abruptly nodded and shut the door.

On the ride back toward the capitol, Audrey asked, "Will they want to talk to me again?"

"I think it's a certainty. Next time it may be the sheriff. He's the one who conducts the investigation. And I wouldn't be surprised if they ask to look through your office."

"Why would they want to do that?"

"You were probably the last one to see her, other than the one who killed her—if she was killed." Stretch took his eyes off the street to look across at his companion. "And you visited with her in your office. Any law officer would want to check it out, just as a matter of proper investigative practices." Eyes back on the street, he asked, "Are you concerned about that?"

"No. Except it makes me seem like a suspect, and I sure don't like that."

"Don't worry too much. The sheriff may yet decide it was an accident. That's possible, you know."

"I surely hope so. The whole thing is beginning to wear on me." She patted his arm. "But thanks, Stretch, for being a friend. And for admitting we are friends when the county attorney asked. I don't know how I'd handle this without you."

Shortly after her return from the county attorney's office, Audrey Welter and her fellow Democratic leaders were focused on the television screen in the Senate president's office when the picture of the attorney general appeared. Henry Sawyer always acted as though he was on stage. His sonorous baritone held the attention of his listeners. He was a Republican so the Democrats watching were skeptical of his motives even before he began to speak.

"The death of Gloria Angel has saddened all of us who knew her. She was an especially talented individual. While the principle responsibility for the investigation into her death rests with the local sheriff, I've directed my staff to provide Sheriff Mendenhall with any and all the assistance that may be helpful to him in his investigation. In addition, if we are asked, my office will assist the county attorney in the prosecution of the perpetrator of the homicide, if that's what it was. That it was a murder, we are not yet certain." The attorney general glanced down at his desk, and up at the camera once again. "I've expressed my sympathies to the members of the family of Gloria Angel. I'm afraid that's small solace to her parents. Our obligation to them is first, to learn if the death was an accident. And second, to find and punish the one responsible for her death if it was not an accident. I will not rest until this matter is properly resolved."

When the television set was turned off, one of the men commented, "He will not rest until he's milked her death for every vote he thinks he can get."

Senator Shea added, "Hell, he was probably getting it on with Gloria himself. He's Montana's worst womanizer.

5

Late in the afternoon, the day after the body of Gloria Angel was found sprawled on the rotunda floor, a knock came on the door of Governor Albert Shewey's office. His secretary stuck her head through the opening. "The sheriff's here, sir. You said you wanted to be interrupted when he arrived."

"Yes. Thank you, Sheila. Please bring him in." The governor put the stack of papers he was reading to one side, brushed his hand over his thinning hair, and straightened his tie. When the peace officer walked through the door, the governor rose. "Sheriff Mendenhall, I've been expecting you."

"Thank you for seeing me, sir. I need to ask a few questions."

"Of course. You're investigating the death of Gloria Angel. I'm sure you understand that I'm deeply distressed by what happened."

"Yes, sir. I realize that."

The governor pointed to one of the side chairs, indicating a place for his visitor to sit. When they were both seated, the sheriff asked, "Governor, Ms. Angel was to meet you at the capitol after her meeting with Senator Audrey Welter. Is that right?"

How in hell does he know about that? He answered, "Gloria and I attended a gathering of supporters that evening. When was that? Night before last? The whole tragedy has me confused as to time." When the sheriff didn't respond, he continued, "I asked her to go to the office of Senator Welter to discuss some environmental legislation in which we both have an interest.

When the gathering ended, Bill Wilcox, another of my aides, gave Gloria a ride to the capitol. I just assumed that he would wait for her."

"Are you saying you weren't at the capitol late that night?"

"That's right. After Gloria and Bill left, I went to the mansion, took a shower, and went to bed. It had been a busy day."

There was a pause before the sheriff spoke again. "Governor, the entry log maintained by the security detail at the capitol shows that you came in through the main doors at about ten o'clock that evening. There's no indication in the log to tell when you left."

There was prolonged silence before the governor responded. "I can't explain that, Sheriff. Someone must have forged my name."

"No, sir. The log entry was made by the night watchman at the desk near the main entry. You apparently identified yourself to him. And the signature on the entry seems to be in your handwriting."

"Then someone led him to believe that it was me, because I wasn't there."

"That's interesting to know, sir. But, as you might expect, he said he recognized you." The sheriff paused. "I suppose he could be wrong. We'll check it out."

The governor leaned forward and said in a harsh voice, "Damn it, Sheriff, I wasn't there. Besides, whenever I enter the capitol, I use the door on the east end near my office. I never use the main entrance."

For a long while the sheriff just stared at the governor's solemn face, then he nodded his head as though making up his mind. "What can you tell us about Ms. Angel that might be helpful?

Governor Shewey slumped back in his chair and blew out

a sigh. "Well, she was extremely intelligent and had a wonderful personality. She was the one I often asked to represent me with important constituents when I couldn't meet with them myself. Gloria understood the things that are of interest to me and could discuss any governmental matter coherently." He thought for a moment. "If you've ever met her, you know she was a beautiful woman. She could charm even my most bitter opponents."

"Why would anyone want to kill her, sir?"

"Was it murder then?"

"Seems so, sir. While the autopsy hasn't been conducted, the preliminary investigation indicates she was probably dead before she went over the railing."

Shewey shifted around in the chair. "So why would anyone want to kill her? I really don't know. She could have had enemies. It's no secret that several men had an interest in her. Perhaps one of them?"

"You would know better than I, sir." The sheriff took a deep breath. "Tell me, sir, who else could help us learn more about Ms. Angel? Who else knew her well enough to provide us with useful information? One of the men you mentioned, perhaps?"

"Sheriff, I didn't keep track of Gloria's social schedule, so I can't answer that question. Perhaps her parents can help you. I understand they're arriving in town today." He paused. "But if you wish, I can ask around and then give you the names of any people that might be of help."

"That would be good, sir." Sheriff Mendenhall rose from his chair. "And I appreciate the chance to visit with you."

Shewey was on his feet. "You're welcome, sheriff. If I can be of more help, please let me know. Of course, I'm anxious that you find Gloria's killer."

"I'm sure we'll talk again, Governor. There is the question of the entry log."

After the sheriff was out of the room and the door closed, Albert Shewey blew out a long breath and growled, "Damn that log!"

Later that afternoon, Loren Hammond, the deputy responsible for securing Gloria Angel's workplace, walked into the sheriff's office. Hammond was an experienced officer in whom the sheriff placed a great deal of trust. The deputy took the seat the sheriff offered, dropped his hat on the floor, and began, "You need to know that the governor has made attempts to get into Gloria Angel's office."

"What kind of attempts?"

"As you directed, we placed secure locks on the door to her office so no one could get in but us. First the governor called me to ask if he could be present when we did an inventory of Ms. Angel's office."

"Did he say why he wanted to be there?"

"Yes. But he was careful about how he said it. The governor told me there were matters that were discussed in his office and among his closest associates that were not intended to be made public."

"What kind of matters?"

"He didn't say."

"And why would matters discussed in his office require the great man himself to be present when an inventory of Gloria Angel's belongings was conducted?"

"Maybe he's concerned that she may have notes that could be embarrassing or harmful to him. Or to others."

"What did you tell him?"

"I said we made a preliminary inventory the day she died, and would make a complete inventory when Gloria's parents could be here. I told him we would let him know when, and that he would be welcome to join us."

"And how did he respond to that?"

"He seemed agitated that her parents would be present. But finally he asked me to let him know when the inventory would be conducted. He thanked me and hung up."

"Anything else I should know?"

"One of the governor's aides asked another deputy for a key to the secure lock. Said he acted at the request of the governor. He didn't get the key."

Sheriff Mendenhall rubbed his chin. He nodded to his deputy. "Good work." He stood and added, "Keep me informed. There may have been something in that woman's possession that could lead us to her killer. I think the governor has something to hide. If not, why did he lie to me this morning?" Detective Hammond rose from his chair but before he could answer, the sheriff added, "Another thing. Do you know that the attorney general has tried to get into her town house? That's what Buzz Kramer reported to me not ten minutes ago. He's the one responsible for the security of her home. I guess the AG called Kramer and asked for the key. Said he needed to get some legal papers he'd given her to deliver to the governor," the sheriff chuckled. "That was one busy woman. The governor and the attorney general hate each other. But it seems they both had something going with Gloria Angel. And she must have been holding something that's a worry to each one of them. Are they worried about the same thing? Or is there more than one thing?" Hammond just shook his head. The sheriff muttered, "I suppose we'll find that out soon enough."

6

Mr. and Mrs. Seth Angel, Gloria's parents arrived in Helena late in the evening and drove directly to the sheriff's office. Sheriff Mendenhall apologized that their daughter's body was not at the local mortuary. He explained that an autopsy at the State Crime Laboratory in Missoula was required to determine the cause of death. Seth took that information in a stoic manner, but his wife burst into tears and wailed mournfully at the thought of any desecration to the body of her only child. The sheriff was at his sympathetic best in listening to the woman's laments while trying to explain the legal process that must be followed.

"After the autopsy is completed—soon I hope—you can make arrangements for her body to be transported to wherever you choose to have her funeral. Burial, of course, will be in accordance with your wishes."

He mentioned the probability that several of her governmental associates would want to attend the service. Finally, he told Seth Angel that his deputies must complete an inventory of Gloria's belongings, both those in her office and home. The inventory was necessary to determine if anything at either place would shed light on the cause of her death. The inventory, he assured them, would be conducted in their presence so they would know that everything belonging to their daughter was preserved and accounted for.

Seth Angel's wide-eyed question was, "You mean someone may have killed her?"

"We don't know yet, but it's something we must consider."

Understanding that her daughter may have been the victim of a murder brought even greater agony to Mrs. Angel. She crumpled downward in the chair and began fresh, keening wails.

7

Four days after the death of Gloria Angel, Stretch was seated at his desk on the Senate floor listening to the debate drone on when a page handed him a note from his secretary. It said, "Call the county attorney as soon as possible." Since the day's debate was near an end, and none of the remaining bills were important to him, he went to his office. Barbara Wilson, the gray-haired, motherly woman upon whom he relied during the legislative sessions, turned from her computer and said, "Hefty Hogan's secretary said it was important."

Stretch went to his desk and punched the numbers into the phone. "Stretch Bruce returning Mr. Hogan's call."

"Oh! Yes, sir. He's anxious to visit with you. I'll get him right away."

After only a moment, Hefty's deep voice came through the phone. "Stretch, my friend, it's nice of you to return the call."

"What's up? They said it was important."

"Two things. First, the autopsy report came back on Gloria Angel. It seems the fall wasn't the thing that killed her."

"Really? What did?"

"The pathologist determined she died from a severe blow to the right side of her head. A massive skull fracture. She suffered another, smaller fracture on the other side of her head. The way her body was lying when she was found indicates the one on the left side came when her head hit the floor of the rotunda. The fall also broke her neck. Right now we're speculating that someone whacked her with the proverbial blunt instrument, perhaps an hour or more before he...or she...pitched Ms. Angel over the balcony railing."

"God, that's awful. Any ideas yet about who might have done it?"

"That's the second thing. Remember that I told you the police found a guy who appeared to be an ordinary transient in the capitol building? You know, during the search after Gloria Angel's body was found? Well, apparently he isn't an ordinary transient. He was dressed like one, smelled like one, and had a scraggly beard like one. And the story he told made him sound like one. So the sheriff turned him loose. But now the sheriff's decided he spoke too well for a bum, more like an educated man. Mendenhall wonders if the guy was trying to be something he wasn't."

"Did the sheriff round him up again to ask more questions?"

"Nope. Can't find him. Must have gotten out of town as soon as he left the jail. They've got the word out to pick him up, but with no result so far. They got his fingerprints off a Pepsi can he handled while he was in custody, ran a check on the prints for priors. It came back negative. So all they have to put on the wire is a description, and the vagrant could change his appearance in an instant simply by cleaning up and putting on other clothes."

"It sounds like he may be the one who did her in."

"Maybe, maybe not. We need to know more about him. One other thing. Sheriff Mendenhall would like to take a look at Senator Welter's office."

"I'm sure Audrey will let him do that. I'll ask her and then call. When would the sheriff want to be there?"

"The sooner, the better. How about this afternoon?"

"I'll talk to Audrey and call you back as soon as I can."

"Thanks, Stretch. We appreciate your help. I doubt they will find anything, but we have to go through the motions."

"I suppose it makes sense that they want to look at my office, but it makes me nervous anyway." Audrey spoke quietly.

Stretch smiled down at her. "What's the harm?' he asked. "At the most they may find Gloria's fingerprints on something, and they already know she was there."

"I understand." Audrey turned to look out the window toward the distant formation of mountains called the Sleeping Giant. "It just makes me feel like a suspect."

"The quicker they do their inspection, the sooner you'll be off any list of suspects, if you were ever on one."

"All right. But let's do it late this afternoon after most of the others have left the building. Call your pal, Hefty Hogan, and tell him to send his thugs a little after five. I'll be waiting for them." She turned back from the window with her head tilted up to look at Stretch. "You'll be there too, won't you?"

"Sure, Audrey, if you want me."

"I want you."

Sheriff Brent Mendenhall and another man dressed in civilian clothes arrived at the open door to Senator Welter's office at five thirty. The sheriff knocked on the doorjamb twice before walking in. He removed his hat and nodded to Audrey. "Ma'am." He shook Senator Bruce's hand. "I understand you represent Senator Welter?"

"Audrey's a friend. I'm a lawyer so she's asked me to be here just in case there's any question."

"I understand." Turning to Audrey, "Is it all right if we look around?" He smiled and added, "Is there anything you think we might break if we touch it?"

That brought a grin to Audrey's face. "No, Sheriff. Have at it.

There's nothing that'll break. But if you don't mind, Stretch and I will stay while you do your search."

"That's fine." The sheriff nodded toward his companion. "This is Deputy Loren Hammond." He gestured an order to the man with a slight jerk of his head. Hammond turned and started moving very slowly to his right, all the while looking carefully at each item of furnishings as well as the walls, ceiling, and floor, especially the floor. The room was little more than a cubbyhole, with a desk, two chairs, a coat rack, and a small bookcase. On top of the bookcase was a vase with artificial flowers, some loose papers and, in the middle, a gold-plated trophy crowned by a tiny figure on skis. The two shelves below held a set of the Montana Code Annotated, a dictionary, the session laws from some previous legislative sessions, and two notebooks.

The sheriff stepped to Audrey's desk and surveyed the surface that held only a laptop computer, telephone, Rolodex, pen and pencil holder, and a stack of legislative bills. Audrey had personalized the desk with three nicely framed color photographs. One showed her standing by a flowing stream with a small child at her side. In another she was wearing ski clothes as she leaned gracefully on ski poles, high on some mountain. The third and obviously the most recent showed Audrey on the same snowy mountain, a handsome young man standing beside her, his arm about her shoulder.

Mendenhall asked. "How about the desk drawers?"

Audrey hesitated briefly before asking, "Why do you need to look in there? Do you think Gloria Angel left a note saying who killed her?"

The sheriff's face remained solemn as he dragged his hand along his chin. "No, of course not. But it's better to be thorough." He backed away from the desk. "The truth is, ma'am, we aren't looking for anything in particular. You told Mr. Hogan Ms.

Angel was here. It's the last place we're sure she was before she died. We think we should go over everything carefully. It's hard to tell what might crop up."

"You're sure now that it was murder and not an accident?"

"The pathologist's report indicated Ms. Angel died from a blow to the head that came before she went over the rail."

Audrey shuddered, looked up at Stretch, and said, "Let's get out of here." Turning back to the sheriff, she said, "Look at anything you want, but I'd rather not be here, after all. It's too much as though you're searching me personally." She turned toward the door, then said over her shoulder, "There's nothing in this room I have to hide."

The sheriff bowed his head ever so slightly. "As you wish, ma'am. We'll be careful not to do any damage, and we'll try to leave everything as we find it."

As they walked down the hallway toward the elevator, Audrey put her arm through that of her companion and said, "Get me out of here, Stretch. I'm scared."

"There's no reason to be scared." He looked down at her. "How about I take you to dinner? We'll both relax and forget that Gloria Angel ever existed."

"Yes, you can take me to dinner. I wish I could forget about her forever."

The roadhouse north of Helena had a dark interior that smelled faintly of spilled beer. They were ushered to a secluded booth near the back. As the youthful waiter stood patiently, Stretch asked Audrey, "Will you have a before-dinner drink?"

"Perhaps a glass of white wine. The house wine will do."

Stretch turned to the young man and said, "Bring us a bottle of your best Chablis." He turned back to Audrey to say, "Good wine is worth the extra cost."

"I suppose. But I don't intend to drink very much of it."

When the glasses were filled, and the waiter had taken his leave, Stretch leaned forward with his arms on the table. "We've known each other for six years. It's a rather strange acquaintance, however. I know a great deal about your political views but very little about you."

"And I know little about you. You're a lawyer, of course, who practices in the big town of Roundup. I've been told that you are a widower and have a married daughter." She leaned in toward Stretch, elbows on the table and hands folded under her chin. "What else would I find interesting?"

"Not much, really. Mine is a pretty quiet life. My daughter married an engineer and lives in Seattle. They have twins, a boy and a girl. I drive out to visit them two or three times a year, and they come to Roundup on a rare occasion."

"You are attractive, so you must not suffer from a lack of female companionship."

"Audrey, I'm fifty-six years old, tall, and skinny. I have a big nose, my face is wrinkled, and I'm losing my hair. Attractive I ain't." He paused. "There. I've told you all about me. Now how about you? You're divorced. You have a good-looking young son. You're a professor of humanities at the university." Senator Bruce sat back in his chair.

"You're wondering what else I'll tell you." Audrey paused to reflect before continuing. "I'm forty-eight years old. I was born and raised in Ohio. The mountains—and my former husband—brought me to Montana. I have degrees from three universities. I enjoy activities that get me out of doors, like riding my bike, hiking, and skiing. I even won a second place trophy in the family ski races at the Snow Bowl. There isn't much else."

Stretch chuckled. "Some lucky legislators and a couple of the lobbyists for environmental organizations have squired you to social functions. It's gotten to be a betting game in the men's washroom to see which one will succeed in getting more than one date. So far it seems that nobody's won."

"So now I'm the butt of schoolboy jokes and gossip, is that it?"

"Not at all. You're respected and admired. We've all just wondered which guy will be fortunate enough to catch you. Perhaps there's a serious contender in Missoula."

"No, Stretch. I've been badly burned once. That should be enough."

"Should be? You mean there's still a chance for some lucky fellow?"

Audrey's laugh was long and melodious. "Who knows? Are you interested?"

"Don't taunt me, woman. I just might be tempted."

Audrey smiled. "And I just might respond." She sighed. "But not until this murder thing is settled and off my mind. It crowds out everything else. I can't even concentrate on the bills in my committees."

Stretch leaned back and reached for the menu. "Let's forget all of it and enjoy a meal. This place is supposed to serve an excellent leg of lamb. How about it?"

"That sounds good. Please order a small serving for me. I'll see if I can concentrate on the food and forget Gloria Angel, at least for a little while."

8

The governor and leaders of both the House and Senate, flew in a state-owned aircraft to the town of Lambert for Gloria Angel's funeral. The Lutheran Church couldn't accommodate Gloria's large extended family and all of her friends. The governor and the legislators were favored with pews near the front of the church, but many local people had to remain outside in the blustery cold and listen to the service over a loudspeaker.

At the cemetery, the minister's final prayer was difficult to hear because of Gloria's mother's sobbing. At the community center, people gathered for a potluck and to reminisce about the life of the beautiful and talented local celebrity. The governor and the legislators murmured their condolences as they filed by Mr. and Mrs. Angel, offering a handshake as they left.

On the flight back to Helena, Stretch thought of a remark once made by an old friend. "The passing of any person is like tossing a pebble into a pond. The waves spread out from the splash and then start to diminish and grow more faint until finally the surface of the pond is still again. It doesn't take long." Stretch had a nagging feeling that in Gloria Angel's case, it might take much more than the usual amount of time for the surface of the capitol pond to become calm once again

9

Seven days after the death of Gloria Angel, an email from the county attorney appeared on Senator Bruce's iPad. It read, "Need to see you pronto. Hefty."

The senator left a message on Hogan's voice mail that he would come to the county attorney's office after the morning committee meetings, at about eleven o'clock. He found himself caught up in a drawn-out public hearing on a bill to impose term limits on Supreme Court Justices. When he finally arrived at Hogan's office, it was ten minutes after noon. Hefty grasped his hand, thumbed in the direction of a chair, and returned to his seat behind his desk.

Stretch apologized for being late. When Hogan waved a dismissive hand, Stretch said, "You sent for me. What's up?"

"Does your lady friend, the senator from Missoula, always leave articles of clothing in her office?"

Stretch paused, puzzled by the question. "How would I know? She may or may not. What difference does it make?"

Hefty fidgeted briefly with a sheet of paper on his desk before responding. "Yesterday an email showed up on my machine out of the blue. I made a copy of it for you to see."

Hogan passed the paper across the desk. Stretch picked it up to read, "CHECK THE SILK SCARF THAT'S IN THE DESK DRAWER AT THAT WELTER WOMAN'S OFFICE."

He looked at the county attorney to ask, "What's this all about?"

"Damned if I know. But we need to get into Senator Welter's office again. Have to follow up."

"Who sent this anyway?" The senator's voice carried a tone of irritation, and his face showed anger.

Hogan's voice remained calm. "Don't know, Stretch. As I said, it just showed up on my machine. As you can see, the sender is someone who calls himself 'Truth,' whatever that means."

Stretch leaned back in his chair, rubbed his hand across the back of his neck as the scowl deepened. "Your guys have already gone over her office. Apparently they didn't find anything they thought was important. What do you expect to learn if they look again and find a woman's scarf in Audrey's office? What the hell would one of her scarves have to do with anything?" He shook the piece of paper, "This doesn't mean a thing. It's either from a crank or from someone who doesn't like Audrey's political views. Hell, it could be some friend of Howard Welter—the same one who called to tell you Audrey Welter killed Gloria Angel."

"You're right, it could be anyone. But we can't simply ignore it. We have to follow up."

Stretch inhaled, held it, and blew out a long breath. When he spoke again, it was with apparent resignation. "Well, I think she'll let the sheriff go through her office again. She won't like it though." He frowned again. "And frankly, Hefty, I don't like it either. It appears that your whole focus is on Senator Audrey Welter."

"It isn't." Hogan leaned back from the desk to ask, "Tell me, Stretch, what would you do if you were county attorney and got this email?"

"Oh hell, you know what I'd do—exactly what you're doing. That's the hell of it. I can't suggest to Audrey that she refuse the request." He stopped short. "It is a request, isn't it? No threats of a warrant?"

"It's just a request, friend." The county attorney smiled and spread his arm widely in a show of openness. "I don't think there's a need for anything other than that. Ms. Welter has been very cooperative so far."

Stretch stood, paper in hand, and said, "Let me know when the sheriff wants to visit Audrey's office." He turned and strode out the door.

Stretch found the senator from Missoula seated at the desk in her office. He knocked on the jamb of the open door and was greeted with her brilliant smile and a friendly, "Hi, Stretch."

Without returning the smile, he closed the door. Stretch pulled a chair around sideways so he could sit with his long legs outstretched, as was his habit. Audrey, watching his actions, could tell he had something serious to discuss. She leaned back and waited for him to speak. Stretch folded his hands across his belt buckle and glanced at the articles on the desktop—some legislative bills in two piles, a tablet on which she had made notes, and a pen lying next to the tablet. His eyes rested for a second on the picture of Audrey with her son. Finally, he turned to look directly into her eyes. "The sheriff wants to get into this office again." He gestured with his chin and said, "Hefty Hogan got an anonymous email telling him to look for a silk scarf in a drawer in that desk."

Audrey's eyebrows rose as she leaned even farther back in her chair. "Silk scarf?" She leaned forward again to search Stretch's face. "What's this all about?"

"I don't know. Maybe you'd better look in the drawers."

Audrey reached to her right to pull open the top drawer and looked down at a phone book, some stationery, and several pencils and pens. Shoving that drawer closed, she pulled the lower one open, glanced at the stack of old legislative bills that it contained, and jammed it closed. With her frustration showing, she yanked open the top and then the lower drawer in the left side of the desk. The top one held a copy of Mason's Rules of Legislative Procedure, a rubber stamp, which might be used to affix her name to a mass mailing, and some envelopes that she knew contained constituent letters yet to be answered. The bottom drawer was empty. Audrey pushed it closed, raised her eyes to look at Stretch. "There isn't any scarf here." She breathed deeply as though she had been holding her breath and added, "I knew there wouldn't be."

"Could it be under something so that you didn't see it just now?"

Audrey's usual pleasant countenance turned to a dark frown. "Do you think I'm trying to hide something?"

"No, of course not. But it would be wise to be certain."

It seemed to Stretch that she stared at him for a whole minute. She almost snarled when she said, "You come look." Her anger was apparent when she yanked at the right-hand top drawer and waited for him to stand and move around to the end of the desk where he could see its contents. The few loose items in the drawer couldn't cover a scarf. Slamming that drawer closed, she pulled at the one below. For a moment she simply looked fixedly at the three-inch pile of bills. She reached down and began to lift them, a few at a time, to place them on the desktop. As the printed sheets were peeled away, it became apparent that something under the pile was causing a slight upward bulge. Audrey ran her finger underneath the rest of the bills, lifted them and held them to the side. Her hand remained rigid as she stared in disbelief at the plum-colored piece of cloth that was smashed nearly flat on the bottom of the drawer.

She dropped the bills on the desktop and moved to grasp the cloth. Stretch quickly reached to stop her. His voice was stern when he commanded, "Don't touch it." He added in a more quiet tone, "It may be evidence that will shed light on Gloria's murder."

Audrey drew her hand away from him with her eyes still on the cloth. She clasped both her arms around her body. "God, Stretch! That thing isn't mine." She raised her eyes to him and whispered, "Someone put it there." Her whole body shuddered. "Someone is trying to make me look like Gloria's murderer."

Stretch placed his hand gently on her shoulder and said, "We don't know that." He squeezed her shoulder. "We don't know what, if anything, that silk cloth might have to do with Gloria Angel."

"Stretch, don't be so dense. Whoever sent the email knew the scarf was in the drawer. And whoever it is must know there is something about the scarf that will implicate me in the murder." Her body shuddered again. "God, Stretch. I'm terrified!"

Stretch let out a deep breath. "You're probably right. The person who sent the email must have hidden the scarf under the old bills where you wouldn't notice it."

She implored, "What do we do now?" Before he could answer, she rattled, "I'll destroy it. I'll put it in my purse right now. Take it to my apartment, and burn it in the fireplace. If it's gone before the sheriff comes to search again, there'll be nothing for him to find." She added quickly. "You and I are the only ones who know that it's here."

Before she touched the scarf, Stretch almost yelled, "Hold it!" He glared fiercely into her eyes. "It's not true that you and I are the only ones who know about it. The one who put it there knows. He may be able to prove, somehow, that the scarf was in the drawer and only disappeared after Hefty warned me, and I warned you."

"Then, for God's sake, what do we do?"

Stretch's cheeks puffed out as he blew. "Let's calm down and think." For a moment he sat with his lips pursed together. At last he said, "Hefty won't be able to get a search warrant on the basis of an email from some unknown person. Any judge would require more than that." After a second, he continued, "He may try to bluff and threaten a warrant, but we can call his bluff and stonewall him. The problem, however, is that the one who sent the email may disclose himself and provide other information. Who knows? A judge may get enough information from some other source to issue a search warrant."

"But, it wouldn't look very good for me when they find the scarf after I refused to let them look for it without a warrant."

"No, it wouldn't. And that's the rub."

"Stretch, we started out trying to show Hogan and the sheriff that we want to be cooperative. Maybe we should continue to do that."

"You mean go to Hefty and tell him what we found?"

"That's one thought." Audrey shook her head. "But I really don't trust Hefty Hogan anymore. And I'm afraid of the sheriff. They both seem to have me in mind as their main suspect. Are they even looking at anyone else as the possible murderer?"

"I asked Hogan the same question. He assured me they're pursuing other leads, too, but he didn't say what they are." Stretch allowed the muscles in his face to relax and reached his hand across the desk as he said, "I certainly understand why you feel as you do about the sheriff and the county attorney. But maybe you're right. Maybe you should let them come here and gather up that scarf. Maybe it would be best to just get it over with. Who could have sent the email, do you suppose?"

Audrey shook her head. "The murderer, of course. Or anyone who doesn't like me or doesn't like my politics." She leaned forward with her elbows on the desk, her face covered by her hands. "Yes, I'm sure the best thing to do is continue our cooperation. But I'm starting to regret going to them in the first place." She sighed, "OK, when do we go to Hogan again?"

"Let me get my coat, and we'll go right now."

She stood and turned for her coat. "All right, let's get this over with."

The moment Senator Bruce walked through the door to his office to gather up his topcoat, his secretary announced, "The sheriff called. He asked if he could visit Audrey Welter's office at four o'clock this afternoon. Is that all right?"

"We're heading for Hefty Hogan's office right now. Please call the sheriff and tell him so. Perhaps he can meet us there."

At the county attorney's office, Hefty approached Audrey with his hand outstretched. "It's good to see you again, Senator."

Audrey deemed his smile to be hypocritical, but she grasped his hand just long enough to be polite and nodded without responding.

Hogan turned to Stretch Bruce. "Senator."

Stretch pointed into the office and said in a curt voice. "We're here to talk." With that he put his hand on the small of Audrey's back and guided her through the door with Hogan trailing behind. Once Hefty was inside, Stretch closed the door firmly, held a chair for Audrey, and then sprawled in another. As Hogan walked around the desk to his chair, Stretch Bruce asked, "The sheriff isn't here?"

"No. Did you expect him?"

"I asked my secretary to call him to meet us."

"Well, he ain't here. Maybe he didn't get the message."

Stretch shrugged and asked, "What have you done to trace that email?"

"Computer experts in our office tell me that they can trace it to the Bozeman library. They have computers for public use."

"If you know where it came from, you should be able to find out who sent it. They must keep a record of the people who use the computers at the library."

"That's what I thought. But apparently anyone can sign up and rent a computer at libraries. And the people who sign up can give any name they choose. No proof of identity is required. And they can use any old name to log on to the Internet. I wouldn't be surprised if there are a lot of John Joneses on the list—maybe even a lot of 'Truths.'"

"Damn it, Hefty, there should be a way to learn the identity of that person." He leaned forward for emphasis. "The email isn't a hell of a lot of value to you until you can verify the sender."

"You mean, I can't get a search warrant based on it?" Hogan nodded his head. "You're right about that." He turned his attention toward Audrey. "You said you want to be cooperative. I'm hoping you still mean it and will let the sheriff go through your office again—without a warrant." When Audrey raised her eyebrows and turned to Stretch without answering, Hogan, too, shifted his gaze to the tall man. "What about it? Can the sheriff take another look?"

Stretch returned his stare without speaking—long enough for Hefty to blink. "Senator Welter has cooperated with you and the sheriff right from the beginning. She's willing to let Mendenhall go over her office one more time." He continued to focus his eyes firmly on the county attorney. "She expects, in return, that you and your people will thoroughly investigate every aspect of the death of Gloria Angel—every bit of evidence, every possible suspect. She guesses, with reason, that you and the sheriff have concluded that she committed the crime and that all you're doing now is trying to prove it."

Hefty Hogan shook his head vigorously. "I've told you before, Stretch, that the sheriff and his men are working as hard as they can to investigate every single possibility." He turned to Audrey. "Senator, no one believes at this time that you are a murderer." The look of skepticism on her face led him to add, "You may not believe that, but it's true. But surely you understand that we have to check out all the information we receive, including anything that involves you."

Stretch leaned forward. "What about that transient? He was in the building and certainly had the opportunity to kill Gloria. What have you learned about him?"

"Nothing." Hefty shook his head slowly. "So far we haven't found him. What would be his motive anyway?"

"Motive? Hell, anything could be his motive." Stretch straightened as he spoke. "Let's suppose he's someone who's angry at Senator Welter's legislative activities. She's been pretty outspoken and aggressive on occasion, especially on matters relating to the environment. Maybe some nutty rancher decided to get even with her because she wants to keep the water in the creek for the fish instead of diverting it into an irrigation ditch."

Hogan laughed and even Audrey grinned at that one. She poked at him with her elbow and said. "You're the only one who'd get that upset at my proposals."

Hefty shook his head. "That's a pretty far fetched-idea, my friend. But I'll mention it to Sheriff Mendenhall although I doubt that he'll take it seriously."

Stretch stood and stepped behind Audrey's chair to hold it as she got to her feet. "Tell the sheriff to be at Audrey's office at four o'clock this afternoon. We'll be waiting."

Sheriff Mendenhall knocked on the door promptly at the appointed hour. He removed his hat and stood with it in his hands. "Thank you for cooperating with us, Senator Welter. I realize this is difficult for you."

His deputy stood at attention near the entry. Stretch leaned against the wall across from the door.

Audrey stood to the side and pointed at her desk. "I guess that's what you came to inspect, isn't it?"

"Yes, ma'am. The email said one of the drawers. May I?"

"Of course, sir. Do what you came to do."

The sheriff pulled open the right top drawer, shuffled the contents around with his hand, and closed it again. He opened the next one below, saw the pile of bills, and paused for a moment. Mendenhall gently lifted the corner of the entire pile. He hesitated at the sight of the plum colored cloth lying on the bottom of the drawer. The law officer looked first at Audrey, then at Stretch, and finally at his deputy. He pulled the cloth upward and held it by one corner between his thumb and forefinger, arm outstretched. To the deputy he growled, "We didn't find this the last time we were here."

"No, sir. But you were the one who looked through the desk."

The sheriff turned with a scowl to Audrey. "Did you put this cloth in here after our last inspection?"

Audrey's face was grim as she replied, "No, Sheriff Mendenhall, I didn't. I apparently had done just as you did. I didn't look under that pile of bills, so it may have been there when you last looked, or it may not have been."

The sheriff appeared loathe to admit that his first search had been less than thorough. There was a note of sheepishness in his voice when he mumbled, "You're probably right. We'll have to take this for analysis, ma'am."

"I realize that, Sheriff. Do what you have to do."

"You don't seem surprised?"

"Surprised that the cloth is there? Of course not. When Senator Bruce told me of the email, I looked and there it was."

She waited only a second before adding in a calm voice. "You needn't ask, sir. That cloth isn't mine, and I had never seen it before I did exactly as you just did. I removed the old legislative bills and found it under them."

Sheriff Mendenhall stood quietly as she spoke before gesturing to his deputy who stepped forward with a pair of tweezers and a clear plastic bag in hand. He plucked the scarf from the sheriff's outstretched hand with the tweezers and dropped it in the transparent container and sealed it. The sheriff pulled a marking pen from his shirt pocket and wrote a description of the contents as well as the date and time on the face of the bag. He also noted that Audrey Welter and Lynn Bruce were present. After Deputy Kramer signed it, he offered the pen to Stretch. Stretch Bruce hesitated before he signed and dated it. When the sheriff turned toward Audrey, Stretch said, "That's not necessary."

Mendenhall shrugged and put the pen back in his shirt pocket. He turned to Audrey, put his finger to the brim of his hat and said, "Thank you, Ms. Welter, for your cooperation. I understand how difficult this is for you. I appreciate your situation and assure you that nothing will be done to implicate you in the murder of Gloria Angel unless I become absolutely certain in my own mind that you did it." He started to turn to the door. "I hope that doesn't happen."

"That's kind of you to say, sir. You can rest assured that you can never conclude that I murdered her—because I didn't do it."

"Take that piece of cloth to the lab, run your analysis, and whatever else you plan to do. Let us know the results, if any, as soon as you receive them." Stretch's voice was authoritative and cold.

"I'll do that, Counselor. I surely will."

10

The following day Stretch sat at his desk on the floor of the Senate, barely hearing the drone of debate on innocuous bills, as the responsibilities of his law practice crept into his mind. His one-man law practice in Roundup had not gone away. While his clients were generally patient, appreciating his service in Helena, there were always matters that required his attention.

A small but very competent staff allowed him to be away from his office for such an extended period of time. Myrtle, the probate paralegal, had been with him for twelve years. Mary, the pleasant-faced receptionist and bill clerk, for seven years. Only Cynthia Weaver, the young lady who handled litigation matters was relatively new to the office. Cynthia was intelligent, ambitious, perceptive, and anxious to learn. During her short period of employment, she had become an almost irreplaceable asset. Each day he received emails from one or more or them with information they had received from clients, with requests for instructions and documents for review. Many required telephone conversations to resolve problems that had arisen. Some of his legal correspondence was prepared by his office staff and forwarded to him for review and mailing. But some of it was also handled by Barbara, his Senate secretary. It was a system that worked, but just barely.

The need to constantly dissect bills that were heard in his committees, the need to review those he must vote on during the floor session, the requirements of his leadership position, and the ordinary demands of his law practice left not nearly enough time to think of the needs of Audrey Welter, his Senate colleague and client. And yet, Audrey's situation seemed, at the moment, the most important of all.

11

A call came from Hogan just as Stretch was about to leave his capitol office for the beginning of the afternoon floor session. The county attorney demanded without preamble, "You better get down here right away."

"Why? What's up?"

"I'll tell you when you get here. How soon will that be?"

"The floor session starts in ten minutes. I'll be busy until about four o'clock. What's so damned important?"

Instead of answering the question, Hogan said brusquely, "If four is the earliest you can get here, it'll have to do." The phone crackled in Stretch's ear as the county attorney slammed the phone into its cradle.

Sheriff Mendenhall was in Hogan's office when the secretary ushered Stretch through the door where he stood for a moment, taking in the situation, then moved to the only remaining chair and focused on Hefty. "All right, you're both here, so it must be something serious. Let's hear it."

The sheriff shifted in his chair. Hefty passed a stapled report across the desk to Stretch. "The analysis of the cloth found in your client's desk disclosed traces of blood."

Stretch picked up the report, looked briefly at the first page, then quickly leafed through the rest. After reaching the last page, he dropped it on the desktop and looked at Hogan, "This doesn't do a great deal for me. I'm not a chemist."

Hogan responded, "Neither am I. But apparently that report tells those who understand it that there is blood on the cloth the sheriff took from Ms. Welter's office."

Stretch's eyebrows went up. "So what? The person who owned the cloth cut herself sometime. What's that got to do with anything?"

Before Hogan could respond, the sheriff leaned forward and said, "Senator Bruce, the blood on the cloth is the same type as the blood of Gloria Angel."

Stretch turned to face the older man, then leaned sideways in his chair and asked, "Type O? The universal type? That doesn't mean anything."

"You're correct, sir. It doesn't mean anything by itself. But we've asked for a DNA test and have reason to believe that test will show the blood came from Ms. Angel. The test will take a couple of weeks."

Hogan rubbed his bald head and interjected himself into the conversation. "We just felt we should put you on notice that the blood may positively link your client to the murder."

Stretch Bruce jerked himself around to face Hogan. His voice dripped sarcasm when he replied, "That's mighty nice of you." His scowl deepened as he continued. "It seems to me that you've made up your minds to charge Audrey Welter with homicide." He swiveled to face the sheriff again. "And having made up your minds, all that you're doing is searching for something to justify what you already plan to do."

The sheriff responded in a calm voice. "That may seem to be the case from your perspective, Senator. But it's not true. We will continue to look at every possibility while we wait for the DNA results." He leaned farther forward and quietly asked, "Would you rather we hadn't invited you here to tell you what we found from the initial blood test?"

Stretch looked back at the older man and shook his head. "Of course not." He was silent again for a long moment. "It's just frustrating to have you continue to focus on Senator Welter." Stretch rose from his chair and turned toward the door. Hogan and the sheriff were immediately on their feet. Before closing the door behind him, Stretch said, "Since you're in a generous frame of mind, let me know the results of the DNA test when you receive them."

The last thing he heard as he strode down the hallway was Hogan's voice calling, "We will, Counselor. Of course, we will."

Stretch met Audrey in the hallway outside their offices. He ushered her into his office. When she remained patiently silent with a quizzical look on her face, he said at last, "They found blood on that scarf."

Audrey's eyes widened, and she sat without moving, waiting to hear what would follow. Stretch pursed his lips, and said, "Apparently it's blood of the same type as that of Gloria Angel."

"What are you telling me?"

Stretch pulled his chair away from the desk and slumped into it. Heaving a sigh, he rubbed his hand across the back of his neck, "Audrey, they think it ties you to Gloria's death."

"How can they think that? It doesn't make sense."

Without answering her question, he continued, "They're having a DNA test done to determine if the blood could have come from Gloria." He sighed again. "They—the county attorney and the sheriff—said it would be a couple of weeks before the test was complete."

Audrey dropped her eyes to her hands clasped tightly together on her lap. She remained rigid for a long minute before slumping in the chair. When she looked at Bruce and spoke, it was with a small voice. "They've decided I killed her, haven't they?"

Her chin began to tremble, and a tear appeared in the corner of her eye. She rose from the chair, turned her back to him, inhaled sharply, then turned again to look at him and say, "God, Stretch, I'm scared." Tears began to run down both cheeks toward the dimples at the corners of her mouth. Her eyes dropped again, and she wiped at the tears with her sleeve. A small whimper escaped her.

Stretch was on his feet and around the desk in an instant. He handed her his handkerchief and then put his arms around her and pulled her close. She leaned against him as sobs racked her body. After a time the sobs diminished, and she put her hands on his chest and pushed herself away. Audrey turned her head to wipe the tears from her face and handed his handkerchief back to him. She sank back into the chair and whispered, "They've decided I'm a murderer. And there isn't anything we can do about it, is there?"

Stretch squatted down so that he was able to look more directly at her. "No, we can't stop them from doing what they're doing." He watched for her reaction before saying, "The only way we can stop them from going ahead with the DNA test is to find the actual killer."

"And we really don't have any way to do that, do we?"

"Not right now." He reached to put his hand on her. "Audrey, I know you didn't kill that woman. And that must become obvious to everyone eventually." He patted her arm, and then rose to stand and look down at her. "The joke will be on Hefty and the sheriff when the DNA test comes back and shows that the blood on the cloth had nothing to do with Gloria Angel." He smiled at the thought of it.

Audrey shook her head and wiped again beneath her eyes. "God, I hope so. What do we do while we wait?"

"We wait. And we go on about our business as state senators.

If I'm correct, you've got some pretty heavy bills about to come out of committee. Those'll keep you busy so you won't have to think about Gloria Angel and DNA tests."

"They'll keep me busy, but they won't keep me from worrying." She stood, reached her hand toward the waist of Senator Bruce. With a smile, she looked up. "Thanks, Stretch, for sticking with me. I don't know what I'd do if you hadn't agreed to help when I asked."

"You'd probably have a better lawyer."

"Maybe, but I doubt it. And no other lawyer could be such a good friend. That's the most important thing." She touched his arm, wiped at the wet beneath her eyes, and walked out the door without looking back.

Stretch sat for a long time as he tried to think of some way—any way—to learn the identity of the one who had actually killed Gloria Angel. In his mind he riffled through the people who might want her dead. One of them was Howard Welter, Audrey's ex-husband. Another might be the governor. Albert Shewey's activities certainly raised questions about his relationship with his dead associate. His thoughts turned to the vagrant found in the capitol. Whoever he was, he had no apparent reason to be there, and it seemed he was something other than his initial appearance indicated. And there may be others of whom he had no knowledge. But there was nothing that Stretch knew about that tied anybody except Audrey to the killing. Despite the scarf and the blood, he remained certain she didn't do it.

At last he decided his advice to Audrey to go about her duties as a state senator was good for him as well. He'd just wait to find out what the DNA test disclosed.

12

The email message read, "Call me as soon as possible." Stretch heaved a tired sigh as he reached for the phone. At the end of the legislative day he didn't feel up to coping with problems at his law office. The receptionist heard his voice and transferred him immediately to the litigation paralegal. His voice was curt when he asked, "What's up, Cynthia?"

"It's the Larsen case, sir. Answers to Interrogatories are due day after tomorrow. Mr. Larsen never gave us the information we needed to complete them, so I called him this morning. He apologized and answered all my questions." She paused and then continued in a rush. "I've prepared a draft. I could FedEx the draft to you for review and signature but you will hardly have time to review it, make the changes, and get them to the Clerk of Court in White Sulphur Springs on time."

Stretch ran the problem around in his mind. Before he could speak, Cynthia offered, "I can drive the draft to Helena tomorrow. You can review my work, and I'll use your laptop to make the changes you need. Then I can file them in White Sulphur as I go through there on my way back to Roundup the next day." When Stretch still didn't respond, she added, "You know what opposing council will do if we're late."

Stretch growled, "Yes, I know very well. The wretch will default us and put us to the work of setting the default aside. He'd love nothing more." He swiveled in his chair to look out the window without focusing on the view. "I hate to put you out.

What about your son? Is there someone who can look after him while you're gone?

"Sir, you know I have a nanny. She's already said she'll stay with Matt." There was brightness in her voice when she added, "It'll solve the problem, sir." Stretch heard her take a breath. "I've only been in Helena once, and I've never been there when the legislature was in session. I'd like to see the place where you spend your time during the winter every other year."

Stretch had to smile at that remark. "All right. I'll reserve a room for you at the Holiday where I stay. When you get to Helena, come to the capitol. My office is on the third floor. Ask anyone you find in the building, and they'll direct you to it."

"I'll find it, sir."

"Cynthia, thank you for arranging all of this. I really appreciate it." Before he dropped the phone in the cradle, he added, "And don't call me 'sir.' I've asked you before. It makes me feel too damn old."

"I'll try to remember, sir."

13

Stretch jumped and turned when Ambrose Swan walked quietly up behind him in the capitol hallway the following morning. The older man grasped his arm and grinned his lopsided grin. "Sorry. Didn't mean to frighten you."

Stretch returned the grin and said, "Not a problem. I just thought you were one of my constituents about to give me hell."

They walked along companionably side by side. Ambrose asked, "Did the law enforcement people ever learn the identity of that transient who was in this building the night Ms. Angel was killed?"

"Not that they've told me."

Swan stopped, then grabbed the senator's arm again to pull him around so they faced one another. "If Senator Welter's bill to prohibit drilling for oil and gas on the state land along the Rocky Mountain Front becomes law, the person who owns the adjacent tract of private land stands to lose any opportunity to have a well drilled on his property, isn't that right?"

"That's what we're told."

"Do you know who that individual is?"

"I've been told his name, but I can't remember it right now."

Swan gave Stretch's coat sleeve a shake. "Could he be the transient?"

Bruce cocked his head, looking puzzled. "What makes you think so?"

"That man, rumor has it, is somewhat unbalanced and has

voiced vague threats about 'getting the one' who is responsible if things don't go his way."

"Ah, come on, Ambrose. There are always rumors of crazy threats. They never mean a thing."

"Maybe not, but how better to 'get' Senator Welter than frame her for a murder?"

Stretch stared at the reporter for a long time. Then he asked, "Do you really believe something like that could've happened?"

"Don't know, Senator. Don't know." He turned to walk back in the direction they had come, then said over his shoulder, "We news people hear things. I just thought I'd pass it along." He left Stretch standing with a quizzical look on his face.

Cynthia was visiting with Barbara when Stretch returned to his office following the completion of the afternoon floor session. "I see you two have made acquaintance."

Barbara said, "Yes. And it's nice to be able to put a face to the lovely voice I've been hearing over the phone."

Cynthia smiled at the compliment and then dug into a large cloth bag she sometimes used as a purse. From it she pulled a packet of papers. Stretch began to read them as he sank into his office chair. Barbara turned back to the constituent letters she was typing, and Cynthia sat silently in one of the hard folding chairs that served for visitors. She understood the need to avoid disturbing either of them. When he turned the last page, Stretch looked across the desk at the young lady with a wide smile. "These are fine. I don't see any need to change them in any way. You've done your usual excellent work." Cynthia's smile glowed as Stretch reached into the inside pocket of his suit jacket for a pen. He affixed his signature to the legal papers with a flourish. He handed the document back to her and turned in his chair. "Leon Larsen provided good information. Those Interrogatories won't help the other side very much."

"No, sir. That was my thought too."

Stretch looked at his watch. "It's close to five o'clock. Let's get you registered at the hotel, and then we'll find some place nice for dinner."

Cynthia stood. "Could you show me some of the capitol on the way out? It's a huge building."

"Surely. We'll tour the Senate and House chambers right now. And maybe I can get us into the governor's office. The governor is always bragging about his availability to the public. We'll test it—but don't hold your breath."

"That isn't necessary, sir. I'm more interested in the place where you work."

He placed his hand on the middle of her back as they turned to the door. "OK. We'll look at some committee rooms too."

"One last request. Can I meet the woman senator you're representing? It would be nice to know what she looks like."

"Let's go see if she's still in her office."

She wasn't. But when they arrived at the balcony overlooking the rotunda, they met Senator Welter coming toward them in the company of a tall, handsome young man. Stretch immediately recognized Audrey's son from the picture on her desk. He introduced Cynthia to Audrey, then extended his hand to her son. "I'm Stretch Bruce, and you must be Senator Welter's son."

"That I am, sir, and I'm pleased to make your acquaintance. Mother speaks highly of you." His grasp was firm. "My name is Logan, by the way."

"It's nice to meet you, too, and as you heard, this is Cynthia Weaver, the one in my law office who does all the work."

The smile that Logan bestowed on Cynthia was the kind that only appears when a young man meets an extremely attractive young woman for the first time. "My, they do have lovely ladies in Roundup, Montana! And talented too!"

Cynthia's blush was barely noticeable. "Thank you, sir. And they have good-looking men in Missoula." She looked confused. "That's where you live, isn't it?"

Logan laughed as he cleared it up. "Well, that's where I grew up. I've lived in Boulder, Colorado, for the last couple of years. I just left a job there." He smiled at his mother as he reached his arm around her shoulder. "Mom says I can hang at her place for a while. I thought I could get in a month of skiing, but she says I'd better spend my time in search for another position."

Stretch felt a need to explain the presence of his paralegal. "Cynthia brought some legal papers that required my signature. We're touring the capitol, and then we need to get her settled in the hotel. After that, I hope she'll accompany me to the Montana Club for dinner. Would you two care to join us?"

Logan answered, "We'd love to." Turning to Audrey, he asked, "Wouldn't we, Mom?"

Audrey laughed the laugh that Stretch had come to enjoy. "Yes, of course. It's nice of you to ask." She smiled at her son and then turned to Stretch, "I'll warn you, though, he eats like a horse. Better bring your checkbook."

Senator Bruce chuckled at that remark. "I believe I can handle it." Grasping Cynthia's upper arm, he smiled down at her. "If we're going to tour this building, we'd better get on with it." Before leaving the other two, he suggested, "How about seven o'clock at the Club?"

Logan answered, "We'll be there."

Audrey and Logan were already seated at a table for four when Stretch and Cynthia arrived. Logan was on his feet in an instant and holding a chair for Cynthia—the one next to his. She favored him with a warm smile as she smoothly assumed her place. Once seated, the young woman offered a nod and another gracious smile to his mother. Stretch watched Logan's mindfulness of Cynthia with some amusement. But then he thought, "Why not? She's a mighty attractive young lady. He'd be an idiot not to pay attention to her." He turned to smile at Audrey, and then he dropped into the remaining chair and muttered, "I must be getting old. This day has worn me down." With a glance out of the corner of his eye at Audrey, he added, "It's those cussed, obstinate Democrats. They show me no mercy."

Audrey's grin was faint but discernible. "It isn't the Democrats that get to you, Senator. It's the Republican Speaker of the House. He's an obstacle to everything that's good for the state." The grin broadened. "Want to fire him?"

Before Stretch could respond to that barb, Cynthia leaned toward her employer wearing a worried look. "I hope my tour of the capitol wasn't an imposition, sir." She shook her head. "I should've realized you would be tired at the end of the day." Stretch's cheerful countenance returned. "Don't concern yourself, Cynthia. I enjoyed showing you Montana's house of government." He reached for the menu. "Let's decide on dinner. Then I'll tell you of an interesting conversation I had with Ambrose Swan."

Audrey dropped her menu. "If Ambrose told you something that has to do with the killing of Gloria Angel, I want to hear it now, not later."

Stretch replaced his own menu, looked around the table, and then focused on Audrey. "Of course you do. Swan mentioned the vagrant that was in the capitol building the night Ms. Angel was murdered. And he wondered if the vagrant could possibly be the man who owns the section of private land, the section that's adjacent to the state land on which your bill would prohibit drilling. They're both parcels of land that some believe could produce oil or gas or both. He said there are rumors that the owner of the private land has threatened to 'get' the one who deprived him of the opportunity to benefit from such production." He paused for effect. "Ambrose wondered if he might have tried to 'get' you, Audrey, by killing Gloria and arranging for the blame to fall on you."

Logan spoke first. "That seems like pure speculation—wild speculation with no substance behind it."

Audrey shifted her eyes from her son to her attorney. "Logan's right. Unless we can show that the vagrant is really that landowner, why even think about it? No jury would consider that theory as an alternative to me as the murderer."

Stretch picked up the menu again. "Of course. I just thought it was an interesting idea." Looking at Logan, he added, "We may want to check it out before the time of the trial—if this ever comes to a trial—just to be certain the vagrant and the landowner aren't one and the same."

He turned his attention to his paralegal. "Cynthia, we've worked together for a long time. It seems strange that I don't know what your favorite foods might be, but they serve excellent prime rib, if that would suit your fancy. Both the chicken and salmon dishes are very good."

"The beef sounds delicious, but let me review the menu before I decide."

Over a cup of coffee after dinner, Logan leaned toward Stretch to say, "Mother has told me about the scarf with the blood on it, the one that was found in one of her desk drawers. That sounds ominous to me. Would you mind sharing with me your thoughts about the seriousness of Mom's situation?"

"The situation is serious. It would be foolish to tell you otherwise. Think of things the way they appear to the law enforcement people. Audrey was the last known person to see Gloria Angel before her death. It has been said that Audrey threatened to kill Gloria. Those remarks were made several years ago but nonetheless they were made, and the county attorney knows about them. And now a scarf with blood on it, blood that may or may not be that of Gloria Angel, has been found in Audrey's desk." Stretch turned his chair to the side to speak to Logan. "In the eyes of the sheriff and the county attorney, all of those things point directly at your mother as the killer."

"Mom said they were doing a DNA test on the blood. If the blood doesn't match that of Gloria Angel, is Mother off the hook, so to speak?"

"If that should be the case, it seems to me it would poke a big hole in any assumption that Audrey is the one responsible for Gloria's death. It probably would not stop the sheriff and his deputies from continuing to look for other things to tie your mother to the killing. It's their job to be thorough."

"And what if the DNA proves to be a match?"

Stretch glanced at Audrey before answering, "If that happens, the situation becomes much worse. I'm not even going to think of that possibility now."

Logan frowned in thought. "At the moment I have lots of free time, and I'd like to help. Is there anything I can do that might make your job easier?"

Stretch smiled in appreciation. "It's good of you to offer. I can't think of anything right now. But both your mother and I will keep the offer in mind."

That seemed to satisfy Logan. He turned to look at Cynthia, paused, and then turned back to Stretch. "You showed this lovely lady the capitol building. Would you mind if I offered to show her some of the nightlife of the capital city? They have a good band playing in a club on the north end of Montana Avenue."

"Don't ask me, son. She's sitting right there. Ask her."

Logan's voice had an eager note. "How about it, Cynthia?"

Cynthia looked first at her employer as though to get permission. She smiled at Logan. "I'd like that. But only for a short while. I have work to do and a long drive tomorrow."

Logan was on his feet. To Stretch he said, "I'll get her back to the hotel at a proper time, sir." He reached to hold the chair for Cynthia, grasped her arm, and escorted her from the room.

Audrey's eyes were big. "Well! It seems my son may be smitten."

"Why wouldn't he be? Cynthia's someone special. But they live in different worlds, so it will probably just be one night of dancing."

"Perhaps you're right." Audrey pushed back her chair to stand. "It's a nice warm winter evening, Stretch. Walk me up and down the Gulch one time, and then you have to drive me back to my apartment. Evidently Logan is so taken with your assistant he forgot that he left me in a lurch—without a car."

"Are you sure you wouldn't like to go dancing?"

Audrey cast a startled glance at him. "You're kidding, of course."

"About the dancing, I am. Can't do it. But I would take you to some dark place for an after-dinner cocktail."

"Nope, Stretch. It's to bed for me." A grin appeared. "Even though the offer might be tempting at some other time."

By eleven o'clock, Stretch found himself acting as he did when his own daughter was still living at home and out late. He felt foolish, looking out the window. Nonetheless, he felt relieved to see Logan drive into the hotel parking lot, watch Cynthia scoot out of the car, and not invite Logan to her room.

14

Stretch understood that a call from Hefty Hogan could only mean bad news for Audrey Welter. Hogan left a message with Stretch's secretary that he wanted to see the senator as soon as possible. The sheriff was again seated in one of the side chairs when Stretch walked in. Without greeting or invitation, Stretch pulled the other chair around so he could face both men. Hogan broke the silence. "We need to bring her in for questioning."

Stretch's face was impassive as he looked across the desk at Hogan. At last he asked with an air of innocence, "Who? Who do you need to bring in for questioning?"

Hefty shifted in his chair and rubbed his bald head, a gesture that seemed to indicate either nervousness or uncertainty. He leaned one elbow on the desk as he said, "Why, Audrey Welter, of course. Your client."

After another long wait, Stretch turned to Sheriff Mendenhall and asked, "Tell me, what has happened to make you decide you need to formally question Senator Welter?"

The sheriff leaned toward Stretch and spoke in a quiet voice. "The DNA test shows the blood on the cloth we found in the senator's office matches that of Gloria Angel." He looked over at Hogan, then back at Bruce. "We need to talk to her, sir. There are questions that must be asked."

Stretch shifted his gaze from the sheriff to the county attorney. The anger that was lurking below the surface was reflected in his grim-lipped countenance. "Senator Welter came to your office voluntarily, right after Gloria Angel was killed. At that time she told you she knew nothing about the manner of her death. What more do you need?"

Hogan started to respond but stopped when the sheriff put up his hand. Mendenhall leaned toward Stretch. "Senator Bruce, the DNA test links your client to the death of Ms. Angel. There may be an explanation for it that will exonerate Senator Welter. But we can't know whether or not that is the case until we question her."

Stretch's eyes remained on the sheriff for a long moment, then shifted to the county attorney. "So you're convinced Audrey is the murderer? Is that right?"

The sheriff again stopped Hogan from answering. "Senator, we're not convinced of anything at this time. We have a job to do. And we're going to do it."

Before Stretch could respond, Hogan jumped in by saying, "That's right. The sheriff and his men have been working hard to solve this crime."

"If they're working so hard, why haven't they learned the identity of the mysterious transient the deputy had in custody and then let walk away?"

Hogan's face reddened as he began to speak. The sheriff held up a hand to stop him. "We made a mistake, sir. I'm willing to admit that. But we haven't given up our attempts to locate him. And we will."

Hogan rubbed at his head again. "Damn it, Stretch, she's got to come in so she can be questioned. And she can do it voluntarily, or we'll get an arrest warrant and drag her in." He waited a second. "Which do you want?"

Stretch Bruce jumped from his chair. The anger in his eyes was reflected in the fierceness of his voice. He leaned over the desk so that his face was about two feet from that of Hefty Hogan.

"All right. First, I'll talk to Senator Welter and recommend that she talk to your boys. Second, if you decide to charge her, no arrest warrant is necessary. The senator is no flight risk, and she will appear in response to a summons." Turning to the sheriff, he asked, "You want her at your office, I suppose?"

Mendenhall, calm of demeanor and voice, replied, "Yes, that would be the place. At her convenience, sir. We'll accommodate Senator Welter's schedule."

The reasonable behavior of the sheriff drained away some of Stretch's fury. He turned to the door, looked back over his shoulder to say to Hogan, "I'll call your office to let you know Audrey's decision."

One Sunday, when he was a small boy, Stretch was enjoying a snowball fight with a friend in the yard that surrounded the church. The day was warm and the snow could be packed into hard balls, easy to throw. Unfortunately, the one he threw the hardest missed his friend and flew through the window of the church rectory. The minister had left the rectory to hold services at an outlying parish so no one but the two boys knew how the window was broken. His friend suggested they just get themselves home and not say a word about it to anyone. That way, there could be no punishment. Stretch spent an agonizing afternoon in his room upstairs under the eaves of the old house in which he lived. His conscience simply would not allow him to hide what he'd done. He had to tell someone and take his punishment. It took him a long time to decide whether he should tell his parents or go directly to the minister. At last he shuffled down the stairs, went to the kitchen to tell his mother he was going out for a while but would be home before supper and trudged slowly along the four blocks to the rectory. Never in his young life had he hated to do anything as much as he hated to face the minister.

Now as he drove from the courthouse to the capitol he remembered that the minister had smiled at his confession, patted him on the head, and acknowledged that he himself had done foolish things as a boy. But then he made Stretch promise to somehow earn a dollar each month for a year and put it in the collection. And he had done it, by agreeing to sweep the church after services, for which he was paid the dollar.

Not since the snowball incident had he faced a task as difficult as telling Audrey of his latest conversation with Hogan and Mendenhall. In his mind's eye he could already see the stricken look that would grip her face as she listened.

If only his current dilemma could be solved as easily as the one with the minister.

He found Audrey in the capitol rotunda, visiting with a group of constituents. Rather than interrupt, he stood near the grand staircase and admired the gracious manner in which she turned her smile from one to the other of the small group of elderly ladies. When one of them asked a question, Audrey focused her eyes and attention directly on that person, as though the question was the most important one she had heard that day. At last, the group leader, a tall, angular woman with long white hair, said in a commanding voice, "That's enough, ladies. We've taken too much of Senator Welter's time. She's assured us the bill to allow clear-cut logging of the state forestlands near Soda Creek will never pass. That's the assurance we came to get." There was a chorus of thanks as the group moved away. Audrey watched them until they disappeared around the staircase.

When she met Stretch near the bottom of the staircase, her smile was radiant. "The thing I enjoy the most about this job is making constituents happy."

Stretch smiled in return but asked, "Should they be happy?

If your prediction is correct and the logging of state forest lands is prohibited, money for education will be lost."

"Oh hell, Senator Bruce, we've been arguing this forever. We can't finance education at the expense of a destroyed environment."

Stretch raised his hands in a gesture of surrender. "All right. I give up. But only because you Democrats control the Senate. Maybe someday we Republicans will have a chance."

"I know. When that day comes, you'll graze off all the grass before you clear-cut all the timber in order to strip-mine the whole state."

Stretch laughed at the old accusation. "Great idea!" The laugh lines in his face fell away, and he reached for her arm to lead her toward the elevator. "Come to my office. We have to talk."

She looked up quickly. "Sounds serious. What's going on?"

He just punched the elevator button. "In my sanctuary. And yes, it is very serious."

With the door to his office closed and locked, they sat facing each other. Stretch drew in a deep breath and then told her of his conversation with the sheriff and the county attorney. The desolate look that darkened Audrey's face was worse than Stretch had anticipated.

She closed her eyes and sat silently a long time. At last she raised her head and muttered in a leaden voice, "So they've decided to charge me with murder."

"That isn't certain, but we may as well get the interview over with." When she sat silently, eyes on her feet, he added with a tinge of urgency, "Having the sheriff arrive with a warrant just won't do."

With a sigh of resignation, she mumbled, "You're right, of course." Audrey covered her face with her hands and shuddered.

"How could this be happening?" She pulled her hands down to look him directly in the eye. "Tell me, Stretch, how can this be happening?" The voice that a short time ago had spoken in calm and even tones now became a soft wail.

Stretch stood, grasped her hands, and pulled her to her feet. Then he gathered her into a close embrace and slowly massaged the small of her back. In a whisper, he said, "I don't know, Audrey. Obviously someone is trying to frame you. We just don't know who or why."

She clung silently to him for a long time before she pulled away and grabbed a handkerchief to wipe her eyes. Then she smiled a tremulous smile and said, "Let's get it over with. Call the sheriff and tell him we'll be there in half an hour."

On the drive from the capitol to the courthouse, Stretch began to think that perhaps he was doing Audrey a disservice. His law practice was generally limited to the affairs of a small ranching community. When he represented someone in a criminal matter, that person had almost always been arrested and charged. With only a sheriff and three deputies, Musselshell County didn't do things the way they did them in the larger cities of Montana. Stretch had never attended a session where his client was to be questioned by law enforcement authorities on suspicion of murder.

Who would do the questioning? Probably the sheriff. Under what circumstances? Don't know. Would Hefty Hogan be there? Probably not, because Hogan wouldn't want to make himself a potential witness by participating in the questioning. Have I made a mistake in advising Audrey to attend the session? he wondered. I hope not. What should I be doing to protect her now that I've signed on? Just have to see how the questioning progresses and make decisions as it goes along.

When he looked across at the small form in the seat beside him, he knew that he couldn't voice his doubts. She needed reassurance and nothing else. Dear God, give me the wisdom to do right for her!

The sheriff's office was in the Criminal Facilities Building next to the courthouse. Stretch turned into the parking lot and maneuvered the Expedition into a slot between a dirty pickup truck and a Cadillac Escalade. A cold west wind tore at his face as he walked around to hold the door for Audrey so she could make the long step to the ground. Wind gusts caused them to stagger as they made their way to the entrance of the tall stone building.

A tall woman in uniform greeted them from behind a high counter above which there was a barrier of bullet proof Plexiglas. Stretch spoke through the small opening in the glass to introduce himself and Audrey. He explained that they were there to see the sheriff at the request of the county attorney. The woman looked more closely at Audrey before nodding silently and gesturing toward some badly worn and scarred benches along the wall. That searching look told them that she knew who they were and why they were there. The uniformed woman spoke quietly into an intercom, listened, and then turned around to say, "Officer Kramer will be with you shortly."

They were barely settled onto one of the benches when a short, overweight man about forty years of age in civilian clothes opened the door next to the counter. Without preamble he said, "C'mon," wheeled around, and retraced his steps. Audrey stared at his retreating form and then glanced up at Stretch, fear evident in her eyes. Stretch squeezed her arm as they rose to follow the officer, who now stood with his arms crossed next to an open door at the end of a long, dim hallway. The two senators entered the interrogation room to find it furnished with nothing more than a table and four chairs, all metal and bolted to the floor. A tall man of spare build stood with his arms crossed near the far end of the table. Stretch noted the mirror along one wall. It was obviously a one-way window that would allow others to observe an interview without detection by the one being questioned.

The short officer followed them through the door and closed it firmly behind them. As Audrey looked uncertainly around, the taller, neatly dressed officer stepped forward and said, "I'm Detective Loren Hammond." Gesturing toward the other man, he added, "This is Detective Buzz Kramer." With a sweep of his hand, he indicated that Audrey and Stretch should take a seat. He slid his narrow frame into the chair at the head of the table while his partner sat at the other end.

The manner of the introduction and the discourteous behavior toward Audrey grated on Stretch's ordinarily calm disposition. Rather than sitting as directed, he stuck his hands in his pockets and growled, "My name's Lynn Bruce. The lady with me is Senator Audrey Welter. We're here voluntarily at the request of County Attorney Hefty Hogan and Sheriff Brent Mendenhall. It would be best if you notified them both that we've arrived."

The short detective leaned back in his chair and clasped his hands over his belly. "The sheriff told us to interrogate *Ms.* Welter." The emphasis, obviously intended to let him know that the title of senator meant nothing to the man, caused Stretch's ire to rise even more. He stepped closer to Detective

Stretch leaned forward with his knuckles on the table to look down on the man as he spoke. "Listen, smart guy, *Ms.* Welter isn't answering any questions from you clowns. Get off your butt and call the sheriff. You have about five seconds to do it before we walk out of here."

Detective Kramer dropped his hands from his belly and glanced toward his partner. Detective Hammond returned the look, then shook his head, and rose from his chair. With arms outstretched and hands held palm down in a calming gesture, he turned his attention first to Audrey and then to Stretch. After a heartbeat he said, "Look, I'm sorry. We've gotten off to a bad start. The customary procedure around here is for us to interrogate suspects. The sheriff doesn't get involved."

Stretch faced Hammond. "If there're going to be any questions asked of *Senator* Welter…" He glanced at Kramer and then back at Hammond. "It'll be with the sheriff present." Standing erect and crossing his arms, he went on. "And come to think of it, the county attorney should be here too. Now get out of here and call 'em. When they get here, Senator Welter may or may not answer questions. She and I will wait in this room for ten minutes, and then we're gone." He looked at his watch to give emphasis to the time allowed.

Detective Kramer shoved his chair back and used clenched fists on the table to help him to his feet. He nodded to his partner and said, "I'll go. You stay."

Stretch's face contorted into a scowl. "Detective Hammond, you go with your buddy. If you're back in ten minutes saying the sheriff and county attorney are on their way, we'll be waiting. If you're not, we're out of here. Now get!"

Kramer's face took on a knowing look. "You're making a mistake. That lady is about to be charged with deliberate homicide. Getting on the wrong side of the sheriff and county attorney isn't going to make it easier for her." As he walked to the door, he said over his shoulder to Audrey, "You better think about it, ma'am."

When they were alone, Stretch saw that Audrey's face was ashen. "My God, Stretch, they're going to charge me with murder!" Her body trembled, and she reached for the back of a chair for support. Tears began to run down her cheeks.

Stretch, his anger diminishing now that the detectives were gone, put an arm around her shoulder and pulled her close. "They're not anywhere near that yet. The sheriff just has to ask you to explain how that scarf with Gloria's blood on it came to be in your desk drawer."

"That's what's so frightening. I can't explain it." Audrey looked up at him and wiped her eyes with the handkerchief he handed her. "I never saw that piece of cloth—never—until you and I started looking through the desk drawers."

"I believe you. Look, just answer the questions as they come. Answer them honestly, as I know you will. Don't let them try to force you to remember something that you can't. If you attempt to create memories where none exist in order to satisfy questions about your activities, you'll make a mistake. That's an old trick that investigators use to catch a person in a lie." When Audrey nodded and sank into a chair, Stretch sat beside her. "Was your office locked after you left the evening Gloria was killed?"

"I can't even remember that." Audrey thought a moment and added, "Maybe not. I never leave anything in there that someone would want to steal. I take my cell phone, my iPad, and laptop to my apartment each night." She shook her head. "There's never anything of value left in the room when I leave."

She lapsed into a silence that Stretch was not inclined to break. At last he looked at his watch. "Time's up. Let's go around to the county attorney's office and get things straight with Hogan. The hell with those two clowns."

"Are you sure that's the thing to do? I don't want to get into any more trouble than I'm in already."

"I'll square it with Hogan." Holding the door, he added, "Lead the way."

As they passed the counter in the front entryway, Stretch said to the woman at the desk, "We'll be at the county attorney's office. Tell Detectives Kramer and Hammond, in case they ask." The woman glared at them for a second and then turned to the intercom. They didn't stay to listen to what she had to say.

Stretch leaned far over Hogan's desk. The county attorney quickly tipped his chair back as though to put distance between them. "Listen, Hefty, Audrey has been cooperative and wants to be helpful. But those detectives told us that you're on the verge of charging her with homicide. Is that correct?"

Hogan turned in the chair, rose to his feet, and moved away from the glowering Bruce. "Look at it from my point of view, counselor. She had the opportunity—they were alone together at about the time the murder occurred. And we've learned she had the motive—Gloria Angel broke up her marriage. We haven't yet learned the means—the way she did it and the instrument she used, but the sheriff and his men are working on it."

"So you do plan to file the charge, is that it?"

"Well now, we're not on the verge of charging her. But the pressure is on to move this along. You can understand that, Stretch." There was a hint of a whine in his deep voice.

Bruce looked at his fellow lawyer for a very long moment, then said, "The pressure may be on, but it isn't in your interest to make the kind of mistake you're apparently about to make." He paused again. "Have you really pursued any other leads, or are you and the sheriff just looking at the easiest suspect as a means of getting the press, the public, Governor Albert Shewey, and Attorney General Henry Sawyer off your backs?"

Anger crept into Hogan's voice. "There isn't any other suspect." He jammed his hands in his pockets, striking a defiant pose. "And the evidence we've found so far is pretty damn convincing. It sure as hell looks like she did it." Both men seemed oblivious to the fact the subject of the discussion, was listening.

"Well, if that's your attitude, we'll leave. Senator Welter isn't answering any questions." He put his hand on Audrey's back to direct her toward the door. "If you decide to file charges and issue an arrest warrant, let me know. Audrey will appear without the need for any political stunt. No perp walk to impress the news people. Agreed?"

Hefty Hogan seemed to relax. "Yes, I understand." He turned toward Audrey and said, "This isn't personal, ma'am. It's what I have to do."

Audrey, standing rigid next to Stretch, took a quick breath and replied, "Obviously, it's very personal to me, sir. I'm the one who is accused of murder. Don't expect me to show concern for your problems."

Stretch guided her gently toward the door as he said again to the county attorney, "No perp walk. Got that?"

"I've got it, Stretch."

Hogan held out his hand, but Bruce ignored it. Instead he scowled and said, "You want to be attorney general. Mess this up, and you're dead meat. You charge a respected state senator with a homicide based on the information you have, the jury will laugh you out of the courtroom. Hell, they may even find you guilty."

Hogan's eyes widened before he stepped forward to slam the door as the two senators left the room.

The moment they were alone in the hallway, Audrey seemed on the verge of collapse. She leaned against the wall with her hands over her face as she began to sob. Stretch put his hands on her shoulders, pulled her close, and stroked her upper arms. The sobbing continued for a full minute. Then she straightened and stepped away, wiped at the tears, and took a deep breath. At last she said, "Let's get out of here before someone sees me." With that she turned and strode purposefully toward the exit.

Stretch followed her out to the parking lot and held her arm as the bitter wind tore at their clothing. Stretch had barely settled himself in the driver's side when she said, "I'll have to resign my Senate seat."

"My goodness, Audrey, there's no reason to do that."

"No. This won't keep. In the morning, the papers will report that I'm a 'person of interest.' Isn't that the euphemism law enforcement people use nowadays instead of calling the person a suspect?"

"Listen, I don't think either Hefty Hogan or Sheriff Mendenhall are dumb enough to put out such a statement. Even if something like that appears on the news, you aren't charged with a crime. And after Hefty thinks about it some more, I'm confident he'll realize he hasn't the evidence he needs to prove a charge of homicide. Better not to do anything in a hasty way."

"You know how it is in this town. It will be on the late news broadcasts tonight that I'm a suspect—by whatever euphemism."

"That may be right. But I still say you should wait before doing anything precipitous."

"I can't wait, Stretch. The presumption of innocence may be good in the courts, but it isn't good enough in the realm of public opinion. You know that. Once this comes out, the people in my district won't want a suspected murderer representing them." She looked directly at him for the first time since they left the detective's room and said, "I'll do a press release right away."

"Don't resign." He straightened in the seat, started the vehicle, and began the exit from the parking lot. With a sideways glance, he added, "Let's do this. I'll arrange for the capital reporters to come to my office. You can make the announcement that the law enforcement people have visited with you and that you have cooperated and will continue to do so. You should tell them of your meeting with Gloria Angel in your office. And then you should walk away and leave the rest to me. I'll take any questions.

That way you can get it over with as soon as possible, and I can take some of the pressure off."

Audrey looked out the side window at the passing scene, thought about the suggestion, then turned back. "Yes. That would probably be better. How soon can you gather the reporters?"

"I don't know. Let's get back to the capitol and find out."

Before Stretch could move, Audrey gasped, "I've got to call Logan and tell him his mother is about to be accused of killing another human being." As she finished, tears again trickled down her cheeks and she leaned toward Stretch and clutched his arm. Her voice was muffled as she spoke, "God! Oh God! How could this be happening?"

Apparently the word was out. Stretch notified the news people that he would have an important announcement in his office at three o'clock. By a quarter to three, the small room was packed with print reporters, all standing and vying for space near the front. Two television crews were struggling to haul their cameras and other sound equipment in through the door—pushing and shoving print reporters in an effort to get some space. Stretch, realizing that a better forum was needed, suggested in a loud voice that they all move to the old Supreme Court chamber. When the crowd seemed reluctant to move, he assured them he would appear in the chamber and at the scheduled time. When the last of the crowd left his office, paraded down the hall and out of sight, he knocked on the door of the ladies room that was nearby. Audrey emerged with a look of determination on her face. She'll need it, Stretch thought.

Rather than take a seat on the high rostrum used by legislators while holding committee meetings, Stretch stood directly in front of the chairs spread across the chamber floor—Audrey at his side. "Thank you all for coming. Senator Audrey Welter will make a short statement. After that, I'll take questions. Senator

Welter will not take any questions, so please don't direct any to her." Turning to Audrey, he said, "Senator Welter?" During the walk down the hall to the chamber, Audrey had gained control over her emotions and prepared herself for the ordeal.

She appeared to be perfectly poised as she moved forward a half step—head held high, posture perfect, hands clasped loosely in front. Her eyes focused on the television cameras. "You all know that Gloria Angel, aide to Governor Albert Shewey, was found dead here in the capitol a few days ago. The sheriff and county attorney have contacted me about the matter because Gloria Angel was in my office at about ten o'clock the night of her death. She was there at the request of the governor to discuss some federal legislation in which both he and I have an interest. The sheriff has inspected my office with my cooperation." She paused for a heartbeat, glanced from one spectator to another, then back at the cameras to continue.

"Senator Bruce and I have been told that a plum-colored silk scarf found in a desk drawer in my office has blood on it. We have just now been told that tests indicate the blood is Gloria Angel's." A murmur arose from the gathered throng and the print reporters began to scribble furiously. Audrey continued. "We've asked you here so I can tell those of you who are in this room and, through you, tell the rest of the world that I did not kill Gloria Angel nor did I have anything to do with her death. I had never seen the plum-colored scarf until it was found in my desk drawer. I don't own it, and I didn't put it there." Audrey turned her eyes from the cameras and scanned the room. "Let me say it again. I had nothing to do with the death of Ms. Angel. I hope the public will keep my statement in mind as events unfold." She stepped back to her place next to Stretch and said, "Thank you for your attention. As Senator Bruce said, I will not answer questions." She turned and quickly left by a side door.

The first question came from a loud-mouthed blogger who liked to think of himself as a legitimate reporter. He shouted after her. "Are they going to charge you?"

Stretch managed to keep his anger under control as he scowled at the man. "You were told Senator Welter would not answer questions." Then he looked around the room and asked, "Other questions?"

The obnoxious one wouldn't be denied. "If she won't answer the question, you answer it."

Senator Bruce stared at the mouthy one without speaking until the man began to squirm. Finally he said, "The county attorney is the one to answer that question. You should know that." And again he asked of the others in the room, "Any other questions?"

Ambrose Swan's voice was gravelly, and his speech was slow as he asked, "Can we assume, Senator Bruce, that you are acting as Senator Welter's attorney? And, if so, can you tell us what will be her defense if she is charged with the death of Gloria Angel?"

Stretch nodded his head as he answered, "Yes, Mr. Swan, I am acting as Senator Welter's lawyer. She asked me to do so because of our association as legislators and because of our friendship." He smiled at the questioner. "As to the defense, why would we even think of such a thing? There has been no accusation that Senator Welter did anything unlawful." Looking around the room as he spoke, Stretch said, "Senator Audrey Welter has told you she had nothing to do with the death of Ms. Angel, and we are certain that will be the conclusion."

Stretch handled several more questions before saying, "That's it for today, folks. I'm sure you will have other opportunities to delve into this as time goes along. Thank you for your attention."

As he turned to leave, the elderly Ambrose Swan stopped him. "Senator Bruce, a moment ago you spoke of your friendship with Senator Welter. Could it be more than friendship? Are you two romantically involved?"

Those who had started for the doors stopped in their tracks, and the room was suddenly silent. Stretch looked across at the questioner for a long time before answering. At last he said, "I've admired Senator Welter since she first came to the Senate. She's personable, intelligent, hard working, and witty. In addition to that, as you all have seen, she is very attractive. Mr. Swan, you are looking at me right now. Do you see anything in an old bald-headed man like me that would generate even a spark of romantic interest in the mind or heart of such a woman?"

Laughter broke out in the room and even Swan chuckled as he responded, "No, sir. I don't find you attractive at all, but that doesn't mean that Senator Welter would not. Perhaps you have virtues that aren't apparent to the rest of us." The laughter grew louder.

"Mr. Swan, if Senator Audrey Welter ever looks at me in a romantic way, I'll call you right away. I'd want you to be the first to hit the news with it. But it just ain't gonna happen."

The crowd was still laughing as the room cleared.

15

"Sheriff Mendenhall, this is Governor Albert Shewey."

"Yes, Governor. What can I do for you?"

"I have a confession to make." After a pause and a forced chuckle, the governor continued. "No, I'm not going to confess to the murder of my assistant, Gloria Angel."

"I hardly thought so, sir."

"The thing is, some time ago you asked me if I was in the capitol building the night of her death, and I told you I was not. Then you said the entry log and the time sheet showed I was there late that evening. You seemed to think I was lying."

"Well, the signature on the entry log is in your handwriting, and the security man verified it was you who was there."

"Yes, I understand. And now I don't deny it. You see, I did go to the capitol after a political dinner that evening for the purpose of picking up Gloria Angel, but somehow I just forgot about it when you asked me the question. Gloria was to meet with Senator Audrey Welter to discuss some legislation of mutual interest. She told me she would wait at the lower entrance. When I got there, she wasn't in sight so I went to Senator Welter's office. The door was closed. Then I walked around in the building to see if I could find her."

"Did you try to open the door to Senator Welter's office?"

"Yes sir, I did. It was locked."

"You said you then walked around the building. Did you find her?"

"No, I never did. I waited in the rotunda for a short while and then decided she had gotten a ride back to the Colonial Hotel with someone else, perhaps with Audrey."

"My understanding, Governor, is that the security people never saw you leave."

"That may be true. I left through the door at the end of the east wing, the one by my office, because that's where my driver was waiting for me."

Brent Mendenhall was silent as he thought about the information. "Well, it's nice of you to call to tell me all of this. I'll pass it along to the county attorney and to my detectives who are investigating the case." He deliberated a moment, then went on, "I may as well tell you that we're inclined to believe Audrey Welter may be implicated in the death of Gloria Angel."

"You think Audrey killed her?"

"We think she may have had something to do with it."

It was the governor's turn to pause in thought. "That's hard to believe. But I'm sure you have compelling evidence, or you wouldn't be telling me this."

"I wouldn't call it compelling evidence, but there are indications that we can't ignore." Mendenhall paused, then added, "Thank you again, Governor, for being so forthright. It helps to clear things up."

"My pleasure, sheriff." After he put the phone back on its cradle, Governor Shewey leaned back in his office chair and blew out a long breath. "Well, I'll be damned. Maybe I haven't as much to worry about as I thought."

16

The single sentence was among the horde of messages from constituents that appeared on Audrey's email. *"I know you didn't kill Gloria Angel, and I'm pretty sure I know who did."* There was no signature. The email identifier showed only mjones@gmail.com. Audrey stared at the message for a long time, then reached for the phone to call across the hallway to the office of Senator Bruce. Stretch, in the process of signing letters to his own constituents, smiled when he heard her voice but then his face turned somber as she related the content of the email message. When Audrey paused in her monologue, he said, "Let's have lunch. Meet me at the doors to the oval parking lot in fifteen minutes."

Audrey replied, "I'll be there."

When they were seated at a rear table in the small eatery in East Helena, five miles away from the prying eyes that seemed to be everywhere near the capitol, Stretch began by saying, "It should be possible to trace that message and find out who sent it."

Audrey shook her head. "Maybe. But we have no way to know where it came from. We don't even know if M Jones is a real name."

Stretch said, "In the mystery novels I read for relaxation, there is always a computer guru—someone who can tap into any computer in the world. We need one of those."

Audrey smiled. "I don't have one of those in my purse. How about you? Know any computer wizards?"

"I wish I did."

The conversation was interrupted by the arrival of a hamburger and fries for Stretch and soup and salad for Audrey. The silence continued as they took the first bites of food, then Audrey wondered, "Who could have sent the message? And how could that person know I didn't kill Gloria—or know who did?"

"Good questions. And why send an email without a signature and some indication of how to find her? Could the person be involved in the death somehow?"

Audrey put her soup spoon on the plate, sat back in her chair and muttered, "I'm not thinking clearly. All I have to do is reply and ask 'mjones' who he or she is. And I'll ask for more information about the killing."

"That makes sense. Maybe the sender will answer. If so, you may solve the mystery and learn who he really is. And maybe learn who killed Gloria Angel." With a smile, he said, "That would be nice."

"Nice? It would be a lot more than nice." Audrey swallowed a bite of salad, put down her fork, and fixed her companion with a sharp look. "Should we tell the county attorney?"

"Not yet. Let's find out as much as possible first. If we can locate the person who sent the message, perhaps we can take that person with us to talk to Hefty and Sheriff Mendenhall. If so, we may be able to lay to rest any notion that you were involved in Gloria's death."

"I'll reply as soon as I get back to my office. And I'll check with a computer person I know at the University to see if he can trace the email." That said, Audrey addressed the remains of her salad greens with vigor. She wasn't going to waste any more time.

At about the same time that Stretch and Audrey finished with lunch, the county attorney walked into his office from an out of town trip to be handed an email printout by his secretary. In his office he read the single line of capital letters. "AUDREY WELTER KILLED THAT WOMAN AND I CAN PROVE IT."

Hogan walked around the desk and slumped into his chair. After glancing at the writing once more, he closed his eyes and sat for a long time without moving. Finally he inhaled deeply before picking up the phone to call Sheriff Mendenhall. When the sheriff came on the line, the county attorney said, "Get over here right away. We've got a break in the Gloria Angel killing."

Later, with Brent Mendenhall seated in a side chair, Hefty leaned forward with his elbows resting on his desk. "We've got to find out who sent that email. It came from a Jsmith@AOL.com."

The sheriff chuckled, "Could it be the same guy who sent the email telling us to look at Audrey Welter's desk?"

"No. That first email came from "Truth."

"Wanna bet it's the same guy? If he's trying to conceal his identity, he wasn't very original in doing it. How many J. Smiths do you know? He's just using a fake name. And "Truth" sounds to me like some kind of screwball idea he thought he'd use to make his first message sound important. "

"The first message was important. It led you to the scarf with Gloria Angel's blood on it." Hefty's face was impassive. "I'm not so sure it's the same person. But this may be the thing that will clinch the case against the Welter woman." Hogan took a deep breath and blew it out. "It's the break I've been hoping for. I have almost enough to charge Senator Welter, and I'm convinced she's our murderer. This dude might be able to clinch it."

"I still think both names are phony. But maybe not." Mendenhall rubbed his jaw before he asked, "You replied to the first email. What did you say?"

"I asked who he is and told him to contact us as soon as possible. That message bounced back, undeliverable."

"Why don't you reply again? Maybe this time it'll get back to the sender. If so, we need to keep up the communication. Sooner or later he or she may come forward in person. When that happens, we'll find out if we've got one informant or two. He said he could prove Audrey Welter did it. That's what was on the email, right?"

"That's what it says. Here, I've printed a copy for you as well as one for my file." Hefty pushed the sheet of paper across the desk.

The sheriff scanned the one line of print, then raised his eyes up to Hogan. "Well my guess is he'll be in touch again. If this guy is real and not just some crank, he wants you to know he has information that you're desperate to get. Maybe he'll ask for money the next time or some other kind of favor. You can't get hurt by replying to the message." Then he looked at Hogan with a solemn face. "But don't be too hasty in your desire to charge Senator Welter with homicide. The governor has left us with a lot of questions."

"What kind of questions?"

"At his press conference right after we found the body, he said he didn't know why Gloria Angel was in the capitol building that night. Then he admitted she was there at his direction. When I first asked him if he was in the building that night, he said he was not. Then, when confronted with the security log, he admitted he was. His explanation was that he simply forgot about it. Seems highly unlikely that he would forget something like that, especially after he'd been told his favorite aide had just been murdered." The sheriff started to say more, then stopped.

Hogan scowled as he asked, "Is there something else I should know?"

Mendenhall didn't respond immediately. "We think someone beat us into Gloria Angel's office after she was killed. The news of her death didn't get out until we had her office secured. If someone was in there, it had to be a person who knew she was dead before the news people found out. Think about it."

"Did you find evidence of anything missing? Or anything destroyed? Any prints?"

"Lots of fingerprints. Most of them were those of Ms. Angel. But there were many others. Hard to know who might have left them or when. But to answer the rest of your question, no, we didn't find evidence of anything missing. But how are we to know? And we didn't find any evidence to lead us to believe anything had been destroyed. But we still think somebody was there for a reason. I have no idea what that might be."

"You think but you're not certain? Hell, that's just speculation!"

"Maybe, but there's one more thing. The governor said he tried the door to Audrey Welter's office while he was in the capitol that night but he couldn't get in because the door was locked. That door wasn't locked when we got there on the morning of the murder, before Ms. Welter arrived. My boys made a trip around the third floor of the capitol looking for anything that would help in the investigation. They tried doors to all of the offices. Many of them were locked. Audrey Welter's wasn't."

"Oh hell, there could be a hundred explanations for that. Maybe Welter came back after she clubbed that woman and didn't lock the door when she left a second time. Or maybe she killed her right in her own office and left the door unlocked in her hurry to escape."

"That's possible, I suppose. But so far the governor's word hasn't been the best. I don't know if the door was really locked when he said it was. The governor's not the only one who concerns us. The attorney general made a real effort to get into Ms. Angel's home."

"What do you mean?"

"Well, first he showed up at the front door of her townhouse the day after her death saying he needed to get a document she was supposed to deliver to him. When my deputy on guard refused to let him in, he got mad as hell and stormed away. Later he called Buzz Kramer, the officer in charge of the house investigation, and tried to sweet talk Buzz into letting him into the house. Buzz had heard about the first attempt and simply told the AG to talk to me. He never contacted me."

"Who the hell knows what Henry Sawyer may be up to? He's a lady's man. Perhaps he's concerned we'll find something to embarrass him. But that isn't any indication of an involvement in Gloria's death. Brent, I'm catching hell from the governor's office, from the press, and even from the attorney general because we haven't charged anyone with this brutal crime. I think I can convince a judge that I have probable cause to charge that Welter woman right now, and I'm inclined to do it. And I'm certain you can fill in the blanks in the case as the investigation goes along." He swiped again at his bald head and looked defiantly at Brent Mendenhall. "Damn it, I'm convinced she did the deed, even if you aren't."

"Well, Hefty, you're the one who has to make the decision about filing charges. Do it if you think you must and if you think you can follow through with a conviction. I intend to continue looking around. Who knows what might turn up? Maybe it'll be something to show with certainty that Audrey Welter is a murderer. Or maybe it'll be something to show that another person did it. If it's the latter, you can always dismiss the Welter charges."

"And look like the biggest fool in the world."

The sheriff's lips barely moved to make a smile. "You said it. I didn't."

Near midnight, the governor sat alone in his study in the governor's mansion and pondered his situation. Gloria Angel was a temptress. He had never intended to speak of his one night of drunken foolishness with that eager woman in Billings. But on the trip to D. C., when he and Gloria were alone after a late meal, remorse over his affair, along with Gloria's habit of quiet listening, had overcome his good judgment. He'd poured out the whole sordid story—how the woman had lured him into her hotel room and how he had simply lost control of his emotions.

He realized that was a mistake when he and Gloria were alone together in his office at the capitol. That day she made it clear that she wanted more from him than her present position as a governor's aide. What more she had in mind was not expressed at the time, but there was an implicit threat that she would expose his indiscretion unless she got it—whatever "it" was. He'd been married for thirty years, and he still loved his wife very much. She was a woman, however, who would not tolerate infidelity for one minute. When she divorced him, she would make it as nasty and costly as possible. And that would not only be the end of his marriage but the end of his political career.

But that wasn't the worst of it. He'd allowed Gloria Angel access to all of his papers, all of his communications, everything about the way he conducted his office. Except one thing. She didn't know, he was certain, about his conversations with the construction contractor and kickbacks from the highway contracts. But could she have somehow learned of them and been able to monitor their conversations? If that information ever became public, it could mean more than the destruction of his marriage; it could lead to criminal penalties.

Governor Shewey rose from the chair and paced across the room. Montana's senior United States senator was seventy-nine years old, and his term expired with the next election. He'd already hinted to the party faithful that he wouldn't run again. The governor was in his first term and could seek re-election. But he also knew the Senate nomination could be his for the asking. So he would have to choose one or the other. He felt confident he could defeat any Republican for either office in the general election.

Until a few days ago Gloria Angel seemed to be the only obstacle between him and a seat in the US Senate. With her death the obstacle was removed—unless she had hidden some writing, or, God forbid, hidden something she had managed to tape. But the inventory of her office didn't disclose anything that threatened him. What, though, of the town house where she lived? Her parents cleaned it out within days of her death and put it up for sale. Apparently they found nothing of a scandalous nature among their daughter's belongings. But maybe they hadn't gone carefully through her papers yet. Something could still come to light to destroy him. At last he sank back into the chair with a feeling of despair and mumbled, "I've done all I can to protect myself from that one night when I blathered foolishly to that woman and from anything else that she may have known." After a long moment, he added, "God, I wish I'd never met that witch."

Two hours later, Attorney General Henry Sawyer paced the floor in his home located on the mountainside, overlooking the city of Helena and the capitol building. Divorced and living alone, it had been easy to become entangled in the web that Gloria Angel wove. He pictured her in his mind. Beautiful beyond description. No one could argue that. But Gloria Angel really was a creature from hell. She could insinuate herself into any situation and then seek to gain advantage from it. He thought back to the night she cozied up to him here in his home and listened as he spoke too freely of his political ambitions. He wanted to be governor. That was no secret. It was expected that he would have no serious Republican opposition in the primary, but it was probable that Albert Shewey would run for re-election as governor. Sawyer knew it was never easy to beat an incumbent. What he needed was an extra something that would create problems for Shewey in the eyes of the electorate. Having listened to his ramblings, Gloria had looked into his eyes and quietly said, "I can help."

Surprise was not an adequate description of his reaction. She worked for the governor. And she had always been a Democrat. Why, he had asked, would she be willing to help him, a Republican? "Just because we're here together like this." And then she smiled an enigmatic smile and added, "I think you will be governor. And I think you will someday get to be United States senator. And I want to take that ride with you." Henry Sawyer was still assimilating her comment when she added, "I have information that will destroy Albert Shewey."

"What kind of information?"

"It's in writing and it's irrefutable."

Damn her soul, he had never gotten anything more out of her. And he hadn't been able to get into either her office or her home to look for whatever was in writing.

"Information that would destroy Albert Shewey." That's what she'd said. It had to be something serious—even criminal in its nature. Henry Sawyer suddenly stopped pacing. Could she also have learned of his arrangement with the wholesaler who provided the beverages for the state liquor stores?

The attorney general resumed his pacing and thought back to a Montana State Bar meeting in Butte when he and a lawyer friend from Missoula watched Gloria Angel work the crowd in the company of Governor Shewey. The friend grinned and asked,

The Body on the Floor of the Rotunda

"Do you think the governor's wife or Audrey Welter's ex-husband will kill that woman first?"

"I can see why the governor's wife would do it, but why Welter's ex?"

The friend's look seemed to ask if Henry Sawyer really didn't know what was going on in the world. "Surely you know that Howard Welter is obsessed with Gloria Angel. Hell, he's been stalking her for months."

"Has she reported him for it?"

"I guess not. None of the authorities seems to be doing anything about it." He chuckled, "Maybe she thinks he's harmless."

"Isn't he?"

"Damn, I hope so. But he's told lots of people that he intends to have her, or no one else can have her either. The friend waved a circle next to his head with his finger. "The guy seems to have gone round the bend."

"How do you know all this?"

"It's all anyone talks about in Missoula whenever Audrey Welter's name appears in the paper. And her name is there almost every day, amidst reports on legislative matters. She knows how to use the press."

That was the end of the conversation, and Henry Sawyer had erased it from his mind until Gloria Angel's body was found. Now it occurred to him that if Hefty Hogan wasn't successful in hanging the killing on Audrey Welter, perhaps he'd go for her ex-husband, Howard Welter.

17

Six days later, Ambrose Swan stopped Stretch in the capitol hallway. After the customary exchange of greetings, Swan glanced around to be certain no one could hear them and asked, "Have you discussed the Angel killing with the sheriff?"

"Only when we've been in the office of the county attorney." Stretch looked perplexed. "Why do you ask?"

Swan was naturally slow of speech. Senator Bruce always thought the old man used the compulsive need of all politicians to fill a void with talk as a means of learning about things best left unmentioned. So Stretch remained silent and waited, lest he be guilty of that mistake. There was a substantial pause before the reporter responded. "You should do it. You may learn things from the sheriff that you won't get from the county attorney."

"What makes you think so?"

"Reporters have sources." Swan paused. "Senator Audrey Welter has always been highly respected and serves the state and its people very well. It would be a shame if the Angel killing were to destroy her. Go talk to Mendenhall. It will be worth your time." With that final admonition Ambrose Swan ambled slowly away, leaving Stretch Bruce staring after his retreating form.

After calling for an appointment, Stretch met with Sheriff Mendenhall later in the afternoon. The sheriff greeted him evenly. When they were seated in Mendenhall's office with the door closed, the officer asked, "What can I do for you?"

"I'm here, as you've surely guessed, about the Angel killing and the perception that Audrey Welter was involved. It appears that the investigation has focused on her alone—to the exclusion of other possibilities. Is that correct?"

"No, it isn't correct. We've followed every lead in an attempt to find the one who did the killing."

"Can you share with me the information you've gathered?"

Sheriff Mendenhall pushed back in his chair and rubbed at his jaw while he thought. At last he asked, "Do you know the county attorney got an email from someone saying they could prove Audrey Welter killed Gloria Angel?"

Stretch's eyes widened slightly. "Another email?" Before the sheriff could speak, he added, "No, I don't know about that. When did the email arrive?"

"A couple of days ago. We don't know for sure who sent it because there was no signature, and it was from JSmith." Mendenhall shook his head, "Of course, the one who sent the message could have used any name other than his own. If so, we may never find him."

"Is that the name that was on the email telling you to look in Audrey's desk for the scarf? And are you sure it's a him and not a her?"

The sheriff smiled as he answered, "No, not quite the same name. The other one was from someone calling himself 'Truth.' And no, I'm not sure it's a man. It could be a woman."

Stretch leaned forward. "Can I get a copy of that message?"

"I'm not sure the county attorney would approve of our conversation. And I'm not certain he would want me to give a copy to you." He reached to his left as he said, "But you'll get it anyway if Ms. Welter is charged. So I'll run this through the copier. I'll be right back." When he returned he handed the copy to Stretch. "Doesn't tell us much, does it?"

Stretch stared at the single line of words and then back at the sheriff. "I agree. It doesn't tell us much. What else should I know?"

"You should know the county attorney replied to the email. JSmith may send more information." The sheriff paused. When he spoke, it was with some evident reluctance. "There are several things that bother me. We've heard conflicting stories from the governor. Nothing to make me think he's involved in the death of Gloria Angel but worrisome enough to make me want to find out more. And the attorney general seems unusually concerned about Ms. Angel's affairs." He stopped, sat back, and clasped his hands across his belly, looking as though he were reluctant to say anything more.

Stretch remained silent and waited for the sheriff to continue. When he didn't speak, Bruce said, "You said you wanted to know more about possible involvement by the governor. What makes you think he's involved in any way?"

The sheriff shook his head. "I didn't say I thought he was involved. I just said we've heard conflicting stories from him."

"Like what?"

"Look, it isn't my job to find a defense for your client. Hogan will probably be mad as hell that I've told you as much as I have." He stood, put his hands in his pockets, turned to look out the window, then jerked his hands abruptly from his pockets, swung back the chair and sat. "It seems to me you should know everything we know. Let me list the things about the governor that concern me. First, the governor said he didn't know why Gloria Angel was in the capitol the night she was killed. Then he remembered he had sent her there. He said he wasn't in the capitol that night, but the log showed he entered at about ten o'clock. Confronted with the log, he admitted to it. Then he said Ms. Welter's office door was locked when he tried to get in as he searched the building for Ms. Angel the night she was killed. But the door wasn't locked when my men and the city police got there first thing after the security man found the body."

Stretch listened in amazement to the monologue. When the sheriff paused, he asked, "Why would he lie?"

"Damned if I know. But it does make me wonder." Mendenhall pursed his lips. "There's one more thing. We think the governor or someone with access to his suite got into Gloria Angel's office after her death and before we got it secured."

"What makes you think so?"

"The office was as neat and tidy as a room could be. Obviously Ms. Angel was a fastidious woman. But one file drawer was partially open. That isn't characteristic of a person of her nature."

"But she could have been in a hurry and left it."

"Of course. It just seems peculiar, that's all." The sheriff leaned back in the chair. "With all the governor's dissembling, it makes me wonder."

"What are you doing about it?"

"Right now, nothing. But as far as I'm concerned, the investigation is ongoing."

Stretch sat for a while, assimilating the information provided by the sheriff. At last he asked, "What about the transient that was in the capitol that night? Did you ever locate him again?"

"Not yet. But the word is out. We'll find him. When we do, I promise you he'll get a more thorough going-over than he got the first time."

"Do you have a picture of him?"

"No. We didn't see any need to take mug shots." The sheriff raised his eyebrows. "Why do you ask?"

"I'm told about a man who owns a section of land north of here. He apparently believes Audrey Welter's legislative efforts may deprive him of the opportunity to lease his land to an oil company. And there's word that he's threatened to do something about it."

The sheriff perked up. "What's his name? We'll check him out."

"I don't know his name, but the boys at the State Lands Department can tell you."

Sheriff Mendenhall returned to his old habit of rubbing his jaw in thought. "Interesting. Probably no connection between him and our transient, but we'll sure as hell find out."

Stretch nodded his approval while asking, "Have any other leads?"

Mendenhall looked sharply at Bruce as he asked, "Do you know Howard Welter, the senator's ex?"

"No, I've never met him. Why do you ask?"

"As you can guess, we've dug into Audrey Welter's past. We know what caused the divorce. Several people have told us that Howard Welter has developed an obsessive hatred for Gloria Angel."

"Really!"

"Welter was in Helena the day of Ms. Angel's death. Stayed at a downtown hotel. One of my deputies went to Missoula to talk to him. He met with the deputy but was evasive during the conversation. The deputy said it was impossible to get a straight answer from the man. We've tried to trace his comings and goings the night of the killing without any luck. He said he was in his room at the time Gloria Angel went over the railing but no one from the hotel can confirm it."

"Well, I'll be damned. I'll have to discuss this with Audrey."

"You do that." The sheriff pushed the chair away from the desk, turned to the side, and crossed his legs. "Now, I've bared my soul to you, what have you got to share with me?"

Stretch grinned. "I don't get something for nothing, is that it?" Before the sheriff could respond, he continued. "As you are well aware, the defense in a criminal matter isn't obligated to give the prosecution anything." When the sheriff remained sober-faced, he dropped the grin and said, "But I appreciate your candor. And there is one thing." He paused for effect. "Hefty isn't the only one getting emails. Audrey received one too. It said, 'I know you didn't kill Gloria Angel, and I know who did.' That email came from mjones—all small letters, all one word. No way to know if that's a real name either."

It was Brent Mendenhall's turn to ponder. At last he said, "I'd sure like to see a copy of that email. It might help us in our investigation. The message may be from a crank but, if it isn't, I need to know."

"Audrey doesn't know I've told you about it. But I'm sure she'll agree that you should get a copy. One of us will drop it off at your office. If you can learn anything that will lead to the real killer, both she and I will be grateful." Stretch leaned forward again and there was earnestness in his voice. "Audrey didn't do it, sheriff. It's important that we find the one who did."

"Well, I won't concede that she didn't do it. There's a lot to show she may have been the one. But I agree we need to look into every possibility."

Stretch asked the question he'd had on his mind when he made the appointment. "Do you know where she was killed? Did the killer club her right there at the rotunda railing where she went over? Or was she beaten to death somewhere else and dragged to the railing and dropped over?"

Mendenhall shook his head. "We don't know the answer to those questions. My guess is that she got whacked somewhere in the general vicinity of the railing but not right beside it. If that happened, the killer either carried or dragged her to the railing and dropped her over. If the killing was done away from the railing, the possibility that your client killed her seems less likely." Looking carefully at Senator Bruce, he asked, "Have you ever tried to pick up a person who was unconscious? Someone who couldn't give you any help? It's damn hard to do." When Stretch didn't respond, he said, "Gloria Angel was a small woman. But so is Audrey Welter. It's hard for me to see how your client could have moved that dead body very far. It's even harder for me to see how she could have lifted Ms. Angel high enough to drop her over the railing. I suppose she could have dragged her to the rail but if that was the case we might have found some scuff marks in the carpet. The police made the first search and didn't find any such marks. But they could've been there and they just missed 'em. It was pretty hectic the morning she was found."

"You're right about the size." The sheriff eyed him. "it seems to me that it would take more muscle than Audrey would have to lift her up onto the railing so she'd fall off the other side.

"Who knows the strength a person might find if she was trying to conceal a murder?"

"Do you think that's why Gloria was dropped onto the rotunda floor?"

"That's the only thing that makes sense. Whoever bashed in Ms. Angel's head wanted us to conclude she fell accidentally and that the fall was what killed her. Might have worked too, if she'd fallen just right."

Stretch shifted in his chair while looking up at the ceiling in thought. "If a blow to her head was what killed her, there should have been blood where the body fell. Didn't the autopsy report show that she'd bled from the nose and ear?" Before the sheriff could answer, Stretch asked, "You didn't find blood on the floor anywhere on the balcony around the rotunda?"

"No, we didn't. And that still bothers me." The sheriff paused again, then reiterated, "But we weren't able to secure the whole capitol building that night. There may have been blood somewhere, but we never got a chance for a thorough examination before the whole place was flooded with people tramping everywhere."

"What about in one of the committee rooms?"

"We've gone over them all without any success in finding blood. And we checked your client's office, as well as the offices of the other Senate leaders at the same time. No blood spots." Mendenhall smiled. "But, counselor, we'll keep working on it."

Stretch said, "Please do." He started to get up from his chair but sat again to ask, "A moment ago you said you had checked into Audrey Welter's background. Did you also check into the background of Gloria Angel?"

"Of course."

"And what did you learn?"

"Well, she grew up in Lambert, near Sidney. She went to MSU at Bozeman because she liked to ski and then became involved in student politics at the university. Before long she was heavily involved in the Democratic Party."

"What about her recent activities? Those are the ones that are important."

"She's been on the governor's staff since he was first elected. And she seems to be on good terms with every elected official in the state, even the Republicans."

"Sheriff, you're evading the question. What have you learned that might shed light on her death?"

The sheriff smiled. "You want to know whom she might have been seeing in a manner that wasn't a part of her professional duties. Someone who might have had a reason to want her out of the way."

"That's right. Let's hear the names."

"The list includes, among others, the governor, the attorney general, the secretary of state." He paused and pursed his lips before he added, "And the Lewis and Clark County Attorney."

Stretch bolted upright in his chair in surprise. "Hefty? Hefty Hogan?"

"Yup." Mendenhall leaned back and crossed his hands over his paunch as before. "Her Rolodex contained the usual list of names and phone numbers. Hefty was on the list." The sheriff considered what to say next. "Ms. Angel kept a diary of her daily doings. Well it really wasn't a diary so much as an appointment book. Her parents have it now, but I kept a copy. It showed not only the official activities related to her job but also a log of her social schedule." He paused again before he added, "And she had a very busy social schedule."

"You mean she was seeing Hefty on the sly?"

"Not necessarily on the sly. But they did share some evening meals in out-of-the-way eating places." Brent hurried to add, "But that wasn't unusual for her. She did the same thing with other officials."

"But Hefty's married!" When the sheriff just shrugged his shoulders, Stretch asked, "What other officials?"

"The governor, for one. It wasn't unusual for them to travel to governmental gatherings together. Everyone knows that."

"C'mon. Who else?"

"She had several evening excursions with the attorney general. Several with the secretary of state. At least one with our senior U. S. senator. And one with the governor of Washington."

Stretch shook his head in wonderment. "She really was a busy girl, wasn't she?'

"She surely was."

Senator Bruce leaned forward to ask, "What does Hefty have to say about all of this?"

"I've never asked him."

Stretch's eyes showed his astonishment. "Never asked him? Why not?"

"Spending time with the deceased doesn't mean a thing. Too many others spent time with that woman."

"Don't you think his relationship with the murder victim might compromise Hefty's thinking?"

"If so, I haven't seen any evidence of it."

Stretch slumped back in his chair as the possible ramifications of the sheriff's disclosure ran through his mind. "I have to think about this."

"I understand." The sheriff rose from his chair and put out a hand. "We've engaged in a lot of speculation. But that's all it is." Upon releasing Stretch's hand, he said, "Put that email in an envelope and mark it 'personal' for me. I'd rather not spread that information around too soon." As Stretch turned toward the door, he added, "If your client gets any more emails, please let me know. And I'll let you know if we find out who sent the emails to the county attorney—unless Hefty Hogan holds out on me."

"Why would Hefty hold out on you, for God's sake?"

"It's simple. Hefty's certain your client did the killing. I'm afraid that our county attorney sees this matter as his free ride into the office of Montana's attorney general. The conviction of a state senator would bring him a lot of publicity that would be helpful in the election campaign. And Hefty knows I'm not absolutely convinced that your client is the killer. That's the reason he may decide to keep information to himself."

"Are you sure he isn't holding out on you for another reason? Because of his involvement with Gloria Angel?"

"So far, I don't think so."

18

Among the members of the Montana legislature there was much idle chatter about the possibility that Audrey Welter killed Gloria Angel. As a consequence, Audrey found her relationship with others in the Senate dramatically changed. They no longer engaged her in the customary camaraderie. Instead she found herself treated politely and cordially but kept at a certain distance. Only Stretch continued to exhibit his usual warmth and friendship.

Their relationship as attorney and client was by now well known and there was no reason for them to conceal it. In the early evening, after the end of the day's session and when Stretch's secretary had left for the day, they closeted themselves in his office. Her first question was, "You've learned something. What is it?"

Stretch leaned back in his chair with his hands clasped behind his head and told her of his conversation with the sheriff, beginning with the part about the email received by the county attorney. He concluded by saying, "The most interesting thing about the conversation is Mendenhall's willingness to share information with me. Most peace officers believe they should avoid, as much as possible, providing information to a defense attorney, at least without first getting permission. It's obvious that Mendenhall isn't sure who did the killing, even if Hefty Hogan is certain you're the one."

Audrey listened in silence, then sighed, "It's comforting to know there's someone besides you who thinks I may not be a killer. I just hope he can keep the county attorney from doing something precipitous. Think about those emails. Doesn't it seem to you that there must have been at least two people—people we don't know about—in the capitol the night Gloria was killed?" When Stretch remained silent, she continued, "Each of those who sent an email must have seen the killing or something revealing about the killing. They may have seen different things or they may have seen the same thing and interpreted it differently. One of them believes that whatever that person saw will clear me. The other thinks whatever *that* person saw will convict me. Who could those people be? And why don't they just come forward and tell what they know?"

"No. It doesn't necessarily follow that two people saw something in the capitol building. The evidence to clear you could be something the killer said to another person. Or the thing that might convict you could be some additional piece of physical evidence, such as the scarf."

Audrey's eyes widened. "My God, Stretch. Do you think some other thing could have been planted in such a way as to make me look guilty?"

"It's possible. After all, it happened with the scarf." He dropped his hands to his knees and leaned forward. "I doubt it. But the hell of it is we just don't know."

He stood and looked down at his client and asked, "Did you respond to the email you received?"

"I did. And it didn't go through, so whoever sent it to me didn't get my reply."

"Give it time, then try again. It might work yet. But we mustn't get our hopes too high. Remember, the person may never respond. In any event, the ones sending the emails might have gotten information from others—the governor for example."

Audrey's reaction was to shake her head. "Perhaps." Then as though struck by another possibility, she asked, "Could the same person have sent both emails—the last one that Hogan got and the one that came to me? If that's the case, it's probably some crank making things up."

"I'm sure Sheriff Mendenhall has asked himself the same question." Stretch's tone of voice emphasized his feelings when he said, "I'm still surprised that the sheriff was so forthcoming with information. But it's clear to me that he has real doubts about your involvement in the death of Gloria Angel.

"Do you really believe he'll help find whoever killed her?"

"Oh, I think he's sincere in wanting to get the killer. Our problem is that Hefty Hogan may have decided you're the guilty party. He doesn't seem to share the sheriff's doubts about that."

Audrey frowned. "You're telling me that the county attorney could charge me with homicide, even though the sheriff still isn't convinced that I'm the one who killed Gloria?"

"Oh, Hefty could charge you whether or not the sheriff thinks you're the killer. But I'm not sure if that's the situation. The sheriff intimated as much." The look of anguish that crept over Audrey's face led Stretch to change the discussion from that depressing prospect. "Could your ex-husband have killed her?"

Audrey looked startled by the question. "Howard?" She shook her head vigorously, "No, Howard isn't the killing kind. Why in the world do you ask?"

"The sheriff knows Howard was in Helena the night of the killing. Your ex was evasive when the sheriff's deputy questioned him. So Mendenhall's suspicions are aroused."

"Stretch, I just can't see Howard hitting anyone hard enough to kill. He's a milquetoast, not a brutal person."

"Have you ever seen him in extreme anger? Most of us act out of character when we're really angry."

"No. I've never seen Howard extremely angry. When he gets mad, he sulks."

"The sheriff said some of Howard's acquaintances stated he had developed an obsessive hatred for Gloria Angel. Could that be true?"

"I suppose it could be. He was infatuated with her at the time our marriage dissolved. I've been told he followed her around for a while after our divorce and began to follow her again recently. It got to the point she told him to stay away or she'd report him as a stalker. But that's all rumor. Since Howard and I never even see each other anymore, much less carry on a conversation, I can't confirm it." She shook her head once again. "It's just hard for me to picture Howard bashing in the head of anyone—no matter how much hatred he might have."

"You may be right about two people being in the capitol and seeing something the night of the murder. That's the scenario most likely to explain the emails."

Audrey nodded as she said, "Even if that's not the case, we need to locate the one who sent the email to me. Damn, I wish I knew how to trace that message through cyberspace, but I guess there isn't any way to do it."

Stretch changed the subject again. "Ambrose Swan didn't have to suggest I visit the sheriff. He did it as a favor. Maybe we should return the favor and tell him about the email you received. If nothing else, he might write about it, and that would make your position look better in the eyes of the public."

Audrey's face took on a pained expression. "Does my position look bad?"

"Perhaps I used the wrong turn of phrase." He leaned forward for emphasis, "I just think it wouldn't hurt to reciprocate his generosity. And if there is some collateral benefit, so much the better."

"I don't know of any reason not to give him a copy of the email. Please deliver it to him. And as soon as possible."

Stretch rose from his chair and said, "I'll do it." He reached for Audrey's hand to help her to her feet. "In the meantime, make some phone calls. See what you can learn about the activities of your ex-husband. No one is in a better position to do that than you are. Despite your belief that he's a milquetoast, he might be the one we're all looking for."

Audrey made a face before she responded. "It seems like spying, but I'll make some inquiries. I have friends who don't like him because of what he did to me. They will be glad, I'm sure, to spill any dirt they can find."

The lead article in the Helena Independent newspaper carried the byline of Ambrose Swan and told of the three emails, one saying Audrey did not kill Gloria Angel, one telling the sheriff to look in Audrey Welter's office where he then found a blood-soaked scarf, and one that stated Audrey was the killer. The article also disclosed much of the other information given to Bruce by Sheriff Mendenhall, but not all of it. No mention was made of Gloria Angel's many social contacts.

As soon as he saw the paper, Hefty Hogan called Swan and angrily demanded to know the source of the reporter's information. Swan politely declined to tell him. Hogan then called Sheriff Mendenhall and screamed at him for disclosing investigative information without the county attorney's approval. Mendenhall listened patiently and then asked, "Are you sure the leak isn't in your office?" Hogan was silent for a second and then angrily dropped the phone in its cradle.

Stretch stopped Swan in the wide hallway between the Senate chamber and the House chamber to thank him for making the public aware of the email proclaiming Audrey's innocence. He added, "I just wish you hadn't felt it necessary to mention the other two emails. They may lead potential jurors to believe she's guilty."

Swan smiled and replied in his gravelly voice, "A newsman is obliged to report all the news. I can't be selective, Senator."

"I know that. But it would have helped the public view of Audrey if the email proclaiming her guilt had appeared in the news at least a day after the one confirming her innocence."

"As I said, I can't be selective, either in what I report or the time in which I report it." He started to walk on toward the stairs to the House gallery, then turned back to say quietly, "But that doesn't mean I can't sometimes tell certain individuals about things I learn—before that information gets out to the public. If something comes along that may affect your Senate friend one way or the other, I just might be tempted to give it to you first."

"Thanks, Ambrose. I can't ask for more."

19

One month after the death of Gloria Angel, Hefty Hogan handed the print-out across his desk to Sheriff Brent Mendenhall. The sheriff read it quickly, then turned his gaze to the county attorney. "Do you really believe this?"

"You're damn right I believe it. The last email like this said to look in her desk. You did and found the bloody scarf." Hefty leaned forward to emphasize his next statement. "I'll get the warrant and you'll serve it. You'll search the Welter woman's car, and I'll bet we find the flashlight that was used to kill Gloria Angel." He leaned back in his chair again with a look of extreme satisfaction. "The minute we have that flashlight in hand, I'm charging her with deliberate homicide."

The sheriff was silent, staring into space. After some deliberation, he asked, "Is this unsigned email enough to convince a judge to issue the search warrant?"

"I think a judge will do it, especially after the first one about the scarf proved to be good information. It clearly connected Audrey Welter to the death of Gloria Angel."

The sheriff thought some more, then intoned, "Suppose we do the search and find a flashlight. And suppose it has no prints on it. And suppose it has no blood on it. What then? It won't do a thing to show that Audrey Welter is a murderer."

Anger blossomed on the face of the county attorney. He straightened himself in the chair. "Listen, Brent. I'm the county attorney. I'll decide what to do with the evidence. Your job is to get it." He pointed across the desk at the law officer and spat, "I'll get the warrant by tomorrow morning. You serve it on Ms. Welter as soon as I get it to you. And you search her car right after that." He ground his teeth together and then growled, "I'm getting damn tired of your attempts to keep me from charging that woman. I don't want any more of it, do you hear?"

Sheriff Mendenhall slowly rose from the chair. He stood with his hands on his hips. "Mr. Hogan, I've been sheriff of this county for twenty years. No one has ever accused me of trying to impede an investigation—because I've never done it. And I'm not doing it now." He leaned over to place his fists on Hefty's desk. "I know my job, sir. And I'll do it the way I believe is correct, regardless of anything you might think or say." When he straightened again, his voice had softened. "Just remember, if charging Senator Welter with homicide turns out to be the biggest mistake of your life, I warned you." With that final remark, he turned and strode purposefully from the county attorney's office.

The warrant was served on Audrey in her office. By the time she found and notified Stretch and they were able to get to where her car was parked, the search was under way. Every window in the capitol seemed to be crowded with people watching the law officers. Audrey, standing close to Stretch's side near the rear of her vehicle, watched as the sheriff's deputies lifted the back hatch and peered down into the opening behind the rear seat. There, next to the spare tire well and in plain sight, was a long, heavy flashlight of the kind that law officers carry—the kind of flashlight they sometimes use as weapons when necessary. Except for the flashlight, the space in behind the seat was empty.

Audrey was shaking her head as she looked up at her companion. "I don't understand it, Stretch. It isn't mine. I never saw it before."

He pulled her closer to comfort her. "I believe you."

Sheriff Mendenhall stepped the four paces that separated them and addressed Audrey after first looking at Stretch. "We'll have to take it in, ma'am, and have it analyzed." Directing his eyes at Stretch again, he added, "I'll let you know the results of the analysis, Mr. Bruce."

"Both Senator Welter and I appreciate that, Sheriff." Even though he knew it was futile to say it, he continued, "That thing doesn't belong to Audrey, and she doesn't know where it came from. Someone is trying to set her up."

"Perhaps, perhaps not. But we found it where the email said we'd find it. Now we have to try to learn why the flashlight is important to the investigation—if it proves to be important. That's what we're obligated to do." He tipped the brim of his hat with his finger and mumbled, "Good day, ma'am."

Audrey squeezed closer to Stretch as she watched Mendenhall walk toward his deputies to give them their final instructions. As the law officers slammed the hatch, she spoke quietly. "I can't go back into the capitol now, Stretch. Everyone in there has been watching. And they're all wondering if the sheriff has finally gotten what he needs to convict me of murder." She turned to look directly at his eyes. "I'm going back to my apartment. Please tell the Senate president why I won't be there for the day's floor session." Before he could answer, she pulled herself away from his side and strode hurriedly to the driver's door of her automobile. A deputy was standing in front of it. "Sorry, Ma'am, but this vehicle must be impounded."

Audrey backed away two steps, then asked, "Impounded? Why for goodness sake?"

"It's evidence, ma'am."

She turned to Stretch with a helpless look. "How in the hell am I to get around without a car?"

Stretch reached an arm around her shoulder. "I'll take you back to your apartment. In the morning we'll arrange for a rental so you'll have transportation."

A shudder racked Audrey's body. "My God, Stretch, how can this be happening? How much worse can it get?"

20

Hefty Hogan's voice was harsh as he spoke into the phone. "Brent, I'm filing a complaint for deliberate homicide today, and I'm naming Audrey Welter as the one who committed the crime." He took a deep breath. "I'm telling you first because of your apparent lack of certainty that she did it." Before the sheriff could respond, he growled, "I expect you to back me up—to continue to look for any additional evidence to support what we already have. Evidence that implicates Senator Welter absolutely."

The sheriff's voice was calm. "You're right when you say I'm not certain the evidence we have is convincing."

"The evidence is circumstantial but its convincing enough." Hogan's voice began to rise. "Damn it, Brent, nothing is ever certain. But we've gotten convictions in other cases on less evidence than we have here."

"You're the lawyer, Hefty. You're the one who decides when you have sufficient evidence to file charges." After a brief pause, the sheriff continued. "I'll keep looking for additional evidence. If I find anything that supports the charge you file, you'll get it. And if I find evidence that contradicts the charge, you'll get that too—and so will Stretch Bruce."

"God damn it! Whose side are you on anyway?"

Mendenhall laughed into the phone. "You know how it is. I'm a peace officer. I'm on the side of all that's right and just." Hogan started to growl a response, but Mendenhall cut it off. "Did you get a response from the email guy this time?"

"No. My email to him didn't go through. That dude must rent a machine to use just the one time and then go to another place the next time."

"Well, he may be back in contact. He better be. Without the information he said he can provide, your case against Audrey Welter is mighty weak."

Hogan yelled, "You're the one who's supposed to do the investigating. You find him. It's your job." He slammed down the phone, breaking the connection.

Hogan's next call was to Senator Bruce's office at the capitol. He asked that his call be returned as soon as possible. That done, he read again the press release his secretary had placed on his desk for review and revision. When the word went out that he was charging a state senator with murder, he wanted it to read just right. After that—the news conference.

Stretch called within the hour. Hogan said they needed to talk and told the senator to be at his office in thirty minutes. When Stretch asked why, Hogan just told him to get himself to the courthouse and dropped the telephone in its cradle.

Stretch's anger was evident when he walked into Hogan's office, and that anger was magnified by Hogan's announcement that he would file charges against Audrey that day. His voice was icy calm, however, when he said, "You're making the worst mistake of your life, don't you realize that?"

Hogan's face turned crimson. "I'm not making a mistake. Your client killed Gloria Angel, and I'll prove it."

"Hefty, you're letting your desire to be attorney general govern your action. You may not even have enough evidence to get past a motion for a directed verdict, much less enough to conviction."

"I know what I'm doing, damn it, so don't lecture me. I only called you down here as a matter of courtesy. I'm suggesting you bring Audrey Welter to the arraignment without any need for the sheriff to pick her up. If you don't like it or she won't come voluntarily, we'll have the perp walk you're so worried about."

"Oh, I'll bring her to the courthouse all right—after I see the charging information and after the arraignment is scheduled—if you're determined to go through with this." Stretch stared at the large man who was now furiously rubbing his baldhead. "Tell me, why are you so hell bent on charging Audrey Welter when Brent Mendenhall still believes there is more to be learned about the circumstances of the killing and seems to believe that some other person may even be the murderer?"

"The hell with Mendenhall. His job is to find evidence for me, and, by God, I intend to see that he does it."

Stretch shook his head in amazement at the statement. Then he said in a voice more quiet than before, "Well, you've obviously made up your mind. Get me a copy of the criminal information and let me know when the arraignment will be held. Audrey and I will be there. Don't expect a plea when the evidence you have is so thin."

"I don't want a plea. I intend to try this one myself. I'm not handing it over to one of my deputies. And I'll get a conviction."

The tall lawyer stared at the man for a long thirty seconds. "And if you don't, your dream of being attorney general goes down the drain. Think about it."

Hogan's anger flared. "Listen! When I get a conviction, I'm a shoo-in. Now, get the hell out of here. You aren't my guardian angel. I'll do what I damn well please."

21

The temperature was ten degrees, but the wind from the north made it feel like twenty below zero when Stretch and Audrey hurried from the parking lot into the courthouse. Hefty Hogan had spread the word that the arraignment of Senator Audrey Welter would take place at ten o'clock in the morning. In the main entry hall, two television cameras were already focused to catch Audrey as she came through the door. Both print and television reporters crowded forward, some trying to push a microphone to her face, each yelling a question. Stretch put his arm around her waist and pushed through the crowd, all the while muttering over and over, "No comment."

The small courtroom of Justice of the Peace Otto Hill had a gloomy appearance. The judge's bench was small, its wood darkened by the years. Every one of the few spectator seats was in use. Onlookers lined the walls. Stretch glanced around as he led his client beyond the swinging gate that separated the working area from the audience. The county attorney rose from his chair and moved toward Stretch with his hand held out. "Good morning, counselor."

As Stretch dutifully responded to the customary gesture, he thought the situation was not unlike that of two gladiators exchanging courtesies before battle. He grasped Hefty's hand and said, "I'd say good morning, but having just come in through the cold and wind, I'm not sure such a greeting is appropriate."

Hefty turned to face Audrey with a smile. "Good morning,

Ms. Welter. I regret that we're here under such circumstances."

Audrey's face remained solemn. "You don't regret it nearly as much as I do, sir." She walked away.

Stretch's voice was measured as he said to Hogan, "We've cooperated in every way, including appearing voluntarily today. I'm assuming you won't resist my request that the senator be released on her own recognizance."

"Ah, c'mon, Stretch. We're talking deliberate homicide here. She's got to post a bond, and a significant one, or sit it out in jail."

"What do you mean significant?"

"Not less than a hundred thousand."

Stretch was so astounded that he couldn't respond for a minute. Then he took a breath and growled, "We'll see what the judge has to say." He wheeled away from Hogan, put his briefcase on the defendant's table, and gestured for Audrey to join him. "Hefty's going to ask the judge to impose a hundred thousand dollar bond for your release pending trial. That's outrageous. I hope to persuade him to release you on your own recognizance."

"What would be customary, if I weren't a public figure?"

"You're a well respected public official. You've lived much of your life in Missoula, own a home, and work there. You have no record of previous wrongdoing. In short, you're not a flight risk." He shook his head. "Hefty knows all of that. The only reason to ask for a bond is to make a point with the public."

"And what's the point?"

"He wants to show that he isn't going to go easy on you just because of who you are."

"Politics as usual." Audrey put her hand on Stretch's arm as she leaned closer. "If the judge imposes a bond of that amount, I can post it." When Stretch raised his eyebrows in inquiry, she added, "I own my home in Missoula, free and clear. It's worth at least three hundred fifty thousand—probably a lot more. That should be sufficient security for the bond, shouldn't it?"

When he hesitated in his response, she added, "And there are other assets too, if that's what's required."

Stretch looked at her in silence, then nodded his head as he said, "The house would do it." Then he growled. "Nevertheless, you shouldn't have to post bond, and I'll do my damnedest to convince the judge."

As he finished speaking, a clerk called, "All rise." Judge Hill, nearly bald with a fringe of snow-white hair, stepped through the door from his chamber and up to the chair behind the bench. After rapping his gavel once, he seated himself, picked up the file and said, "This is the time set for case No. Cr. 14—632, State of Montana vs. Audrey Welter." He turned to Hogan and asked, "This is an arraignment on a charge of deliberate homicide. Is that so, Mr. County Attorney?"

Hogan was swift to his feet. "It is, Your Honor."

The judge then turned toward Stretch and Audrey, with a wisp of a smile. "I know who both of you are, of course, because of your legislative service." He looked down at the file, then raised his eyes toward Audrey to say, "Ms. Welter, you are the defendant. Is that correct?"

Stretch was on his feet immediately to respond. "Yes, Your Honor. Senator Welter is the defendant. She has appeared voluntarily for this proceeding."

"I take it you are representing her, Mr. Bruce?" The statement came as a question.

"Yes, sir, I am."

"Very well." The smile disappeared from his round face and took on a businesslike appearance. He picked up the file and scanned a document. To Audrey, he said, "The county attorney has charged you with the crime of deliberate homicide. Do you understand the charge?"

Audrey rose to her feet. "Yes, Your Honor, I do."

Turning to Stretch, he asked, "Do you wish to have the charging documents read?"

"That isn't necessary, Your Honor. I've seen them and so has my client. We waive the reading."

Turning to Audrey again, the judge asked, "You've had adequate opportunity to discuss the case with your attorney?"

Audrey's back was ramrod straight, her head was held high, and her hands were clasped together firmly in front. "I have, Your Honor."

"If that's the case, Ms. Welter, I must ask how you plead."

Her answer was spoken with quiet assurance. "I plead not guilty, Your Honor."

The judge nodded his head, dropped the file on the desk, and turned toward Hogan. "We must discuss the matter of bond. What is your recommendation as to the amount of a bond—if any, Mr. County Attorney?"

Hogan puffed himself up, rather like a pouter pigeon and launched into a monologue. "As you know, Your Honor, this is a case that potentially carries the most severe penalty. The murder was gruesome. The victim was a prominent person, not only here in Montana but on the national scene as well. The public outcry has been intense."

Before he could go farther, Judge Hill put up one hand to stop him. "No need for all of that. I read the newspapers, counselor. What is your recommendation as to bail?"

Hefty seemed taken aback but regrouped and leaned forward with his knuckles on the desk. "Section 46-9-301 (5) of the Montana codes governs. It states that bail must be commensurate with the nature of the offense. As I said, the murder of Gloria Angel was gruesome and committed in the most public of Montana places. I recommend that the court impose a bond in the amount of one million dollars."

Stretch's head swiveled to look at the county attorney. He spat, "That's ridiculous!"

Hefty shouted, "It's not ridiculous, Your Honor." He pointed in Audrey's direction. "That woman is facing the gallows. She has every reason to run!"

Judge Hill motioned with his hand for Hefty to quiet down. "That's enough, Mr. Hogan." He turned to Stretch. "And what do you recommend, Mr. Bruce?"

"With reference to the statute just quoted by the county attorney, subsections (7), (8), (9), and (10) provide guidance for the court. Senator Welter has no prior record, she's resided in the city of Missoula for several years, and is a member of the faculty at the University of Montana. She owns her home in that community, and her son lives with her. Finally, Your Honor, the defendant is a member of the Montana State Senate. She is not a flight risk. I recommend release on her own recognizance." He paused for an instant then asked, "Shall I give more reasons for release, Your Honor?"

"The reasons are indeed apparent, Mr. Bruce." Turning once again to the county attorney, he went on, "Mr. Hogan, first of all, your information doesn't set forth any aggravating circumstances that would make this a death penalty case. Until such circumstances are included in an amended information, if you ever file one, this isn't a capital case to which the death penalty applies. Secondly, given the background of the defendant, the knowledge of the law she's surely gathered from her legislative experience, as well as the firm ties she has to the Missoula university community, I believe it's highly unlikely that she'll flee the jurisdiction of the court." He paused, then directed his comment to the defendant. "Ms. Welter, will you voluntarily appear at all court hearings in this matter?"

"I will, Your Honor."

"Will you remain in touch with your attorney at all times until this matter is resolved?"

"Of course, Your Honor."

"Do you agree to refrain from criminal conduct of any kind during the pendency of this proceeding?"

"Certainly, Your Honor."

"All right. The defendant is released on her own recognizance." He turned again to Audrey. "Please understand if you fail to do any of the things to which you have just agreed, the county attorney may bring you back in here and once again ask for a substantial bond."

"I understand, Your Honor."

The judge smiled. "There being nothing more before the court, we're adjourned." He pushed himself from his seat and banged the gavel one final time.

Two uniformed deputies approached. One held a pair of handcuffs in his hands. The other, an imposing figure with his thumbs hooked through the belt holding his sidearm, announced, "We have to take the accused in for booking." Stretch stepped between them and his client to say, "No need for that, gentlemen. I'll walk Senator Welter across to the Criminal Facilities Building."

Just as the tall deputy put out an arm as though to push Stretch away, Sheriff Mendenhall walked up to the group. "I'll handle it." He touched his hat with his index finger. "If you and Ms. Welter will follow me, I'll run interference through the news folks out front." With that, he forced his way through the crowd with Stretch and Audrey close behind. One man jammed a microphone in Stretch's face and screamed over the noise of the crowd, "Isn't it true she got off without a bond only because she's a state senator?" Stretch elbowed his way past the newsman who yelled, "Isn't it correct that you public officials always get preferential treatment by the courts?"

At the corridor leading from the courthouse to the Criminal Facilities Building, the Sheriff directed a deputy to block the doorway to the trailing reporters. They went through a second door at the end of the corridor where Sheriff Mendenhall turned to Audrey and said, "Ms. Welter, the law requires that you be booked. The booking includes the taking of your fingerprints and your photograph."

Audrey, badly shaken by the court proceedings and the noise of the crowd, seemed to lack comprehension of the things the Sheriff was saying. Stretch, still grasping her arm, gave it a squeeze and said, "Come along, Senator, I'll stay with you."

In a small cluttered room, a technician rolled Audrey's fingers and thumb across the inkpad and imprinted them on the form that would then become part of her criminal file. She was photographed, both full faced and in profile, in front of a white mat. Throughout the process she moved as though in a trance.

When the booking was completed, the sheriff led the way to the doorway from the building. He stepped to one side and bobbed his head toward Audrey in what was almost a small bow. "Ms. Welter, I'm sorry you had to endure this." He reached for his jaw, rubbed it, then nodded again. "I've always admired your work as a member of the Senate." With that he turned on his heel and started back toward his office.

Stretch waited only an instant before calling after him, "Thanks for making it as painless as possible." Mendenhall waved an arm and continued walking without looking back.

Stretch opened the door, relieved to see that the cold had chased the news people away. During the walk to the parking lot against the bitter wind, Audrey huddled close to Stretch's side. When they were finally inside the car with the heater going,

Audrey sat for a full minute, staring down at her hands. When she looked up at Stretch, she said in a flat voice, "Now I have no choice but to resign."

"I'd try to dissuade you, but you're probably right. It would be difficult for you to serve effectively with this charge constantly on your mind."

"That's true, of course. But of more importance is my obligation to be fair to my constituents. They wouldn't elect a senator who was charged with murder so they shouldn't be burdened with one who is." She brushed away the tear that formed at the corner of her eye. "I'll get the resignation prepared right away. Will you file it with the secretary of state for me, please?"

"Of course."

The tears began to flow and she put her hands to her face to cover them. Stretch reached across to put his hand on her shoulder. Audrey dug in her purse for a handkerchief to wipe away the tears. She looked at her companion through red eyes. "I'll get out of town as quickly as I can in order to avoid any more pressure from the press." She dropped her head and wiped again at her face with the handkerchief. "I have a cabin up the Blackfoot River from Missoula. It's isolated and that's where I'll go." She thought for a moment. "The judge directed me to keep in touch with you. There's no phone at the cabin. You'll have my cell phone number and my email address. The reception isn't perfect at the cabin, but it works most of the time. I'll be sure to call you at least once a day, even if it means a trip to the public phone at the store in Potomac. I had a satellite dish for Internet access installed a couple of years ago, so we'll have email."

"It may not be wise to stay there alone. Is there someone who can spend time with you at the cabin?"

"Logan, of course. He's been in the east the past few days.

But he's a great kid, and he'll provide lots of support."

"He certainly seems to be a fine young man. Will he be back in Montana soon?"

"Maybe tomorrow." She sighed. "If necessary, he'll stay with me until this all ends." More tears formed and began to trickle down her cheek. "God! I wonder how it will end."

"It will end the way it should. We have to believe that." Stretch started to back the Expedition from its parking place, then stopped, reached for Audrey's hand and said, "I'd do anything to make this all go away—to make it as though it had never happened."

She squeezed his fingers. "Stretch, just do everything you can to protect me now that it has happened. That's all I ask."

22

The headline on the front page of the Helena Independent Record read "SENATOR CHARGED WITH MURDER." Her picture—the mug shot taken during the booking process—was directly under the headline. It portrayed an Audrey Welter that Stretch did not know. In the grainy black and white photo, her cheeks seemed to be sunken; her hair was disheveled; her eyes were lifeless. Audrey's appearance in the mug shot was that of a criminal. Exactly like the criminals pictured on wanted posters found in post offices.

Stretch cursed, wadded the paper in a ball, and hurled it across the room. Everyone in Lewis and Clark County would see the picture. Every potential juror would conclude that Audrey was guilty as sin. Talk about tainting the jury pool! Hefty Hogan had done it beautifully.

Audrey returned to Missoula in the early morning hours of the day after the arraignment. Logan welcomed his mother at the door and smothered her in a warm embrace. She closed her eyes and let him hold her for a full two minutes. She finally pulled away to look up at him. "Thank you for coming. But I'm sorry to interrupt your life. This wasn't ever supposed to happen."

Logan smiled as he gave her one more quick squeeze. "Hey, Mom. What's a child for?"

"Not to be forced to give support to a mother who is accused of murder."

Logan and Audrey sat on the davenport. "I know you couldn't hurt anyone. God, Mom, you couldn't even spank me when I was bad."

"Well, you were seldom bad. And you've grown up to be a fine adult so the upbringing must have been adequate."

"Do you want to tell me about the arraignment now?"

"Not now. I have to unpack and pack again. I told Stretch Bruce that I'd be at the cabin on the Blackfoot tomorrow."

"That's moving pretty fast. Can't you take a day or two here to relax and regroup?"

"No. I need to get away from everyone but you—as soon as possible."

She began to gather the clothes and other things she wished to take to the cabin. But the work was interrupted by a barrage of telephone calls. Some were from friends offering support. One was from a man who screamed that she was a murderer and would burn in hell. After that call, she allowed Logan to answer the phone. Even worse were the curious who knocked on her door as though they were old friends.

Early the following morning, Audrey and Logan escaped from Missoula to the seclusion and solitude of a cabin located on a mountainside above the Blackfoot River. Once there she used her cell phone for outgoing calls to Stretch once a day. That arrangement was less than perfect. All too often when she called, Stretch was busy with legislative matters or away from both his office and his hotel room. They exchanged emails, but she couldn't depend on a reliable Internet connection in stormy weather. Heavy clouds and snow often blocked the satellite signal. The situation caused them both considerable frustration.

Logan made it his job to keep Audrey busy with various wintertime activities, carefully avoiding discussion of the terrifying prospect that awaited his mother.

Rumors flew at the capitol. Speculation about Gloria Angel's death filled the newspaper. The flashlight found in Audrey Welter's car took center stage the same day Hefty Hogan sent Stretch an email. "They didn't find any fingerprints on the flashlight or on the batteries that were in it. She tried to wipe everything clean, but she missed a smudge of blood on the barrel of the light. The blood is Gloria Angel's."

Representing a client accused of murder is a difficult task under the best of circumstances. Doing it while performing legislative duties compounds the difficulty beyond measure. And the long distance to his office in Roundup, one hundred sixty miles to the east, where his small staff was located, created additional problems for Stretch in dealing with the murder case. He worked with Cynthia to prepare the customary demand for production of evidence related to the killing of Gloria Angel. When the demand was served on the county attorney, Stretch got a call from Hogan. "Damn it Stretch, you don't have to do it the hard way. This ain't New York. We don't need demands for production. All you have to do is ask to look at the file and you'll see everything we've got."

"Can't afford to take a chance, Hefty. But since you've offered, when can I go through your file?"

"Any time at your convenience. I'm cooperative. When is good for you?"

"I'll be in your office tomorrow morning, early."

"How early?"

"At eight o'clock. Then I should be able to make it back to the capitol for a committee meeting at ten."

"You've got it."

"Since you're cooperative, you won't object if I visit with Sheriff Mendenhall from time to time, of course." Hogan didn't respond. He just severed the telephone connection.

THE BODY ON THE FLOOR OF THE ROTUNDA

Ambrose Swan approached Stretch at the end of the day's floor session. The reporter pulled him into a private niche. Swan spoke quietly while looking out of the corner of his eye to be certain no one else heard his remarks. "Do you know that there was a young woman in this building the night Gloria Angel was killed?"

Stretch's eyes widened. "No, I haven't heard about any young woman. Who is she?"

"Don't know a name. May be just a rumor." Swan cast a furtive glance up and down the hallway. "If it's true, I don't think the law enforcement people know about her."

"I'll be damned."

Swan smiled. "I'm just sharing things that I've heard. There may be nothing to it." He patted the senator on the arm and walked away.

The county attorney's file lay on his desk, halfway between them. Stretch Bruce was having a difficult time maintaining his composure while staring at the smug look on Hogan's face. "Hefty, there's not a damn thing in this file that says the sheriff's investigated anyone other than Senator Welter."

"Why would we investigate anyone else? We've got all we need—means, motive, and opportunity. We've got your client cold, Stretch." Hefty leaned his bulky body forward with his arms on the desk so they could see eye to eye. "The fact Gloria Angel was with Ms. Welter right before she was killed may not mean much by itself. And the fact that Ms. Welter threatened to kill Ms. Angel wouldn't carry much weight with a jury by itself. But the blood on the scarf and the blood on the flashlight are the clinchers. Before this comes to trial, we'll have found the email guy. It's only a matter of time. That person's story will be the nail in your client's coffin. Even if we don't find the guy, your client's dead meat." He leaned back in his chair with his hands clasped over his belly and gazed at Stretch with a self-satisfied smile.

Senator Bruce remained still for a moment, then leaned far back in his own chair and clasped his hands behind his head. After looking at Hogan for a couple more seconds, he asked, "You still want to be attorney general?"

"What's that got to do with this case?"

"You blow this one, pal, and you're the one that's dead meat."

"How am I going to blow it? I tell you, this is a no-brainer. Your client did it, and the jury won't be out more than ten minutes before they return with a guilty verdict."

Stretch waited another long moment before speaking again. "And where will you be if we provide an explanation for the scarf and the flashlight? An explanation that doesn't implicate Senator Welter? And what if you never find the email sender? Or what if you find him and he proves to be the murderer or someone connected to the murderer? Then what will you do? You've committed yourself to a course of action based upon an expectation that evidence will appear."

"I'll have the evidence."

"Maybe, maybe not." Stretch leaned forward to stare across the desk. "The press has already made a big thing of the lies told by our illustrious Governor Al Shewey. Tell me, if he isn't involved somehow in the killing, why the lies?" As Hogan inhaled to answer, Stretch cut him off. "By now everyone knows that Howard Welter hated Gloria Angel and that he never got over the divorce from Audrey Welter. Could he have done the killing and then sent the emails in order to frame Audrey? He would have known how to get into her office and plant the scarf. And he would have been able to get into her automobile to plant the flashlight. And he doesn't have an alibi." Stretch took a breath and then went on. "What of the transient who was in the capitol that night?

You've never found him. Could he have some tie to Al Shewey?" Another pause while staring at the county attorney. "And think some more about Shewey. He's a big man and better able to heave Gloria Angel over the railing than tiny Audrey Welter." Stretch shook his head as though in disgust. "What will the press report about your investigative efforts if Audrey walks? And about your ability as a prosecutor? About your qualifications for the office of attorney general? Have you thought of that?" Stretch waited and then grinned as Hogan shifted uncomfortably in his chair. "Isn't a pleasant thought, is it, Hefty?"

"Well, the sheriff got it straightened out with Shewey. He just forgot some things."

Stretch snorted, "You bet! Just forgot!" Then he started turning the pages in the file lying before him on the desk. He found nothing about a young woman who was in the capitol building the night of the killing. He considered telling Hogan of Ambrose Swan's rumor but decided the information might be of use at some later time. Instead he rose from his chair and looked down at Hogan, still seated across the desk, "What about Gloria Angel? Have you thoroughly delved into her past? Who might she have offended or threatened?" Before Hogan could respond, Stretch added with a devilish look, "Which one of her dinner companions may have reason to worry that their time together might become public knowledge?" He watched as Hogan's face began to color. "It seems to me that someone who wants to look good when running for attorney general would cover all the bases. Not just hope the first guess is the right one."

When the door closed, Hogan snatched the telephone from its cradle, punched the intercom and yelled, "Get me the sheriff! Right now!"

Minutes later, Sheriff Mendenhall sat, unruffled, in Hogan's office as the county attorney ranted. When Hefty finally stopped talking, the sheriff nodded his head and said, "We haven't been sitting on our dollar watch. All those people have been interviewed, and we've given copies of the reports to you."

"What about Gloria Angel's love life? There are some, Republicans mostly, who believe she and Shewey had a little something going on the side. Anything more on that?"

The sheriff shook his head. "I don't believe it. Shewey isn't about to do anything to jeopardize his chance at re-election or a seat in the United States Senate."

"Well, work on it. Let's not have anything jump up and bite us. I'm certain we can nail Audrey Welter with this murder, neat and clean. But I don't want to give Stretch Bruce any wiggle room—wiggle room from something we don't know about."

Mendenhall stood before he answered, "We're still looking at everything." He looked down at the county attorney seated across the desk. "How hard do you really want me to dig into Gloria Angel's social activities?"

"Dig damn hard."

"And what am I supposed to do when your name surfaces in connection with her?"

Hogan's eyelids dropped, and he tucked his head down and to one side before he looked up at the sheriff and asked, "What do you mean?"

"Her diary says you two spent some evenings together."

The county attorney inhaled sharply. Then his face turned red with anger. "God damn it! That isn't a diary, it's an appointment book."

"Well, by whatever name, you know she kept one." The sheriff waited for a response but Hogan's breath had become labored, and he sat without moving. When Hefty didn't speak, Mendenhall added, "All the diary says is that you and Ms. Angel had dinner together a few times."

"Brent, that's all there was to it. We went to dinner. Nothing more."

Sheriff Mendenhall nodded. As he turned to leave he said, "You told me to keep working. That order is hardly necessary because I've never felt we know all we need to know about the death of Ms. Angel." From the door he said, "It's always possible we'll find something that will help Ms. Welter."

The county attorney growled, "If any such thing exists, I want to know so I can be prepared to deal with it." Hefty stared at the sheriff. "We're going to send her to the pen for a long time, Brent. Let's be certain we do this in a systematic and methodical manner. No basis for reversal. Not one single thing on which an appellate court could hang its hat." Before Mendenhall could leave the room, he growled, "My dinners with Gloria Angel had nothing to do with her death. Don't get any wrong ideas about that."

23

"Stretch? This is Audrey. I'm sorry I've been hard to reach, but I've just had to hide myself away from everybody and everything."

"That's understandable. You don't need to apologize for anything." Stretch paused. "But, it would be helpful if we could get together to discuss a number of matters."

"I don't want to come to Helena or even Missoula. I've been branded a murderer, and it shows in the way people look at me. That's hard to take."

"I really wish I could ease that burden."

"A quick trial with an acquittal would do it." Audrey's anger and frustration colored her usual calm manner of speaking.

"I still hope we dig up something to make a trial unnecessary. But in either case, we need to prepare." Stretch hesitated. "The legislature's mid-term break starts this weekend. Could you drive to my house near Roundup? It's a place where we can have some peace and quiet."

There was a long pause. "Senator Bruce, I know your intentions are honorable, but what about public perceptions? Won't that hurt my defense?"

"There isn't any need for the world to know you're there." Then, after a quiet chuckle, "How can you be sure my intentions are honorable?"

"You're a Republican, Stretch. Doesn't the old joke say only Democrats know how to have fun?"

Senator Bruce chuckled. "Don't bet on it. But you're safe for now. All I can concentrate on at the moment is the trial."

"All right, Stretch. Logan is leaving for a few days, so this is a good time. I'll meet you there sometime Saturday."

After a long, tiring drive Audrey caught her first glimpse of the house in which Stretch lived. It was a large two-story structure, painted in earth tones and obviously built many years in the past as a home for a rancher. The moment the Subaru came to rest near the front door, her host hurried across the broad porch and down a walkway to the gate in a picket fence. Stretch took her hand as she stepped out onto ground that was whitened by a light cover of snow. Stretch put an arm around her shoulder and gestured toward his home. "It will be a pleasure to have such a lovely lady grace this house."

Audrey smiled. "I've been curious to see the place you call home when you're not in Helena.

Inside, Stretch took her coat and hung it in a nearby closet. "Let me show you around, and then we'll share a cup of coffee while we talk. In the morning I'll take you for a casual drive through some of the Bull Mountains. We should see both mule deer and antelope in abundance. Maybe some elk. This evening, however, I promise you a real ranch dinner."

Stretch had always appreciated Audrey's striking good looks. Today, her attire was appropriate to the season and the setting—copper-colored wool slacks, a warm chocolate brown sweater over a light tan high-collared blouse.

Now they sat, coffee cups before them, at a kitchen table placed before a large window that provided a southerly view of the nearby, hard frozen Musselshell River. The low hills that were the beginnings of the Bull Mountains lay just beyond the river. In mid-winter and after recent snow, the world was a brilliant white beneath the afternoon sun.

Audrey shoved her coffee cup to one side and said, "Okay, what's the first thing we need to discuss?"

The smile that had remained on his face since her arrival slipped into a frown. "An omnibus and scheduling conference is scheduled for early April. As you probably know, the prosecution must bring the case to trial within six months of the filing of the charges or the court will dismiss them. We're already a month and a half down that road."

"What are you suggesting?"

"I think you should waive speedy trial. It's almost impossible for me to get ready to defend you properly while the legislature is in session. More importantly, we should do some investigating. Sheriff Mendenhall has been more cooperative than we have any right to expect. But we shouldn't rely on him."

"I'm certainly in favor of a proper investigation, but I'm extremely anxious to get it all over with."

"What we really need to do is find out how someone managed to place the incriminating objects in both your office and your car. And when they did so. The blood on the scarf and flashlight are almost certainly Gloria's. While DNA tests aren't foolproof, they're nearly so. It may be wise to seek out another expert to do an independent analysis just to be sure no mistake was made." He leaned back in his chair. "What if the flashlight was used to kill Gloria Angel right there in your office? Did anyone ever test the carpet in your office for blood stains?"

"Not that I know of. I know they didn't do it any time during a legislative day. They might have done it at night or over a weekend."

Stretch was grim-faced as he said, "If they did, Hefty had better disclose their findings." Then he reached for a tablet and pen. "Let's go through your activities the night you met with Gloria and the morning afterward when her body was found.

And do it step by step. Without leaving out one single thing. You talk, and I'll take notes."

Audrey nodded, rose to her feet and began to pace the floor. The pacing continued as she spoke. Stretch only interrupted when he felt a need for clarification. At last she stopped her monologue, paused with a frown, and returned to her chair. Once settled, she looked directly at Stretch. "I don't think I left out a single thing."

He placed the notepad on his lap. "Thank you for telling me all of it. I have a better understanding of the things that happened that night."

"Will my telling be of benefit to you during a trial?"

"He cocked his head to one side and smiled. "It surely will."

They sat in silence until Stretch leaned back with his hands behind his head. "That really brings us to another matter. As I said, we may need to retain an expert to analyze the blood found on the scarf and on the flashlight, just to be certain the state's analysis is correct. And there will be other expenses that come along. As an example, we may need to hire someone to interview everybody else who might have been involved in this matter in any way. People like Governor Shewey. Or the vagrant who was in the capitol that night. Or the attorney general. Maybe even your ex-husband."

"Investigate Howard? You still think Howard might have done it?"

"He had a motive."

She wrinkled her nose as though in disgust. "I guess he had a motive, all right." Then she added, "But isn't the sheriff doing all of that?"

"As I've said, the sheriff has been generous in sharing information with us, but we can't rely on him or any other person in the law enforcement establishment to provide you with a defense. The county attorney thinks he already has his killer. In his mind, you're the one who did it. While the sheriff and his deputies may make some pretense of looking for an alternative, it may not be a very diligent effort."

"Could I do some of the investigating?"

Stretch smiled. "Audrey, anything you found would be suspect simply because you're the one charged with the crime."

"You're right, of course. And, besides, I don't really want to talk to anyone about what happened. I just want to hide at my cabin until this is over." She raised her eyebrows as she asked, "How about you?"

"I'm still busy with the legislative session. I'll interview as many of Hefty's witnesses as possible before the trial. But if I discovered something that might be helpful, I could become a witness. That's a real concern." Stretch got up and walked to the window and stood with his hands in his pockets. "Sheriff Mendenhall has been cooperative. And Ambrose Swan has been helpful. Ambrose seems to have resources available that he won't discuss. I have to finish out the second half of the legislative session. If either one of them discovers any new evidence—good or bad—I'll be in Helena to intercept it." He gave his head a shake. "At least I hope I can intercept it." When Audrey remained silent and sober-faced, he added, "I suppose we could hire a private investigator, but I don't know of one that I'm absolutely certain would do a decent job." He paused. "And such an investigator would cost money, with a substantial retainer up-front."

Audrey smiled. "I've wondered when we would finally talk about fees. You've never asked me for a retainer."

"No, I haven't. I've been reluctant to discuss fees with you."

"Why not? I'm your client, and I expect to pay the same as any other client."

"I understand, but our relationship is somehow different."

"Well, what would be your fee arrangement with any other person in my situation?"

Stretch hesitated. "For this kind of case and from anyone else I would demand a retainer of twenty thousand dollars. And I would charge an hourly fee of three hundred dollars for work up to time of trial. Trial time costs more."

"Then that's what I'll pay. Stretch, you don't know much about me." Audrey leaned forward, elbows on the table. "Listen, I can afford whatever is necessary for a proper defense. You'll get a check for the retainer before I leave here, and I expect to receive a monthly statement for the time you spend." She paused. "I don't often discuss my finances with others, but you need to know how I'm situated. I inherited a substantial estate when my parents died, and I've lived rather frugally and invested carefully."

Her face turned grim. "Sometimes I think the money was the thing that Howard was really after. You can be sure he didn't get any of it in the divorce." Then her face relaxed again, and she smiled and reached to pat his hand. "Wipe that distressed look from your face, Senator. If you think we should have an investigator, hire one. If not, don't. I trust your judgment. Now let's discuss whatever else you think is important. I'm leaving tomorrow, you know." She turned and pointed out the window toward the timbered hills of the Bull Mountains. "You promised me a scenic drive through the countryside in the morning, with wild animals to see. And you also promised to cook the world's most delicious beef entrée for the meal this evening. Isn't that the way you described it? Or is my memory faulty?"

"Nope, I promised and I'll deliver."

The promised dinner consisted of roast beef tenderloin, browned potatoes, a green salad, and warm, fresh bread from the bread machine. When dishes were done, Audrey, weary from a long, emotionally draining day, retired to the guest bedroom.

24

The fragrance of hot coffee led Audrey to the kitchen. Stretch, dressed comfortably in a flannel shirt hanging over a pair of old denim pants, turned to smile. "I hope scrambled eggs, bacon, toast, and fruit juice will make a suitable breakfast." He smiled and added, "My, but you look lovely!"

Looking down at her denim jeans, Audrey felt a slight blush redden her cheeks. "Why, thank you, good sir." With a grin, she crossed to stand beside him at the stove where he was about to break eggs into a pan. "I seldom have more than a cup of coffee and a roll for breakfast. But your suggestion sounds wonderful this morning. It must be the country air and a good night's sleep."

"Did you sleep well then?"

"Better than I have since the day Gloria Angel was found on the rotunda floor." Audrey filled two coffee mugs and handed one to Stretch, before sitting at the kitchen table. Comfortably relaxed, she sipped coffee and watched Stretch. In short order he placed two plates of food on the small round table. "It smells as good as it looks." Then her smile flashed again as she said, "You cook. This house is as neat and tidy as it can be. No wonder you've never remarried. You don't need a wife."

"It isn't very hard to keep things clean when I'm the only one around. All I have to do is pick up after myself. But in truth, ma'am, it is lonesome out here."

Audrey put her fork on her plate and leaned toward him. "Tell me about your wife."

Stretch sat a moment in remembrance. "Rosalind was the most comfortable of companions. She seldom displayed an ill temper—and then only when I deserved some scolding." He paused as he pictured her in his memory. "I thought she was the most beautiful girl in the world when I first saw her, and she became more beautiful in my eyes each day of our marriage."

"And you have a daughter. Does she resemble her mother?"

The smile returned to Stretch's face. "Yes, thank God. She doesn't resemble her father."

Audrey began to pick at her food again as she asked, "You have a nice home and a thriving law practice. You're extremely personable. Surely there have been a lot of women who would like to be Mrs. Lynn Bruce."

The smile broadened as he looked at her. "I'm not as young as I used to be, and certainly not handsome. No reasonable woman would have me."

"Beauty—or lack of it—is in the eye of the beholder." Audrey swallowed a bite of toast and then sipped from the coffee mug. "I'm sorry, Stretch. I have no right to pry into your private life." They ate in silence, devouring the meal, until she pushed her plate aside, walked to the carafe, and carried it back to the table to refill both mugs. Back in her chair, she asked, "What more should we discuss before our tour of the Bull Mountains and before I take myself back to the solitude of my cabin."

"We've concentrated too much on the scarf and on the flashlight. Let's think for a while about other aspects of the case." Stretch retrieved his tablet from a cabinet and returned to sit again across from Audrey.

"The county attorney feels he has three facts upon which he can convince a jury that you are the one who dropped Gloria over the railing." He glanced from the notes to her face as he enumerated them. "You were the last one to see her—as far as he knows—before her death. You have a motive to want her dead. Gloria caused your divorce. Two items bearing her blood were found in your possession." When she started to protest, he added quickly, "I know, they weren't in your actual possession, but Hefty will do his best to convince the jury that they were yours."

"I'm certain of that."

"Hefty believes he has all the elements needed to persuade a jury—opportunity, motive, means. Let's take the three items one at a time as though at trial. First, Hefty will try to convince the jury that you were the last one to see Audrey alive. We can refute that insinuation by pointing out that you voluntarily went to the county attorney and told him of that conversation."

"How will that get into evidence? Will it just be my testimony?"

"If I have to, I'll call Hefty to testify. He won't want to become a witness so he won't attempt to deny that you came to him voluntarily."

"OK. What's next?"

"Motive. It appears certain there will be at least one person willing to testify that you threatened to kill Gloria Angel. I don't have any names yet, but Hogan has to disclose them."

"I can probably guess who they'll be. But let's wait and see."

Stretch nodded. "You're right. Let's not speculate. I think the county attorney is doing too much of that." He glanced at his notes again. "The scarf and flashlight were in your desk and in your car, respectively. You can't deny those things. He'll try to overplay that information. And he'll do his best to show that even if it may have been rather easy for someone to plant the scarf in the desk, assuming the door was unlocked, he'll argue no one but you could have gotten into your car without a key. You always lock your car, don't you?"

"Yes, at least I normally do. That's a real problem, isn't it?"

"Correct. We just said we shouldn't speculate. But there is nothing we can do at this time but speculate on how someone was able to get into your car when it was always locked. Perhaps that person used a shim. Who knows?"

"Maybe. That's the most difficult thing to deal with, isn't it?"

"It certainly is one difficult thing. We can counter the assertion that you were the last one to see Gloria by letting the jury know that the governor was also in the building that night, as was the transient. And, as Ambrose Swan whispered to me, there may have been a young woman there as well."

"You sent me an email about that. Have you found out any more?"

"Not a thing. I'm hoping Ambrose may learn more and share it with us."

Stretch scanned his notes, then looked up to say, "We can counter the assertion that you killed her because of the divorce by using testimony that shows your ex had come to hate the woman." He stopped, dropped his pen, and rubbed the back of his neck. "But the scarf and the flashlight are a real problem." He picked up the pen and then dropped it again in seeming frustration. "I keep hoping the one who sent you the email will follow up."

"That may be a forlorn hope." Audrey traced a finger around the rim of her coffee mug. "Can you talk to Mr. Hogan's blood analysis expert? The one who will testify it's Gloria's blood on the scarf and flashlight?"

"Of course. And I will. And after that, we'll decide if we should try to get someone of our own to contradict him."

"Is that fair? Is that the way the law works? Each side gets someone to tell the jury what that side wants them to hear? Doesn't that encourage a lying contest—our word against your word?"

"Yup, that's about the way it works. Don't let it shock you. Such an expert will cost money."

"Stretch, I thought I made myself clear. Get whatever you need. I can handle it."

"You may know that the name Bruce is Scottish. I hate to waste money, even your money."

"It's comforting to know that. But don't be so tight-fisted as to cost me life in prison." She inhaled sharply. "God, Stretch, the thought that I might be convicted scares me to death."

"Of course it does. That's the reason we're having this conversation. So we can plan a defense that will be successful."

She shuddered, clasped her arms around her chest, and said, "This whole thing is just eating me up. Last night was the first good sleep I've had since it all began."

Stretch leaned toward her and smiled, "Then the trip to my house had some benefit."

"Yes, it certainly had that benefit." She rose and refilled the coffee mugs once again. Easing back into her chair, she muttered, "The only way to ensure I'm not convicted is to find the real killer." She turned to look directly at her host. "Who might that be? What can we do to find that person?"

"We've discussed the possibilities." Stretch sipped at the coffee. "We know about your ex-husband, of course. There's the notion he was so angry at Gloria that he could have killed her. What have you learned about that?"

"Just as there are those around the campus who will say bad things about me, there are others who will say bad things about Howard. I've made some inquiries. Some rumors are afoot that he'd threatened Gloria, and there is some talk that he's actually stalked her. But those are just rumors. There are also rumors that he threatened harm to me on occasion. There's nothing of substance to any of it that I've been able to find."

The Body on the Floor of the Rotunda

"Keep asking. See if you can learn who his closest confidant might be. Then see if you can find someone who can get him to talk. You might get some important information that way."

"I know who the confidant is. It's another professor in his department. Getting to him is another matter. But it makes sense to try, and I'll do it."

Stretched paused. "There's one thing we really haven't given enough consideration. It's the timing of Gloria's death."

"What do you mean?'

"You said she left your office about ten o'clock. Is that right?"

"Yes, it was about that time."

"Think about it. Her body was found at about twelve thirty the next morning."

Audrey's eyes widened. "My God, Stretch, I hadn't thought about the time in between."

"It's important. The security people have a routine as they walk the capitol building at night. Gloria's body wasn't on the rotunda floor when one of them passed through at eleven thirty."

Audrey leaned back abruptly and asked, "What was she doing between the time she left my office and the time her body was found?"

"That's part of the question. Another part is where was she? And the third, who was she with?"

"She may have been in her office in the governor's suite."

Stretch nodded. "That's a reasonable assumption. Who else might have been in the governor's suite?"

At that question, Audrey sat bolt upright and inhaled. "Albert Shewey. The governor!"

"Makes you think, doesn't it? I really don't know Shewey. The only time I've even been in his presence very long is when he called the party leaders to his office to discuss legislative matters." He paused. "You must know him much better. After all, he's the head of your party, and you've helped him a great deal since he's been in office. And you'd hoped to discuss your concerns about drilling along the Rocky Mountain Front with him on the night Gloria was killed."

Audrey was silent for several seconds. "It's hard to know a person through casual contacts, and that's really all I've had with the governor. The time I've spent with him has generally been in the presence of others. At such times, he's always wearing his public face. Only once were we alone together. He came to Missoula for a gathering at the University campus and, after the meeting was over, I gave him a ride to the airport. He was genial but quiet during the trip." Audrey leaned back in the chair and shook her head. "I don't know Albert Shewey very well, but it's hard to think of him as a murderer."

"Is that party loyalty talking?"

"No, I'm not that stuck on party loyalty, especially when my whole life is at stake. But he just doesn't seem like the kind who could beat another person to death."

"Maybe, maybe not." Stretch cleared his throat. "There's another possibility." When she only stared and waited, he went on to ask, "What if she left the capitol right after she left your office? Where could she have gone?" Then, after another pause, "And could someone have seen her at a place away from the capitol between the time she left and the time she was dropped over the balustrade?"

"My God, Stretch! Could that have happened?"

"Who knows?" Stretch leaned back in his chair as he said, "Maybe that's how your email correspondent knows you aren't the murderer. Maybe that person saw Gloria somewhere. And with someone. Maybe that person even saw them go back into the capitol together just before she was killed. It's a certainty she had a key and could have gotten in through one of the east doors, away from the security desk at the main entrance.

Audrey's face brightened. "Now you're thinking the right way. Someone killed Gloria Angel, and it wasn't Audrey Welter. We know that. So let's find the one who did the killing instead of trying to plan a court defense to a murder charge." The excitement lasted only the briefest of moments. But then she slumped, was silent, and finally mused, "Who am I kidding? There may not be anyone other than the killer who knows where Gloria was after she left my office. It's extremely unlikely we'll ever find anyone who can clear me. I don't even know how or where to look."

Stretch reached out to touch her hand. "Send another response to your email person." Drawing his hand back, he added, "Learn what you can about your ex-husband's threats. And give some more thought to the governor's activities. Those are all things that may help." He turned the chair again to stretch his legs. "Ambrose Swan has been awfully interested in this whole matter—more so than its news value seems to justify. For some reason, he wants to be helpful. And reporters have sources of information not available to anyone else. When I get back to Helena, I'll talk with him some more. Who knows? He may be able to find out something that will identify the killer."

"I'm sure he'd like to be the one to do so. It would be the greatest news story of the year. Every other newsman in Montana would envy him."

Stretch smiled. "Ambrose is long in the tooth. I think he's beyond seeking the envy of his fellows. But there's no question he'd like to score a big story." Stretch stood. "As I said, I'll talk to him when I get back to Helena on Monday."

Audrey reached for the cups and carried them to the sink. "It's a long drive back to Missoula. Let's make that tour through the hills a short one."

Stepping from the Expedition, Audrey stretched to loosen her muscles. "The drive over the ranch land was scenic and enjoyable. But you have no business calling those little hills the Bull Mountains. We have real mountains in western Montana."

Stretch grinned. "We must do with what we have for mountains here in Musselshell County."

Audrey turned for the house. "I'll gather my belongings. It's time for me to be on my way." She dragged her finger along his upper arm as she passed by on the way to the bedroom and said, "You've been a most generous host, Senator. I'm glad we had this visit."

Stretch carried the large bag to her car and loaded it into the rear compartment, the one where the flashlight had been found. Audrey climbed in and started the motor. She lowered the window and looked up at Stretch, standing with his hands in his pockets and his shoulders hunched against the wind. "Mr. Bruce, last night before I went to sleep I fantasized that you acted like a teen-ager and came prowling into my bedroom. And I fantasized that I acted like a teen-ager and welcomed you to my bed." Before he could think of a response, she grinned a wide grin, put the car in gear, and drove away, leaving Stretch Bruce wondering if he had been an absolute fool.

Back in the kitchen, he stood by the table he had just shared with Audrey and groaned, "God, I'm tired of living alone in this big house."

25

After the mid-session break, Ambrose Swan stepped from the pressroom, caught Stretch by the arm, and muttered, "Let's have a visit." He led the senator to a quiet place beneath a stairway leading to the fourth floor. The reporter leaned close and whispered, "Howard Welter was stalking Gloria Angel."

"Stalking? Honestly? As in following her?" His voice was louder than he intended.

Swan put a finger to his lips and spoke in a soft voice. "Apparently, Audrey Welter's ex-husband began following Gloria a few months ago. Not only did he follow her almost everywhere she went, but he would park near her townhouse night after night to watch her visitors come and go."

"How'd you find this out?" And then without waiting for an answer, Stretch asked, "Did she report him to the authorities?"

Swan scowled, "No, she didn't report what he was doing to the authorities either here or in Missoula where he lives."

Stretch asked, "I wonder why not." Then he added quickly, "Maybe she didn't realize she was being stalked."

"That's possible. But if it was blatant enough so others were aware of it, she must have known."

"That doesn't mean he was the one who killed her though, does it?"

Before he answered, Ambrose Swan looked carefully again to make certain no one was near and listening. "Maybe not. But he was in Helena the night she died. And his car was seen parked behind the capitol that night, at about ten o'clock."

Stretch's eyebrows went up as he realized the significance of the statement. "So he was following Gloria when she went to visit Audrey."

"It would seem that way." Swan grinned and then leaned toward Stretch and added just before he turned to walk away. "Don't you wonder if he followed her after that? And if so, don't you also wonder where they went?" With that final remark, the old reporter walked back toward the pressroom.

Stretch lingered only briefly under the staircase, pondering the question Ambrose had offered. Could Howard Welter really be Gloria Angel's killer? And if he wasn't the killer, was it possible that he knew whether or not Gloria left the capitol after her visit with Audrey? Could he know the person she left with? How could he find out if the two of them were together at any time the night of the murder?

The short, unkempt blogger accosted Stretch when he stepped into the hallway and shouted, "Senator Bruce, what's the latest in your defense of Audrey Welter? Have you found someone else who you'll claim was the killer?"

"You should ask the law enforcement authorities if they've found the real killer. Have you done that?"

"You still insist she didn't do it?"

"That's right. She didn't do it." Stretch brushed past the man while giving him the slightest shove with his elbow as he went by. He turned through the doors leading to his office, wishing he could devote all his time and efforts to Audrey's defense while realizing that the most demanding part of the legislative session was now upon him. His duties would consume nearly all of his time and most of his energy.

26

The rules of the Montana legislature required that all bills passed by the Senate (except for spending bills) be transferred to the House of Representatives on or before the mid-session break. And all the bills from the House (except for tax and spending bills) had to arrive at the Senate before that date. After the break, each House concentrated its efforts on transmitted bills and on money matters. The money matters demanded the most time and attention from the tax and appropriation committees as well as from the legislative leaders. Montana faced a revenue shortfall that aggravated the contentious task.

The senatorial district that Stretch Bruce represented included the Bull Mountains where several underground mines once produced prodigious amounts of coal. It also included some of the areas to the east where coal was now being strip-mined in large quantities for shipment to mid-west electrical generation plants as well as to foreign countries. And it included the oil-producing areas north and east of Roundup. He viewed these natural resources as providing a bountiful source of state revenue flowing from the taxes that were imposed upon their extraction. Because of that belief, he sponsored several measures intended to stimulate both the mining and the drilling that brought forth revenue-producing minerals. He believed the production could and should be done in an environmentally sound manner. There were many in Montana, well represented in the legislature, who believed that any production of natural resources was inherently damaging to the environment. The ones who harbored this belief not only opposed the efforts of Stretch Bruce and others like him, but sponsored legislation to restrict if not prohibit the exploitation of the minerals.

Audrey Welter had sponsored three of the bills. Two of them had died in the Senate but one—the one that would prevent exploration for gas on state land along the Rocky Mountain Front—had survived and would be debated in the House of Representatives. Now she was no longer a member of the Senate. Her replacement, George Peterson (the Missoula County Commissioners had chosen a man, much to Audrey's distress) was lacking in persuasive talents. Her absence grated on Stretch, despite the fact that he viewed Audrey's bill as totally wrong-headed. He wondered if some influential Democrat in the house would carry the bill in a persuasive manner. And he wondered if he should, because of her situation, suggest to some house Republicans that they not resist passage of the bill too vigorously. No. He couldn't do that. Her absence increased his anger—anger at Hefty Hogan. She should never have been charged with a crime, and she should never have felt obligated to resign her Senate seat.

The demands upon every member of the state legislature during the latter part of the session were daunting, and upon the leaders, they could be overwhelming. As a consequence, Stretch was unable to devote time to the preparation of Audrey's defense.

Late one night, after a long day filled with the review of bills, committee meetings in which debate dragged on interminably, party discussions during which other Republican senators complained bitterly about the treatment of their pet bills by the Democratic majority, heated exchanges with the Republican leaders of the House regarding political strategy, and lively discussions with the leaders of the Democrats in the Senate about the scheduling and debate of various bills, sleep did not come easily to Senator Bruce.

He found questions relating to the killing of Gloria Angel playing over and over in his mind. Who actually murdered that woman? If Howard Welter was stalking her, could he have gone from stalking to homicide? What of the vagrant who had so conveniently disappeared? And what of the young woman Ambrose Swan had heard was in the building the night of the murder? Could she have been involved? Or could she have seen something that would lead to the killer? And what of the dissembling of the governor? Why would he lie if he had no involvement in Gloria's death? And what about the unusual interest of the attorney general in Gloria's affairs? Each night before he slept, he resolved to pursue the answers to the questions, but when each new day arrived, the press of legislative matters left him with no time and little energy for the practice of law. And then the following night his conscience would plague him about his neglect of the defense of his client.

27

The ninety-day legislative session was grinding to its finish. Although controversy continued to rage regarding the method by which the budget would be balanced, Stretch was confident that an agreement could be reached. He felt it was his duty, as Republican leader in the Senate, to find a compromise. If he were successful, it would allow the legislature to adjourn.

Stretch began by asking Norman Fraker, the senator from Big Horn County, to share a cup of coffee. He asked the craggy-faced cattle rancher about the winter conditions in his part of the state and listened to all of Fraker's woes.

After three cups of coffee, Fraker abruptly stopped talking about matters in his home district. He pushed back in his chair and said with a grin, "You ain't buying me coffee to listen to my problems. You're being generous because you want my vote on the income tax bill."

"Yup, Norman, that's what I want." Stretch stopped short, leaned back slightly, and said, "No. That's not what I want. That's what I need. And I need more than that. I also need the votes of three of your friends."

The Big Horn County rancher dropped his arms loosely over the side of his chair. "Damn it man, it's tough to go against the party line."

Stretch nodded his head slowly, his voice full of sympathy. "I know it is. But you've done it in the past. And so have I. And neither one of us has been drummed out of our party."

"We ain't been drummed out yet. But there's always the first time. This is a vote where the governor and all the other Democratic honchos insist on holding the line. They're thinking about the next election. You know that."

"Of course. Everyone is thinking about the next election, except people like you and me. Folks in both our districts send us here to do what we believe is right. They'll continue to vote for us as long as they think we're trying to do the right thing—even if it doesn't fit the party line."

Fraker grabbed the arms of the chair with both hands and straightened his back. He croaked a throaty laugh. "That's the way, Stretch. Make it look easy. Why don't you wave the American flag too, while you're at it?" He stood and shook the minority leader's hand. "Thanks for the coffee, Senator. I'll think about the vote. And I'll talk to three of the guys on my side of the aisle. They may go along."

Larry Sloan stuck his head in the door to Stretch's office. "Your lady friend's bill to stop oil and gas drilling passed the House." He growled. "Five of my Republicans jumped ship and voted for it." He pushed himself away from the door. "I hope you're happy." Sloan stomped off down the corridor leaving Stretch to realize that he was indeed happy and to wonder how that could be.

The legislative session ended in the early afternoon. Senator Fraker and his three colleagues joined with the Republicans on the income tax bill. Their action brought the fury of the Democratic leadership and the governor down on them in full force. But, as Stretch knew, they were all from safe senatorial districts and could act independently when they felt it was the right thing to do.

When the Senate finally adjourned, Stretch reached to grasp

the hand of his Democratic counterpart, the majority leader, standing across the aisle. "Well, Pat, we survived another one."

"So we did. Now all we have to do is explain to the news people why we did the things we did."

Stretched grinned. "That's your job. Those of us in the minority don't have to explain anything—just howl that you Democrats did it all wrong."

"As the saying goes in politics, 'it was ever thus.' When you're in Butte, give me a call. I'm good for lunch." He was three steps up the aisle toward the doors when he stopped and turned around. "You know, Stretch, we're all expecting you to take care of Audrey Welter. I don't know who killed Gloria Angel, but I damn sure know Audrey didn't do it." He moved back down the aisle and reached for Senator Bruce's hand once again. "If I can help you in any way, please call me." He gave the hand a squeeze before he released the grip. "I mean it, friend." With a final pat on the arm, the Irishman strode through the doors, leaving Stretch Bruce as the last member standing on the Senate floor.

Barbara, his Senate secretary, was busy stuffing papers in boxes when he arrived back at his office. In her usual efficient way, she had categorized the detritus from the legislative session so that each box was labeled to match its contents. One box contained all the information and other legal documents pertaining to Audrey Welter's homicide case. Stretch fell wearily into the chair behind his desk as Barbara went about her task. Before him were the last of the letters that he had dictated, all correctly prepared for signature, each accompanied by an addressed envelope. The secretary shoved the final packet of paper into the last box and pushed the lid firmly into place. She brushed her hands one against the other to remove dust and nodded toward the correspondence. "If you'll sign those, I'll mail them on my way out."

Stretch reached to the inside pocket of his sport coat for a pen. After he scribbled his signature on the letters, he smiled a tired smile at Barbara. "I can't thank you enough for all that you've done for me."

"Nonsense! I enjoy the excitement of the legislature. And you're a nice man to work for. I'll bet the folks on your staff in Roundup all say the same thing."

Stretch leaned forward to rest his forearms on the desk top. "I'm a holdover senator so I'll be back here again in two years. Will you be my secretary again?"

"Of course I will." Barbara reached to the rack for her coat. Stretch scrambled to hold the garment as she shrugged into it. Grabbing her purse from the desk where she'd worked for the past four months, she said, "When you come to town, please call me. I'll be curious to know about the defense of your friend Audrey." A smile appeared on a usually somber face. "The news folks aren't always accurate in the things they report, you know." She was out the door and gone before Stretch could respond.

Stretch placed the call to Audrey late in the evening while sitting on the edge of the bed in his hotel room. Her voice, when she answered, so lifted his spirits that he found himself smiling into the mouthpiece of the telephone. It was clear that her interest in legislative matters had not diminished when her first words were, "So, Senator Bruce, you succeeded once again. You've saved your rich friends from paying their fair share of the income tax, and you've burdened local taxpayers with more of the state's responsibility to fund education."

He chuckled softly. "The art of compromise, Senator Welter. Without it, nothing would get done."

"I guess. But one of these days, there has to be an accounting. And please remember, I'm not a senator anymore."

Stretch sighed. "You don't know how much I wish you were. We've had the tax and school finance discussions many times before without resolving our differences, haven't we?"

"Yes, of course, Stretch. I'm sorry I brought it up. I know from experience that the last days of any session are exhausting." After a slight hesitation, she said, "I'm sure there's another reason for your call."

"Yes, there is. We need to visit again. The session is over. Could we get together somewhere in the next day or so?"

"I visited your house the last time. Would you come to my cabin for this next visit?"

"I could do that." He added quickly, "Our visit shouldn't take long. If I get there in the morning, I can leave and return to Helena in the evening."

Audrey's laugh had a lilt when she teased, "You're worried again about sleeping arrangements, aren't you?" After waiting for some word from Stretch, she said, "There are two bedrooms here, sir, and my son is gone for a few days."

"If that's the case, and I won't have to hurry away the same day I get to your place, would you mind if we put my visit off for a few days? I need to return to Roundup to catch up on things there. I've allowed my regular practice to languish. After I get my affairs at the office back in order, I could drive to the Blackfoot."

"I understand. And I'm at your disposal. After all, you're the only thing standing between me and life in prison." Fear crept into her voice.

"That's another reason to get back home. In the quiet of my law office, I can thoroughly review the evidence that Hefty Hogan thinks will lead to a conviction. It's been too hectic here in Helena to get that done."

"Just call to let me know when you'll arrive, so I can have enough food to keep a man happy."

"Of course. Give me directions so I can find you. I'm not well acquainted with your part of the world."

Stretch walked one more time around the hotel room to be certain he'd packed all his belongings. He dropped the key on the table, together with the final tip for the maid. A warm April wind gusted a whirl of parking lot dust when he stepped across the asphalt to his automobile. As he reached his Expedition, a vintage Chevrolet pulled in beside it. Ambrose Swan waved from behind the steering wheel and then heaved his body forward to get himself out onto the pavement. Once standing, he grumbled, "Every day it gets harder to get out of that damn car. The seat's too close to the ground."

"Better get yourself a new one." Stretch grinned and gestured to a huge Lincoln Navigator parked nearby and added, "One like that, maybe. It's high enough."

Swan snorted and ducked away from another gust of wind that carried dirt. He turned toward Stretch while shielding his eyes from the morning sun. "Can you think of a reason the governor and the attorney general would meet quietly at a remote cabin in the woods out by Canyon Ferry Lake?"

Stretch frowned and shook his head.

"Try this. Mightn't they both want to put the Gloria Angel murder to rest as quickly as possible?"

"I suppose they might. Is that what you think?"

Swan got into his car. Looking through the open window, he asked, "It just seems strange, doesn't it, that two politicians, a Republican and a Democrat, both of whom are hungering for the next step up the political ladder, are huddled together at a place so remote that no one is likely to learn of it?"

"You're right. It's strange." Stretch leaned both hands on the bottom of the open car window as he looked in at Ambrose

Swan. "If their get-together was such a secret, how do you know it happened?"

"Contacts and sources, Senator, contacts and sources." Swan turned the key and started the engine. "Convicting your client would be the quickest and easiest way to put the murder to rest. Think about it." He gunned the engine and backed away, leaving Stretch to wonder if there could be some kind of conspiracy to use Audrey Welter as a scapegoat so the real murderer would never be found. And to ponder the larger question, what person would receive the most benefit from her conviction?

28

Late in the evening, after everyone else had left the law office, Stretch sat with an elbow on the desk and his chin resting in his hand as he leafed his way through the material delivered to his office by Hefty Hogan in response to his discovery requests. There wasn't much to review. He was well acquainted with the charging information and affidavits that were filed in their support. He felt no need to spend time on them.

The autopsy report seemed straightforward. The pathologist described severe trauma to one side of the deceased's head, concluding that it was the cause of death. He characterized the trauma to the other side of her head and the injuries to her body as post death and consistent with a fall from the gallery overlooking the capitol rotunda.

Of particular interest in the report were statements regarding blood on the exterior of the body. Apparently there was a flow of blood from the woman's nose, a small flow from her ear, and a somewhat smaller flow from one corner of her mouth. Neither the pathologist's report nor the report of the sheriff's deputies made any mention of blood where the body was found. The deputies' reports listed no other place in the capitol where traces of blood were found. If no blood was found in the capitol, how does anyone know that Gloria Angel was killed there? He was certain he would think of more questions for the pathologist before the trial began, all of them asked for the purpose of distancing his client from the cause of death.

The investigative reports prepared by the sheriff and his deputies were interesting for other reasons. The sheriff's notes of the initial conversation with Audrey Welter were extensive and appeared to be in keeping with Stretch's remembrance of the actual conversation. He made a note to himself to take a copy to Audrey when he visited her.

The list of the furnishings in Audrey's office seemed to be correct. With regard to the scarf, the reports stated that care was taken to ensure there was no contamination when it was delivered to the laboratory for testing. No copy of the email—the one that precipitated the collection of the scarf for testing—was contained in the material provided by Hogan.

The sheriff's records of his conversations with the governor were extensive, and his skepticism at some of the governor's statements crept into his writing. Stretch smiled to himself, thinking they provided ample fodder for cross-examination.

The deputy's notes of his questioning of the vagrant found in the capitol were brief. The vagrant's name—as shown on the affidavit—was Kevin Palmer. He had no documents to prove that was his legal name. His age was shown as forty-two. The notes gave a vague physical description of the man. He was about five feet ten inches tall and weighed about two hundred twenty pounds. Stretch read what appeared to be an effort at a verbatim recital of the questions posed to Palmer and the answers that he gave. Nothing in them seemed to help or hurt Audrey.

The questioning continued until the deputy apparently concluded the man had nothing to offer regarding the death of Gloria Angel.

At that point the notes ended abruptly as though the story told by the vagrant wasn't worth more of the law officer's time.

There was a scribbling that showed that a deputy interviewed Howard Welter. There was no evidence of a transcription of the conversation, and the scribbling concluded by stating that no usable information was gathered.

Only after her belongings had been inventoried were Gloria Angel's parents allowed to gather the possessions from her office. In addition to the appointment book, the inventory consisted mostly of correspondence, office memos, personal writings, some books, and several decorative items including pictures taken of her with the governor and other public figures. The notes that accompanied the inventory showed that the sheriff had retained the appointment book with the permission of Ms. Angel's parents. It appeared that no inventory was compiled of the belongings, if any, that were taken from Gloria's townhouse before her parents cleaned it out and closed it up. At least, no such list of belongings was among the discovery documents.

Putting the last of the many papers to one side, Stretch leaned back and stared at the ceiling—deep in contemplation. While the county attorney would call a number of witnesses to testify at the Welter trial, in the end his case came down to the same facts that had been evident from the beginning. Audrey was the last known person to see the victim. A scarf with Gloria Angel's blood on it was found in Audrey's desk, and a flashlight with Gloria's blood on it was found in Audrey's car. Audrey's rage at Gloria Angel for destroying her marriage supplied the motive. Motive, means, and opportunity. The classic things law enforcement looked for when a homicide occurred.

The defense tactic, then, must be to explain away each of the three things that the county attorney would use to justify a conviction. In addition, Stretch must constantly remind the jury that there was nothing in the evidence to directly connect Audrey with the killing.

On the face of it, the county attorney had a reasonable chance of convincing twelve jurors to convict, based on the evidence shown in the discovery documents. Explaining away the bloody scarf and the bloody flashlight would be difficult but might not be impossible. In the end, though, Audrey was right when she said, "We have to find the real killer." The only possible way to find the killer seemed to be in locating the person who sent the email to Audrey, stating that he—or she—knew Audrey didn't kill Gloria Angel. But there didn't seem to be any way to find out who sent that message. Evidently it came from the Billings Public Library. The librarian said there was no way to determine who was using the library computers at the time the message was sent.

It was time for another conversation with his client.

29

Stretch stopped for lunch at his usual restaurant in Helena. There he found Ambrose Swan seated at a small table for two. The reporter waved an invitation for Stretch to join him. Without preamble, the newsman said, "I've been coming here for lunch for a week, hoping to catch you."

Stretch smiled. "Well, you've caught me. Now what're you going to do with me? Throw me back in the water 'cause I'm too small a fish?"

"You ain't a small fish, Senator." Swan shifted in his chair and shoved the plate aside. "You ever hear of a guy named Donald Kastner?"

Stretch cocked his head to one side in thought. "Nope, never heard of him."

"He's the guy who owns that tract of land next to the state section along the Rocky Mountain Front. You know, the land that can't be explored for oil and gas because Audrey Welter's bill passed the legislature and was signed by the governor?"

"What about him?"

Swan leaned back in his chair and picked at his lunch. Then he leaned forward and said in a conspiratorial manner, "I think it would be worth your while to find out what kind of person he is."

"And why do you say that?"

The reporter shoved his chair back and pushed down on the table as he struggled to his feet. "Remember, I admire your client. Find out about Donald Kastner. Talk to the head of the Land

Department. Ask what Kastner threatened to do to your lady not long before Gloria Angel was killed. It might help your case. And it can't hurt." With that the older man turned and shuffled away. Stretch followed Swan with his eyes. Better plan a stop at the Land Department on my return through Helena, he decided.

    A winding gravel track lined by a dense growth of willows led from the paved road to Audrey's country retreat. The cabin itself—a long, low one-story log building—was perched on a prominent rise next to a small stream that flowed northward into the Blackfoot River. When his vehicle emerged from a growth of willows, Stretch found the structure framed squarely in the windshield. With four huge evergreen trees rising behind the cabin and the willows and several aspen trees along the nearby creek with their early-season multihued leaves gently shimmering, the image was one of a western landscape done in oil by a master. Audrey, standing on the deck, was dressed in cinnamon-colored western jeans, a blouse the color of ginger— accented by a silken tie of scarlet red. The colors of her clothing seemed to perfectly complement the cabin's varied shades of brown. Stretch thought her appearance suitable for the cover of a fashion magazine.

    She remained on the deck as Stretch pulled his vehicle alongside her Subaru and hauled his lengthy frame from behind the steering wheel. One look at the smile on her face, and he hurried up the steep, flat-stone walk. He bounded up the three steps to the deck to meet her. For the briefest of moments they stood facing each other without speaking. Concern about the criminal charges hanging over Audrey's head had wreaked subtle changes in her appearance. Stretch saw worry lines around her mouth and across her brow where none had existed before. He felt an overwhelming desire to put his arms around her and gather her to his chest in a comforting embrace. At the moment when he began to reach out to her, she moved back a step and put out her hand. "Welcome, sir, to my hideaway."

Stretch quickly regained his professional composure, grasped her hand, and smiled. "I've been anxious to see your hideaway." Turning to face the wide Blackfoot Valley and the rugged mountains of the Swan Range in the distance, he added, "It's easy to understand why you enjoy your time here."

Audrey moved beside him to share the view. "I would be enjoying both my time and the view a great deal more were it not for the purpose that brings you here—to save me from the clutches of the law." Then she touched him on his arm and said, "You've had a long drive, and it's a warm spring day." She gestured toward a couple of rustic wooden rocking chairs and added, "Rest and rock while I fetch something from the refrigerator."

The pleasant mid-April sun drifted slowly toward the western horizon. With tall glasses of iced tea and a plate of fresh baked sugar cookies on a table between them, they gazed quietly for a time at the spacious panorama that lay to the north. Stretch reached with his left hand for a cookie just as Audrey broke the silence. "And your law practice? Did it survive your absence once again?"

"Things were no worse when I got back to Roundup this time than they've been after any other legislative session. Except for your matter, of course." When Audrey's face darkened, he waited for her to speak. Instead, she placed her glass on the table and crossed her arms in a protective posture. When she remained silent, he continued. "I went through all the investigative material given to us by Hefty Hogan. As you know, the rules of procedure require him to disclose all the information in his possession that bears upon your guilt or innocence in any way. There is nothing there that you and I haven't discussed before."

"Is that good or bad?"

"It's good that only three things—actually four things—seem to implicate you in the death of Gloria Angel, and you know what they are."

Her posture remained rigid as she said, "But those facts may be enough for a jury to convict me. Isn't that right?"

"That's the hell of it, Audrey. I'd like to think a jury wouldn't convict on that evidence alone. But twelve people could."

Audrey's shoulders trembled in an involuntary shudder. "They could. That's the thought that haunts me. And terrifies me." She reached across the table toward him. "God, Stretch! Have you any idea what it's like to be in my position?" Without giving him time to respond, she continued, "Try as I might, I can't put the thought of conviction out of my mind during the day. And night is even worse. When I finally do drop off, it's only for a short time. Then I come awake from dreams of prison—or worse."

Stretch grasped her hand and gave it a gentle squeeze. "Nothing has changed since we last visited. No one has come forward to provide information that would clear you. There are only two ways to eliminate the uncertainty of a trial. One is to find the actual killer."

When he paused, she asked, "And the other way?"

"Try to work out a plea agreement with Hefty Hogan."

Audrey's body stiffened again, and her face froze into a cold mask. "You mean plead guilty in exchange for a lesser sentence, don't you?"

"Yes. That's what a plea bargain amounts to."

She bolted from her chair and stood with her hands on her hips—her face an ashen mask. Leaning over him, she spat, "I won't plead guilty to something I didn't do. Don't ever mention it again." She turned toward the door leading into the cabin and barked, "Bring your belongings. I'll show you the guest bedroom."

Stretch slumped in the chair. Her intense reaction was unexpected and seemed completely out of character. At some point he was obligated to discuss the possibility of a plea agreement with her. When he spoke of such a bargain, it had been on impulse. He wished he'd waited to mention it until the trial was nearer at hand and until he had some idea if Hefty Hogan was amenable to negotiation. But it was done, and she had made plain her feelings. He wouldn't mention it again.

Stretch lugged a garment bag and his briefcase from the car, up the cabin steps, and through the entry into a broad open room. Audrey, arms still crossed in a defiant posture, stood near a door to the far right. Stretch followed her along a short hallway past an open door to a large bedroom on one side, past a door into a bathroom on the other, and finally to a second bedroom at the far end.

Audrey stepped into the room and gestured toward a closet to indicate the place where he could hang his clothing. Without meeting his eyes, she said, "I'm sure you saw the bathroom as you went by." She stopped, and turned to look directly at him. "The kitchen is at the far end. Dinner will be ready before too long." Finally the corners of her mouth relaxed and turned up in a slight smile. "My offerings may not be as good as yours, but they will have to do. There's no other place to eat for twenty miles."

The realization that Audrey's anger had subsided brought a rush of relief to Stretch. His smile was broad. "I'm sure the food will be as appealing as the one who prepares it."

That brought the usual winning smile to his hostess's lips. "All right, Stretch Bruce. I understand you were only doing what you have to do when you suggested I plead guilty. And I'm sorry if I sounded a little huffy. You don't have to lay the compliments on quite that thick in an effort to placate me." Her moccasins made a brushing sound on the carpet as she walked back down the hallway.

Stretch slipped the garment bag from his shoulder and called after her, "If I can have a few minutes to clean up from my travels, I'll join you in the kitchen. Perhaps I can help with something."

"It's your turn to relax. Let me wait on you. Who knows? You may like it."

Stretch grinned in relief. Her pique had passed, and the evening could be comfortable after all. He changed into Wrangler jeans and a flannel shirt. While putting on his shoes, he wished he'd brought his own comfortable moccasins. Refreshed and dressed, he strode back along the hallway to the wide-open living area where he paused, hands in his pockets, to survey the room and its furnishings. It was arranged as a combination living room and office, all of which was decorated in a western motif.

Windows, taller than they were wide, provided a view of the wide Blackfoot valley. Near one end of the room and in front of one of the windows was a flat-surfaced desk on which stood a computer, neatly stacked papers, and a book that appeared to be a small dictionary. A long credenza was perpendicular to the outside wall, creating an illusion of separation of an office from the adjacent living area. The credenza had several pictures arranged along its top. Included among them were the ones of Audrey and her son that Stretch had seen in her office in the capitol. Standing near the office chair was a spotting scope set up for ready use. Audrey must be a bird watcher. Several prints of western paintings graced the walls.

A pleasant aroma drifted from the kitchen. Audrey, wearing an apron, stood near the stove, spatula in hand. She turned to face him and wiped her sleeve across her brow. "I hope you like trout because that's the entree for the evening,"

"Did you catch them yourself?"

With a quiet laugh, she said. "As a matter of fact, I did." Turning her attention back to the pan, she added, "Only yesterday and especially for this meal. They should be tasty if you like trout. I've never asked if you do."

"I do, and I don't get to eat it often enough. The river near where I live is too warm for trout."

"Your bad luck. Maybe you should move to western Montana where the fishing is great, the golf is better, and the skiing is the best."

"Is that an invitation of some kind?" Stretch watched with pleasure as the smile lines formed around her mouth.

"Take it as such, if you wish." Audrey lifted the side of one fish with the spatula. "This will be ready in a couple of minutes. White wine with fish is what I'm always told." She pointed with her elbow toward the refrigerator. "You have a choice—Riesling or Sauvignon blanc." She mimicked John Wayne when she added, "Pick your poison, partner."

Stretch found a corkscrew and opened a bottle. He sniffed the cork and sighed—for Audrey's benefit. Better let her know he appreciated the wine. He carefully filled the two wine glasses and placed them on the snowy white linen tablecloth. Audrey took two potatoes from the oven and put one on each plate. She retrieved steamed broccoli from the microwave and hot bread from the warming oven. Finally, she scooped two large trout, perfectly browned, onto the plates. The warmth from the stove had brought moisture to her forehead, and she blew upward at a wisp of hair that had fallen near her eyes. Audrey gestured for Stretch to be seated. Instead, he stepped around to hold the chair for her. Audrey smiled at the courtly gesture.

With his hands resting on his lap, he waited for her to begin. She hesitated for a heartbeat. "Do you ever pray before a meal?"

The question was so unexpected that it caused Stretch to blink. He recovered quickly. "I've gotten out of the habit." Then he hurried to add, "Please say grace, if you will. We should appreciate the food that God gives us. And prayer will do me good."

With his head down, he listened as Audrey quietly recited the common prayer remembered from his childhood, "Come Lord Jesus, be our guest. And let this food to us be blessed. Amen."

Eyes raised again, Audrey spread a napkin over her lap. Her face carried a worn appearance when she told him, "I've said more prayers than that lately—serious prayers."

Before he could reply, she deliberately wiped away the worried look and smiled across the table. "But let's enjoy the meal."

They ate in a silence broken only by the compliments that Stretch offered for the perfect manner in which the fish was prepared. In response to his question, she acknowledged that the bread was fresh baked and that she made it herself. She did confess to the use of a bread machine. Nevertheless, the admission led to more compliments. When his plate was clean, Stretch pushed his chair back and leaned forward with his elbows on the table. "Tell me about yourself. Where were you born?"

As she spread butter over the last morsel of bread, Audrey spoke without raising her eyes. "I was born in Columbus, Ohio. My father was an accountant. My mother was a homemaker." She told him of her history, her sister and her family in Ohio, and ended by talking about her son.

"Logan's a handsome young man and seems to have his mother's intelligence."

"He's wonderful. There's no other way to describe him. He has never caused me a bit of trouble and was an excellent student. Logan graduated from Stanford two years ago. He's an accountant—like his grandfather."

"A person doesn't get into Stanford unless he's exceptional."

"He's exceptional." Audrey pushed her chair back from the table. "He treats me wonderfully. I don't know how I would have survived the first few days after the arraignment had Logan not been here." Standing, she asked, "Coffee? It's decaf." She crossed to the counter, poured the mahogany-colored liquid into mugs, and carried them to the table. "Of course, you'd expect a mother to say her child is exceptional. But in the case of Logan, it's true."

"Knowing his mother, I'm sure it's true."

"You are full of compliments this evening, Senator." Her smile widened. "And I'm in a mood to appreciate them."

They sipped coffee in silence, each seemingly at ease in the company of the other and feeling no need for forced conversation. At last Audrey said, "It's a warm evening, and the sun will slide behind the mountains in a few minutes. Let's move out on the porch and enjoy the sunset."

With Audrey seated beside him, Stretch rocked the chair contentedly. The cool evening air, carrying the freshness of spring, acted as a gentle narcotic. The upcoming trial—the purpose for his visit—slipped slowly from his thoughts. His mind wandered as he absorbed the magnificence of the landscape around him. The mental meandering eventually coalesced into a picture of himself free of life's anxieties, with Audrey at his side as a warm and affectionate companion. Their time could be spent in peaceful settings—with nothing to cause either of them concern.

His reverie was broken when Audrey shivered and said, "The night air still has a winter bite to it."

Stretch rose quickly and offered a hand to help her to her feet. She led the way back to the sitting area, gestured for him to take one of the comfortable chairs, and seated herself on the couch, her hands folded together on her lap. With her eyes on her hands, she took a deep breath and let it out. At last she looked directly into his eyes and said, "I know you came to talk about preparations for the trial. But could we defer that discussion until tomorrow? This has been a pleasant interlude. I'd prefer to savor it as long as possible."

Stretch returned her gaze without responding for so long that she wondered if he had been listening. When he spoke, it was to say, "Gracious lady, this evening will remain in my mind forever. It's the most pleasant I've spent in a long time." His earnestness showed as he leaned forward. "Of course we can delay any discussion that might spoil it. I want to hold this feeling for as long as I can."

Audrey's shoulders relaxed, and the corners of her mouth turned up in the beginnings of a smile. "But what shall we do now? I've shown you all the sights."

What shall we do now? The parting remarks she made as she left his home near Roundup came immediately to Stretch's mind. She had spoken of a fantasy in which he crept into her room during the night—and in the fantasy she welcomed him. The thought left him temporarily speechless, wondering if she was offering an invitation.

Apparently his look reflected his thoughts, for she said, "It's much too early for bed."

Stretch stumbled out a question. "What would you be doing if I weren't here?"

Audrey's laugh was as melodious as ever. "I'd probably watch a James Bond movie on DVD. Would you like to do that? I have the complete set."

"I haven't seen a Bond movie for years. If you have the complete set you must have the earliest ones, how about watching one of those?"

By the end of the movie, Stretch was completely relaxed and found that he was sleepy even though it was much earlier than he ordinarily retired. Audrey stood and faced him as he rose from the chair. Putting her hands on his upper arms, she said, "Senator Bruce, I may have misled you with my parting comments when I left your house. So let's understand each other. My bedroom is there." She poked an elbow in one direction. "And your bedroom is there." She poked the elbow in the other direction. "And the twain shall not meet. Understood?"

Stretch put his hands on her shoulders and grinned down at her upturned face. "Understood." His grin widened. "But I must admit to harboring some fanciful ideas on my drive over here."

Audrey dropped her hands "Well, put those fanciful ideas out of your mind. In the morning we must spend our time discussing my fate."

Sleep came slowly to Senator Bruce. Intoxicating images of his client, images that had nothing to do with her legal problems, refused to leave his mind.

30

"Who benefits if you are convicted of killing Gloria Angel?" Audrey stared at Stretch until he answered his own question. "Obviously the real killer benefits. Whoever that person might be is home free if a jury finds you guilty."

Audrey nodded. "That's true. But we don't know who the killer is so we don't know who will benefit, do we?"

"Among the ones who had access to the building that night, which one or ones might benefit from her death?" Stretch held up a thumb as though beginning to tick off numbers. "There's the vagrant. So far as we know there was no connection between him and Gloria Angel. Unless he was an impulse killer or maybe a contract killer, there really isn't any reason to think he did it."

"I wish we knew more about the guy. From what I've heard about him, he's seems a little strange."

"Let's think about others." He raised a finger beside the thumb. "The governor's behavior has been odd. His stories have been totally inconsistent. And he had a closer relationship with Gloria than anyone else."

"It's hard to imagine Albert Shewey bludgeoning someone to death. He just doesn't fit the picture of a murderer.

"Perhaps not, but we can't count him out." Another finger appeared. "It seems Gloria had something going with the attorney general. While there is no indication he was at the capitol that night, his behavior makes me wonder if she was somehow a threat to him. Could he have a reason to want her dead?"

"God, Stretch, I don't know. He's a Republican, one of your guys. You know him a lot better than I do. Could he kill someone?"

"Damned if I know. I guess it depends on the seriousness of the threat. His whole life is politics, and he wants to be governor. I suppose if Gloria knew something that could jeopardize his political future and if she threatened to expose him, he could become desperate enough to do her in." Stretch sipped from his cup. "There's another thing. Ambrose Swan told me that Shewey and Sawyer gathered in a remote cabin about the time the legislative session ended. He refused to tell me how he knew of their get-together, but he must have felt it had something to do with your case. There was no other reason for him to mention it to me." He raised his eyebrows as he asked, "Could both of them be involved in the killing? And be in cahoots?"

"Ah c'mon, Senator. That's stretching it too far. Shewey wants to be a United States senator. Sawyer wants to be governor. If they're in cahoots, it's because they've made some kind of deal to further their mutual political ambitions. That would be understandable." Audrey's face twisted into a smirk. "It's not unheard of in this state for that kind of conniving to take place. Just read Montana history." Audrey got to her feet. Pacing across the kitchen, she added, "No, I can't imagine any of our elected officials murdering Gloria Angel or anyone else. I've had political differences with both Albert Shewey and Henry Sawyer. But that's all they were, political differences. There's nothing special in my association with either of them. Nothing to make either of them want to frame me for murder."

"I suppose you're right. But Ambrose must have thought otherwise. And he has a better nose for foul odors in the capital city than anyone. Think about it. They may not have intended to frame you. If either of them is responsible for Gloria's death, you may have just been unlucky and provided a target of opportunity."

"Forget it, Counselor. You're not going to find the killer by digging under that rock."

Stretch's eyes lingered on her trim silhouette, framed in the window, as he smiled and admitted, "You're probably right. As far as Hefty Hogan knows, you were the one who saw her last."

She turned back to face him. "What about Hogan? I don't trust him. Could he have something to do with her death?"

"Funny you should ask." Stretch beckoned her back to the chair. As she passed the coffee maker she picked up the pot and refilled their mugs. When she was seated, Stretch continued, "The sheriff said Hogan was one of several prominent people with whom Gloria Angel shared quiet dinners in out-of-the-way places. Ambrose Swan mentioned it one time too."

Audrey shook her head. "How does the sheriff learn such things? And does either he or Ambrose really have any way of knowing if they're true?"

"The sheriff found it in her appointment book. Ambrose has been around Helena for years and years. He knows everyone. And he's liked by everyone. My guess is that people just trust him and tell him things they wouldn't tell anybody else."

Stretch draped one arm over the back of the chair. "And, how about this? Ambrose caught me at the restaurant when I stopped in Helena on my way over here. He told me I should learn more about the man who owns the section of land that's off limits to drilling because of your Save the Rocky Mountain Front bill. The man's name is Donald Kastner. It seems Kastner has made threatening remarks about you at some time or another."

Audrey sat bolt upright. "Threatened me?"

"That's what Ambrose indicated. He told me to talk to the head of the Land Department to find out exactly what words the guy used."

"Did you talk to him?"

"No. It was late, and I was anxious to finish the drive over here." When Audry showed no reaction, he added, "I'll stop at the Land Department on my way back."

"Why is Ambrose Swan giving you so much information? What's he up to?"

Stretch shook his head and chuckled. "I don't know. But that old newsman is certainly trying to be helpful to us. He has told me several times how much he admires you. You must have been good to him along the way. Did you make it a habit to slip him choice news items before any other reporter got them?"

"Not that I can remember. I always liked him because he wasn't pushy. And he always reported fairly. Those are qualities any office holder comes to appreciate."

"We've digressed from our discussion of those who were in the capitol that night. What about the young woman Ambrose mentioned? Could she have done it?"

Audrey shook her head. "That's silly! Ambrose Swan only said there was a rumor that a young woman was in the capitol building that night. As far as I know, it's never been confirmed." Eyebrows raised, she asked, "Has it?"

"Not that I've heard."

"Then why waste time thinking about it? If the sheriff hasn't confirmed her existence by now, the rumor must be false."

Stretch nodded. Then to change the conversation, he reached for a briefcase resting against the leg of his chair. "Let's discuss other things." He pulled out two thick packets of papers. "I made copies of all the information that the county attorney provided. One copy is for you to review in a thorough manner after I'm gone." He pushed a bundle of papers to Audrey's side of the table. "But let's discuss them while I'm here so I can get your reaction to my observations."

Audrey picked up the papers and slowly riffled through the beginning pages to get a first look. Then she raised her eyes. "What is all this stuff?"

"The top document is the autopsy report. It's written in the usual medical mumbo-jumbo. In essence, however, the pathologist concluded that Gloria died from a blow to the head."

"That's something anyone could figure out."

"Well, it's something we've all assumed, but there was always a possibility that she died of some other cause—until the cause of death was confirmed."

"All right, Counselor, does the report help or harm my defense?"

"In my view, it doesn't do either. But Hogan has to question the pathologist at the trial and introduce the report as an exhibit to prove the cause of death. That's why he enclosed the report with his other disclosure documents."

"If there isn't any question about the cause of death, why must it be proven?"

"We're going to make Hogan prove everything. There is no reason to concede one single fact. Who knows? The pathologist may slip and say something that will be helpful. We're not going to forego that possibility, remote as it may seem."

Audrey nodded. "So it's your intention to try to raise a question about each bit of evidence that Hogan wishes to offer?"

"We may not be able to blow smoke all the time, but we can try. Unless we are able to identify the real killer, we have to do everything we can at the trial to show that the state's case is full of holes. We do that by questioning each bit of evidence as Hogan offers it." Stretch added in a grim voice, "It's not the best defense against an accusation of criminal conduct. But it's the only one we have at the moment. If it doesn't work, you will be convicted of homicide."

Audrey straightened and her eyes widened. She clasped her arms tightly across her chest and glanced around the room as though looking for escape. She pulled her arms away and lowered her face into the palms of her hands, elbows braced on the table and sighed. "I've always understood that, but to hear it spoken out loud is really unsettling."

"I'm sure it is." Stretch reached a hand across the table. "And I wish I didn't have to say it. But both of us must always keep it in mind."

Audrey sat silently for a long time, then looked up, and began massaging one hand with the other. At last she asked, "What else is in the material you've given me?"

"Notes of your conversation with Hefty Hogan, his notes from the time when you told him of Gloria's visit to your office. He didn't make any notes while we were talking so he must have dictated them right after we left. Please read the notes at your leisure to be certain they are accurate."

"What else?"

"The sheriff and his deputy made an inventory of the items they saw in your office, both when they were first there and when they came for the scarf. You should look that over carefully too."

"Is that all?"

"No. There are notes from the sheriff's conversations with the governor. A deputy's notes of his questioning of the vagrant. And there's an inventory of the things found in Gloria Angel's office. There's no inventory of Gloria's belongings from her townhouse. And the record of the interview with your ex-husband is all but worthless. A deputy questioned him."

"And Howard proclaimed his innocence?"

"That's my understanding. Have you learned any more about the stalking accusation?"

Audrey shook her head. "Just rumors. Nothing of substance."

Stretch waited for her to elaborate. When she remained immobile, he changed the subject. "What is most curious is that Hefty provided no notes or memoranda of the email he said he received from someone saying that person could prove you were the killer."

Audrey raised her eyes. "Shouldn't he have made a record of a communication like that?"

"He sure should have. But maybe he just figured that so long as I knew about the email, he didn't need to formally disclose its existence. Maybe we can make something of his sloppy work—if he tries to bring it up at trial."

"What if the person that sent the emails really surfaces and starts telling Hogan things that aren't true?"

"Could happen, I suppose. We'd demand a continuance to interview the sender and try to make him out a liar. We can't anticipate what might be said. We'll just have to wait and tackle it head on if it does happen." Stretch slid down in the chair, extended his legs and crossed his ankles. With his hands clasped on his stomach, he asked, "What about the person who sent you the email? I assume you haven't heard anything further or you would have told me."

"Nothing. I haven't received any more emails, and I don't know how to find out who sent the one I received."

"Well, perhaps whoever sent it will surface again. Let's hope so and also hope that person really can provide evidence that you didn't kill anyone."

Audrey stood and stretched her back. "This hasn't been the greatest conversation I've ever had." She looked down at her lawyer. "What else do I need to know before I drag you out of this house for a walk up the creek to a beaver dam? Sometimes, when I'm quiet, I get to watch those busy little beasts at their work. It's a nice morning, and we might be lucky."

The Body on the Floor of the Rotunda

Stretch unfolded his long frame to its full height. "The judge has set a scheduling conference for the end of the month. During the conference he'll give us a trial date. The date for the trial will probably be in the fall. Is there any period of time that would be really bad for you? A time when someone may have planned to visit you? Your sister, for example?"

She shook her head. "No, Stretch, there's nothing I need to do that's more important. Let's just get this thing over and done. I'm in limbo right now. I can't keep going like I've been. I need to know whether I'll be exonerated or sent to jail." She reached for his hand and led him toward the door. "Now let's enjoy this lovely day for a while before you drive away. Time spent out of doors helps me blank this murder accusation from my mind, at least for a short while."

31

Stretch arrived back in Helena shortly after noon. After a quick lunch he went to the Land Department offices. At the receptionist's desk, he identified himself as a state senator and asked if he could see Dave Bowman, head of the Lands Administration Division. Since no bureaucrat ever wants to antagonize a member of the legislature, he was promptly shown to Bowman's office. Bowman, short and rotund, stood at the door. "Good to see you again, Senator. You're back in Helena so soon after the session?"

Stretch gripped his hand. "Can't stay away. Can I have a few minutes of your time?"

"Always time for a member of the legislature. What can I do for you?"

Stretch seated himself and assumed his relaxed pose. His relationship with the folks at the Land Department had always been good, and he liked Dave Bowman. "I've heard that a man named Donald Kastner has threatened Audrey Welter. Do you know anything about that?"

Bowman leaned forward with his elbows on the desk. "As a matter of fact, I do. Donald Kastner is a very strange person. As you probably know, he owns a chunk of land next to the state section north of here where the oil companies wanted to drill." Bowman grimaced. "But Audrey Welter put a stop to that, didn't she?"

"Yup, she did. Or at least a bill she introduced became a law that stopped drilling on the state land."

"Well, the exploration companies aren't interested in Kastner's land without the state section. So, Senator Welter's efforts, in Kastner's view, effectively deprived him of the possibility of getting a lot of oil and gas money from his land. For some reason, he thought those of us in the Land Department were pushing her proposal. He would show up here, red-faced in anger, and would rant about a conspiracy to deprive him of his property rights."

"When was this?"

"It happened more than once. But the first time was early in January, right after the papers reported that Senator Welter had introduced the bill."

"Did he say the same things each time he was here?"

"Essentially. He was so irrational that I didn't want to talk to him after his first visit. But he'd storm in here and frighten the receptionist. So I told her to bring him to my office any time he arrived. I believed I could handle him better than anyone else."

"Did he ever threaten Audrey Welter in your presence?"

Bowman's eyes widened. "Oh yes! He surely did. He would tear in here, calling her foul names. Then when the Senate committee voted to pass the bill and send it to the floor, he was in here again, shouting the most vulgar kinds of things about her. I tried to calm him down, but he kept it up and finally screeched that he would make her pay for what she was doing to him." He sat back in his chair and shook his head as though in disbelief. "I finally had to call the police to get rid of him."

"Did the police know of the threats against Senator Welter?"

"Of course. He was still making them while they were escorting him out." Bowman's lips turned up in a ghost of a smile. "Well, they really didn't escort him so much as drag him. Two cops had a hold of him, one by each arm."

Stretch looked across the desk with his lips pursed. "No one told Senator Welter of this. Didn't you think you should warn her?"

"I assumed the police would do it. That's their job, isn't it?"

"If it is, they didn't do it." Stretch pulled his feet near the chair and dropped his hands on his knees as though to rise. He stopped and asked. "Have there been any threats lately? Has he been back here since the police dragged him out?"

"No, thank God. We haven't seen him since that day." Bowman took a deep breath. "I hope I never see that man again. He's a husky dude, and he's scary!"

"Tell me more about him. What does he look like?"

"He's about forty-five years old, I'd guess. And about five foot ten. Weighs about two hundred twenty pounds. Wears old clothes that haven't been washed for months. He stinks—literally." Bowman thought a moment. "The thing is, he's extremely intelligent, and he must have had an education. When he was at his worst, the manner of speaking was that of an illiterate. But when he was somewhat calm, he used words only an educated person would know and use." After a head shake, he added, "Except for the vulgarities, of course. They seemed to be a regular part of his vocabulary. "

"Do you think he's capable of doing harm to Audrey Welter? Or Gloria Angel?"

Bowman leaned toward Stretch "I sure as hell do. I'm telling you, man, that guy is scary."

Stretch started the engine of the Expedition but, instead of driving away from the land office, he sat for a time in thought. His intention had been to finish his drive to Roundup. But curiosity led him instead to turn the vehicle up the hill toward the capitol. He found a parking spot and tramped the long walk up the curved driveway to the entrance under the massive front steps of the building. From there it was a climb up a side stairway to the rotunda and another climb up the grand staircase to the legislative chambers and the pressroom.

Luck was with him. He found Ambrose Swan sitting before a computer, spectacles perched low on his nose. Swan looked over his shoulder when Stretch came through the door and held up one hand to show that he didn't want to be interrupted. He squinted at the computer screen, deleted a paragraph, and reinserted it farther down on the page. The old man typed a final sentence and squinted some more as he read it over. He jammed the print button with a flourish before swiveling his chair to face Stretch. "Welcome back to the seat of government. But I'll guess you're more interested in legal matters on this day than in governmental matters."

"Your guess is a good one." He nodded back toward the door. "It's my turn to buy lunch. You get to pick the place."

"Let me see. What's the most expensive eatery in town? Wherever it is, that's where I want to go—so long as you're buying."

"They're all expensive for a country lawyer from Roundup. How about the Montana Club? We can get a table in a corner and visit without anyone overhearing us."

"So it's a secret conversation you're after. Mysteries! I love mysteries."

"The only mystery in my mind is how you learn all the secrets of this place before anyone else. Maybe I can add one to your list." As they reached the elevator, he added, "I'll drive."

Another cold April wind had arrived, and they both ducked their heads to keep the blowing dirt out of their eyes as they crossed the street from the parking garage to the door of the Montana Club. At Stretch's request, they were ushered to a table in a far corner of the bar area, away from the main part of the dining room. At one thirty in the afternoon most of the diners had left, so they had no concern that their conversation would be overheard. The lawyer delayed the questions he had for the newsman until they had ordered, received their meal, and finished eating. Then he leaned an elbow on the table and rested his chin on one fist. Before he could speak, Swan brushed at the shock of white hair that persisted in falling down toward his eyes and grinned. "I take it you learned something about Donald Kastner."

"I did. And now I have more questions. What more can you tell me about the man?"

The old reporter's smile widened. "Not a hell of a lot. You talked to the folks at the Land Department?"

"I talked to Dave Bowman, and he told me about the threats Kastner made—the threats to do harm to Audrey Welter. But that doesn't mean he made any attempt to carry them out. Listen, Ambrose, you must have heard something that made you think Kastner was somehow implicated in the death of Gloria Angel. Am I right?"

"I hear rumors. Sometimes I try to verify them. Sometimes I just send them along to someone else to do the verifying."

Stretch leaned back and took a breath. "You aren't helping much. I need to know what, if anything, that man had to do with Gloria Angel's death."

Swan shook his head. "I don't know of anything." Then his face took on a conspiratorial look. "What has our good Sheriff Mendenhall done about it? Has he checked him out to see if Kastner was the transient they found in the capitol building the night Ms. Angel was killed?"

Stretch cocked an eyebrow. "I don't know. Hell, I don't even know if he's aware of the threats that Kastner made. The city police knew about them. But they may never have told the sheriff. I guess the sheriff's people didn't take a picture of the transient. The only way to know if Kastner is the transient is to have one of the deputies who dragged him out of the basement go find Kastner. The deputy could tell if they're one and the same person."

"I'd say you better get yourself to the sheriff's office and discuss this with Brent." Swan grinned. "For some reason, old Brent doesn't seem to believe your client is a murderer. And that's driving the county attorney crazy." The venerable reporter pushed himself away from the table and said, "I've got a meeting with the head of the Department of Natural Resources."

As Stretch walked the reporter toward the door, he asked, "What other rumors have you heard that I should know about?"

"None. But if I hear of any, you can be sure I'll call."

There was a hint of anger on Brent Mendenhall's face. He didn't like the possibility that the transient might be a person who was frequently in the capital city. And he didn't like the fact that he hadn't been informed about threats to a legislator. When Stretch finished telling of his conversation with Dave Bowman, the sheriff growled, "You can be certain that we'll learn all there is to know about Mr. Kastner." He reached to shake Stretch's hand. "And thanks for bringing this to me instead of to the county attorney. We'll let him know what we find. And I'll keep you informed."

Outside in the Expedition, Stretch pondered on the sheriff's remarks. It was clear that communication between the sheriff and the county attorney wasn't the best—and he wondered why that would be.

32

Judge Milton Hasting's secretary led Stretch to a small room used by the judge for scheduling conferences. County Attorney Hefty Hogan and a young man with blond hair and a carefully trimmed beard were already in the room, sitting side by side at a round table. Hogan remained seated when Stretch entered. He merely nodded his head in recognition and then poked his elbow toward his companion. "Meet Ellis Bradley. He's one of my deputies."

The deputy stood to take Stretch's hand and said in a respectful voice, "I've admired your work in the legislature, Senator."

Stretch pulled out a chair next to Bradley and dropped his briefcase on the floor beside it. "Thank you. I enjoy my activities in the Senate. But today we're dealing with legal, not legislative, matters." He turned to Hogan. "Am I at the right place at the right time? We seem to be without a judge."

With his chair pushed back and hands clasped at his stomach, Hogan appeared calm and assured. "The judge was on the telephone when we got here. His secretary said we wouldn't have to wait very long. This conference shouldn't take long either."

"I agree. I assume you're ready to go to trial?" It was said more as a question than a statement.

"Yup! We can try this one tomorrow if that's what you and the judge want." He turned to his companion. "Isn't that right, Ellis?"

Ellis smiled deferentially at the county attorney. "Well, maybe not tomorrow but very soon." He turned to Stretch. "Mr. Hogan has asked me to sit second chair with him at Ms. Welter's trial. I've been doing a lot of the preparatory work." The young man's voice revealed some pride in his involvement in a matter of such consequence.

Stretch started to reply but was stopped when Judge Hastings bustled into the room, followed by a court reporter. The judge, wearing a dark brown suit, immediately dropped into the remaining chair, opened the file to look at the case heading, mumbling as he read.

"Good afternoon, gentlemen." He seemed surprised to find Ellis Bradley as part of the gathering. He put out his hand. "I don't believe we've met. Am I correct about that?"

"I'm Ellis Bradley, Your Honor. I've only appeared in your court one time. I was representing the state in a bail matter, and it only took a couple of minutes."

The judge nodded, then glanced at Hefty Hogan. "We're here to schedule a trial in the Welter matter. Am I to take it that Mr. Bradley will be participating in that trial, Mr. Hogan?"

"Yes, sir. Ellis has been doing much of the work to get ready, and I've asked him to assist me during the actual trial itself."

"So, you intend to try this one yourself? As lead attorney? Not one of your older, more experienced deputies?"

Hogan's displeasure at the insinuation was evident by the way he clenched his jaw before he spoke. "Yes, Your Honor. I'm going to try it, and I'm going to convict Mr. Bruce's client of deliberate homicide."

The corners of Judge Hastings's lips turned up and a twinkle appeared in his eyes. "Well, you've charged her. It's not likely that you'd have done so unless you felt you could convict." Then he added, "But it doesn't always come out that way, does it?"

Hefty's face began to redden. "Not always. But we've got Ms. Welter cold. No jury will acquit her after they hear the evidence we intend to present."

The judge seemed to be amused by Hefty's arrogance. "I can guess, Mr. Bruce, that you disagree. Is my guess correct?"

"It is, Your Honor. With all due respect to my colleague, Mr. Hogan, he's full of hot air. And he knows it."

The judge's smile turned into a chuckle. "Well, now that you two have established your positions regarding the outcome, perhaps we should discuss a time for the beginning." He pulled a sheet from the file and glanced at the notations on it. "My secretary has listed some dates from my calendar that are available." He stopped, as though realizing he'd missed something, and then turned his eyes to Hogan. "How many days do you think the trial will take?"

Hefty looked at Ellis Bradley, and then back at the judge. "It should take four days, Your Honor."

Turning to Stretch, the judge asked, "And you, Mr. Bruce, what do you think?"

"I don't know how long it will take Mr. Hogan to put on his case in chief, but the defense should not take more than two days, assuming there are no interruptions during those days."

"How about it, Mr. Hogan? Can you handle your end in two days?"

"I was thinking three, Your Honor."

The judge followed his index finger with his eyes as he ran it down the sheet with the open dates. Toward the bottom his finger stopped. "It sounds to me like you're thinking it will take five days to empanel a jury and take the testimony. We'd better set aside another day or two for jury deliberations. I've seven open days beginning on Monday, July twenty-seventh. Would those days work for you, gentlemen?"

Stretch was quick to say, "Yes, sir. I can try the case at any date that accommodates your schedule."

Hefty said, "Those dates suit me fine, Your Honor."

The judge smiled. "Well, that was easily settled." Pushing the paper aside, he asked, "What other matters need to be discussed? Are there any pretrial motions for me to decide?"

Hogan shook his head, "None from my side, Your Honor."

The judge turned again to Stretch, "Mr. Bruce?"

"I've filed none to this date, Your Honor, but I plan to file some motions between now and the time of trial. If I do so, it'll be done in time for Mr. Hogan to respond and for the court to schedule a motion hearing and issue a decision."

"Very good." Turning now to Hogan, Judge Hastings asked, "What about discovery? Have you received discovery requests? And have you responded fully to them?"

"We've received requests, and we've given Mr. Bruce everything we have in terms of evidence. I've held nothing from him."

The judge smiled as though he was giving a blessing. "That's the way it should be done." Turning to Stretch, he asked, "Are you satisfied that you've received everything your discovery requests require?"

"Because I don't know what Mr. Hogan knows, I can't say that I have. But since Hefty says he's given us everything, I have to take his word for it."

"You sound skeptical."

Stretch shook his head. "I'm not trying to insinuate that Mr. Hogan will deliberately withhold exculpatory evidence. I don't believe he will." Turning to the county attorney, he added, "You understand that the discovery requests are continuing? You'll supplement them if and when you discover any new evidence?"

There was anger in Hefty Hogan's voice when he replied, "Of

course I will. I don't need any lawyer from a town the size of Roundup preaching to me about the rules."

The judge, no longer smiling, raised his hands, palms out, as he said, "All right, gentlemen. That's enough." He looked from one to the other. "Is there anything further?" When neither of the principal attorneys answered, he turned to Ellis Bradley with his pleasant smile showing again. "There seem to be more and more young lawyers in town, and I lose track of them. Next time I'll remember who you are."

Ellis grinned and said, "Please don't let it worry you, sir. I know how busy you are. You don't have time to learn all of our names."

Judge Hastings pushed himself erect and reached to shake hands with Stretch and then Hefty. Finally he grasped Ellis's hand. "The trial of Senator Welter portends to be a media event here in Montana. After it's over, young man, I'm sure I'll remember you very well." Without a backward glance, he stepped into his office and closed the door.

All three lawyers had scrambled to their feet together with the judge. Stretch reached for his briefcase, pulled a yellow tablet from it, and wrote the trial date across the top. He jammed it back in the case and turned to the county attorney. "Good to see you again, Hefty." He turned to Ellis Bradley, shook hands with him, and said with a wide grin, "Try to keep your boss honest, will you?"

Bradley laughed softly at the joke. "I'll do my best, sir. But he's hard to manage." When he noticed that Hogan wasn't smiling, his own smile disappeared.

Stretch shrugged his shoulders and started for the door. Without looking back, he recited the standard lawyer's parting statement. "Gentlemen, I'll see you in court."

The Body on the Floor of the Rotunda

Stretch enjoyed a leisurely spring drive from Helena to Roundup through a countryside clothed in green—fresh green grass, fields of green alfalfa, and green winter wheat—all of them in varying hues. After looking to his left at the glistening snowfields on the Big Snowy Mountains and to his right at the shimmering trees along the winding Musselshell River he heaved a sigh and mumbled, "I'm sure glad that I live in Montana."

33

It had been a long and arduous negotiation, and Stretch was exhausted when he returned to his office at nine o'clock in the evening. His client, Harvey Jordan, finally agreed to settle a lawsuit brought by a Californian who had tried to buy Jordan's ranch. The man from California had made a small earnest money payment at the time the parties signed a buy-and-sell agreement. He was obligated by the agreement to make a much larger payment thirty days later. The second payment was never made because the Californian said that Jordan had misled him as to the value of the haying machinery included in the transaction. The suit had little merit, and the lawyer from Billings who represented the man from California knew it. Jordan had his back up, and it took eight hours of persuasion before Stretch could convince the old rancher that he should return a small part of the earnest money to the purported buyer instead of paying a larger amount to Stretch to take the matter to trial. And it took even longer for the Billings lawyer to convince his client that he should accept the amount that was offered.

Despite the late hour, Cynthia was waiting when he shuffled through the door. As he trudged to his desk, she leaned with her shoulder against her office door frame. She stepped along the hallway, followed him into his office, and waited for him to drop into his chair. Then she sat primly on the edge of a chair across from him. Without preamble, she asked, "Well, did you settle?"

"Yes, we settled."

"Was old man Jordan satisfied?"

"No, of course not. He had to agree to pay money to a man he's come to hate." Stretch leaned his left elbow on the desk and rubbed his right hand over his face. With a sigh, he continued, "No, he wasn't satisfied, and he only agreed to do it after I convinced him that there are other, more reliable buyers out there. And after I suggested that there could be one of them who would pay more than the Californian, a lot more."

"Is that true? That he can get more money than was offered? It seemed like an awful lot to me."

"I really believe he can. The ranch is in the foothills of the mountains and has a creek full of trout running through it. It has a resident elk herd that Harvey hates because they compete for feed with his cattle and raise hell with his fences. But those elk will help convince some wealthy city dude that he has to own the ranch." Stretch smiled at Cynthia. "Harvey made that deal with the Californian without talking to me or even talking to a good realtor." Stretch straightened in his chair. "Harvey's old and doesn't have a child to take over the place. He decided to sell and now he's learned a lesson. I gave him the names of three good ranch realtors. He'll list his ranch with one of them. And I'm sure the old boy will bring any new sale agreement to me to review before he signs it."

Cynthia dropped her eyes to her hands that were fidgeting in her lap. "I hate to bring this up, but we have lots to do to get ready for the trial of Audrey Welter."

Sudden, defensive anger came over Stretch, sharpening his voice. "Damn it, Cynthia, I know we have a lot to do. You don't have to remind me."

The minute he said it, he was sorry. A crestfallen look appeared on her face. He leaned forward and spoke with earnestness. "Cynthia, I'm sorry. I didn't mean to offend you. It's been a long day, and I'm tired—if that's any excuse." He took a deep breath and let it out. "I appreciate the fact that you waited here in the office to find out how the Jordan matter came out. And I know we need to prepare for the Welter trial. It's coming up much too fast. But right now I need to get some rest. And you should be home with your son." He stepped around the desk to take her hand and help her to her feet. Her stricken look remained unchanged and she refused to meet his eyes. Stretch said earnestly, "I really am sorry. I can't say anything more than that. Will you forgive me, please?"

The nod of her head was almost imperceptible as she withdrew her hand and walked quietly across to her office. His shoulders drooped, and he slouched back into his chair. His attention was immediately drawn to the stack of papers centered on his desk, directly in front of his chair. With a heavy heart, he crossed his arms on the desk top and dropped his head to rest his brow on them. Why, oh why, had he chosen this night to scold Cynthia? Or any night for that matter? She was as close to a perfect employee as he had ever found. Her analytical skills were excellent, and he frequently used her as a sounding board when he was attempting to dissect the critical elements of an intricate legal question. If a particular court decision was needed, she would find just such a case and often more than one. Cynthia routinely prepared drafts of pleadings that seldom required revision. She could prepare almost any other kind of legal document as well. But most of all, she was a warm and gentle person, and didn't deserve his wrath.

Stretch lifted his head and glanced at all the documents that cried out for his immediate attention. The next day was filled with appointments, leaving little time for him to deal with the paperwork. He puffed out a sigh, strode down the hall, and knocked softly on Cynthia's door. For a moment there was no sound, and he wondered if she had left the office so quietly that he hadn't heard her. Then the door opened, but not fully. She stood holding the knob as though prepared to slam it shut.

"I'd take it back if I could," he said."

She moved to close the door, but he put his hand out to hold it and added quickly, "I know it's late, but would you come with me to the Candy Corner for a sundae or milkshake?"

Cynthia let go of the doorknob and wrapped her arms across her chest.

"If you'd rather, we could go to the Sportsman for a drink instead. I'd like to make it up to you—show you that I really am sorry for a remark I truly regret."

Cynthia remained as rigid as a statue. At last she looked up at him. "No drinks. But it might be okay to go for a milkshake."

When they began their stroll through the warm evening air, she stuck her arm through his and patted his arm with her other hand. "You're forgiven. And a trip to the Candy Corner will be fun. Thanks for inviting me."

Hillary Brown, the clerk of court, had held the office for at least twenty years. She was about sixty years old, and her demeanor was always brusque, never smiling. The clerk responded in monosyllables to most inquiries. Stretch handed her the petition to open an estate and asked that the filing fee be billed to his office. The clerk was stone-faced as always while she filled in the case number on the face of the petition. Stretch thanked her and turned to the door to leave. Before he could complete the exit, she said to his back, "Are you trying to beat the time of the young man who's been seeing that girl?"

"What girl?"

"Cynthia, of course. What other girl do you take to the Candy Corner to giggle with over milkshakes?"

Stretch was speechless for a full minute. When he spoke, the tone of his voice disclosed his exasperation. "Hillary, I invited Cynthia to the Candy Corner to thank her for all the good work she does at my law office." He scowled. "And we weren't giggling."

"That isn't what the whole town is saying. The story I hear is that she was glowing as though you'd already proposed and she'd accepted."

"That's nonsense." He slapped the counter once with the file folder he held in his hands and stalked toward the door.

The clerk stopped him by saying, "Stretch Bruce, a very nice-looking young man has been visiting Cynthia over the last few weeks. He's from out of town. You may be afraid he'll marry her, and you'll lose your most reliable assistant. But that doesn't give you any right to try to butter her up to make her think you're interested in her in a romantic way—just to keep her from running off with someone else."

Stretch turned back to face the clerk across the counter. "Good God, Hillary! She's half my age. What would I do with a woman in her twenties, one that's especially attractive at that? I'm sure as the dickens not trying to romance her. I just took her for a milkshake, for God's sake!" The lawyer began to turn away but stopped in his tracks. "Some young man has been calling on Cynthia?"

"Sure has. He's taken her to Billings at least twice—one time with Matt, her son." The clerk cocked her head to one side. "I can't believe you haven't noticed the spring in her step and the glow on her face."

"Glow on her face?"

"Like a woman in love." Hillary smiled. "I think it's wonderful. The young fellow seems like someone worthy of her. Up till now, the only men who've tried to date her have been ranch hands and oil field monkeys."

"Well, thanks for telling me." He turned and hurried out the door.

It wasn't terribly hot, but a warm front had blown in from the west as he ambled along the sidewalk toward his office. With each step, the words of the clerk echoed in his mind. Cynthia had a suitor and might get married. That certainly was possible. He knew that several of the young bachelors had an eye on her. She had spoken to him about dates with one or another of them, rather like she might have discussed them with a father. If there was someone for whom she had serious feelings, why hadn't she mentioned it to him? Did he dare raise the matter with her?

When he arrived at the door to his office building, he still didn't know how to handle the situation. To avoid a decision, he hurried through the reception area to his private office and closed the door. He punched the phone and told the receptionist that he didn't want any interruptions. He would just put the whole matter off for another day.

34

Weeks passed and Cynthia never mentioned any young man. Stretch's feelings were slightly bruised to think that she wouldn't confide in him. However, with the Welter trial only a month away, he put Cynthia's private life out of his mind.

Cynthia prepared drafts of proposed jury instructions and a proposed verdict for Stretch's review. The Lewis and Clark County clerk of court had sent the list of potential jurors together with the jurors' responses to the standard questionnaires. Cynthia read through the questionnaires and highlighted the names of those who, at least in her mind, might be a problem for the defense. The information received from Hefty Hogan was categorized, tabbed, and indexed by Cynthia and placed in sub-files. In a section of the trial notebook, she listed the prosecution witnesses, and after each witness, she'd prepared a set of suggested questions for Stretch's consideration and elaboration. The section for defense witnesses contained only one name—Audrey Welter—and there were no suggested questions following that name. All of the material was organized in the trial notebook so that any of the material could be readily accessed during the trial itself. The completed notebook had been sitting on Stretch's credenza for two weeks.

Late in the day, after the last client had departed, he picked up the notebook and slowly leafed through the material, beginning with the charging information and ending with the draft verdict. Once again, he marveled at Cynthia's efficiency.

As he worked his way through the mass of paper, he made notes on sticky tabs at the places where he felt some change, deletion, or addition should be made. Cynthia's work product was, as usual, excellent.

He stared at the ceiling and thought through the course that the trial would follow. Hefty would call his witnesses, one after another, all tending to show that Audrey and only Audrey had the motive, the opportunity, and the means to murder Gloria Angel. Stretch's defense strategy had to be the old, worn, 'Some other dude did it' tactic. He would cross-examine each of the prosecution witnesses in an attempt to discredit that person's testimony and cast doubt on the accusation that Audrey Welter was the killer.

What was discouraging to contemplate was the fact that he had only the testimony of Audrey to counteract that evidence. And her testimony, like that of any other defendant, would appear to the jurors as self-serving and therefore less than credible.

The person who sent the email to Audrey could be the key. But if that person didn't come forward voluntarily, he knew of no way to find him—or her. Like it or not, the case would turn on the believability of Audrey Welter. It was time to arrange for a meeting to plan her testimony. He'd try to contact her on her cell phone in the morning. A warm glow had come over him at the prospect of time in the company of his one-time Senate colleague.

Early the next morning, Stretch shuffled through the monthly statements that Mary, the receptionist, had prepared and left on the desk. Satisfied that they were correct, he walked them back to her for mailing. Then it was time to call Audrey. Before his hand reached the telephone, Mary buzzed him to say that Audrey was on the line. A tingle of excitement coursed through him when he heard her voice. "Counselor, it's time we got together to discuss my testimony. After all, I seem to be about the only witness that you have."

"Of course we need to talk. I was about to call to ask when we might meet. At your convenience, of course."

"As you know, my thoughts are filled with only one thing—this damn trial. So I can meet with you at any time you suggest."

Stretch glanced at his scheduling calendar. Today and tomorrow were busy. After that, three days were free.

"Well, I suggest we meet in Helena the day after tomorrow. Would that work for you?"

"Surely. Will you be there by noon? And if so, can we have lunch?"

"Lunch sounds great."

"I plan to stay at the Colonial. Could we have lunch there?"

"That would be good. I'll make a room reservation at the same place since I'm staying over too." He hesitated. "I'm anxious to see you, Audrey."

Her laugh was throaty and spontaneous. "And I'm anxious to see you, sir. You're good company—for a Republican."

Stretch felt foolish when he realized he'd been sitting with the phone in his hands as his thoughts wandered down a path that had nothing to do with the law.

35

Cynthia stood in Stretch's doorway. "Mary said you are going to Helena in the morning to meet with Mrs. Welter." Stretch thought there was a hint of accusation in her voice.

"Yes. I've made arrangements for a visit to discuss her testimony. The trial date is bearing down on us, and she's the only real witness we have."

Cynthia stared at him, obviously thinking of something. Then she asked, "When you say 'we' do you mean the litigation team here in the office or are you referring to just you and Mrs. Welter?"

Stretch raised his eyebrows. "I guess I mean both. Why do you ask?"

Cynthia stepped the rest of the way into the room and stood with her arms crossed. "The last three times you've tried a case you've asked me to sit in with you. You said you wanted me there in case there was something I could do to help. I think I've been able to help on at least a couple of occasions."

Are you asking if I want you to go to Helena with me for the Welter trial?"

"Something like that. It's an interesting case. And, since it's out of town, you won't have your regular staff nearby to prepare any last minute documents you might need. I could bring my laptop and perform those tasks for you. I'm sure I could find a printer I could use to print documents directly from my laptop. *If* I'm there with you to use it, of course."

"Cynthia, I really hadn't thought that far ahead. What about your son? The trial will take several days."

A look of impatience crossed Cynthia's face. "We've discussed this before. Mrs. Whelan has been my nanny ever since I came to work here. You know that. She's already said she'd care for Matt if I'm gone for a few days." There was a glint in her eye as she leaned forward ever so slightly and added, "So you needn't leave me behind on that account."

Cynthia was right about his possible need for her help. And there she was, wanting him to say she could be part of the trial team. "You're right, of course, about the possible need for document preparation." The corner of his lips turned up in the beginnings of a smile. "And if I remember correctly, at the last trial you made some good suggestions about questions to ask on cross examination. All right. We'll do it together as we've done in the past."

Before he could say more, Cynthia said, "I've already reserved a suite, two bedrooms and a sitting room at the Holiday Inn on Last Chance Gulch for the dates of the trial. We can use the sitting room for an office while the trial is going on." As she waited for his response, the look on her face was one of uncertainty.

Stretch put her concern to rest by smiling. "Thank you for being your usual efficient self." Then he added, "We'll need to drive over there a couple of days before the trial. And we'd better plan on a couple of extra days in case something delays the verdict."

"Like a hung jury, you mean?"

"That's always a possibility. Or the jury might take a long time to reach a verdict. Or the testimony may take more time than we think. Who knows what could cause delay? But we should be prepared for it, just in case."

Cynthia's wide sunny smile crinkled her nose and showed

her white even teeth. "You won't be sorry if you take me with you. I'll make myself useful."

"I'm sure you will."

Cynthia shifted uneasily, cleared her throat, and said, "And maybe I should go with you to visit with Mrs. Welter tomorrow."

"Tomorrow? Visit with Audrey?"

"Yes, to visit with Mrs. Welter and to listen to her testimony. I can be of more assistance to you if I know what's going on." She paused. "And I don't really know what's going on. Except for that quick trip to Helena, all I know is the stuff in the trial notebook."

Stretch rubbed at the back of his neck at this completely unexpected development. He wondered what Audrey's reaction would be if he arrived with Cynthia in tow. And he realized how much he wanted to spend time alone with Audrey. "Let me think about it, Cynthia, I need to discuss it with Senator Welter."

A look of disappointment flashed briefly across Cynthia's face. Then she brightened, stood, and said, "I understand. Let me know if you want me to go—so I can tell Mrs. Whelan."

When she was back down the hallway and had closed the door to her office, he quickly closed the door to his. Then he dialed Audrey's number. It rang only once before Audrey punched in with a cheery "Hello!"

"This is your favorite attorney, again."

"My goodness. I was just about to call you."

Stretch blinked. "Okay. You go first."

He waited while Audrey took a breath. "Would you mind if my son, Logan, joined us tomorrow? He just called to tell me he'll arrive back here at the cabin this evening."

"No. Of course not. In fact, it would be wise to involve him in our discussions. He may be able to offer some help."

"I'm so glad you feel that way. I was almost afraid to ask. Now, it's your turn. Why did you call?"

Stretch laughed. "For the same reason. You've met Cynthia, the young lady who works with me on litigation matters. She should be with us when we talk about your testimony. I plan to bring her to Helena to help with the trial. The more she knows, the more help she can be."

"Stretch, is it possible that you don't know that Logan has been driving to Roundup to visit her?"

"Logan? He's the one I've been hearing about?"

"He is. I saw his admiration of her when they first met. Now I believe he's truly smitten."

"Do you approve?"

"Why wouldn't I? She seemed like a very intelligent young woman. And she has a charming personality."

"Well, she's all of that. But Cynthia has no education beyond high school." After a moment's silence he added, "And she has a son."

"Logan knows all of that." Audrey's chuckle came through the phone. "And he even appears to like Matt. That's Cynthia's son's name, isn't it?"

"Yes, that's his name." He took a breath. "Frankly, I'm glad they seem to hit it off. Your son appears to be special, and so is Cynthia."

Audrey chuckled. "I'm glad too. But tomorrow we may find that they are more interested in their own conversations than in our discussion about the trial."

Stretch laughed. "Young love. May it always exist."

"Indeed!" Audrey's voice turned serious. "Of course you should bring Cynthia with you tomorrow. I want all the help I can get. And Logan may even give her some time to provide that help."

When the conversation came to an end, and the phone was back in its cradle, Stretch took a deep breath. "I'll be damned!"

Standing in the doorway to Cynthia's office, he smiled and said, "As usual, you're right. You should make the trip to Helena to meet with Audrey. And she agrees." He jammed his hands into his pockets and added, "It seems she knows all about you—including the fact that her son Logan has been making trips to Roundup to visit you and Matt."

From the startled look, Stretch could tell that Cynthia hoped he wouldn't find out about the visits. When she spoke, it was with her eyes on the floor. "He's a nice man. He treats me like I was a queen or something." She raised her eyes with a defiant look. "And he likes Matt, and Matt thinks he's great."

"Cynthia, I'm glad you two enjoy the each other's company."

"Will he be in Helena with his mother tomorrow?"

"Yup. He'll be there. And I'm glad about that too. Audrey needs his support."

Cynthia pushed back from the desk and got to her feet. "Thank you, sir, for letting me go with you to Helena. It will be interesting to learn more about the trial of such a difficult case."

"Should I pick you up in the morning? Or would you rather that we meet here at the office?"

"I'll be here—and ready to go."

"Please make reservations for a room for each of us at the Colonial Inn. That's where Audrey and Logan will be staying."

"Yes, sir. I'll do it right away." As Stretch walked across the hallway, he heard her add, "I like Logan. But you should watch your step, sir. His mother may have more in mind for you than just a trial."

36

The rains came during the night and continued into the next day. The trip over narrow, crooked U. S. Highway 12 from Roundup to Helena in the lashing downpour took an hour longer than usual. The rain died away on the outskirts of the capital city, leaving behind only a chilly wind. Stretch pulled into the parking lot at the Colonial a few minutes before noon. He worried that Audrey would grow impatient, maybe even angry, if she and her son found themselves waiting overly long in the restaurant. He carried his and Cynthia's travel bags into the lobby, with Cynthia toting a case full of litigation material leading the way. They registered and hurried down the long corridor to their rooms, one across the hallway from the other.

After holding the door for Cynthia and depositing her bag on a bed, Stretch went to his room and found—beside the usual bed, bureau, and television set—a desk and a worktable where he could set up his laptop using the hotel's wifi.

Having told Cynthia that he'd meet her in the lobby, he started in that direction. Rounding a curve in the hallway, he encountered Audrey and Logan, their bags on the floor and fumbling with a key to the door. Without thinking, Stretch reached his arm around Audrey's shoulder and pulled her to him in a gentle hug. As he looked down at the upturned face, he found the impulse to kiss her almost irresistible. When he felt her resistance, he thought of her son. Stretch stepped quickly back and put out his hand. "It's good to see you again, Logan."

Logan looked confused by the familiarity with which Stretch greeted his mother, but he grasped Stretch's hand in a firm grip. "And I'm glad to see you again, sir."

At that moment, Cynthia strolled around the corridor's curve. Stretch grasped her arm and said. "I'm sure you both remember Cynthia Weaver."

Logan confessed. "Perhaps you don't know it, sir, but I've been to Roundup to see Cynthia a couple of times lately."

Cynthia smiled at Logan and then cast a guilty look at Stretch. "I only told Mr. Bruce about that yesterday."

Logan eyed his mother. "Well, truth be known, I hadn't told mother about it either. She thinks I've been job hunting in Billings."

Stretch and Audrey exchanged a smile. Audrey laughed and squeezed Logan's arm. "Can't fool your mother. Both Stretch and I know about these…ah…trysts." She grasped Cynthia's hand, and with a bright smile, added, "And I approve."

Cynthia's smile was equally bright "He's been awfully nice to me, Mrs. Welter."

Stretch turned to Audrey. "We'll let you two get settled. Meet us in the restaurant when it's convenient."

"Twenty minutes?"

"Twenty minutes will be fine. Look for us in one of the back booths. I'll probably have a coffee cup in hand."

"We won't be long. There is much to discuss."

Their lunch was interrupted twice, both times by capitol lobbyists well known to the senators. Each lobbyist offered warm greetings, and each carefully avoided mentioning Audrey's legal difficulty. She breathed a sigh when the last one drifted away. "I've begun to hate to come to this town. I get the feeling that everyone here thinks I'm a criminal—a murderer. Did you notice how artificial the greeting of those men sounded?" Looking down at her plate, she added, "But what else could they do?"

"That's the question, isn't it? To offer sympathy may have seemed even more artificial."

"I just hope I can avoid as much contact with my old legislative associates as possible until this thing is resolved."

Logan, seated quietly by her side, reached his arm across the back of her chair and gave her shoulder a pat. She smiled and looked across at Stretch. "That's what we're here to do—decide how to resolve this murder charge so that everyone knows I'm innocent."

"Of course." Stretch leaned forward. "Have you ever testified in court?"

A look of distaste came over her face. "Only at the time of my divorce. Even though Howard filed for the divorce, and we had settled all the property matters before the day of the hearing, my lawyer insisted I be there to testify that the property settlement was satisfactory." She glanced at her son and patted his hand.

"Was there any cross examination?"

"No, of course not. Why do you ask?"

"When the time comes for your testimony, I'll ask you questions. We'll go over the questions several times so that you can have answers framed in your mind. After that, Hefty Hogan will have his chance. He will not be gentle. And he'll use every trick in a lawyer's book in his attempt to get you to contradict yourself, to get you to say something you don't want to say, or to make you look like you're hiding something. Anything that might cause the jurors to question your testimony."

"I know that. I know he'll use any tactic he can get away with in order to convict me. He thinks it will further his political ambitions." She frowned. "I've never really hated anyone, not even Gloria Angel. But I'm close to hating that man."

"He'll try to take advantage of that. He'll hope that in your anger you'll say something that you would never say when you were in a quiet state of mind."

Audrey's lips turned up ever so slightly as she asked, "This is just the first of several times you're going to tell me that I have to control my emotions—my temper—isn't it?"

"That's correct. If we're to be successful, the jurors have to believe you. Conviction will surely come if they decide your testimony can't be trusted."

Audrey's eyes widened, and she inhaled quickly. For a whole minute she sat unmoving before slumping. "You just dumped the whole load on me. You know that, don't you?" Logan put his arm around her shoulder. She placed her hand over his. "I understand, of course. No one can carry the load but me. But you have to help me. You have to give me the best preparation possible. Anticipate everything Hefty Hogan will do and tell me how I'm to respond. And you have to do it over and over again until I've got it down cold."

"That we'll do. But your testimony can't sound like it's memorized. It has to be given naturally." He smiled. "Audrey, I've listened to your presentations in the Senate. You have a wonderful and convincing way of speaking." When she took a breath to respond, he held up his hand to stop her. "We'll go over everything that we believe will come out in the trial several times. Not only your testimony—everything. By the time you take the witness stand, you'll know exactly what you need to say and how to say it. I have the greatest confidence in your ability to handle Hefty Hogan, no matter what he tries to do."

Audrey smiled at the compliment. Turning to Cynthia, she asked, "Are you always so quiet? You haven't said a word since we arrived."

"I've nothing to offer, Mrs. Welter. I'm just here to listen, so

I can prepare documents for Mr. Bruce when they're needed."

"He speaks highly of you. He's said how much he appreciates all you do to make his practice more manageable. And anything that helps Mr. Bruce helps me, so I'm glad you're here." Then she pushed herself away from the table and said, "Well, let's get started. The sooner we begin, the better we can prepare."

They spent the afternoon in Stretch's room while he and Audrey went over all of the material disclosed by the county attorney. Cynthia and Logan sat quietly near the window. As they examined each document, Stretch scribbled some possible questions that he might ask of Hogan's witnesses to carry a document into evidence. He then read each one of them to Audrey. The process gave Audrey a sense of Stretch's mental processes in preparing for trial. He was pleased that she wasn't reluctant to offer suggestions.

Audrey stood and paced the room from time to time, but Stretch remained at his work, head down, with his hand occasionally rubbing his neck. He only looked up now and then to discuss a point with his client. At mid-afternoon Audrey stopped her pacing and turned to Stretch. "Logan and Cynthia need a break."

Turning to her son, she said, "Take the young lady somewhere for some refreshment. Stretch and I have to suffer through this, but you two do not."

Logan stood, smiled at Cynthia and asked, "How about it? Want to go for coffee? Or something else?"

Cynthia cast a questioning glance at Stretch. He nodded. He didn't dare admit that he'd like to join them.

By five o'clock Stretch's head hurt and his back ached from sitting so long in the uncomfortable chair. Audrey was standing at the window when he rose unsteadily and said, "That's enough for today." He moved to her side to join her in looking across the broad valley toward the Big Belt Mountains in the distance. They stood in silence until he said, "We need to relax. Where would you like to go for dinner?"

Audrey turned to face him. "Let's find a place where we won't be bothered."

"How about that place out in Clancy? I can't remember the name. The food there is supposed to be good."

"The Gold Digger? It's as good a place as any. And it's casual so I can wear jeans." She strode across the room to reach for her purse on the bureau next to the television. "I wonder where Logan and Cynthia have wandered off to."

There was a knock, and the door opened. Cynthia, glowing, moved into the room with Logan close behind. The young man's demeanor matched hers. Before either Stretch or Audrey could ask, he explained, "We went to Reeder's Alley. Cynthia'd never been there. We got to visiting and didn't realize so much time had passed."

Cynthia looked at Stretch. "I hope you'll forgive me. I know I should've been here in case you needed something. That's the reason you brought me to Helena."

Stretch smiled. "It's fine. There was no need for you to sit in this dull room and listen to us groan."

Audrey winked at her son before turning to Stretch. "I need to freshen up." With a glance at her watch, she added. "Meet us in the lobby at five forty-five, if that works." Her son trailed her out the door.

They sat at a table reserved for non-smokers, but smoke from the gaming area tainted the air. It had been a long afternoon, and neither Stretch nor Audrey was disposed to engage in much idle talk. Cynthia and Logan, on the other hand, carried on a lively discussion. The meal, when it was served, brought their verbal exchanges to an end. The group ate in silence until after-dinner coffee and tea were served. At last, Stretch stirred himself to say, "Cynthia made reservations for us for the duration of the trial at the Holiday Inn on the mall. It's close enough to the courthouse that we can hoof it from one to the other." Directing his look at Audrey, he added, "It would be best if you stayed there too. Can we make reservations there for both of you? We should spend a day or two together before the trial begins. There will be some final matters to address."

Audrey nodded. "It makes sense for us to be at the same place. And to devote adequate time to review my testimony and the other evidence just before the trial begins." She took a breath. "But I can make reservations for both Logan and me before we leave town tomorrow." She patted her son's hand. "And Logan's mother really needs and appreciates his support. The thought of room reservations makes what's about to happen to me seem even more imminent and real." She slowly shook her head. "God, I hope I can get through this with some dignity."

For a moment it appeared that she would break down in tears. Then she gathered herself, looked across at Stretch, and offered a weak smile. "Most of the time I'm able to control my emotions. But now and then the notion that I might be convicted just comes crashing through—and I lose it." At Stretch's look of alarm, she reached across to put her hand over his. "Don't worry. I'll maintain my composure whenever anyone associated with the trial is in sight. But if I break apart when it's just you and me, I hope you will understand."

"Of course I understand. Anytime there are no outsiders around and you feel the need to let it all go, please do it. You can't keep it inside all the time. Logan will be here to help. And if there's no one else, I'm here to lean on."

"Before this is done, sir, I'll probably lean on you so much you'll wish you'd never known me."

"Not a chance of that, gracious lady. Not a chance."

The following morning Stretch led Audrey through the questions he would ask when she took the witness stand. Logan and Cynthia listened, as would the members of the jury. Then he pretended to be Hefty Hogan and did his best to anticipate the questions the county attorney would ask and the manner in which he would ask them. He was brusque. He was insulting. He was demeaning. And he cut her off in the middle of her answers. By the end of the morning, Audrey was near tears with frustration because she wasn't allowed to just respond to the questions in their entirety and in a way that reflected the truth. When at last Stretch sat back in his chair and lapsed into silence, Audrey relaxed. After a time, she raised her head to look at Stretch with a wan smile. "At least it's good to get an idea of what it will be like." She stood and rubbed her hands up and down her arms. "But I imagine the real thing will be even worse."

"Unfortunately, it will be much worse, simply because it's mean old Hefty Hogan asking the questions instead of gentle old Stretch Bruce." He pushed himself from the chair, stood, and stretched his back. "But you held your composure very well just now. And you have time to reflect on this session and prepare for the real thing." He started to reach for her, stopped to look at Logan and Cynthia, then withdrew his hand and said, "You'll do all right, Senator. I know you will."

Audrey looked up at his sober face as she reached out to put her hands on his waist. Her voice was a whisper. "Take care of me, Stretch. Please take care of me."

37

Ambrose Swan called Stretch at the Holiday Inn the evening before the trial. Without preamble, the old reporter said, "You know they never found that man, Donald Kastner. You remember, the one who was furious over Senator Welter's bill to prohibit drilling for oil and gas."

"Yes, I remember."

"It seems he's disappeared. The sheriff's deputies went to Kastner's place to determine whether he was the vagrant who spent the night in the capitol. But he wasn't at the shack he lives in, and no one in that community has seen him since the day Gloria Angel was killed." The reporter waited for Stretch to comment. When he didn't, Swan chuckled, "It kind of makes you think, doesn't it?"

"It sure as hell does."

Ambrose Swan's chuckle turned to a laugh. "I just thought you should know."

38

The trial would begin at nine o'clock that morning. To avoid the press and the curious, Audrey and Logan joined Stretch and Cynthia for breakfast in the hotel room reserved for use as an office. There was little conversation. Audrey's possible fate hovered over them like a specter. Stretch kept the conversation on the things they could expect when they arrived at the courthouse.

Logan ate quietly, shifting a concerned look at his mother from time to time as he downed breakfast burritos. Cynthia attacked her waffle with a purpose. Stretch nibbled a small portion of the eggs and bacon on the plate before him. Audrey didn't even try to eat. She drank a small glass of orange juice and then sipped black coffee.

Stretch pushed his plate away and turned to the side to extend his legs. He leaned his elbow on the table as he recited things he had already said. "The judge didn't grant our motion to exclude the bloody flashlight as evidence. You will remember I had argued that the search warrant was flawed because the information on which it was based came from an unknown person by way of a blind email. Hefty, of course, countered that the earlier information from the same unknown person led to the discovery of the bloody scarf. Therefore the second email was basis enough for the warrant. Turning squarely to Audrey, he said, "I've already apologized to you for not requiring the sheriff and his men to secure a warrant before they searched your desk that second time. I doubt that they could have gotten such a warrant based on a single, blind email. And, of course, without the scarf, the second warrant would never have been issued." He took a deep breath. "But it's done, and I can't undo it." A wry smile crossed his face. "I've also said you can use the things I did as evidence of incompetent counsel, in the event of a conviction."

A scowl darkened Audrey's visage. "Don't even mention conviction right now!"

Stretch straightened in the chair. "That's the last time I'll say the word." He signed the check and then got to his feet. "Time to get moving. We never want to offend the judge by being late for court."

Evidently the media people hadn't realized that Audrey was staying at the Holiday Inn. No one bothered them on the walk along the mall and up the steep sidewalk to the courthouse. But the print reporters and television personalities with their camera crews would almost certainly be stationed outside the courthouse, waiting for the celebrity defendant to appear. He told Audrey that he would lead the way through the crowd. She was to remain behind him. Cynthia and Logan would bring up the rear. None of them was to say a word to anyone as they pushed their way through the throng.

The day was sunny, and the walk would have been pleasant on any other occasion. As they approached the old stone building, Stretch was surprised to see a deputy sheriff standing near the front door. The officer moved toward them with a grin and said, "The reporters are all at the back entrance by the parking lot." His laugh was soft. "You bamboozled them by coming this way." He held the door and said, "Sheriff Mendenhall sent me to run interference, in case it's needed."

Stretch and his entourage were spotted at the foot of the stairway leading to the upper floors. Reporters, screeching questions, led the throng that broke in their direction. Sheriff Mendenhall, trailing three more deputies and hurrying to get in front of Stretch, gestured to his men and muttered, "Two in front. Two in back. And have your batons at the ready." Then he turned to face the clambering throng and shouted, "Back, all of you." When there wasn't any movement by those of the crowd that were closest to him, he spoke loudly. "I mean what I say. Get back now and leave these people alone. If you don't, my deputies are directed to use force to move you." He waited a second before poking his baton at the nearest reporter. He growled, "Move!"

The reporter flinched backward, convincing the others that the sheriff was serious. Although there was a lot of grumbling and grousing, the throng stumbled back. A few of the more obstreperous barked questions at Audrey's retreating back.

Through the wide doors to the courtroom, Stretch could see that it was filled with people. The level of the conversation was subdued, a strange contrast to the noise they had just endured. Stretch heaved a sigh and dropped his briefcase. He turned to Sheriff Mendenhall, reached for his hand, and said, "I can't thank you enough for what you just did. I'm not sure we could have made it in here without your help."

"Not at all. If your client had been held in the jail, as most defendants are, we would've escorted her to the courtroom. So it seemed right to make sure she got here without too much trouble. And besides, we have an obligation to keep the peace and, with a crowd like that, there was a possibility that something could go wrong and somebody could be injured." His craggy face showed a slight grin. "We in law enforcement want your client safely in this room, ready for trial. We don't want anything to happen to arouse more public sympathy for her than she already has."

"She has public sympathy?"

Mendenhall snorted, "Of course she has. She's attractive and a well respected senator. Gloria Angel's death happened months ago. You know how it is. People forget about the victim and focus their attention on the accused. When that person is as popular a figure as Senator Welter, she generates a lot of sympathy."

Before the conversation went any further, Hefty Hogan bustled into the room, followed by his youthful deputy. He strode right past Stretch and the others, banged open the small gate that divided the working part of the courtroom from the audience section, and dropped a large notebook on the counsel table nearest the door. Ellis Bradley, struggling along behind with another notebook and a large briefcase, had to step aside quickly as Hogan whipped back through the gate and strode toward Stretch with his hand out. Mendenhall nodded to the county attorney, swung about abruptly, and left the room.

Stretch shook Hefty's proffered hand as courtesy required. When Hefty spoke, he had a gleam in his eye, and a chortle in his voice. "Ever since I heard all the talk about how you got that murderer off down in Roundup, I've wanted to get you in the courtroom. The press made it sound like you're the best trial lawyer in Montana." There was mockery in his voice. "Time to test our relative trial skills, isn't it?"

Stretch frowned as he glanced back toward Logan and Audrey. "I've never thought of a trial as some kind of test of lawyerly skills. There's too much at stake for games."

Hogan finally seemed to realize the impression his remark had made on Audrey Welter. The foolish grin faded away, and he pushed by Stretch and reached in her direction. "No offense meant, ma'am. Just lawyers being lawyers."

Audrey pointedly ignored his outstretched hand. As she looked him directly in the eye, she said, "This may be a game to you, sir. But I assure you, it's no game to me."

The county attorney inhaled for a response, but before he

could speak, Cynthia grasped Audrey's arm and tugged. Audrey jerked her arm away. She immediately realized that Cynthia was trying to rescue her and followed the paralegal past the two lawyers and into the well of the courtroom. Cynthia snagged the briefcase that Stretch had been carrying. Toting the case, she led Audrey to the counsel table farthest from the door. Once there, she pulled back a chair for Audrey to sit. Audrey smiled at the younger woman and settled into the chair. She sat stiffly with her eyes focused on her clenched fists that rested on the tabletop. Cynthia slid onto the chair beside her and began the process of emptying the briefcases.

Hogan's eyes followed Audrey as she passed by, then he turned back to Bruce. "It seems I've offended that lady."

Stretch didn't try to hide his anger. "Hefty, you're an obtuse dunce." He brushed by the county attorney. "You were a dunce in law school, and you haven't improved a damn bit." Hogan's jaw dropped, and his face reddened, giving Stretch a brief sense of satisfaction. But as Stretch joined the two women at the counsel table, the seriousness of the moment drove any feeling of triumph from his mind.

The judge had granted permission for Cynthia to sit at the counsel table. Audrey sat between Stretch and Cynthia so he could converse with her should it be necessary. Cynthia would keep track of exhibits and take extensive notes of the testimony of each witness. If she needed to convey something of importance to Stretch, she would pass a note. While a witness was on the stand, there would be no oral communication between the lawyer, his client, and his assistant unless it was of utmost importance. Logan sat in the audience directly behind his mother.

Ellis Bradley had just finished arranging the prosecution's trial material on the counsel table when the court recorder carried her machine to her place next to the clerk's desk. Hogan, having passed one more morsel of information to a reporter, stepped before the bar and settled himself next to his deputy. The clerk of court entered the room and called, "All rise!"

Judge Milton Hastings, white-haired but tall and erect, walked from his chamber and climbed the two steps to stand behind the bench. He stood still for a second or two, looking out across the room that was filled with potential jurors, newspeople, and the simply curious—all of them standing. The judge shifted his gaze to the counsel tables to confirm that the people necessary for the beginning of the trial were in their places. At last he sank into his chair, gave a gentle tap with his gavel, and said in a soft voice, "Court's in session. Please be seated."

The judge reached to grasp the file that the clerk offered to him. After opening the cover, he raised his eyes to look first at Hogan, then at Stretch Bruce. "This is case number Cr-14-632, State of Montana vs. Audrey Welter. And this is the time set for trial. Is that correct, Gentlemen?"

Hogan was on his feet in an instant. "Correct, Your Honor."

Stretch placed his hands on the arm of the chair and raised himself to stand erect. "That is correct."

"Very well. Are there any motions to be handled before we begin with the jurors?"

"The standard motion, Your Honor." Stretch stood with his hands clasped behind his back. "The defense moves the court for an order that each and every witness, excepting only the witness who is testifying, be excluded from the courtroom during the time when testimony is taking place."

Hogan's look was one of disgust. "It's a needless requirement, Your Honor. But, with the understanding that any witness who has testified and who will not be called to testify again may be allowed to sit in on the remainder of the proceedings, the prosecution doesn't object."

Judge Hastings smiled. "It's good that we can begin the day on a friendly note of agreement." He raised his eyes to the audience. "I want to make it clear right at the outset that all witnesses are to remain out of the courtroom until the bailiff calls you to testify." There was some shuffling of feet by the audience. The judge turned his attention to the clerk, "All right, Mary. Let's call the jurors."

Selecting a jury in a county with as many people as Lewis and Clark was a new experience for Stretch. In Musselshell County, with its four thousand people, he had a pretty good idea of the opinions and prejudices of most of those to whom he would address his questions. The process would be different for him in Helena where he knew not a single one of the people who had been called to serve as possible jurors. It was a concern that Hefty had the advantage of knowing some of them.

Stretch, Audrey, and Cynthia had all studied the juror questionnaires that the clerk of court provided in an attempt to determine which of those on the jury panel would be the best from Audrey's standpoint and which would be the worst. In a further attempt to help him make a reasoned choice of jurors, Stretch had mailed the list to Ambrose Swan and asked if the reporter could provide more detailed information about any of the ones listed. A couple of days later, Swan returned the list with accompanying notes that told much about the personal lives of several members of the panel. All of the information was helpful but not definitive of which names to strike or which he would absolutely want to keep on the jury.

Stretch and Cynthia had spent a considerable amount of time discussing the kind of juror that would be best for their client. They decided it was hard to predict. Some women might be jealous of Audrey's success as a senator but others might be offended by Gloria Angel's lifestyle. Some older men would probably find Audrey attractive which, alone, might lead them to believe her testimony. Gloria Angel was such a beautiful young woman that younger men might see Audrey as jealous and vindictive—enough to want to do her in. In the end they concluded that the only people who absolutely should be excluded were those who hated every living environmentalist.

Jury selection went much more smoothly than Stretch had expected. He thought that Hogan would spend a great deal of time questioning prospective jurors in an attempt to discern if any were sympathetic to Audrey because of her public service, if for no other reason. However, the county attorney seemed to know a great deal about each of those on the panel and only challenged one woman for cause. She was large and florid and dressed in a three-colored ensemble—red, white and blue. When the county attorney asked if she knew Gloria Angel, she replied in a fierce voice, "Gloria Angel was a bad person." Then she pointed at Audrey and added, "And Senator Welter may be the only honest politician this state ever had!"

After the ripple of laughter that flowed through the courtroom subsided, Hefty made his motion to have her excused. Stretch thought he might as well see if he could score some more points for his client. Rising to his feet he asked, "May I inquire, Your Honor?"

"You may."

"Mrs. Thompson, I appreciate your feelings about my client. I share those feelings. Tell me, though, what makes you think Gloria Angel was a bad person?"

"The whole town knows she was sleeping with every one of those no good politicians—like the governor and the attorney general."

"How do you know that was the case, Mrs. Thompson. You don't have any direct knowledge of Ms. Angel's habits, do you?"

"Don't have to have direct knowledge. Just know it's true."

This wasn't really helping Audrey. Stretch stepped away from the table to stand directly in front of her. "You understand, don't you, that it won't be your responsibility to decide whose life style is good or bad? If you are picked to be on the jury, your responsibility will only be to decide if the prosecution has presented evidence—evidence beyond a reasonable doubt—that Audrey Welter killed Gloria Angel?"

The woman struck a defiant pose. "You bet, I know that."

"And can you set aside any feelings that you presently have about either Ms. Angel or Ms. Welter in making that decision?"

"I can try. But I'll tell you, I admire that woman sitting there. She's always done the right thing in the legislature." Her eyes squinted, and her voice became even more strident. "I can't say the same thing about your legislative performance, buster."

This time the laughter was loud and long. Even Audrey chuckled at that remark. Judge Hastings rapped the gavel to restore the quiet. Then a broad smile deepened the wrinkles around his mouth. "Mr. Bruce. Are you sure you want to ask any more questions of Mrs. Thompson?"

Stretch could do nothing but smile at the juror. "No, Your Honor. I have no more questions. And I don't resist Mr. Hogan's request that Mrs. Thompson be excused."

The judge turned his charming smile to the large woman and said, "You're excused from jury duty, ma'am. You may leave now if you choose. Or you're welcome to stay and watch the proceedings. The clerk of court will send you a check for your service to the community and for being here today."

Hefty quickly finished his questioning of the members of the panel, turned toward the bench, and solemnly announced, "Pass the jury for cause, Your Honor."

Stretch's voir dire of the panel went smoothly. Not a one

of them gave any concrete indication of a bias that would lead the judge to excuse that person for cause. When both the prosecution and defense had used their preemptory challenges, the final twelve jurors were seated in the jury box. Two alternates, a man and a woman, sat in folding chairs beside the box. Of the twelve, five were men. Among the men were two retirees, a student at Carroll College, an older accountant, and a middle age stonemason. Among the women, one was a young housewife who said she had three children. She maintained she could concentrate on the evidence without concern about the welfare of her children because her mother would care for them. Of the other six, one was an older housewife, two were retired government workers, two were current government workers, one was a registered nurse.

After the clerk administered the oath to the twelve jurors and the two alternates, Judge Hastings looked up at the clock that hung above the balcony at the rear of the room and said, "It's eleven-forty. We will recess until one thirty." He turned to direct his attention to the jurors. "All of you must be back here in the courtroom at that time. Don't be late." Then the judge, for the first of many times, admonished them not to discuss anything about the case with anyone else until all of the evidence was in and he had released them to go to the jury room to deliberate. He emphasized especially that they were not to discuss the case with their spouses. Finally he concluded with a smile, "I realize there isn't anything of consequence to discuss as yet. But you may as well become accustomed to the idea that you must not discuss anything about the case until I tell you otherwise." As the judge started to rise from his chair, he added, "Now go and have a good lunch. The opening statements will begin when we reconvene."

39

Hefty's opening statement was short and exactly as Stretch had anticipated. He told the jurors they would learn about Audrey's meeting with the dead woman, about the scarf and the flashlight, and about Audrey's threats to kill Gloria Angel. He listed the witnesses who would testify for the state—belaboring the fact that many of them were officers of the law.

Stretch responded by emphasizing reasonable doubt and telling the jurors that they would find lots of it among the bits and pieces of evidence the state would try to cobble together in an attempt to prove that his client was a killer. Looking from one to another of the jurors, he asked each of them to keep an open mind throughout the state's presentation of its evidence and to then listen carefully to the evidence provided in defense. If they did so and weighed one against the other, he concluded, they would have no trouble in finding the defendant innocent of the crime of which she was accused.

Hefty stood and pronounced loudly as though to impress upon everyone the importance of the moment, "The state calls Sheriff Brent Mendenhall."

The sheriff, wearing a neatly pressed uniform, stood erect while the clerk administered the oath. Then he mounted the witness chair, turned left to nod to the judge, and turned right to nod to the jurors. Finally, he sat comfortably and relaxed with his hands clasped in his lap and turned his attention to the county attorney.

Hogan stood beside his seat, holding a yellow tablet. On it Stretch glimpsed what appeared to be series of questions written in the county attorney's hand. After leading the sheriff though a recitation of his qualifications for his position and of the history that led him into law enforcement, Hefty stated, "Sheriff, I'm going to ask you to tell us everything that you did in your investigation of the death of Gloria Angel from the time you first learned of her death." This was followed by a series of questions that led the lawman through his activities immediately after the capitol security guard found the body and called the death in to the sheriff's office.

The sheriff spoke slowly and just loudly enough for the jurors to hear without straining. He told of arriving at the capitol with his deputies where they observed the body lying on the hard tile of the rotunda floor. He told of his cooperation with the chief of police to secure the area where the body was lying, as well as the balcony area directly above it. He explained that Ms. Angel's office was sealed and that a deputy was sent to seal the dead woman's townhouse. Finally he described the body as he observed it. The description was given in a matter-of-fact manner that, Stretch thought, did little to convey the horror that the sight of the dead woman must have presented. He also told of the searches of Senator Audrey Welter's capitol office and that the searches were made with her permission.

Stretch rose to his feet the minute the county attorney finished his direct examination. His voice was measured as he asked, "Sheriff Mendenhall, did you have a warrant that permitted you to search Ms. Welter's office on the first occasion?"

Answering in the same calm manner, the sheriff said, "No, sir, we did not."

"If you didn't have a warrant, how was it that you were able to search the office, not once but twice?"

"As I told the jury when Mr. Hogan asked, Ms. Welter allowed us to make the searches without a warrant."

Bruce let time go by for the jury to consider the answer. After the pause he said, with his eyebrows raised in question, "Without a warrant?"

The lawman's voice remained calm. "Yes, sir. Without a warrant."

"Was she present when you conducted your search?"

The sheriff allowed a gentle smile to cross his lips. "She was there part of the time. You'll remember, counselor, that you were present too."

Stretch returned the smile. "Indeed I was." Then his countenance turned somber as he asked, "She could have stopped you at any time if she had chosen to do so, couldn't she?"

"Yes, sir. That's right, she could have."

Stretch stepped around the desk corner to move closer to the witness, but his question carried no hostility. "Sheriff, a guilty person would never have allowed such a search, would she?"

Hefty started to rise for an objection, but the sheriff's response was too quick. Without a change in his demeanor or expression, Mendenhall answered, "Who knows what a guilty person might do?"

The response brought a few chuckles from the jury and the audience. Stretch ignored the noise. "Had Ms. Welter known that the bloody scarf was in the drawer of her desk, she could have destroyed it—destroyed it before you made the first search and surely before you made the second search. And if she'd destroyed it, you would never have known it existed, would you?"

Hogan half rose to his feet to say, "Objection, Your Honor. Multiple questions."

Judge Hastings turned to Stretch and said in his quiet voice, "Sustained. One question at a time, Mr. Bruce."

Stretch acknowledged the rebuke with a nod to the judge and then faced the sheriff again, "If Ms. Welter was the one who killed Gloria Angel and wanted to conceal what she'd done, she could have destroyed the scarf, couldn't she?"

"There's no reason for me to believe she couldn't have."

Stretch took a step closer to the witness chair. "Isn't it true, Sheriff, that the county attorney told me of an email message he received, an email saying a second search of Ms. Welter's office should be made?"

The detective shook his head. "I don't know about that for sure. I believe that's what happened."

"Since Ms. Welter was my client, isn't it reasonable that I'd have told her of the email that carried the message."

"Yes, That's reasonable."

"So, she knew you wanted to search a second time. Did she try to prevent you from doing so?"

"No, sir. She did just as she did the first time we went to her office. She allowed us to look at anything we wanted."

"And that time you found the scarf, right?"

"Yes, sir. That's correct."

"Sheriff, let's get this straight. Audrey Welter knew you wanted to search her office, not once but twice. She didn't make you get a search warrant. And she let you look wherever you wished. Does that sound like the behavior of an intelligent person such as Senator Audrey Welter, if she had really killed Gloria Angel?"

The sheriff's face remained impassive as he admitted, "No, Mr. Bruce, it does not."

Stretch walked back to the counsel table to sip from a glass. While doing so, he glanced at the jurors in an attempt to determine if they were paying attention. None of them seemed bored. Stretch turned, crossed his arms, and looked squarely at the law officer. Sheriff Mendenhall returned his gaze without a blink. Finally, Stretch asked, "Isn't it true, sir, that Ms. Welter voluntarily went to the county attorney and told him of her meeting with Gloria Angel shortly after Ms. Angel's body was found on the rotunda floor?"

"That's what I was told."

The judge shifted his eyes from the witness to Hefty Hogan, as if expecting an objection to the hearsay statement. When Hogan remained seated, giving no indication that he wished to object, Judge Hastings' eyebrows went up. He shook his head ever so slightly and returned his attention to Stretch.

"You never would have learned of the meeting that Audrey Welter had with Gloria Angel had Ms. Welter not told Mr. Hogan about it, would you?"

The sheriff smiled again. "We might have. The governor knew they were to meet, and someone may have seen them together."

"It's been a long time since Ms. Angel died. No one has come forward to say they actually saw the two women together just before she was killed, have they?"

"No sir, no one has done that."

"Sheriff, you and Detective Hammond never would have conducted the first search of Ms. Welter's office had she not told the county attorney of her late night meeting with Gloria Angel, would you?"

"We might have after the governor told us the two women were planning to meet that night."

"Might have?"

"Yes, sir. We might have wanted to search the office. But then again we might not."

"Can you think of any reason why, if Ms. Welter was the murderer, she would have attracted the attention of the law enforcement authorities by volunteering the very information that the county attorney now wants to use to convict her?"

The sheriff's response was calm as before. "Mr. Bruce, I have no idea what might have been in your client's mind."

Stretch stared back at the man for a second. "I'll grant you that." He dropped his hands and clasped them together behind his back. "So let's review what happened and let the jury decide. First, Gloria Angel was found dead on the capitol floor. Right?"

"That's what happened."

"Then before you had a chance to do much in the way of investigation—before you talked to the governor—Audrey Welter went to the county attorney and told him of her meeting with the dead woman, isn't that correct?"

Hogan interjected himself into the proceedings from his place at the counsel table. "Objection." He stood and continued, "Asked and answered."

The judge turned and stared at him for a long moment before he said, "That isn't the objection I had expected, Mr. Hogan." The implication was clear to both Hogan and Bruce. The judge was wondering why Hogan wasn't objecting to hearsay testimony.

"Perhaps not, Your Honor. But it's the objection I'm making."

Judge Hastings remained still for a moment before a look flashed across his face that told the lawyers that the judge suddenly realized what was going on. Hogan didn't want to object to hearsay testimony and then find himself on the witness stand. The ends of his lips turned up in a small smile. "I see, sir." He leaned his head toward Stretch Bruce with an inquiring look as though to ask, "What about the objection?"

Stretch turned from the sheriff to speak directly to Judge Hastings. "We need to put the sequence of events in context for the benefit of the jury, Your Honor. It's important that they understand what happened and in what order."

The judge held his gaze for a moment before giving a slight nod. "Although I think they've got the sequence, Mr. Bruce, I'll allow it. The objection is overruled."

"Thank you, Your Honor." Turning quickly back to Mendenhall, he asked, "Do you remember the question?"

"Yes, I remember the question." The sheriff leaned back with his hands relaxed on the arms of the witness chair. "And to answer the question, I've been told your client went to the county attorney early on the morning we found Gloria Angel's body."

"And you had no reason other than that visit to make the first search of Ms. Welter's office, did you?"

"At that time? No, sir, I didn't."

"Senator Welter was in her office when you conducted the search?"

"Yes, sir, you and Ms. Welter were in the office when we arrived."

"And she didn't interfere with the search in any way?"

"No, Mr. Bruce, she didn't."

"Your search was thorough, wasn't it?"

The sheriff's face briefly showed an indication of agitation, then relaxed again. "At the time I thought it was."

"Did you go through the desk drawers at that time?"

The brief look of agitation returned. "Yes, sir. I did."

"Did you find a bloody scarf?"

The sheriff seemed to find a need to defend his actions. "No, I didn't find the scarf at that time." When Stretch started to speak, the sheriff held up his hand. "If I may explain." Before Stretch could stop him, he continued, "The scarf, when I found it during the later search, was under a pile of paper. I could very easily have missed it during the first search."

Moving toward the witness, Stretch asked, "So—either the scarf wasn't there—or the search wasn't very good, is that right?"

The sheriff smiled. "If that's the way you want to put it."

Stretch continued to pursue the line of questions. "But it was in the desk drawer the next time you searched, wasn't it?"

"It was there, under the pile of old legislative bills. I've already told you that."

Hogan was on his feet. "Sheriff Mendenhall is correct, Your Honor. All these questions have been asked and answered."

"Yes, they have, Mr. Bruce. Move on to something else."

Stretch acknowledged the admonition with a nod. "Let's discuss another part of your investigation. Who else have you questioned in regard to the death of Ms. Angel?"

"My deputies have questioned several people. But I've only personally questioned one other person."

"And who is that person?"

"Governor Albert Shewey."

Hogan's voice was so loud it startled the sheriff. "Objection! Beyond the scope of the direct examination. And whatever the sheriff might have heard from the governor has nothing to do with the guilt or innocence of the defendant in this case. It's irrelevant."

Stretch's calm voice contrasted with the strident one of Hefty Hogan. "Not so, Your Honor. First of all, the county attorney opened his direct examination by stating he was going to ask the sheriff about everything the sheriff did in his investigation from the time the body of Ms. Angel was found. I'm just following up on that statement so the jury will be fully informed. And, Your Honor, the defense is entitled to delve into anything that may provide another explanation for the death of the governor's private assistant."

The judge gave Hogan a stern look. "You did open the door, Mr. County Attorney." Turning toward Stretch Bruce, he added, "Of course you're entitled to pursue alternate theories. The objection is overruled. You may continue, Mr. Bruce."

Stretch let a little time lapse for the jury to ponder before he directed the next question to the sheriff. "The governor gave you some inconsistent statements, didn't he?"

"Yes, Mr. Bruce. He did."

"First he told you he wasn't in the capitol building the night Gloria Angel was killed, and when you confronted him with his signature on the entry log, he admitted he had lied, didn't he?"

"He didn't admit that he lied, Counselor. He said his memory was faulty."

"In the end, however, he admitted he was in the building near the time Ms. Angel was killed, didn't he?"

"Yes. That's correct."

"And he sneaked out of the building sometime later?"

"I don't know that he sneaked out. He didn't leave by the main entry, or at least the security folks said he didn't. And there's no entry in the log to show that he did." The sheriff looked toward the jurors when he added, "He told me he left by the east door, the one near his office."

"No one knows what time he left or if he had blood on his clothing, do they?"

Hogan was shouting again. "Objection, Your Honor. There is nothing to implicate Governor Shewey in the killing of Gloria Angel. She was his trusted assistant, for God's sake! The governor wouldn't kill her."

Stretch Bruce walked to a position directly in front of the bench and planted his feet firmly. "Exactly, Your Honor. She was his trusted assistant. She knew a great deal about him. It's possible that she knew too much."

Hefty yelped. "Pure speculation—speculation of the worst kind! Your Honor, Mr. Bruce should be sanctioned for even suggesting such a thing!"

The judge held up his hand. "That's enough, Mr. Hogan. The defense in a criminal trial is entitled to present alternate theories. Surely you know that."

Hefty's face was red. "I know that, Your Honor. But the theories should have some substance, not just slanderous statements about the holder of the highest office in this state."

There was impatience in the judge's voice. "I said, that's enough, sir." Turning to Mendenhall, he asked, "Do you remember the question, sheriff?"

"I do, Your Honor."

"Then answer it."

"As far as I know, no one saw the governor leave the building that night. Obviously, if no one saw him, no one can know if he had blood on his clothes."

Stretch left his place in front of the judge to stand before the witness. "Sheriff, a technician scanned Senator Welter's office for traces of blood. Isn't that right?'

Mendenhall's posture was again relaxed. "That was done, yes, sir."

"Then why didn't you make a search of the governor's belongings for blood traces?"

"It seemed a senseless thing to do. If there was any blood on the governor's clothes, it's not likely we would have found it. Clothing can be destroyed."

"A guilty person would destroy evidence to protect himself. Is that what you're saying?"

The sheriff showed no sign that he was concerned about his answer. "It's possible."

"For some reason you and the county attorney believe that the governor would protect himself if he killed Ms. Angel but Audrey Welter would not. Is that right?"

The sheriff looked across at Hogan, then back at Bruce. "I

can't speak for the county attorney." Leaning forward he said, "But Mr. Bruce, I won't pretend to know whether or not Ms. Welter put the scarf in the desk drawer. I'm only here to testify about the things I found—things based on my own knowledge."

Stretch could hardly keep from turning to look at the jurors. He never expected the sheriff would come so close to an expression of doubt about Audrey's guilt. He did glance at Hogan. The man's face was crimson. His seething anger was apparent in the glare he directed at Mendenhall.

Stretch decided to stop while he was ahead. He smiled collegially at the witness. "Thank you, Sheriff Mendenhall." Then turning to Judge Hastings, he said, "I have no more questions for the sheriff, Your Honor."

Hefty Hogan jumped from his chair, rushed around the counsel table, and nearly collided with Stretch. His voice, when he spoke, was loud and harsh. "Sheriff Mendenhall, neither you nor your deputies have found anything at all to indicate that Governor Shewey killed Gloria Angel, have you?"

The sheriff's demeanor didn't change. "No, Mr. Hogan, we have not."

Anger was still reflected in the county attorney's voice. "But your officers found something other than the scarf to prove Audrey killed that woman, didn't you?"

"Objection!" Because Stretch had spoken so calmly up to that point, the sharp interjection caused all eyes to jerk toward him. "The sheriff can only testify to those things about which he has personal knowledge. He can't testify about something his deputies might have done."

"That's correct, Mr. Hogan. If there is something that the sheriff's deputies have to offer, it can come from them. You do intend to call them as witnesses, don't you?"

"Yes, sir. Two deputies will testify."

"Very good. The objection is sustained. Please continue."

Hogan seemed nonplussed. He turned and leaned over the table to whisper to Ellis Bradley who listened, scanned the notes he'd been making, and then shook his head. Hefty straightened and seemed to ponder. The appearance of anger had disappeared, replaced by the look of confidence he'd carried into the courtroom. He focused on the judge when he said, "I have no more questions for Sheriff Mendenhall."

The judge glanced at the clock hanging high above the courtroom balcony, and turned to the jury. "It's nearly five o'clock. We'll adjourn until nine o'clock in the morning. Please remember the admonition not to discuss this matter with anyone until I say you may do so. And please be on time for court tomorrow." He rose from his chair, gently tapped the gavel, and said, "We stand adjourned."

Stretch was somewhat surprised to find the sheriff and two deputies waiting to escort him, his assistant, his client, and her son through the crowd and halfway down the steep hill toward their hotel. The sheriff stopped when it was apparent that no one was following who might bother the group. Stretch shook Mendenhall's hand and thanked him. "After our session a few minutes ago, I didn't expect you to be so accommodating."

With the thumb of his left hand hooked in the belt that now held his sidearm, Mendenhall said, "You have a job, Mr. Bruce, and I have a job. If we both do our jobs correctly, maybe justice will prevail." He nodded a goodbye, and turned to give orders to his deputies.

Stretch needed time alone, time to think without interruption. Back at the hotel he suggested that they all meet again in the lobby at six thirty to decide about dinner. Audrey, too, was relieved to have an hour to relax. Logan eyed Stretch as he reached to take Cynthia's arm. "Okay if I steal your assistant for a few minutes, Counselor?"

Concern about neglect of her duties showed on Cynthia's face. Stretch, seeing it, smiled at his paralegal and waved his arm. "Go with my blessing."

Stretch stood for a moment and watched them disappear from sight. The attraction of Logan to Cynthia and she to him was clearly evident. Stretch found that it pleased him. His youthful assistant had lacked male companionship of the quality of Audrey's son for a long time. Let her enjoy it.

In his room Stretch shed his courtroom clothes and changed into his sweats. Slipping on a pair of Reeboks, he rode the elevator to the ground floor and hurried out onto the mall. After strolling up the gulch for about two minutes to warm up, he began a jog that lasted for another two minutes. Stretch maintained the walk and jog routine for only a short distance. He'd been neglecting any effort to keep in shape and his breathing soon became a series of gasps. The upward climb through the mall and beyond proved much steeper than he had anticipated. Stretch did an about face, stopped, and turned to gaze across the wide view of the Helena valley spread in panorama before him. Mountains stood shoulder to shoulder in every direction, and Hauser Lake glistened in the distance. When his breathing returned to normal, he began again the walk and jog, this time downhill, retracing the course he'd followed from the hotel.

Back in his room, he discarded the sweaty clothes. The hot water of the shower washed the perspiration from his body and cleansed his mind of personal recriminations over mistakes he'd made in court that day. He had never tried a case without doing something that, in retrospect, seemed not only wrong, but foolishly wrong, and he always spent time berating himself afterward. He just couldn't help it.

In fresh clothes and with a fresh frame of mind, Stretch

greeted his companions and tucked Audrey's arm in his. He led them to his SUV, determined that nothing would prevent him from enjoying a relaxing meal in the company of two attractive women and a handsome and personable young man.

Audrey suggested the dining room of the Great Northern Hotel at the lower end of the gulch where they might eat without too much interference from others. Most of the patrons at that hour would be out-of-town guests of the hotel and were likely to respect their privacy—if they recognized them at all. Comfortably seated in one of the back corners with her son on one side and Cynthia on the other, Audrey reached across the table to place her hand on her lawyer's forearm, "You were magnificent! The sheriff all but told the jury that he doesn't believe I'm guilty."

Logan said, "I liked the part when you made that county attorney mad. His display of anger didn't help his case, did it?"

Stretch smiled. "No. I don't think Mr. Hogan's anger helped his case. But it probably didn't hurt it much either. And Sheriff Mendenhall is only one witness. I don't believe his testimony damaged our case. And it may have helped. But there will be other witnesses, and they may not be as accommodating."

Cynthia was sober-faced as she spoke to Audrey. "As good as the sheriff's statements sounded, they don't eliminate the fact that the bloody scarf and flashlight were found where it's logical that you would leave them. Those facts tie you to the killing of Gloria Angel." Turning to Stretch, she added, "And we still have nothing to link the killing to any other person, do we?"

Before Stretch could answer, Audrey spoke with some impatience. "Maybe not, but Senator Bruce sure helped my case by his examination of the sheriff." Turning to Stretch, she added, "Reasonable doubt. That's all we have to create. Am I right?" Without giving the lawyer a chance to respond, she continued, "The sheriff provided some doubt. Now we just have to create some more." She patted his arm. "You've done great so far. And I'm certain you'll keep it up."

"Audrey's right about reasonable doubt. Our objective is to create it. But Cynthia's right about the physical evidence. It's damning. The 'some other dude did it' defense isn't the best we could wish for. We aren't able to show means, motive, or opportunity for any of the other possible suspects, including the governor. But it's all we have for a defense right now." He leaned toward his client and spoke in an earnest voice. "I don't want to dampen your enthusiasm, but you must be realistic."

The starch seemed to go out of Audrey's body. "I know you're right, of course." She pushed at the eating utensils before her. "You just ruined my appetite." Her son immediately rubbed her shoulder, giving the support only he could give.

None of them ate much of their food, and the little that was eaten was eaten in silence. Stretch looked at his watch. "It's getting late, and we all must be fresh tomorrow. We need to get back to the hotel and into bed."

Audrey pushed back from the table. "You're right. But I won't sleep."

40

When they walked through the front door of the courthouse the following morning, Stretch was relieved to find that the mob that had besieged them the day before had melted away. A few curious county workers peeked from office doors. Only the rude blogger yelled questions—to which he received no response. Evidence, Stretch thought, of the short attention span of the residents and newspeople of any capital city in America.

Ambrose Swan was the only other person waiting for them in the lobby. He gestured with his chin toward a quiet corner. Stretch turned to Logan and the women and said, "Go on up to the courtroom. I'll join you in a minute." As Stretch sidled up the reporter, Swan said in a low voice, "As you could have guessed, it was about money."

"What about money?"

"The secret meeting between the governor and the attorney general, remember? Money. That's what they were discussing."

"So what?"

Swan smiled. "Neither of those dudes is wealthy. Where would you look for loose change in government? A place where a little money might be snagged for a more personal use."

"What do you mean?"

The smile grew wider. "Contracts for highway construction involve a lot of money. And the liquor monopoly requires the handling of lots of cash. A little bird told me Governor Albert Shewey may have found a way to slip a straw into that highway honey pot and take a sip. And Sawyer may be doing the same with the booze pot. And neither of them is really aware of what the other is doing. But apparently each has suspicions about the other."

Skepticism spread across Stretch's face. "Would either one of them do that and risk his political future? Shewey hungers to be a United States senator, and Sawyer drools at the thought of being governor."

Swan muttered, "The need for money can make people do strange things. Don't know if any of it is true. Just thought you should be aware of what I heard. It might be something you can use to help Senator Welter." Swan turned to walk away, "She's a quality person. Hefty Hogan shouldn't be allowed to crawl over her back into the office of attorney general."

A police photographer took the stand and described how he photographed the dead woman as she lay on the floor of the rotunda, before the body was disturbed. Hogan presented a packet of the pictures to the judge and then walked across to hand another packet to Bruce. Then the county attorney presented eight pictures to the photographer, one by one. The man stated that he indeed was the one who had taken each picture and that it accurately portrayed both the scene and the body as they were at the time each picture was taken. After all of the pictures were identified, the county attorney held the originals in the air and said, "Your Honor, I offer State's exhibits 1 through 8 into evidence."

Stretch hurriedly shuffled through the photographs. When he reached the last of them, he sprang to his feet. "Your Honor, may we have a sidebar?"

The judge raised his eyebrows. He glanced at Hogan, then back at Bruce and nodded. When Stretch and Hefty, with Ellis

Bradley at his side, were huddled close to the judge's bench on the corner away from the jury, Stretch growled, "Your Honor, Mr. Hogan only gave me three of these pictures before today. They were the least offensive of the lot. The county attorney indicated they were sufficient to allow the jury to understand the situation, as it was when Gloria Angel's body was found. Now he wants to introduce five more." Stretch shoved two of them along the top of the bench toward the judge. "These are taken in such a way as to emphasize the legs and crotch area of the woman's body. It's an attempt to make the death scene more gruesome than it actually was. The only purpose for their introduction would be to inflame the jury."

Hefty started to respond, but Bruce put out a hand to stop him. Pushing the remaining three pictures to the judge, he growled, "And these focus directly on the dead woman's head in such a way as to focus attention on the blood that flowed from the nose, ear, and mouth of the deceased. In the three full body pictures, those provided to me by Mr. Hogan, the blood can also be seen but in such a way that shows that the flow of blood was miniscule. These three extra pictures create an apparent distortion of the amount of blood that came from the body. They're nothing but inflammatory."

Hogan maintained his composure, and his voice was calm when he said, "The pictures are of the body as it was found. They are a true and accurate portrayal. And they will give the jury a proper understanding of the situation the night this poor woman was killed." A touch of a smile crossed his lips. "And, Your Honor, the pictures are needed for the pathologist to describe his work. They're clearly admissible."

Judge Hastings scowled at the county attorney. "Did you or did you not provide copies of all these pictures to Mr. Bruce?"

Hogan began to reply in a stammer, then seemed to gain

control. "Maybe I didn't, Your Honor. But there was no intent to deceive the defense. It must have been an oversight by my deputy. He handled the organization of the exhibits." He didn't even look at Ellis Bradley as he made the accusation. Bradley shifted his feet but remained silent. Loyal warrior falling on his sword.

Hefty seemed to gain confidence as he went along. "And there really isn't any prejudice to the defendant. Mr. Bruce still has a chance to cross examine the photographer." That remark was followed by a sickly kind of grin. "Perhaps the folks in Musselshell County where Mr. Bruce ordinarily practices law are more easily offended than those here in Lewis and Clark County."

The deepening scowl on the judge's face told both lawyers that he wasn't pleased by the explanation, especially the last flippant remark. "Mr. Hogan, you've been county attorney for a long time now. You know the rules—or at least you should know the rules." Judge Hastings sat for a long minute, just staring at the county attorney. "It seems to me that I can do one of three things. I can refuse to admit the pictures. Or I can sanction you, Mr. Hogan, and admit the pictures. Or I can let you off with a warning and admit the pictures." He held Hefty's gaze for a full twenty seconds. Turning at last to Stretch, he said, "I'm doing the latter, Mr. Bruce. I don't believe the pictures are unduly prejudicial. You can cross-examine the photographer, as is your right, to show that the five to which you object are not truly representative of the actual situation. And, Mr. Hogan is probably correct that the pictures may be needed by the pathologist." Turning back to Hogan, he said in a stern voice. "You get a warning, sir. Never again come into my courtroom without full disclosure to the defense. Is that clear?"

Hogan almost bowed to show he was properly chastened. "Very clear, Your Honor. It will never happen again."

"I certainly hope not." Turning to Bruce, the judge said, "All the pictures are admitted. As I said, I don't think they are unduly prejudicial."

Stretch took the defeat gracefully. "Perhaps, Your Honor. I just hope the jurors can look at them dispassionately."

Upon returning to the counsel table, Hogan turned to the judge and stood for a second before asking, "May I publish the pictures to the jury at this time, Your Honor. It will be a help to them, I believe, in following the testimony of the next witness."

Judge Hastings glanced toward Bruce as though expecting an objection. But Stretch, realizing the jurors would see them sooner or later, made no move to object. The judge then turned to the county attorney and said, "You may."

Hogan handed the pictures, one by one, to the woman juror sitting at the end of the first row. After looking at the first of them, she passed it to her seatmate, who then handed it to his seatmate. The jurors passed the second picture and the ones that followed in the same way, taking time to study each of them carefully. Stretch and Hogan, as well as Audrey, Logan, Cynthia, and Ellis Bradley, followed the progression of the photographs from one juror to the next, attempting to discern the reaction of each. Stretch concluded the men spent time on the ones showing the dead woman's legs. The women seemed to focus more on the blood. When all of the pictures were back in the hands of the first juror, Hogan collected the packet and placed them on the clerk's desk.

The State Medical Examiner was next to take the witness stand. He had a youthful appearance—slender body, light blond hair, glasses with round frames, and an unlined face. When he recited his education, credentials, and experience, however, it became apparent that he was nearly fifty years old. The man sat hunched over as he explained how he conducted his examination of the body and of his finding that Ms. Angel died, not from the fall onto the rotunda floor, but from a blow to the head that must have occurred before she fell. Hogan never once asked the Medical Examiner to use the photographs as a means to clarify any part of his testimony. Stretch decided that a time might come when it would be helpful to remind the judge how the county attorney misled the court.

Stretch had consulted with an independent pathologist from Billings before the trial. That individual stated with some certainty that the report of the man now on the witness stand conformed to professional standards and seemed correct in all aspects. That information, as well as the knowledge that to question the witness or to mention the objectionable pictures would only emphasize them in the minds of the jurors, led Stretch to forgo any cross examination of the pathologist.

Loren Hammond was next on the stand. The tall detective had accompanied the sheriff during the searches of Audrey's office and was the officer most reasonable when Stretch and Audrey went to the courthouse so she might be questioned. The manner in which he took the oath and then seated himself comfortably attested to his experience as a witness in criminal trials. In a quiet and professional manner, he described how he walked through every hallway and looked into every unlocked office in the capitol immediately after arriving at the scene. When asked, he stated he did not accompany the laboratory technician as the technician luminoled those places where there was a possibility that blood from Ms. Angel might be found. Deputy Buzz Kramer was the one assigned to that task.

Hammond spoke of accompanying the sheriff to Audrey Welter's capitol office and of a search that disclosed nothing in the office that was of help in finding Gloria Angel's killer. Finally, he told of the second search and stated that he saw the sheriff find the scarf with blood on it in Audrey's desk.

Hogan gathered a clear plastic bag in his fist and approached the witness. "Detective Hammond, you mentioned a scarf that the sheriff found in a desk drawer in the defendant's office. I'm showing you what is marked as State's Exhibit 9. Do you recognize it?"

Hammond asked, "May I take it out of the bag to be certain?"

"Yes, you may."

The detective pulled the silken material from the holder and shook it so that the scarf was hanging free of any folds. After looking at all parts of the material carefully, he looked up at Hogan and said, "Yes, sir. I recognize this as the scarf found in Ms. Welter's office."

Hogan wanted to nail it down. "How can you be certain it's the same scarf? There must be many like it."

"The blood stains are there." He tried to hold one corner of the scarf and point to a discolored spot, but the loose material folded so that the spot wasn't visible. Hogan came to his rescue, grasped the material by two corners, and held it up so the jury could easily see what the detective was trying to show. Hammond used his index finger to point to three small dark blotches at different places on the scarf while saying, "The stains tell me it's the same scarf. They are in the same shape and the same location as when I placed the scarf in the evidence bag after the sheriff handed it to me at Ms. Welter's office." He turned to the jurors. "I marked the bag with my initials at that time."

Hefty folded the material and returned it to the bag. "Your Honor, we offer State's Exhibit 9 into evidence."

Stretch was standing. Judge Hastings turned to him, eyebrows raised. "Mr. Bruce?"

"May I inquire, Your Honor?"

"Of course."

The lawyer reached to grasp the bag from the clerk's table

where Hogan had dropped it. Holding it up before the witness and so the jury could see it, he asked, "You don't know of your own knowledge that there is blood on this scarf, do you?"

"No, sir. I only know what the lab tech said."

"And the day you and the sheriff found it, you didn't know what the stains might be, did you?"

"No, sir. I didn't."

"And you didn't know at that time and still don't know how the scarf got into the desk drawer, do you?"

"No, Mr. Bruce. I don't know that for certain."

"Detective Hammond, the only reason you were searching the desk was because of an email from some unknown person, a person who may even be the killer? Isn't that right?"

"It's my understanding that the identity of the person who sent the email isn't known." He turned to look at the jurors. "I won't speculate as to whether or not someone other than the defendant was the killer."

"But it's possible that the sender was the killer. You'll admit that, won't you, sir?"

"Anything's possible, Mr. Bruce." He turned again to the jurors. "But we wouldn't be here if the county attorney didn't believe he could prove Audrey Welter was the one who killed Gloria Angel."

Stretch cursed himself. Should have stopped him from expanding on the answer. But he couldn't let it end there. "That proof must be beyond a reasonable doubt. It can't be based on guesswork or speculation, isn't that right?"

"You're the lawyer. You know that the judge will give that instruction to the jury."

Better quit before I do more damage, Stretch thought. "I have no objection to the introduction of the exhibit."

Judge Hastings looked at the clock on the wall. He said to the whole room, "My clerk tells me there is a matter that requires my immediate attention. We'll take a fifteen-minute break." Turning to the jurors, he added, "Remember my admonition." With a rap of the gavel, he strode briskly from the room.

Stretch took the opportunity to find the men's restroom. A reporter from the local paper caught him near the door and tried to get a newsworthy comment. Stretch brushed him aside. When he walked back through the doors into the courtroom, he saw Audrey standing alone near the counsel table. Cynthia was next to the railing in conversation with Logan.

The jurors returned to the box. The judge climbed to the bench and rapped his gavel. "Mr. Hammond, you understand that you're still under oath?"

"Yes, Your Honor. I understand."

"Mr. Hogan may have more questions for you."

Hogan rose slowly from his chair and asked questions to lead Hammond through the remainder of his involvement in the investigation of Gloria Angel's death. Finally he said, "I have no more questions of Detective Hammond, Your Honor."

Stretch stepped around the end of the counsel table but remained some distance from the witness. "Detective Hammond, you and I have met before, haven't we?"

"Yes, sir, we have. We first met in your client's office."

"We met again when Audrey Welter voluntarily went to the sheriff's office to answer any questions that the sheriff might have, questions about her activities the night Gloria Angel was killed. Isn't that right?"

Hammond nodded his head even as Stretch was finishing the question. "Yes, sir. That is correct."

"She wasn't under a subpoena or any kind of court order to testify at that time, was she?"

"No, sir. Not that I know of."

"You've been in law enforcement for a long time, haven't you, sir?"

Hammond turned to the jurors to answer. "I've been in law enforcement for more than fifteen years."

"In your years of experience, has any person, who later proved to be guilty of the crime, voluntarily appeared before you for questioning about a murder he or she had committed?"

Hogan growled, "Objection! He's being asked to speculate about the guilt or innocence of the defendant in this case."

"Not so, Your Honor. I'm asking Detective Hammond to testify as to a fact, a fact of which he surely has knowledge."

"Overruled."

"Have you ever had that happen, Detective Hammond?"

The law officer turned his eyes away from Bruce to stare at the far wall. After some thought, he turned back to the lawyer. "No, Mr. Bruce, I don't believe I have."

"Guilty people don't do that kind of thing, do they?"

Hogan was on his feet this time. "Objection, Your Honor. Now Mr. Bruce really is asking this witness to speculate on the things guilty people may or may not do."

Stretch made no attempt to argue. The question had made the point with the jury. Audrey had done what no guilty person would do. "I withdraw the question, Your Honor."

Having achieved as much as possible from that line, Stretch moved to another part of the detective's direct testimony. "You told the jury that you searched every unlocked office in the capitol building shortly after the body of Ms. Angel was found. Is that correct?"

"Yes, sir. That's what I testified, and that's what I did."

Stretch moved a step closer to the witness. "Did you search the office of Ms. Welter?"

As he did before, Hammond took time to think. At last

he looked at the jurors and then back at Stretch. "You know, Mr. Bruce, I don't know if the door to her office was locked or unlocked. At that time, I didn't know which office was Ms. Welter's. I only learned which one was hers when the sheriff and I went to search it the first time."

"So it's entirely possible that the door to Senator Welter's office was unlocked at the time someone killed Gloria Angel."

"As I said, I don't know if it was locked or not."

"If it was unlocked, the killer could have easily walked in and put the bloody scarf in her desk drawer right after he committed the crime, isn't that right?"

"I suppose that could have happened." He emphasized the word 'suppose.'

Stretch turned to the jurors for only a second, then back to face the witness. "If that could have happened then, it's possible, and maybe even probable, that Audrey had nothing to do with the death of Gloria Angel, isn't that right?"

Hammond refused to react. His voice remained calm. "Again, Mr. Bruce, anything is possible."

There wasn't much more to be gained from that line of questions.

After a moment of silence, he asked, "Isn't it true that when you conducted a search of Gloria Angel's office right after Ms. Angel's death, you found one file drawer partially open and with a file out of place?"

Hammond reflected for a moment, then answered, "Yes, sir. Now that you mention it, one file drawer was slightly open, and one corner of a file folder was sticking up. The file wasn't flush with the bottom of the holder."

"Why did that catch your eye?"

Hammond's face brightened in a touch of a smile. "Because everything else was so neat. It appeared that Ms. Angel kept her entire office extremely tidy. Every other thing seemed to be in its proper place."

"Who had a key and could have gotten into that office to search the files?"

The smile left the detective's face abruptly. He shifted in the chair. "The governor had a key, of course. I don't know if other members of the governor's staff might have had a key."

"The governor." Stretch paused to let the jurors think about it. "And the governor was running around in the building at the time of Ms. Angel's death, wasn't he?"

"I can't say that he was running around, sir. He was in the building that night. That's all I've been told."

Stretch crossed his arms and stared at the detective. He walked to the counsel table to whisper a question to Cynthia. She scanned her notes and then shook her head. Stretch smiled his thanks and turned to Audrey to whisper again. She, too, shook her head. Stretch straightened and turned to the judge. "I have no more questions for Detective Hammond."

Judge Hastings looked at the clock on the far wall. He turned to Hefty. "We're approaching the noon hour. Mr. Hogan, will your next witness take much time?"

"Yes, sir. The next witness will be Detective Kramer. I expect his testimony will take a considerable amount of time. And then there's Mr. Bruce's cross. I don't know how long it will take." He hesitated. "If the time he took with Loren Hammond is any indication, he may take all day tomorrow."

Hastings smiled. "Well, Mr. Bruce wants to be thorough, I suppose." Turning to the jury, he recited his admonition and added, "We'll be in recess until one thirty." With a bang of the judge's gavel, the morning proceedings came to an end.

41

Court reconvened. Detective Buzz Kramer swore to tell the truth and took the stand. While Loren Hammond had been dressed in a tailored business suit, Kramer wore a herringbone sport coat, white necktie with pictures of fishhooks on it and wrinkled brown slacks. His manner of walk suggested an attempt at a swagger. Once in the witness chair, he leaned way back, tucked his chin down so that he was looking out from under his eyebrows, and folded his arms across his chest as though challenging anyone, including the county attorney, to ask the wrong question.

Hogan led him though a description of his actions the morning Gloria Angel's body was found and his investigative duties thereafter. Kramer responded to each question in a gruff manner, offering no detail beyond that required to answer. The man had a habit of turning his head slightly to one side and answering while looking upward at Hefty out of the corner of his eye. The direct examination didn't take long.

As Hogan turned away, Kramer looked at Stretch and began shifting in the chair and clenching and unclenching his fists. Stretch rose slowly from his chair and walked around the counsel table to stand in front of him. "Detective, you and I have met before, haven't we?"

Kramer seemed to flinch at the question. He pulled in a breath and finally responded. "Yes, we have."

"We met when Senator Welter voluntarily went to the sheriff's office to answer questions, isn't that right?"

Kramer ground his teeth for a heartbeat before answering. "Yes." After a brief pause, he added, "But she didn't answer any questions."

"That's because your behavior was so rude and reprehensible that I took her away, isn't that right?"

More teeth grinding. "I didn't think I was rude. I was just doing my duty like I always do."

"You always behave in a rude manner when a person voluntarily appears to answer questions about a crime?"

"It ain't often that we have to deal with volunteers. Most times we've brought 'em in, usually in cuffs."

"It's such a rare thing to have someone volunteer to answer questions that you didn't know how to handle it. Is that what you're saying?"

Kramer slumped back in the chair and mumbled, "Maybe."

"Detective Kramer, you were the one who assisted the technician in a search of the capitol for blood spots after the body of Ms. Angel was found, is that right?"

"Yes. I took him to the places I thought we should check."

"For the benefit of the jury, how do you conduct such a check?"

"The tech used luminol to test in any area where we thought there might be traces of blood."

"And if there are blood traces, the luminol will differentiate them from other compounds, is that right?"

"Yes, sir. That's the way it works."

"Did you check Senator Welter's office?"

Kramer took a breath and blew it slowly out again. "Yes, we did."

"And what did you find?"

"Nothing."

"No traces of blood in Ms. Welter's office?"

"That's what I said."

Stretch walked back to perch himself on the corner of the counsel table. "Where else did you check for traces of blood?"

"In Gloria Angel's office." He paused. "And on the balcony overlooking the place where the body was found."

Stretch pushed away from the table to stand erect. "Is that the balcony on the third floor, at the place where the Centennial Bell is located?"

"Yes, sir. We believe she was pitched over from that location."

Stretch took a step forward. "And did you find blood at any place on the balcony?"

Kramer shook his head. "No, sir. We didn't."

"Not on the floor on either side of the bell and not at any place on the railing?"

"As I said, we didn't find any traces of blood."

Bruce moved one step closer. "Did you also check on the balcony on the fourth floor that overlooks the rotunda?"

The detective blinked a couple of times and then seemed to hesitate. "No. We didn't check up there."

"But Ms. Angel could have fallen from that balcony, couldn't she?"

Kramer's discomfort was evident as he tucked his chin even farther down and twisted to one side. At last he said, "I guess that's possible."

Stretch took another step. "Isn't it correct, sir, that the third floor balcony juts out at the place where the bell is located?"

"What do you mean, juts out?"

"The railing is not straight from pillar to pillar. It curves outward and around the bell." Stretch drew a picture with his arms. "Isn't that correct?"

Kramer scrunched up his face as he tried to recollect. "That may be right." He nodded. "Yes. It does bulge out a little."

Bruce crossed his arms and stood as though in contemplation. "The body of Gloria Angel was found almost directly below that bulge, not off to one side. Isn't that correct?"

The detective squirmed and then chewed on his cheek for a full second as he thought. "Yes. No wait, I believe she was maybe a little way out in front instead of directly below the bulge. Maybe a little out in front."

"The bell fills the bulge. Tell me, sir, how Ms. Angel's body could have gotten over the bell to fall from the third floor to the place where it was found?"

Kramer straightened and leaned forward for the first time. "Someone pitched her body over." He thrust his head forward as he added quickly, "And that someone was your client."

Stretch stood quietly and stared at the detective in response to that remark. Then he asked in a patient voice. "Isn't there a more reasonable explanation? Isn't it more likely that Ms. Angel fell from the fourth floor balcony rather than the third floor balcony?"

Still sitting stiffly erect, Kramer replied, "Fourth floor, third floor. What difference does it make? She was dead before she went over the railing."

"Was she, sir? Suppose she accidentally fell over the fourth floor railing and hit her head on the third floor railing on the way down—hit her head on the railing where the bulge is located. That would explain the blow that the pathologist said killed her, wouldn't it?"

"Objection!" Hogan seemed to think his objection would carry more weight if it was spoken in a shout. "Speculation. You warned him, Your Honor.

Stretch's voice was calm when he faced the judge. "The defense is allowed to present alternate theories of death. I'm only asking the witness if a sequence of events is possible." As the judge started to turn his gaze toward Hogan, Stretch continued, "If what I'm suggesting is what actually happened, there wasn't any murder, only an accident."

Hogan's face reddened. "There's not a single bit of evidence to support such a notion, Your Honor. It's ridiculous!"

Stretch smiled when the judge turned to him. "But what evidence might there have been, Your Honor, if Detective Kramer had investigated the fourth floor balcony? Who knows what might have been found? Neither he nor any other officer thought to do so because they were focused on Audrey Welter as a murderer. They assumed right from the beginning that she was somehow responsible for Gloria Welter's death and they assumed it was caused by a fall over the third floor railing. After all, the third floor railing is near Senator Welter's office." He looked sideways at Hefty. "It's what happens when people in law enforcement jump to conclusions."

Hogan was out from behind the counsel table and charging toward the judge's bench. "We didn't jump to any conclusions." He wheeled and pointed his finger at Audrey while looking at the jury. "The evidence is clear. That woman had a scarf with Gloria Angel's blood on it hidden in her desk. And she had the flashlight in her automobile that she'd used to bash in Gloria Angel's head." His chest was heaving. "The evidence is irrefutable."

Stretch's calm voice was such a contrast to Hogan's yelping that the attention of everyone in the courtroom immediately focused on him. "I have a motion to make, Your Honor, out of the presence of the jury."

The scowl of displeasure on Judge Hastings' face crowded the wrinkles together, making deep lines from brow to chin. "I'm certain that you do, Mr. Bruce." Turning to the jurors, he said, "We'll be in recess for a time. Please return to the jury room. The bailiff will let you know when we're ready to resume. And don't forget my admonition not to discuss the case." He turned to the lawyers and growled, "In my chambers—now."

Judge Hastings stood behind the desk, waiting as Stretch Bruce followed Hogan and Ellis Bradley through the door. Once the court reporter was in place, he pointed a finger at the county attorney without preamble and growled, "Mr. Bruce is about to move for a mistrial because of your unwarranted outburst." Turning to Stretch, he asked, "Isn't that why you asked for this recess, Mr. Bruce?"

"Yes, Your Honor, it is. The remarks made by Mr. Hogan are about as prejudicial as any can be."

The judge turned to the county attorney for a response. Hefty's effort to control his anger and to regain his composure was apparent. He was still breathing heavily when he spoke. "Not so, Your Honor. I could make those same remarks during my closing argument. That the jurors heard them now makes no difference."

Stretch swiveled his head from side to side. "It certainly does make a difference. Any evidence that is produced from this point forward will be tainted by the remarks." His eyes moved from the judge to the court reporter and back to the judge. "I move for a mistrial, Your Honor. The motion is based upon the prejudicial remarks made by the county attorney in the presence of the jury."

Judge Hastings pulled out his chair, sat down, and leaned his elbows on the desk. He gestured to the others to be seated as well. His face had resumed its accustomed placid appearance. He turned to Stretch and looked at him quietly for a full twenty seconds. In a solemn voice, he asked, "Do you really want a mistrial, sir? Do you want to do this all over again, leaving your client in a life of uncertainty?"

The question was so unexpected that Stretch didn't know how to answer. In fact he didn't want a mistrial. He made the motion because it was necessary to preserve the issue should an appeal be necessary. How could he admit that to the judge? He knew his reply sounded weak as soon as it was out. "I made the motion, Your Honor."

A hint of a smile crossed the judge's lips as though acknowledging the lawyer's dilemma. "All right. I'm going to deny the motion—for now. You may renew the motion later, if you choose." He turned to address the county attorney in a stern voice. "I'm disappointed in you, Mr. Hogan. You've tried cases in my court for several years now and never until this case have you acted in such an unprofessional manner." He held Hefty's eyes for a long moment. "I expect you to control your emotions from now until this trial is over. Do you understand, sir?"

Hogan dropped his eyes to the floor and mumbled, "I understand, Your Honor. And I apologize to the court." Turning to Stretch, he added, "And also to the counsel for the defendant."

Judge Hastings pushed back from his desk and rose to his feet. "Very well." Directing his speech to Stretch, he noted, "I'll instruct the jury to ignore Mr. Hogan's remarks." Striding toward the door, he added, "Now let's get on with it. We can't keep the jury waiting."

With the jurors once again in place, the judge leaned in their direction as he spoke. "Before the recess, Mr. Hogan made some remarks that should have been reserved until all of the evidence was in. You are not to take those remarks as facts nor are you to let them influence the way in which you listen to and interpret the remainder of the evidence that will be brought to you. Is that clear?" After peering at the nodding heads of those in the jury box, he turned to Detective Kramer to remind him that he was still under oath. Then he said, "Mr. Bruce, please continue."

Stretch moved to the front of the witness, stared at him until he blinked, then said, "Mr. Kramer, I asked you if Ms. Angel could have fallen from the fourth floor balcony. And I asked if she could have hit her head on the railing of the third floor balcony, thus receiving the blow that the pathologist has said killed her. What is your answer, sir?"

Having had time to think about the question, Kramer said, "I suppose something like that might have happened." Before Stretch could stop him, he rushed to add, "But it's not at all likely that a body going over the upper railing would fall straight down. More likely, she would fall out and away from the railing below." With a look of satisfaction, he sat back in his chair, crossed one foot over his knee, and grabbed it with his hand.

"Some things just aren't likely. Is that what you're saying?"

Kramer tried to appear bored. "I guess."

Stretch walked back to heft a haunch onto the corner of the counsel table. If Kramer wanted to appear at ease, so would he. "It's also unlikely that a woman the size of Audrey Welter could hoist a dead body and drop it over the third floor railing, isn't it?"

The detective gave some thought to the question. "Well now, Mr. Bruce, I don't know anything about your client's abilities. For all I know she could do it without any trouble."

There was anger in Stretch's voice when he asked, "Detective Kramer, how easy is it to lift and carry a limp body?"

The lawman released his foot and dropped it to the floor. He leaned to one side with his elbow on the arm of the witness chair. "It depends."

"Depends on what, sir?"

Kramer straightened in the chair again and looked toward the jurors, then back at Bruce. "It depends on how you go about it. I can do it."

"Easily?"

"Well, it's never easy. But it can be done."

Turning to his paralegal, Stretch asked, "Cynthia, would you please stand?" When she did so, he turned again to the witness. "Detective Kramer, Miss Weaver is about the same size as Gloria Angel, isn't she?"

Kramer leaned forward to look across the open space. He looked sideways at Bruce to ask, "Could she step out from behind the table so I can see her?" Cynthia smiled at the jurors and then walked out into the open area in front of the jury box. She stood quietly with her hands clasped in front. Kramer's gaze traveled over her from top to bottom, and his face took on a look that approached a leer. Then he jerked around to say, "I don't know if she's the same size as the dead woman or not."

"Don't be cute, sir. Cynthia is small and trim. Gloria Angel was small and trim. There can't be more than ten pounds difference between them, can there?"

"Well, Ms. Angel was dead when I saw her body, but I guess she and that woman are near to the same size."

Stretch stood and gestured toward Cynthia with his elbow. "Detective Kramer, I'd like you to show the jurors how easy it is to pick up a limp body. Ms. Weaver will be the body." There was risk in his request. Kramer might just demonstrate that it was easy. He, Audrey, and Cynthia had discussed the gambit and decided it was worth the risk. If Kramer was unsuccessful or had a great deal of trouble, the jury would understand that Audrey would surely have more difficulty. Stretch had asked Cynthia if she would be willing to play the role of a dead woman. She thought it would be fun to be a real part of the trial. Stretch wasn't sure if the judge would allow the demonstration, but he'd suggested Cynthia wear slacks to avoid as much embarrassment as possible in case the judge consented to the demonstration. At a nod from her employer, she dropped to the floor, directly in front of the jury box, resting on her left side.

Hogan was on his feet. "Now he's going too far, Your

The Body on the Floor of the Rotunda 291

Honor. What's this have to do with the guilt or innocence of the defendant, anyway?"

Judge Hastings' eyebrows went up. "Is that an objection, Mr. Hogan?"

"It is. Lack of relevance. Likely to confuse the jury."

Stretch stood calmly, arms still crossed. "The prosecution seems to believe that Audrey Welter whapped Gloria Angel and killed her. Then, they seem to believe, she dragged the body from—somewhere—and tossed it over the third floor railing. Detective Kramer is about to show the jurors how that might be done. It's a permissible demonstration."

A flicker of a smile crossed the judge's face. "I'll allow it."

Stretch pointed at Cynthia. "There's your limp body. Please step down from the chair and show the jurors how you can pick her up. When you've done that, show how you could toss her over the railing in front of the jury box, please."

Buzz Kramer looked over at the county attorney as though seeking help. Seeing only a stony face, he slowly turned and pushed himself up from the chair. The short, stocky man stood with his hands on his hips while looking down at Cynthia. He hitched up his pants and took a deep breath. With a final glance at the jurors, he leaned over to reach for Cynthia's right arm. With his hands grasping her wrist, he tried to pull the arm up so he could drag it over his shoulder. Cynthia, playing her role to perfection, allowed all her weight to hang on the arm as though her body had no bones. Kramer easily lifted her upper torso off the ground but he was unable to get his shoulder under her armpit so as to pull her body onto his back. He released his grasp and Cynthia, still playing the limp dead body, flopped to the floor. Glancing again at the jurors, Kramer squatted beside Cynthia and reached under her shoulders with his left hand and under her knees with his right arm. When he tried to rise from the floor while lifting her body, she simply relaxed her torso at the waist and slipped between his arms, back to the floor. All of the jurors watched the deputy. Stretch watched the jurors. He was pleased to see some of them start to smile when the second effort failed. The detective stood with his breath coming in short bursts. He looked down at Cynthia for second. Turning to the judge, he mumbled, "It's been a long time since I was a rookie and had to learn the fireman's carry." Turning to face the jurors, he spoke more clearly. "But if it's done right, it's possible to pick up a dead body."

Stretch didn't make it easy. He waited for a full half minute before saying, "You may take the stand again." He gestured for Cynthia to return to her place. She rose from the floor, smiled at the jurors, brushed at her clothing, and took her seat next to Audrey. Stretch returned his attention to Detective Kramer. "Do you have any reason to believe that Ms. Welter knows how to perform the fireman's carry?"

Kramer, still trying to catch his breath, puffed out an answer. "No, sir. But who knows? She might."

Stretch placed his hands on his hips, glanced at the judge, then at Hogan, then turned to the jurors and shrugged. Three of the men were smiling faint smiles. They understood.

"The sheriff testified that no one checked the governor's belongings for blood, and you let the vagrant get away without proper investigation. You don't really know if all the evidence points to Ms. Welter, do you?"

Kramer growled, "There's no evidence that points in the direction of either the governor or that man, Kastner."

"There may not be now, but there may have been if proper investigation procedures had been followed early on, right?"

Hogan was on his feet. "Objection! Mr. Bruce is arguing with the witness."

The Body on the Floor of the Rotunda

Judge Hastings said, "You're right." Turning to Stretch, he added, "Enough of that, sir. Move on."

"Yes, sir." Stretch walked to the clerk's table and asked for the bag containing the flashlight that Hogan had introduced into evidence during his direct examination of Kramer. Returning his attention to the detective, he asked, "You were the one who broke into Senator Welter's auto and took this flashlight?"

"Objection!" Hogan was up and around the table and rushing toward the judge's bench. "Detective Kramer didn't break into that car. He went in under a search warrant. He had every legal right to do what he did."

Judge Hastings inhaled to speak, only to see Stretch stare at the county attorney and growl, "Yes, that's right. Under another search warrant that was based on a tip from some phantom whose reliability is completely unknown." Turning to the judge, he continued, "The state's whole case is built on that kind of tip, Your Honor. They are baseless, and any evidence of any kind generated by them should be excluded. And if they're excluded, the charges against my client should be dismissed."

Judge Hastings leaned forward with his elbows on his desk. This time his scowl was directed at Stretch. "Mr. Bruce, you made your motion to exclude the evidence prior to trial, and I denied it. I'm not going to change my mind now. The reliability of the tipster is evidenced by the fact the items were found where the sheriff's officers were told they would be." The frown intensified and made the wrinkles on his forehead even deeper. "As to Mr. Hogan's objection—more of a complaint than an objection. But nevertheless, he's right. You accused the officer of committing a crime." Leaning forward for emphasis, he added, "Don't do it again, sir. Am I understood?"

Stretch dropped his head. "You are, Your Honor."

The judge turned to the jurors, scowl gone. "Mr. Bruce

seemed to imply that Detective Kramer broke into Ms. Welter's auto and, by doing so, broke the law. The implication is not correct, and you are directed to ignore it." Facing Stretch again, he said, "Now, sir, please continue."

Kramer smirked after the judge rebuked Senator Bruce. Stretch ignored it and held up the bag that contained the flashlight for both the detective and the jurors to see. "You found this in Ms. Welter's Subaru. Correct?"

"I've already testified that I did." When Stretch didn't ask another question right away, he filled the void by adding, "The Subaru is a hatchback, and it was behind the rear seat."

"This is the kind of heavy flashlight that law officers carry, isn't it?"

"Yes. Lots of us do, but not all of us."

"It's as good as the old time sap that cops used to carry—good to club people with, isn't it?"

"Law officers carry the lights to use in the dark. And, yes, if we need to subdue someone, we can use the light for that purpose."

"It's more likely that this flashlight belongs to a law officer than to a lady college professor, isn't it?"

"It was in her car, sir. It's hers."

"So you said." He paused. "And you said you found it behind the rear seat. What else did you find back there?"

Kramer hesitated. "Nothing. Nothing at all."

"Just this flashlight, lying there in plain sight, all by itself?"

"Yes sir, it was all by itself."

Stretch lowered the evidence bag to his side as he asked, "Did you search the rest of the car?"

"Yes. Once we were in the car, we searched all of it."

"What else did you find just lying around in Ms. Welter's private automobile?"

Kramer scowled. "As I said, it's standard procedure to search a vehicle thoroughly after we get a warrant." Then he remembered the question. "But we didn't find anything else loose in her car."

"Nice and neat, wasn't it?"

"Yes, sir. It was."

"Didn't you think it was strange, if she was a murderer, that Audrey Welter would leave the flashlight, the thing that could tie her to a killing, lying in plain view when she was so careful to put everything else away?"

"I guess I didn't think about it one way or another."

"What do you think about it at this moment?"

Hefty's objection was more muted than before. "Objection. What Detective Kramer thinks is of no probative value."

Before the judge could rule, Stretch said, "Withdraw the question." To ask the question was enough. The answer was immaterial.

Crossing his arms again, Bruce asked, "What makes you think that Senator Welter left the flashlight where you found it?"

Kramer shook his head as though in disgust at the question. "It was her car, sir. That's why."

"Who's to say that someone else didn't put it there? Someone who wanted to make Ms. Welter look like a killer?"

Kramer thought before he answered. "The car was locked."

"It was locked?"

"Yes sir. We had to use a shim to get into it."

"So you really did break into the car, didn't you?"

The detective squirmed. "Well, that woman wasn't there to open it for us. We had a warrant and had to get in."

"You're telling me it's possible for anyone to enter a locked car if they have the proper tool?"

Kramer looked past Stretch at Hogan. Finally, he said, "Sure. Anyone can break into a car if they know how."

"So anyone could have entered Ms. Welter's car and left the flashlight. Right?"

Kramer was trapped and didn't like it. He looked over at Hogan again, then back at Bruce. "I suppose that's possible."

"Do you know if Ms. Welter's car was locked at all times?"

The detective shuffled his feet as he tried to think of a good answer. "She doesn't seem like a person who would leave her car unlocked."

"But for all you know, she could leave it unlocked from time to time. Isn't that right?"

Kramer resigned himself to the answer. "She could."

Stretch took a step toward the witness. "And anytime the car was unlocked, it would be easy for someone who wanted to incriminate Ms. Welter to open the hatch and drop the flashlight where you found it. Right?"

Kramer nodded, his face blank.

"You've testified many times, sir. You know you have to answer out loud."

The detective pulled back and grunted, "Right. Someone might have put it there."

"And that someone could very well have been the unknown tipster, the one who sent you looking for it. Isn't that right, too, officer?"

Kramer glanced quickly at Hogan, then back at Bruce before he said, "I don't know about that."

"Don't try to be evasive and don't look at Mr. Hogan for help. Answer the question."

"I guess if the car was left unlocked, someone could have put the flashlight in there."

"And that someone could have been the unknown tipster. Right?"

The law officer ground his teeth but finally muttered, "Yes."

"And it could have been Donald Kastner, the man who threatened Senator Welter, couldn't it?"

The detective gave up trying to be evasive. "Yes."

"Or the vagrant, if the vagrant wasn't Donald Kastner?"

"Yes."

"Or even Governor Albert Shewey?"

Kramer directed a pleading look at Hogan. The county attorney rose to his feet as he said, "Objection!" Standing erect, he continued, "This is the second time that Mr. Bruce has insinuated that the governor had something to do with the killing of Gloria Angel. He should be admonished, Your Honor."

Stretch didn't move from the place he was standing. "It's a simple question. Could Governor Albert Shewey have placed the flashlight in Senator Welter's unlocked car? The detective should be able to answer a question as uncomplicated as that."

"Mr. Bruce is correct, Mr. Hogan. The objection is overruled." Turning toward the witness, the judge said, "Answer the question, Mr. Kramer."

Having swiveled his head to look at the judge, Kramer now jerked it back around, anger evident in his voice. "The answer is yes. Are you satisfied?"

Stretch chose to let it go and stood for a long time, just looking at the sheriff's detective. Then he asked, in a quiet voice, "And fingerprints, Detective Kramer. Did you find Senator Welter's fingerprints on the flashlight?"

Kramer's face was red as he tried to control his anger. "You've seen the reports. You know we didn't." He leaned forward and spat, "But she could have scrubbed them or worn gloves when she whacked the Angel woman."

"Or she may never have touched the flashlight. Right, sir?"

The detective sat back with his lips pressed together and took his time to answer. "Yes, Mr. Bruce. That's possible."

"Detective Kramer, you're correct in saying that I've seen the investigative reports. In looking through them, I found that forensics tests were conducted on the clothing of Gloria Angel. Mention is made in the reports of foreign fibers clinging to Ms. Angel's clothing, apparently fibers from clothing of others. Are you aware of the results of the tests for foreign fiber?"

"What do you mean, 'foreign fibers'?"

"Fibers that could have come from the clothing of the one who picked her up and pitched her over the railing—if that's what happened."

"I've read the reports. I don't remember anything about fiber tests but if you say they were there, I won't argue. "

"The fibers could lead to the one who killed Gloria Angel, couldn't they, sir?"

Kramer maintained a stoic pose. "Perhaps."

"All that needed to be done was compare the fibers with the clothing of those who might have come in contact with Miss Angel that evening. Was such a comparison made with any of the clothing of Governor Shewey?"

The detective shifted in the chair. "Not to my knowledge."

Stretch crossed his arms as he asked. "Wouldn't it have been a matter of good investigative practices to have done so?"

"Why do that? There was no reason to suspect the governor."

"He was in the capitol building that evening. Prudence would seem to dictate that all possibilities be pursued. Evidently that was not done. Am I right?"

Kramer was tired and angry. "If it ain't in the report, it wasn't done. That's all I can tell you."

"So are we to conclude that no attempt was made through forensics examinations to determine who, if anyone, pitched Ms. Angel's body over the balcony railing? No tests on the governor's belongings to determine if the fibers found on Miss Angel's clothing came from the governor? No tests to check the vagrant's hair or clothing. Not even any tests of hair or fiber that might have come from Audrey Welter. Right?"

"If the reports didn't mention any tests, I guess none were made."

"Another opportunity to learn vital information that was ignored. Is that right?"

Hogan squawked. "The man has said that's not his job. How can he answer such a question? I object, Your Honor."

Stretch looked from Hogan to the judge and smiled. "I withdraw the question, Your Honor."

As Stretch turned back toward the counsel table he scanned the faces of the jurors slowly. Then he leaned with his fist on the counsel table to whisper a question to Cynthia. She shuffled through her notes and shook her head. He smiled, stood erect and pivoted to face the bench. "I have no more questions for Detective Kramer, Your Honor."

Judge Hastings looked relieved. After a quick glance at the clock, he turned to Hefty and asked, "Any redirect, Mr. Hogan?"

The county attorney seemed to hesitate. He leaned toward Ellis Bradley who said something in his ear. Hogan shook his head. Bradley offered something else, and Hogan shook it off with a scowl. At last he stood and said, "No redirect, Your Honor."

Judge Hastings leaned back in his chair and turned to the jurors with a sigh. "I realize it's late—well past five o'clock. But it seemed wise to let Mr. Bruce finish his questioning of the detective. We'll be in recess until nine o'clock in the morning. Don't forget my admonition not to discuss the case as yet."

42

Plates pushed aside, they drank coffee and rehashed the day's events. Audrey laughed as she described Detective Kramer's efforts to pick up a limp woman. Turning to Cynthia, she giggled, "I thought letting your head loll toward the floor when he tried to pull you up by the arm was classic. But it might have been better if you'd let your mouth hang open and drooled."

Cynthia chuckled at the thought, and then shuddered at the memory of Hogan's hand on her. "What a creep," she muttered. After glancing at Logan, she looked at Stretch and posed the question that had been on her mind since the trial ended for the day. "What will Howard Welter say tomorrow when he takes the stand?"

Audrey was quick with the answer. "He'll swear that I said I'd kill Gloria Angel." She clenched her teeth as she shook her head. "Howard can't accept the fact that Gloria Angel made a fool of him, and he can't stand the fact that I've done fine without him. He's a bitter man." She turned a grief-stricken look at her son. "I hate it that you have to listen to me say such a thing about your father."

Logan slid the chair close to his mother and put his arm around her shoulder. "Mom, I know what happened." His hug was gentle. "I want you to understand about my feelings toward Dad. The foolishness with Gloria Angel was wrong and hurtful to you." He looked directly at his mother and added, "But I don't believe he killed her. It just isn't something he could do."

Audrey patted him on the knee. "I've said the same thing to Mr. Bruce. Howard just isn't a violent person."

Stretch waited in silence. When neither spoke again, he leaned Audrey's way. "I've asked before, but I'm asking again. Did you say in his presence that you could kill Gloria Angel?"

"Damn it, Stretch, I can't remember. I may have, but I don't think so." She took a deep breath. "It was a long time ago—in another world."

"If you said it, where would you have done so? In your home? In the presence of others?"

"Not in the presence of others. I'm certain of that. If I said it in his presence, it would have been in our home when I confronted him about his dalliance with that woman. I was just so damn angry at the time."

Stretch focused on Audrey for a long minute. Then he asked, "Can you handle it when your ex-husband is asked questions by the county attorney?"

"It won't be pleasant, but I can handle it."

"How about when I try to rough him up? Try to get him to contradict himself?"

Audrey's grimace showed her teeth. "Do your damnedest. It's my life on the line, not his."

Turning to Logan, he asked again, "Can you tolerate the kind of verbal abuse your father may suffer tomorrow? Or would it be better if you weren't in the courtroom?"

Logan shook his head as he spoke. "This whole affair has been painful for me. But I'm an adult. And Mom needs me there for support. I'll be in the courtroom."

Stretch nodded, leaned back, and changed the subject. "Of more importance will be the testimony of the other person who apparently heard you threaten to kill Gloria. What can we expect?"

"We can expect the witness to be Samuel Broeder." Bitterness was reflected in her voice as she added, "He was one of my close associates in the Humanities Department, and I thought he was a friend. I was so mixed up and distressed at the time that I really wasn't rational. And I needed to confide in someone. Fine friend! The next thing I knew, he was repeating the things I'd said to anyone who would listen." She added quickly, "And I did say in his presence that I could kill Gloria Angel. There's no denying it. And I won't try to deny it if Hefty Hogan asks me."

"Heat of passion." Stretch paused. "Most of us have said something in the heat of passion that we didn't really mean. But once said, there's no recalling, as we've discussed. We may or may not want you to testify. That decision will be made when the time arrives."

"Damn it, Stretch. I want to tell my story. No one else can do it for me."

"I understand." His smile was gentle. "But if asking you to be a witness will do more harm than good, we ain't a gonna do it."

Logan put his hand up as though to ask permission to interrupt. "Isn't that a problem though? Who else is there to testify for Mom?

"You've seen our witness list. We can call the security people to testify that the governor signed in that night and sneaked out. We can ask the State Land guy to tell of the threats that Robert Kastner made toward your mother. We have two people who will tell how Howard Welter was obsessed with Gloria. We can muddy the water. But we don't have the one witness we really need—the one who sent the email saying he or she could prove Audrey is innocent."

Cynthia mused, "There must be some way to find out who it is." She slumped in the chair, resigned. "I know. We've tried, and time is running out."

43

Stretch was surprised to see that Howard Welter, who'd refused to meet with him before the trial, didn't fit the man he imagined Audrey would marry. He was short, nearly bald with a chubby face, wore round-rimmed glasses, and flaunted a ragged mustache. His jacket and pants were rumpled. The knot of his tie was not centered at his throat. All in all, it seemed to Stretch that the man was trying to create the image of the proverbial college professor. Welter shuffled to the witness stand without a glance at Audrey. Nor did he look toward Logan who was seated in the audience section directly behind his mother. Once in the witness chair, he turned his head toward Hefty Hogan so that there wasn't a chance he might meet Audrey's gaze.

Hogan stood behind the counsel table and led him through the introductory questions, then asked, "You and the defendant were once man and wife. Is that correct?"

"That's correct." He managed not to look in her direction.

"You've been divorced for how long?"

"About three years."

"Was the divorce amicable?"

Howard Welter shook his head vigorously. "No. Not at all. It was very bitter on her part."

"By 'her,' you mean Ms. Welter?"

"I do."

Hogan glanced down at the notes on his tablet. "Is your former wife present in the courtroom?"

For the first time, Howard was forced to look directly at Audrey. "Yes, she's sitting by the tall lawyer."

Hefty turned his body partially toward the jurors while still facing the witness. "What caused Ms. Welter to feel the bitterness that you've described?"

Welter shuffled his feet and squirmed in the chair. "She seemed to think I'd been having an affair with Gloria Angel."

"Was that true?"

Howard attempted to draw himself up into indignation. "Of course not. Gloria and I were friends—nothing more."

Hogan waited for a long moment before turning directly to the witness. "At any time during your marriage, did Ms. Welter threaten Gloria Angel in any way?"

"Yes, sir. She did."

"What did she say?"

Stretch made the objection knowing it was futile, but he wanted to let the jury know this wasn't going to be easy. "Objection. Hearsay."

Hefty was ready. "Admission against interest, Your Honor. Exception to the hearsay rule."

Stretch rose to his feet. "Not so. An admission implies that an event has occurred. Even if Senator Welter made the kind of remark that the county attorney seems to be seeking, it could not have been an admission."

The judge looked at Stretch out of the corner of his eye. "I'll admit it. The objection is overruled."

Stretch was quick to speak again. "Objection on other grounds. Spousal privilege. One spouse can't testify against the other. It's even more sacred than other privileged statements."

Hogan's irritation was evident in the reddening of his face. "They're no longer married, Your Honor. The privilege doesn't apply."

Stretch again. "Oh yes it does! The remarks were made during the marital state. He just testified to that. The privilege survives the divorce. *Kemp v. Kemp.* Affirmed by the Supreme Court only a year ago, Your Honor."

Hogan waved his hand as though to brush away the objection. "She made the same threats to others. By doing so, she waived any privilege that may have existed." He stepped toward the judge's bench in his earnestness. "We'll bring one of the others in here to tell of those threats."

The judge shifted his eyes from Hogan to Bruce and back. "Assuming you will bring the other witnesses to testify to similar remarks, I'll let it in. Objection overruled." Turning to Welter, he said, "You may answer the question, if you remember what it is."

Howard turned to face the judge to listen, then turned back to Hogan. "I remember." He gave one quick glance out of the corner of his eye at Audrey without turning his head. "She said she could kill Gloria Angel."

Hefty Hogan decided to leave it on that note. "Nothing more from the witness, Your Honor."

Stretch was slow to rise from his chair. He stepped around the corner of the counsel table and stopped. For a full minute he stood with his arms crossed, staring at Howard Welter. Welter, seeming to anticipate the worst, tried to push himself back in the witness chair as far as he could go. When Stretch spoke, his voice was gentle. "So you and Gloria were just friends, is that right?"

Howard's eyes darted toward the county attorney, then back to Bruce. "Yes, that's what I said."

"But what you said wasn't the truth, was it?"

"What do you mean?"

"You were the one who told Audrey that you wanted a divorce because you were going to marry Gloria Angel, isn't that right?"

Welter's eyes darted to Hogan and then back to Stretch. "Well…" He rubbed his hands together as though to buy time. "Well, we did discuss marriage once." He hurried to add, "But it was only in jest."

"You mean that you and Miss Angel discussed the possibility of marrying one another. Is that what you're telling us?"

The darting eyes went to the jury and back. "Something like that."

"What you just told the county attorney isn't true, is it? When you said your wife asked for the divorce?"

Howard Welter turned and looked up at the judge as though asking for help. When he found no help there, he sagged in seeming resignation to his fate. "No. I was telling the truth. You see, when I told her about Gloria Angel, she grew angry and said she wouldn't put up with it and would divorce me." His face took on a haggard look. "She told me to get out and not come back." For the first time he looked directly at Audrey, then at the jurors and then back at Stretch. "You see, she owned the house. What could I do?"

"And that's all there was to the conversation, wasn't it?"

"At that time? Yes."

"Your wife didn't say she could kill Gloria Angel at that time, did she?"

A quick look at Audrey again. "No. Not at that time."

"And not at any other time in your presence, did she, Mr. Welter?" Stretch took a step toward the witness. "You're under oath, sir." He took one more step. "After that, you and Senator Welter were only together in the presence of your lawyers, right?"

Hogan was on his feet. "Objection, multiple questions."

Stretch looked at the judge and said, "He's right, Your Honor. I apologize." Turning his attention to Welter, he asked, "Did Audrey Welter ever say in your presence that she would kill Gloria Angel?" He stood quietly while Howard shifted in the chair. Then he again reminded the witness, "You're under oath, sir."

"Well, no. She didn't say it in my presence." Howard directed a hurried additional remark toward the jurors, "But she said it to others who told me."

Stretch backed away and stood with his coat held open by the hands on his hips. "So, sir, you weren't telling the truth when the county attorney asked you if you had heard Senator Welter say she could kill Gloria Angel. Right?"

"I guess so. But as I say, she told others."

"Not you. Just others?"

"Yes."

Stretch took a slow walk by the jury and around the counsel table to his chair, giving the jurors time to think about the county attorney's witness. Then standing with his hands on the back of the chair, turned again to Welter. "You were in Helena the day Ms. Angel was found dead, weren't you, sir?"

Welter swallowed hard. "Well, yes. I was in town." Before Stretch could ask the next question, he hurried to say, "But I didn't see Gloria that day."

"But you wanted to see her, didn't you?"

"No. No. I just happened to be in town. That's all."

Stretch waited again. Let him sweat. "Isn't it true, sir, that you were in your automobile behind the capitol late in the evening of Ms. Angel's death?"

Welter was perspiring. He pulled a handkerchief from his coat pocket and wiped his face. Once finished, he said, "Well, I may have been."

"You were there at the capitol, sir, because you hoped to find Gloria Angel. Isn't that true?"

The man shifted around in the chair. At last he admitted, "I probably thought it would be nice to talk to her again."

"And you went up to the east door of the capitol building and beat on it, hoping she would hear you and open the door, didn't you?"

Welter seemed to give up. He looked down, "Yes. I did that."

Stretch waited a long time before he asked the last question. "And she let you in, sir, didn't she?" Another long pause before he added, "And that's when you killed her."

Hogan was on his feet yelling, "Objection. That's not a question. That's an accusation of murder. That man in the witness chair isn't the killer. She is!" In his anger he started toward Audrey while pointing with his outstretched arm.

Bang! The judge's gavel smacked the bench and his voice when he spoke was loud. "Sit down, Mr. Hogan." Hefty stopped in mid-stride. The judge turned his attention to Stretch. "Mr. Hogan's correct and you know it, sir. The statement was improper. Mr. Welter is not on trial." Then turning to the jury, he said, "You are to ignore the statement just made by Mr. Bruce. It is not evidence, and you are only allowed to consider evidence during your deliberations. And only evidence presented in this courtroom." Then he looked to be certain Hogan was back behind the counsel table. Satisfied, he said to Stretch in his normal voice, "You may continue, Mr. Bruce, but please remember the rules."

"I will do that, Your Honor. And I have no more questions of Mr. Welter." Pulling the counsel chair out, he turned his head so the jury couldn't see his face, looked in Hefty's direction, and winked.

The Judge turned to Hogan. "Redirect, sir?"

The county attorney was on his feet, anger evident in his appearance and movement. He marched around the counsel table to stand directly in front of Howard Welter. Hands on his hips, he asked, "Did you kill Gloria Angel?"

Welter straightened in the chair, took a breath, held it for a second, and then blew it out. That done, he seemed to crumple downward once again. "I loved her." A tear formed in the corner of his eye. He took a deep breath and whimpered a second time, "I loved her."

Hogan seemed momentarily nonplussed by the confession. He waited, and then asked again, "Did you kill her, sir?"

Welter looked up at the county attorney and blinked his eyes as though attempting to grasp the question. It was a long ten seconds before he dropped his eyes again and answered in a flat, dull voice. "No."

Hogan, with an expectant look on his face, waited for more. When Howard Welter remained slumped in the witness chair, one tear coursing down his cheek, Hefty turned to the judge. "No more questions, Your Honor."

Judge Hastings turned to Stretch. "Re-direct, Mr. Bruce?"

"No, Your Honor."

The judge leaned toward Howard Welter and said, "You may step down, sir. And you're excused. You may leave the courtroom if you wish."

Welter wiped at his eye before sliding from the witness chair and stumbling through the gate into the audience section—without a glance at his former wife or his son.

It seemed to Stretch that a great deal of time passed while everyone in the room, including the judge, stared at the man as he trudged to the door. When he was out of sight at last, the judge shifted in his chair and looked back at Hogan to ask, "You have another witness?"

Hefty stirred himself, rose from his chair, and said, "The state calls Samuel Broeder."

Samuel Broeder was tall and burly. His long hair was tied in a ponytail. He displayed a drooping gray mustache. His dress, like that of Howard Welter, was rumpled. The shoes he wore looked like they had never been shined. But he smiled broadly at Hefty Hogan as the county attorney stood before him and asked about his background and education. Broeder came from a family of academics and spoke with pride of his undergraduate education at Princeton University and his graduate degree from Yale. He finished by turning to the jurors to say, "I received my doctorate from Stanford." The smile dimmed when not one juror seemed to be impressed by that statement. It brightened again as he turned back toward Hogan for the next question.

"Doctor Broeder, you know the defendant, Audrey Welter, do you not?"

"Oh yes, sir. Audrey and I are compatriots in the Humanities Department at the university and good friends."

"Do you see yourself as someone she would confide in?" The professor looked toward Audrey and smiled. She remained stone-faced as she returned his gaze. Broeder turned back to Hogan. "She often confided in me. Yes, sir."

"What, if anything, did she ever say to you about Gloria Angel?"

The professor shifted in his chair and turned to look at the jurors as he answered, "She said some pretty unkind things about Gloria Angel. The woman had destroyed her marriage, you see, and she was terribly upset."

Hogan turned to face both the witness and the jurors. "How upset, sir?"

"Well, I think it's fair to say she was furious."

"Furious enough to do what?"

Professor Broeder turned to stare at Audrey for a long moment, smiling as though he was asked to tell the time of day. Then he addressed the jurors. "She said she could kill Gloria Angel." He looked again at Audrey and shook his head, but the smile remained. She stared back at him, upright, and unmoving.

"How many times did you hear Ms. Welter say she could kill Gloria Angel, Doctor Broeder?"

"More than once." He peered upward in thought. "I believe she said it three times."

"In your presence each time?"

The witness vigorously nodded his head. "Only in my presence." Then before Hefty could stop him, "I never heard her say it when anyone else could hear."

"So, Doctor Broeder, Audrey Welter was extraordinarily angry at Gloria Angel. So angry she wanted to kill her. Is that your testimony?" Hefty sneaked a quick peek at the jurors as he finished the question.

"Objection. Mr. Hogan is mischaracterizing the testimony of the witness," Stretch said, rising from his chair.

Hogan's response was immediate. "Not so, Your Honor. Professor Broeder told us that Audrey Welter wanted Gloria Angel dead. He may not have used those exact words, but Ms. Welter's intent was clear."

Stretch looked toward the jurors and then at Hogan. "Ah c'mon, Hefty. The testimony was that Audrey said she could kill Gloria Angel. That's considerably different from saying, she wanted to kill her." Turning to the judge, he added, "The first is the kind of statement any person could make in a moment of pique or anger. The second seems to imply intent. There's a world of difference between the actual testimony of the witness and the words that Mr. Hogan is trying to put in Ms. Welter's mouth through the testimony of this witness."

As Hefty began his response the judge raised his hand to stop him. "I agree with Mr. Bruce." Turning to the jurors he said, "Please disregard the implication that was contained in the last question of Mr. Hogan. Bear in mind only the things the witness actually said." Then to the county attorney, he said, "Please rephrase the question, sir. Or ask another."

Hefty shoved his hands in his pockets and thought briefly. "She said she could kill Gloria Angel. There's no question in your mind about that, is there, sir?"

"Those were her exact words as I remember them."

Hogan returned to the counsel table. "No more questions."

Stretch shoved the chair back, rose, and stood for a long moment staring at the witness. Professor Broeder's relaxed pose disappeared, and he straightened in the chair as he waited for the lawyer to ask a question. His eyes fluttered from Hogan to Audrey and back to Hogan until they at last focused on the tall man standing before him. The smile weakened into a foolish grin. When Stretch Bruce finally spoke, the man gave a little start.

"So, Professor, you are a close friend of Audrey Welter. Is that your testimony?"

Broeder leaned forward as he answered. "Yes. Yes, that's what I said."

"In spite of that fact, you refused to talk to me about the testimony you would give when I called you on the telephone several days ago, didn't you?"

The man leaned back and clasped his hands tightly together. "I wasn't sure I should."

"Not sure you should help your good friend by telling her lawyer what you intended to say today?"

"No." He looked across at Hogan. "I wasn't sure the county attorney would approve."

"Did Mr. Hogan tell you not to discuss the matter with me?"

"Well, no. But he had told me my testimony was crucial."

"So, you understood that your testimony would be crucial to the county attorney's case—crucial in his attempt to convict your good friend of murder—and you didn't want to risk anything that would make your testimony less convincing. Is that what you're saying?"

"Objection!" Hefty was on his feet. "That's not what the witness said." He shook his finger at Bruce and barked, "He's been trying to confuse the jury ever since this trial began."

Judge Hastings frowned and, with his palm, signaled the county attorney to hold on. "You made your objection, sir. That's enough. We don't need any courtroom histrionics." Turning to Stretch, he said, "The objection is well taken and sustained, Mr. Bruce. Now, please continue with a proper question."

Stretch accepted the admonition with his usual nod and turned again to the man on the witness stand. "You've said you consider yourself a good friend of Audrey Welter. The kind of friend in whom one could confide?"

"Yes, sir. I'm certain she believes me to be such a friend."

"Didn't she confide in you about her marital difficulties with the expectation that the conversation would be held in confidence?"

Broeder's eyes widened, and he looked toward the jury with a sickly smile. Turning back to Stretch, with the smile still on his face, he responded, "Well, we had often shared confidences. It wasn't something new."

"When, in her pain and anger, she told you she could kill Gloria Angel, did you really believe, sir, that she expected you to speak of that comment to several of your associates on the university campus?"

The professor, smile gone, looked down as he rubbed his hands together. "Well, I guess I assumed she might have told others as well as me."

"That isn't what I asked. Did you believe Audrey expected *you* to tell others of her remark, a remark made in a moment of extreme stress?"

Broeder raised his eyes. "Well, if you put it that way, I guess she didn't."

Stretch moved around the corner of the table to stand directly before the witness chair. "No, of course not. She spoke to you thinking she could trust you, didn't she?"

"I guess so."

Stretch raised his voice. "But you violated that trust just as soon as an opportunity presented itself, didn't you? You told the first person you encountered that Audrey was going to kill Gloria Angel, isn't that so?"

"Not the first person. And I don't think I used those words—that she was going to kill someone." The smile was gone.

Stretch crossed his arms and watched Broeder's eyes blink rapidly as he waited for the next question. "Audrey Welter was hurt and angry when she told you all of this, wasn't she?"

The professor nodded his head vigorously. "Yes, sir. It was obvious that she was."

Stretch moved back to lean against the counsel table. "Professor Broeder, how long ago did Audrey tell you she could kill Gloria Angel?"

The professor raised his eyes to the ceiling in thought. "I believe it was three years ago." A pause. "It may have been four years ago. I don't remember for certain."

"If I told you that she and Howard were divorced three years ago, would that help?"

"Yes. Then it must have been three years ago that we had our talk."

Stretch moved a step closer. "At that time, you really didn't believe that your friend intended to kill Gloria Angel, did you?"

"Objection. The witness can't know what was in the mind of Audrey Welter. Calls for speculation." Hogan struggled to his feet as he spoke.

The Body on the Floor of the Rotunda

There was a note of patience in the voice of Stretch Bruce. "I asked if the professor really believed that Audrey Welter intended to kill Gloria Angel. He can answer that."

Judge Hastings face remained passive. "I agree. Overruled." Turning to the witness he said, "Please answer the question. Did you believe, at the time of your conversation, that Ms. Welter intended to kill Gloria Angel?"

Broeder turned his eyes from the judge to Bruce. "No. I never believed she would kill anyone." He looked at Audrey and added quickly, "She's too gentle. She never acts irrationally. She's too intelligent. She immediately engrossed herself in her activities at the university and here in the capital city. She simply put the matter of Howard's affair behind her and moved on." Turning to the jurors, he added, "It's the kind of person she is."

Stretch waited a long time before he turned to look toward the jury. After a second or two, he turned toward the bench to say, "I have no more questions for the professor, Your Honor."

The judge raised his eyebrows and asked of Hogan, "Redirect?"

Hefty fiddled with his pen for a moment, looked down at the notes on the pad before him and finally stood to say, "No redirect, Your Honor." After a long wait he turned from the witness to scan the jurors. Finally he shifted his eyes to the judge. "And the state rests."

Judge Hastings straightened in his chair, looked up at the clock, and then turned his attention to the jurors. "It's ten to eleven o'clock. I have things to discuss with the attorneys so we'll recess at this time. And my time will be occupied the rest of the day by an unexpected matter that demands my attention. So please enjoy the afternoon and return refreshed in the morning at nine o'clock. Remember my admonition not to discuss anything about this trial until I tell you it is all right to do so.

And don't forget my admonition to avoid watching anything on the television or read anything in the newspapers about the trial. Remember. You've been here in the courtroom. You know more than anyone else about the things that have happened. You don't need to hear it—incorrectly—from others." He stood and rapped the gavel. "We're in recess until tomorrow morning at nine." Glancing first at Stretch Bruce and then at Hefty Hogan, he said, "In my chambers, gentlemen."

The judge gestured for the attorneys to be seated as he shrugged out of his black robe. He sank slowly into the tall chair behind his desk and turned to Stretch to say, "I assume, Mr. Bruce, you have a motion to make."

"I do, Your Honor. The usual one. This time the motion has merit." He paused to glance at Hefty before speaking again to the judge. "I move for a not guilty directed verdict. Based on the evidence presented by the state, the jury can only conclude that there is reasonable doubt that Audrey Welter committed the crime with which she has been charged."

Hogan leaned forward to reply in a rush. "We've proven means, motive, and opportunity, Your Honor. The defendant had the means—the flashlight in her possession on which was found the blood of Gloria Angel. She had the opportunity—she was the last person to see Ms. Angel before she was killed. A scarf with the dead woman's blood on it was in her possession. And we heard she had the motive—Audrey Welter hated the woman who destroyed her marriage. Certainly the jury could, and I'm certain will, return a verdict of guilty—no matter what kind of case the defense may present." The county attorney sat back as he concluded, "The motion should be denied."

The judge had been resting his chin on his fist as Hogan spoke. Now he raised his head to look sideways at Stretch Bruce. "Your response?"

"The response is obvious. The only way the sheriff knew of the late night meeting of Audrey Welter and Gloria Angel was because Audrey told Mr. Hogan about it. Not the act of a guilty person. The scarf in Senator Welter's desk wasn't found during the first search. It was found during a second search only after some unknown person told the authorities to look again. That very person could have placed it in that drawer at any time between the first search and the second. There is nothing, other than the place where it was found, to tie it to my client. And the reasonable question to be asked is, 'Would a guilty person leave that scarf in the desk drawer, not hide it or destroy it?' The answer is obvious."

Hogan interrupted to say, "That's for the jury to decide."

Stretch sat patiently and listened, then returned his attention to the judge. "With regard to the flashlight, it, too, was only found after an anonymous tip. It wasn't found until several days had passed and under circumstances that defy the conclusion that Audrey Welter left it in her car. It was the only loose item the officers found in an otherwise orderly vehicle. Again, the tipster could have very easily placed it there with the intent to incriminate my client."

Hogan reiterated, "That, too, is for the jury to decide."

Stretch leaned forward with his elbows on his knees. "As far as motive is concerned, the jury heard only one witness who seemed to imply a motive. And that witness, the professor, admitted that he didn't believe Audrey meant it when she said in anger that she could kill Gloria Angel." He paused. "Three years passed between the time the remark was made and the death of Ms. Angel. If Audrey Welter's anger was so great as to really wish the death of the woman who destroyed her marriage, reason tells us she would not have waited three years to get her revenge."

Hogan started to speak but the judge stopped him with his

hand and straightened in the chair. "All that you say is true, Mr. Bruce. But Mr. Hogan is correct—these are matters for the jury to decide. Your motion is denied. Now, Counselor, how long do you think your case in chief will take?"

Stretch didn't hesitate. "Tomorrow and most of the next day."

"With time left to argue instructions?" The judge grinned as he asked.

"I doubt that, Your Honor."

"All right. We'll see how it goes." He leaned back and clasped his hands over his belt. "Except for a few minor lapses, you both have performed professionally. I appreciate that." Turning to Bradley with a warm smile, he asked, "Is the county attorney going to let you do anything? How can I find out how good a lawyer you are if you just sit at the counsel table taking notes?"

Bradley first looked at his employer, and then stammered, "There has been nothing for me to do so far, sir."

Hogan jumped in. "Ellis is a good lawyer, Your Honor. And he'll get his chance, but probably not during this trial."

"I'm sure he'll get his chance." The judge waved his hand toward the door to dismiss them. "Please be on time in the morning, gentlemen."

44

Stretch was tired. Since the press and everyone else seemed to have forgotten them, he suggested they eat the evening meal in the hotel restaurant. Both Audrey and Stretch ordered light meals and hardly touched their food. Logan and Cynthia ordered the evening's special, some kind of Mexican dish that Stretch didn't recognize. They both attacked it in a hungry manner. When the plates were cleared, and a cup of steaming tea was before Audrey and coffee before each of the others, Stretch looked across the table at Logan and said, "I'm sorry about your father. Listening to his testimony must have been excruciatingly painful for you."

Logan dropped his head and rubbed his hands up and down his thighs. When he raised his eyes to Stretch, the pain was obvious. "I wanted to run up there, grab him, and drag him out of that room. I wanted to do something—anything—to save him from all of that." Logan swallowed hard and shook his head. "But don't think I blame you, sir. You did what you had to do to save my mother."

Before Stretch could respond, Audrey broke in to say, "Seeing Howard being battered and humiliated was hard for me too, Stretch. I don't hate him. And I surely felt sorry for him before it was over and done."

Stretch looked from mother to son and back again. "In order to give the jury something to think about beside the evidence the state is presenting, I felt I had to make the case that someone else had the motive and the opportunity. Today that someone else just happened to be your ex-husband." After a slight pause, he added, "It wasn't fun for me either."

Audrey reached across to pat his hand. "We all know that. Don't feel badly about what you did. It was the cross examination the situation required. After all, my life is on the line."

Stretch leaned back in his chair and changed the subject. "Hogan's done. Has he made his case?"

Logan answered first. "He's done some of the things we always knew he could do. He placed the silk scarf in Mother's desk. And he placed the flashlight in her car. But he failed miserably in trying to prove that mother wanted to murder Gloria Angel. He didn't, in my view, prove that she had a motive."

Audrey nodded her head in agreement. "That's true." She smiled her appreciation at Stretch. "And it's because of your cross-examination that he failed." The smile broadened. "You've been wonderful throughout this whole ordeal, Senator. Even better than when you were blasting my proposals in the legislature. I especially liked the admissions you extracted from the sheriff and his deputies. It appeared that they did a sloppy job."

All eyes turned to Cynthia for her reaction. With her eyes on her hands holding her cup, she seemed reluctant to offer it. Finally Stretch said, "Please share your thoughts."

Cynthia raised her eyes and turned to look at Audrey. "Mr. Bruce did as he always does in court—he made the witnesses for the other side appear to be unreliable." Turning to Logan, she said, "I'm sorry he made things so hard for your father. But the fact remains that there is no other person we can pin the crime on. Not even your father, although Mr. Bruce intimated that he may have been the killer. The scarf and the flashlight with Gloria Angel's blood on them tie your mother firmly to the murder. No amount of cross-examination could change that. I wish it weren't so, but it is."

The Body on the Floor of the Rotunda   321

"Cynthia's right." Stretch shoved his coffee cup and saucer aside. "We begin to put on our case first thing in the morning, and we have some decisions to make." Stretch rubbed his hand across his forehead, wishing to relieve his weariness. "Should we call the State Lands fellow to testify? Or have we already taken care of the threat made by Kastner? Should we call the governor and try to make him look like a liar? Or would that only appear to be mean spirited when we can't really connect him to the killing?" Finally, he looked at Audrey. "And—the big question—shall I ask you to take the stand, and let you tell your story?"

Audrey touched his hand. "I've told you all along that I have to tell my story. And I'm prepared to do so. Now that I've watched Mr. Hogan in action, I feel that I can handle his cross-examination. I've seen the impression a witness makes when he loses his composure, and I believe I can retain mine." After a deep sigh, she said softly, "And it's really my task to convince the jury that I didn't commit murder." She looked hard at Stretch. "You can't do that for me. I must do it for myself."

Logan's face contorted into a look of agony. "God, Mom. Are you sure? Hefty Hogan will do his best to give you hell."

Audrey reached for her son. "I'm sure. But, if that man tries too hard, he may make the jurors feel sorry for me."

Stretch nodded. "I agree with you, Audrey. I'd hoped it wouldn't be necessary for you to testify, but it is. And I'm confident you will do well." After a glance from mother to son, he asked, "What sequence should we use in the testimony? Who should we call to the stand first?"

Cynthia spoke first. "The jury is just waiting for Audrey. All they want is to hear what she has to say. The other witnesses won't mean a thing to them until they've heard her. Once they hear her story, they may be inclined to look for someone else—possibly the governor—as the killer. She should be the first witness."

"I agree with Cynthia," Audrey hurried to say. "The verdict really depends on my testimony. I want to get on the witness stand, give that testimony, and be done with it. After that, the other witnesses might possibly lend support to the idea that I'm innocent."

Stretch used the table to push himself erect. "I agree. Audrey will be the first witness tomorrow morning. And there isn't any sense in going over the things you'll be asked. We've been over that time and again. What you need is rest—as do we all." Reaching for his client's hand to help her to her feet, he said, "But rest for you is the most important. Do you have a sedative you could take to help you sleep?"

"No, Stretch, I never use such a crutch. I just have to make it through tonight and tomorrow. Then it will be in hands of the jury—or maybe in the hands of God."

Alone in her room, Audrey brushed her hair as her mind ran to her former husband. Howard—the poor, sad soul. He didn't kill Gloria. He wouldn't have the gumption to do such a thing. She made a few more strokes with the brush, and then stopped. I thought I loved him once upon a time. Now I wonder why.

Just as Stretch was removing his tie, a knock came on the door to his hotel room. He turned the knob to find Ambrose Swan standing silently in the hallway. The old reporter handed him an envelope and muttered, "This appeared in my box at the capitol press room. I don't know who put it there." Then he turned and disappeared around the corner of the hallway.

45

Stretch and the others were huddled in the hotel suite after picking at the breakfast delivered by room service. On the table, amidst the debris of the meal, lay a copy of a single sheet of flowered stationery bearing the printed name "Gloria Angel" in the top left corner. The writing below the printing was in a feminine hand, neat and graceful.

> *Both Al and Henry have been milking the state for money—the governor from highway funds—the AG from the liquor funds. Neither of them knows for sure what the other is up to. Written proof of this is in a safe deposit box held in my name at the First National Bank of White Sulphur Springs. There is also a tape explaining how each one of them is getting it done.*
> *January 18 GA*

Cynthia asked. "Is that Gloria Angel's handwriting? Do any of you know?"

Stretch looked at Audrey who shook her head. "I've seen her handwriting on some notes, but I can't swear this is something she wrote." She picked up the paper, read it again, and then turned to Stretch to ask, "Who do you suppose could have given this to Ambrose? Why him? And why now?"

"Who knows? But right now I'm trying to figure out how to use it. If I try to offer this writing into evidence using Audrey as the vehicle, Hefty will object that there is no foundation, and the judge will agree. If we do as we've discussed and put the governor on the stand, I could ask him to identify the handwriting. Considering the things that writing contains, he'll deny that it's Gloria's writing and that it's a blatant attempt by someone to discredit him."

Cynthia reached across the low table to pluck the paper from Audrey's grasp. "For goodness sake, Mr. Bruce! Who could identify your handwriting? I could. So could Mary or Myrtle—the people who work in your office and see your handwriting every day. So who can identify Gloria Angel's handwriting? The secretary in the governor's office—the one who handles Gloria's correspondence. That person would have seen her handwriting on just about every piece of paper that came across the secretary's desk—whether it was a scribbled memorandum, her signature on a letter, or corrections to something produced by the secretary for Gloria's review. And probably on other things—notes from Gloria or jottings on sticky tabs." She looked at Audrey. "And I'm the one to find that person and get her to tell me what we need to hear—one poor secretary sympathizing with another." Cynthia turned to Stretch. "Once I get that secretary committed, you can put her on the stand to authenticate the handwriting on this note. Am I right?"

There was a look of skepticism on Stretch's face. "You think you can do that?"

Cynthia was on her feet, still grasping the handwritten memo. "Let me show you, sir." She grabbed her purse as she headed for the door. "I'll make a couple more copies of this to take with me. Then I'll bring this copy and a couple more back to you for safekeeping." And she was gone.

Logan half rose from his chair to go with her, but Audrey put out a hand to stop him. "She has to do it alone." Stretch was still looking at the door when Audrey added, "That's a mighty talented young woman. You're lucky to have her."

Stretch dropped his elbows on the table. "Don't I know it! But I don't know how she expects to get anyone in the governor's office to read that note and then swear its Gloria's writing. To do so would wreck the governor's political ambitions. And he's the boss up there."

Audrey reached to pat Stretch's arm. "I don't know what she has in mind, but she certainly seemed determined. I'm willing to bet she succeeds."

Stretch smiled and placed his hand over hers. "That's a nice compliment. I'll make sure Cynthia knows about it." He pulled his hand away as he leaned back with a frown. "But I still must find some way to get the writing before the court. I need a witness." He stared at the wall for a second, brightened, and turned to Logan. "Ambrose Swan! Would you go to the pressroom in the capitol and find him? Tell Ambrose I need him to explain to the jury how that piece of paper came into his possession. He should bring the original with him. And don't let him put you off. Tell him Audrey's fate may rest on his testimony."

Logan rose from his chair and put his hand on his mother's shoulder. "God, Mom. This may be the thing we've needed! Political corruption. A couple of other people for the jurors to focus on as the possible murderer instead of you!"

Stretch hated to dampen the young man's enthusiasm, but the need to be realistic remained. "We can infer that the information in the note could damage the governor so badly that he'd kill to keep it secret. But that's just another diversion. We're still stuck with the fact that we have no direct evidence that the governor or anyone else killed Gloria Angel."

Logan refused to be deflated. "It's something. Something is better than nothing."

"Indeed it is. And we'll use it if you and Cynthia are both successful." Stretch waved a hand. "Young man, be on your way."

Logan was out the door in an instant.

Stretch turned to Audrey. "This changes the way we had planned our defense. After you'd completed your testimony, it was my intention to put the governor on the stand and make him admit to his indiscretions—or lies—about his activities the night Gloria was murdered. The idea was to show that he had the opportunity to kill her. But if that piece of paper is authentic, we may want to present the authentication before we question old Albert Shewey. Can't decide that unless and until Cynthia does the job."

Audrey asked, "So what do you plan instead?"

"If we must, right after you, we'll go with the man from the Land Department. Have him tell of Robert Kastner's threats to you. Our strategy has to remain the same—try to show that there were others who had the opportunity, or the reason, or the means to kill Gloria Angel." He sighed. "It's risky because it doesn't allow the jury to focus on one individual as the alternative to you—as I've said a thousand times by now. But it's the best we can do."

Audrey clutched his arm. "Will it be enough? Tell me it will be enough!"

Stretch reached for her hand. "We must be confident that your testimony will convince the jury that you could not and did not kill anyone." He stood and looked down at her. "It's time we get ourselves to the courthouse."

Audrey appeared to be completely composed as she settled into the witness chair. With her hands resting on the chair arms, she smiled an almost imperceptible smile at Stretch.

"Ms. Welter, did you murder Gloria Angel?"

"No, Mr. Bruce, I did not."

"Did you have anything to do with her death?"

"No, sir, I did not."

Stretch moved along the counsel table to a place near the jury box. He wanted the jurors to see more of her face than just the profile. She turned her head to follow him, nodded to the jurors, and then shifted her attention back to her attorney.

He said, "You've heard other witnesses testify that you went to the county attorney voluntarily to tell him of your late night visit with Gloria Angel. Was that testimony substantially correct?"

"Yes, it was. I told him about that visit almost before the public was aware of her death."

"Why did you do that?"

"I thought it would be helpful to him to know about it right away—that it might help in the investigation into the cause of her death."

Stretch assumed a relaxed pose with his arms crossed and asked, "When you learned the sheriff wanted to search your office, did you object?"

Audrey shook her head. "No, sir. I told him to look anywhere he wanted—and he did."

"Without a search warrant?"

"Well, if he had one, he didn't show it to me."

Stretch nodded. "During the first search of your office, the sheriff found nothing of interest to him, did he?"

"No, he did not."

Stretch was pleased with Audrey's demeanor. She focused her eyes on him most of the time but would occasionally turn to speak in the direction of the jury. She appeared to be absolutely confident and forthright in her answers.

"What about the second search? What did the sheriff find in your office?"

"He found a silken scarf, plum-colored, under a pile of old legislative bills in one drawer of my desk."

Stretch stepped forward for emphasis. "Ms. Welter, did you place that scarf in the drawer?"

Turning to the jury, she answered, "No, I did not."

"Do you know who put the scarf in the drawer?"

Audrey shook her head vigorously. "No, I don't." Turning slightly toward the jury, she added, "I wish I knew who did."

Stretch stepped back beside the counsel table to break up the cadence of the questioning. "Were you ever served with a search warrant?"

Audrey Welter nodded her head. "Yes, I was. Some time after the death of Gloria Angel, I was served with a warrant allowing the authorities to search my automobile."

"And the flashlight that was found in your car when that search was made? Did you place it there?"

"No, Mr. Bruce. I didn't place the flashlight in my car. And I wish I knew who did."

"Had you ever seen it before?"

"No, never." Audrey shifted in the chair, crossed her legs, and ran her hand down her skirt in a reflexive action.

Stretch waited until she was settled again. "Professor Broeder told the jury that you said you could kill Gloria Welter. Did you say that?

Without any show of reluctance, she answered, "Yes, sir. I did say that in the presence of the professor. More than once. I was extremely distressed at the time."

"Were you angry?"

Audrey turned again to the jury. "Yes. I was very angry and upset."

"Did you really mean to kill Gloria Angel, even at the time you made that remark?"

"No, of course not. It was just one of the things a person sometimes says in anger." With a glance from one juror to another, she added, "Obviously, I wish I hadn't said it."

"Did you have any reason to kill Gloria Angel on the day of her death?"

"No. Of course not. By that time any anger I ever felt about her affair with my ex-husband was long forgotten."

Stretch waited a heartbeat for the jury to contemplate that statement before stepping closer to the witness. "Ms. Welter, tell us of your meeting with Gloria Angel on the night of her death. Why did you meet?"

Audrey dropped her eyes to her hands, then upward again. "She came to my office to discuss some thoughts I had about environmental legislation that I hoped the governor would convey to our congressional delegation."

"How long was she there?"

"She arrived at my office at about nine thirty and stayed less than half an hour. She looked at her watch as if she were preparing to meet someone and got up and left."

"Did you see where she went?"

The answer was again directed to the jurors. "No, she walked out the door without looking back at me. I heard the click of her heels as she walked down the hallway in the direction of the rotunda balcony. I never saw her again."

Stretch stood directly before the witness chair. "Ms. Welter, let me ask you again, Did you kill Gloria Angel that night—in your office or elsewhere?"

"No, Mr. Bruce, I didn't kill Gloria Angel." Audrey took a breath and continued, "She was a very talented person. Her death was a loss for us all."

Stretch glanced toward the counsel table, realized that Cynthia was elsewhere engaged, stopped to think for a minute, and then turned his eyes to the judge. "I have no more questions for Ms. Welter, Your Honor."

Hefty Hogan stood, stared a moment at Audrey, then swept around the counsel table to stand directly in front of the witness chair, a look of calculation on his face. "Ms. Welter, you and Mr. Bruce are romantically involved, aren't you?"

The question was so unexpected that Stretch was slow to his feet. Before he could get the word "objection" out of his mouth, Audrey—staring calmly at the county attorney—replied, "No, sir, Mr. Bruce and I are not romantically involved." Hefty inhaled to ask another question, but Audrey spoke again before he had the chance. "Why, Mr. Hogan, would you ask such a question? A question that has nothing to do with the death of Gloria Angel?"

The crimson color began at Hefty's shirt collar and moved slowly upward to cover his face and even his baldpate. He had expected the question to rattle the witness. Instead, the question he received in response left him speechless—for a heartbeat. His voice rose as he spat, "I'll ask the questions, you answer them. Got it?"

"Yes, Mr. Hogan. I understand the procedure." Audrey spoke calmly and quietly. "Please go ahead and ask your questions, sir. I'm prepared to answer them truthfully."

The county attorney had expected to catch Audrey off-guard, confuse her if not make her angry. He had hoped, just as Stretch had predicted, to get her to blurt out something damaging to her defense. Frustration at her careful and measured response was evident when he growled, "You're damn right I'll ask the questions."

Stretch was on his feet. "Objection, Your Honor."

The judge reacted slowly, and the county attorney seemed

not to hear Stretch's objection. Anger was evident as his voice grew louder, "You killed that woman, didn't you? Why don't you admit it?"

Audrey's reply was given in the same calm voice she'd displayed throughout her testimony. "I did not kill Gloria Angel." Turning toward the jurors, she added, "I've already told you that."

Hefty's huge body seemed to expand in size as his frustrations grew. "The scarf that was found in your desk is yours, isn't it? And you used it to wipe up the blood after you bludgeoned Ms. Angel with the flashlight, didn't you?"

"You've asked two questions, sir. I'll answer them in order." Turning to the jury, she said, "The scarf with blood on it is not mine. I had never seen it before I found it under a pile of bills in my desk drawer. And since I didn't bludgeon Gloria Angel with a flashlight, I didn't use the scarf to wipe up any blood."

Hogan's frustration grew to anger and was intensified by the quiet manner in which Audrey spoke. She was thwarting his attempt to make her lose control. He stepped closer to the witness chair and snarled, "You said you could kill Gloria Angel. And you did kill her, didn't you?"

Audrey turned to look at the jurors, one after another. Then she turned back to Hogan and answered patiently, "As I've already testified, I did not kill Ms. Angel." The look she gave him seemed to infer pity. "I did say I could kill Ms. Angel. I said it in a time of anger." She paused only an eye blink. "You are displaying anger now, sir. And I can't help but believe it's affecting your performance. It demonstrates how a person can do something in anger that he wouldn't do otherwise."

Hogan trembled as he moved even closer to the witness. His size made the movement appear menacing. He snarled, "You're trying to blame that woman's death on someone else, aren't you? Anyone else—even Governor Albert Shewey, aren't you?"

"I haven't accused anyone of murder, sir." She looked at Stretch, then at the jury, then back to the county attorney. "And, Mr. Hogan, if the kind of questions you have asked me are an indication of your legal ability, you certainly are not qualified to be the attorney general of the State of Montana."

Hefty Hogan clenched his fists and lunged toward the witness stand. It appeared that he was about to attack Audrey Welter. Stretch jumped from his chair, rushed around the corner of the counsel table, and grabbed at Hogan's coat sleeve. The bulky man jerked away and snarled over his shoulder at Bruce, "Get away from me."

At that moment Judge Hastings banged his gavel while half-standing. "Recess!" His voice was sharp enough to penetrate the county attorney's befuddled mind. Hogan stopped, looked startled, and seemed to realize what he'd done. The judge pointed at the attorneys. "It's eleven o'clock. We'll be in recess until one thirty." He gave the jury the customary admonition. Banging the gavel again, he ordered, "Gentlemen, in my office—immediately."

Stretch looked over his shoulder to see Cynthia and Logan coming through the doors to the courtroom. Both were smiling.

Judge Hastings did not display his usual placid countenance. First he pointed a finger at Hefty Hogan. "Ms. Welter is correct, sir. That is no way to conduct the cross-examination of a witness if you hope to extract a useful answer. You appeared to be on the verge of assaulting her. You've come close to forcing me to declare a mistrial. I'll have no more of it. Do you understand?"

Hogan's breathing was labored. Either unable or unwilling to answer, he just glowered at the judge. Ellis Bradley, believing he should do something but at a loss for what it should be, finally grabbed at the back of Hefty's jacket and said, "The judge asked a question, sir."

The gesture brought the county attorney's mind back from wherever it had retreated. He batted his eyes and then puffed, "Yes, Your Honor. I understand."

The judge, still scowling, added, "I suggest that you discuss your cross-examination with your deputy. He may help you decide if it is in your interest to question Ms. Welter any further. Perhaps he should do it, assuming Mr. Bruce doesn't object. But if you decide to ask more questions, your deputy may be able to help you frame them." Turning to the deputy county attorney, "Mr. Bradley, please share with your employer the impression that he is making upon the members of the jury."

The judge turned to focus on Stretch. "Mr. Bruce, your client has been impertinent in the remarks she's made to the county attorney. When you return to the courtroom, remind her—forcefully—that she is to answer questions, not to offer gratuitous observations." The unaccustomed scowl remained on his face as he added, "Gentlemen, when court convenes again, I expect professionalism from all of you."

Cynthia and Logan were telling Audrey of their success when Stretch joined them. Cynthia sparkled when she said, "I've got the secretary who can verify Gloria's handwriting. She's ticked at the governor and is about to quit her job. She's out in the hallway, ready to tell the court that this note is in Gloria Angel's handwriting."

Logan chimed in to say, "And Ambrose Swan will be here shortly. He was reluctant but agreed to testify if his testimony is important to Mom's defense. He said a conviction would be a real miscarriage of justice." Turning to his mother, he grinned. "I think he's enamored with you, Mom."

Audrey smiled in return. "Don't be foolish, Logan." Sober-faced again, she turned to Stretch and asked, "What was that all about? With the judge?"

Stretch gently grasped her upper arm for emphasis. "For one thing, he directed me to instruct you to just answer the questions. You are to stop making statements." He gave the arm a squeeze. "And he meant it."

"That man left himself wide open."

"I agree. But, Audrey, this isn't the State Senate where such exchanges are normal. This is a trial, and you are a witness. Your role is limited to answering the questions asked of you."

"All right. I'll be good. But it won't be easy to do if he continues to behave as he has been."

"Please be good. It's in your interest to do so." Stretch looked off into the distance. "Hefty's actions baffle me. Surely he must understand the detrimental effect his behavior could have on the jury." He paused and then asked rhetorically, "Can his desire to be attorney general be so compelling as to make him lose control like that?" Stretch paused before turning to Cynthia. "Good work in getting the handwriting witness. You'd better tell her we don't know how long it will be before she's to testify. Probably at least a couple of hours." He shifted his attention to Logan. "And it may be at least that long before we need Ambrose Swan." Looking from one to the other, he added, "But please ask them to stay close so we can call them whenever their testimony is needed."

46

The jury trailed back into the room as Stretch finished speaking. Hogan and Bradley moved to the counsel table from the far corner of the courtroom where they had been in intense conversation. The bailiff called, "All rise." Court was again in session.

Judge Milton Hastings resumed his place and spoke in his customary quiet voice, "Mr. Hogan, you may continue your examination of Ms. Welter."

Hefty, now calm of appearance, stood to say, "I have no further questions of the witness, Your Honor."

Hastings's face showed no emotion at the announcement. "Re-direct, Mr. Bruce?"

"None, sir."

"Very well. Ms. Welter, you may step down and return to your seat." To Stretch he said, "Call your next witness, Mr. Bruce."

Stretch stood. "I expected Mr. Hogan to take more time, Your Honor. May I have a couple of minutes? My next witness is, I believe, in the lobby. I'll go and get him."

"Please do."

Stretch leaned over the rail to whisper to Logan. "The governor's presence in the courtroom won't be required until late this afternoon. Please call the governor's office, make apologies, and explain that in any trial it's impossible to know with certainty when a witness will be needed." He searched in the trial notebook and scribbled on a scrap of paper. "Here's the phone number."

Standing next to the courtroom doorway, with a highway patrol officer hovering nearby, was Governor Albert Shewey. Stretch at first looked past him for Ambrose Swan, then did a double take and stared at the governor. Shewey, standing with his hands on his hips, glared at the lawyer. Stretch squared himself to face the man. "Governor, your testimony won't be needed for some time, probably not until late this afternoon. We have a call in to your office to let you know, but obviously, we're too late. I apologize for any inconvenience the delay might cause."

Anger covered Shewey's face. "You're damn right it causes inconvenience. I don't have time to waste on this accursed trial." He was breathing rapidly. "It doesn't interest me."

"Really? I rather thought you would have a concern for a fellow Democrat who has been so helpful to you with legislative matters."

That remark seemed to give the governor pause. "Of course, I like and admire Senator Welter." The scowl returned. "But I don't know what I can say that will help her."

"When the time comes, sir, just answer the questions truthfully. The truth may help." Stretch nodded and moved away.

Governor Shewey looked at the clock on the wall, then jerked his head for his driver to follow, and strode toward the stairway—nearly colliding with Ambrose Swan who was hurrying in the other direction.

Swan saw Stretch, grabbed him by the arm, and hissed, "Come with me." The old reporter then dragged the lawyer across the hallway to the men's room. When they were inside, Swan looked in each stall to ensure they were alone before leaning against the door to keep anyone from entering. His chest heaved from the exertion. After resting for a moment, Swan finally said, "I was afraid I'd miss you."

"What the hell's going on?"

"Who's your next witness?"

"You are. Why?"

Ambrose grabbed a lapel of the lawyer's suit coat. "Forget that. As soon as you get back to your table, I'll bring a woman into the courtroom. You call her as your next witness."

"Who is she? And what will she say?"

"Can't tell you right now. Just do as I say, and you won't be sorry. I promise." Swan dropped his hand from the jacket and brushed at the lapel as though to straighten any wrinkle he may have caused. He turned at the door. "Senator Bruce, if you sincerely want to help Senator Welter, get the woman that I bring to you on the witness stand. And once she's on the stand, just let her tell her story. You can do that, can't you? Just keep asking her, 'And then what happened?'" With that final instruction, he ducked out the door and down the stairs.

Stretch left the restroom and scanned the hallway. No one new was in sight. He stood frozen in confused contemplation. What the hell was that all about? No idea. But Ambrose Swan had been so consistently helpful, Stretch couldn't ignore him. He hustled back to the counsel table and said to the judge, "It will be a minute or two, Your Honor."

"I hope it isn't more than that, Mr. Bruce. We can't wait all day."

"I understand, Your Honor. I'm sure the witness will be in the room shortly." He dropped in the chair and leaned toward Audrey. In a quiet whisper and in as few words as possible he told her what had happened. "I'm not certain I should call the witness as he suggested, not knowing what she'll say. Whatever she says might be devastating to you. Perhaps I should ignore Swan's suggestion—but if I do, will we miss a bit of testimony that might be crucial."

Audrey didn't hesitate. "Do just what Ambrose says. He's

been trying to help me ever since Gloria died and especially since Hogan began to focus on me as the killer." Her voice was earnest. "Do exactly what he told you, Stretch. If it's wrong, I'll take the blame."

Stretch was still rolling the whole notion around in his mind when the door to the courtroom opened. Ambrose Swan ushered a tall, slender young woman into the room. With his hand on her upper arm, he led her to the gate through the barrier. She was neatly dressed. While her facial features were of youthful beauty, they bore the appearance of either consternation or fear. She looked at the judge, apparently expecting some guidance from him. Stretch quickly moved to her side and asked in his quietest voice, "What's your name?"

She turned, hesitated, and then replied, "Sylvia Partington."

Stretch pointed to the witness chair and said, "You'll need to sit there." Directing her attention to the clerk, he added, "The clerk will administer the oath. After that, go sit in the chair."

She nodded and gathered herself as she stepped forward, raised her hand, and listened as the clerk recited the oath. The response was a mumbled, "I do." She turned again to Stretch for reassurance. He gestured once more toward the witness stand. Her movements were graceful as she stepped up the one step and settled into the chair. The troubled look remained and her hands were clenched tightly together in her lap.

Stretch began with the usual request. "Please state your name for the court record."

Looking directly at him, she replied in a very soft voice, "My name is Sylvia Partington."

"Miss Partington, would you please speak a little more loudly so the jurors can be sure to hear you?"

In a little above a whisper, she replied. "I'll try."

"Thank you, please do. Where do you live, ma'am?"

Her voice gathered some strength. "My home is in Billings." She glanced at the jury. "I worked here in Helena for a short time last winter."

Stretch stood perplexed, wondering what to ask when there was no way of knowing what the woman wanted to say. Before he could ask any questions, Hefty Hogan rose to his feet to growl, "Sidebar, Your Honor."

The Judge frowned at the interruption, but nodded for the lawyers to approach the bench. When Hefty and Stretch were standing side by side at the end of the bench, Judge Hastings asked, "Well, Mr. Hogan?"

"I object to the testimony of this witness."

Stretch understood. Hogan was taken by surprise. And the witness was someone about whom he had no knowledge, a person who might destroy his case. He was stalling for time to figure out what was happening and what to do.

Hefty continued, "The existence of the witness was not disclosed prior to trial. And we've received no indication as to what her testimony might be. It's ambush, pure and simple, Your Honor, and should not be permitted."

Stretch groaned aloud. "Ah c'mon, Hefty. I only found out about this witness a few minutes ago. I'm not trying to ambush anybody."

Judge Hastings scowled at Stretch. "Mr. Bruce, you are to address the court and the court only. You know that."

Stretch presented the expected contrite expression when he answered, "I do, Your Honor. And I apologize."

Addressing Stretch again, the judge asked, "What is this young woman going to tell the jurors that will help them decide whether Ms. Welter is guilty or not?"

"The truth is, Your Honor, I don't know. But I'm confident she should be heard."

"You don't know? Aren't you running the risk of bringing testimony to the court that could convict your client?"

"I'm aware of the risk, and I'm willing to take it. And so is my client."

The judge shook his head. "Well, you're an experienced lawyer. I have to assume you know what you're doing." Turning to Hogan, Hastings said, "Isn't it your responsibility as county attorney to conduct a complete investigation? If this witness has information that relates to the guilt or innocence of Ms. Welter, shouldn't you have found her?"

Hogan refused to back off. "We conducted a thorough investigation, Your Honor. But we never heard of a Sylvia Partington from any source connected to the Angel murder." Then he hurried to add in a more strident tone. "At least we should be given time to find out about her. I move for a recess until tomorrow morning so we can do just that."

Stretch spoke quietly. "Let's listen to her testimony first. Then the county attorney will be in a better position to decide if he needs a continuance." With a glance from Hogan to Judge Hastings, he added, "And for the court to decide if one is warranted."

The judge pondered only a moment. "What Mr. Bruce suggests makes sense." Directing his gaze toward Hefty, he continued, "If, after listening to her testimony on direct examination a recess seems warranted, you can delay any cross-examination. And both the investigation and the cross should be more effective. They will be based on more information than you have right now, sir." Speaking more loudly so the jurors could hear, he said, "The objection is overruled. Mr. Bruce, you may continue asking questions of Ms. Partington."

At the counsel table Hogan leaned across to whisper to Ellis Bradley. Stretch chuckled as he guessed what was said.

Standing once more in front of the witness stand, Stretch wondered what questions to ask of Ms. Partington. He decided to take a guess. "You're here because you can tell the jury something about the death of Gloria Angel, is that right?"

"Yes, sir. That's correct."

She wasn't going to provide much help. "Why do you know something about Ms. Angel's death?"

"I worked as an intern in the office of the secretary of state. Gloria—Ms. Angel—and I got acquainted and then became friends. She seemed to take a liking to me because of my interest in the political process. I think I reminded her of herself at a younger age."

"How does your friendship with Ms. Angel help the jury in this case?"

Miss Partington dropped her eyes to her hands, squeezed her elbows against her sides, and looked as though she would cry. In a quiet voice, she said, "I saw her get killed."

Until that instant there had been silence in the room, broken only by the voices of the lawyer and the witness. The silence was instantly broken by excited murmurs. This is the kind of testimony the audience had been waiting for. The statement was just as unexpected to Stretch Bruce as it was to the others in the room. His first instinct was to look at Hogan for his reaction.

The big man's eyes were wide, and his face had gone a pasty white. Stretch could only guess what was going through Hogan's mind. If the witness said that someone other than Audrey Welter killed Gloria Angel, the testimony would destroy Hogan's case—and dash his chances to become the next attorney general.

Stretch returned his attention to the witness. "Can you tell us what you saw?" With the question Ms. Partington appeared about to dissolve into tears. Stretch asked gently, "Ms. Partington, would you like a few minutes to compose yourself?"

The young woman reached in a jacket pocket for a handkerchief. Tears began to flow. "Yes, please." She sniffled. "This is difficult."

Stretch turned to the judge. "Your Honor, may we have a ten-minute recess?"

Judge Hastings turned to Hefty Hogan for an objection. The county attorney sat motionless, staring with a slightly open mouth at the woman on the witness stand. When he didn't speak, the judge asked, "Mr. Hogan, any objection?"

Still Hogan sat, unmoving as stone. Ellis Bradley sensed that Hogan wasn't listening to the judge's inquiry. He half rose from the chair. "No, Your Honor. There is no objection."

The judge frowned slightly as he regarded Hogan. Then he turned to the jury. "Very well. We'll be in recess for ten minutes."

Stretch moved closer to the witness stand and spoke quietly to Ms. Partington. "You can step down and move around if you wish." When she didn't move, he asked, "How can I make this easier for you?"

She sniffled and wiped her eyes. "You can't, Mr. Bruce. I just have to get through it. I'll try to do better when we begin again."

"If you need another break, just tell me. I'll square it with the judge."

The sniffles seemed to subside as Ms. Partington blotted her eyes with a handkerchief. "Thank you for making it as easy for me as possible." Rather than bother her with questions or conversation, Stretch stepped away to allow time for Ms. Partington to compose herself.

In due course the bailiff escorted the jurors back to the box, and Judge Hastings climbed to the bench. He spoke softy to the woman on the stand. "Are you more comfortable now?"

She turned to face him, still wiping at her eye. "Yes, sir. And I'll try to do better from now on."

The judge smiled sympathetically and murmured, "You'll do fine." Then he turned to Stretch, who was standing before his counsel table. He started to speak but stopped, mouth half open. He'd noticed that Hefty Hogan wasn't where he belonged. He frowned and asked Ellis Bradley, "Where's the county attorney?"

Bradley stood. There was a touch of bewilderment in his voice when he said, "Your Honor, I don't know. He just stood up and said, 'I'm not feeling well. You can handle this witness.' And then he left."

"He left you alone? To continue the trial? With no more guidance than that?"

"Yes, sir."

Judge Hastings was obviously nonplussed. He leaned back in his chair and stared in thought toward the windows on the side of the room. After a full minute he returned his attention to the youthful deputy county attorney. "Mr. Bradley, do you feel comfortable doing what Mr. Hogan asked?"

Bradley pulled himself up a little taller. "Why, yes, Your Honor. After all I'm licensed to practice law. And I know how to cross-examine a witness."

Turning to Stretch, the judge said, "Mr. Bruce, we must find out about Mr. Hogan." He pointed at the bailiff. "Send someone to locate the county attorney. Bring him back here, if he's not incapacitated. If he can't come back, return and tell me what his condition is." After a moment of thought, he looked at Stretch. "Well, Mr. Bruce, since Mr. Bradley is comfortable with his new responsibility, you may continue to question Ms. Partington."

The young woman seemed more at ease. For that reason, so was Stretch. He put his hands in his pockets and asked, "Where were we?" Then he quickly added, "Ah, yes. You said you saw Gloria Angel get killed. Then I asked you to tell us exactly what you saw. Can you do that?"

The young woman took a deep breath. She raised her eyes to look at Stretch and asked, "Can I just tell you what happened in the way that I want to?"

"Of course, you can." He waited for her to speak. When she hesitated, he asked, "Perhaps you can start by telling us why you were in the capitol the night Ms. Angel was killed."

Sylvia took another long breath. "I wanted some quiet time and a quiet place to work on my master's thesis. So I stayed at the secretary of state's office late that night. About ten thirty I needed to use the restroom. I found Gloria in there. We visited in the usual way but when she reached for the door, Gloria held up a sheet of paper she was carrying and said, 'This is insurance. I may need it sometime.' I didn't know what she meant."

Sylvia Partington shifted in the chair. "A little later I came down the corridor from the secretary of state's offices and had just reached the outlet into the rotunda when something high up near the balcony caught my eye. I looked up and saw her body roll over the fourth floor railing." The tears came again. The handkerchief dabbed at her eyes. "I saw the clothes she was wearing—the clothes I'd just seen on her in the rest room. I saw her hair blowing outward as she fell. And then I saw her body hit the floor." More tears fell, and she choked, "My God! It was awful. The sight of the body falling—just—falling. It seemed to take forever." She gulped. "And then the sound. God! The awful, sickening sound when her body struck the tile." Ms. Partington struggled for composure for a few seconds, glanced toward the jurors, and then continued to speak in a soft voice. "I had no way to know she was dead before she went over the rail. But I was certain she couldn't have survived the fall—the crushing blow when she landed." Looking directly at Stretch, the young woman pulled her body erect. "Then I looked up and saw a man leaning over the railing, watching to see where she landed."

The great temptation was to ask, "Who was the man?" But Stretch remembered Ambrose Swan's admonition. He simply asked, "What did you do then?"

She shuddered. "I was frightened. I was scared the man might have seen me. And I knew if he saw me, he might recognize me. I knew if that happened, I'd be the next one he killed."

"What did you do?"

"I ducked back into one of the doorways in the corridor leading back to the secretary of state's suite."

"And then what did you do?"

"I thought of the paper Gloria showed me. Her insurance. And I wondered if it might still be in her office." She glanced again at the jurors. "I waited a long time. After awhile, when I hadn't heard or seen anything more of the man who dropped her off the balcony, I dashed down the other corridor to her office in the governor's suite."

"How did you get in?"

"I had a key. Sometimes I'd helped Gloria with political matters. She had a key made so I could fetch things for her."

"What did you find when you got into Ms. Angel's office?"

"She kept her personal papers, along with matters relating to her work, in a file cabinet. But I found nothing in the cabinet. A small bag she sometimes used to carry spare footgear was by her desk. For some reason, I opened it. No shoes were in it, but the covering on the bottom was askew. Under that covering I found a single sheet of paper with her handwriting on it. The writing told of things the governor and the attorney general were up to."

Now Stretch knew who delivered the paper to Swan. He picked up the copy Swan had given him, walked to the witness stand, and handed it to Ms. Partington.

"Is this a copy of the paper you found?"

After little more than a glance, she said, "Yes, sir. That's a copy of the paper I got from Gloria Angel's bag that night."

"Where is the original?"

"Earlier today, I gave it to Ambrose Swan. I felt confident he would get it to the official in government who should have it. Everyone at the capitol seemed to trust him—even the legislators who always complained so much about the press."

Stretch went back to the counsel table and carried another copy of the paper to Ellis Bradley and handed a third to the judge. Before either Stretch or Sylvia Partington could speak, Bradley was on his feet. "Sidebar, Your Honor?"

The judge didn't even hesitate. "More than a sidebar is needed, Mr. Bradley." Turning to the jurors, he said, "We'll be in recess for fifteen minutes. Remember my admonition." Turning to the lawyers, he grunted, "In my office, gentlemen."

Stretch said quietly to Ms. Partington, "This won't take long. You can get down from that chair if you like. But you're still a witness, under oath, so please don't leave the room."

As soon as the door was closed, Judge Hastings asked Stretch. "What's going on here, Counselor?"

"Your Honor, Ambrose Swan came to me at the last break and said he had a witness crucial to this matter. He didn't tell me her name or anything about her." He glanced at Bradley. "Earlier today he'd given me the copy of that sheet of paper. At the time I didn't know how it came to be in Swan's possession. Ms. Partington just testified that it came from Gloria Angel's office. My paralegal has found a secretary familiar with Gloria Angel's handwriting who will testify that the writing is hers."

Turning to Ellis Bradley, the judge said, "You asked for a side bar. What for?"

"Your Honor, Mr. Bruce is about to offer this..." He glanced at the sheet in his hand as though wondering how to characterize the writing, "this scrap of paper into evidence. I strongly object. Neither the piece of paper itself nor the writing upon it tells us anything that will help the jury decide the guilt or innocence of the defendant." His voice became more urgent. "And to make this writing public is to accuse the governor and attorney general of political corruption or worse—without any foundation or basis in fact."

Stretch's head was moving from side to side. "Your Honor, the writing shows a strong motivation for someone other than Audrey Welter to kill Ms. Angel. Otherwise why would she have told Ms. Partington the writing was 'insurance?'"

Bradley was young but not slow. "She could have meant insurance against job loss. Or insurance against the disclosure of something detrimental to her—an illicit affair—criminal activity."

Stretch's response was immediate. "What Mr. Bradley says would be true if Gloria Angel hadn't been murdered right after she characterized the writing as insurance. She must have known she was in some danger because she knew about the shenanigans of the two highest officials of this state."

Bradley inhaled to respond, but stopped when the judge held up his hand. "Mr. Bruce, do you intend to offer the writing into evidence?"

"Yes sir. I do."

"Then, Mr. Bradley, you may offer your objection for the record at that time. But you need to know that I will allow the exhibit. I'll allow it, but only as something found among Gloria Angel's possessions that may have a bearing on her death. Not, however, as something that speaks the truth about the activities of the governor and attorney general. And I'll so instruct the jury." Nodding toward the door to indicate the two lawyers should leave, he added, "Now, let's reconvene."

With the judge back on the bench, Stretch handed the "insurance" memo to the clerk and said, "Please mark this as the defendant's first exhibit. Then, with the memo in hand, he said to the judge, "I offer Defendant's Exhibit A into evidence."

Bradley spoke his objection with fervor. Judge Hastings overruled the objection. Then he leaned toward the jury box and took some time to explain the purpose for which the jurors might consider the writing on the paper. He then gave great emphasis to his explanation that they could not assume that the statement on the paper with regard to the governor and the attorney general was true—it may in fact be untrue. He stared at the jurors one by one, evidently to be certain they understood. At last he turned to Stretch Bruce to say, "You may continue, Counselor."

Stretch asked, "May I circulate the exhibit to the jury at this time, Your Honor?"

"You may."

The jurors were ready and anxious. He handed the sheet of paper bearing the writing of Gloria Angel to the juror seated closest to the bench. Then he stepped back to watch as it was passed from hand to hand. The expressions on the faces of the jurors as they read the writing ran from wonder to disgust. When the paper came back to Stretch, he returned it to the clerk. He resumed his position in front of the witness stand and smiled at Ms. Partington. "Before the recess, you'd told us about finding the paper that the jurors have just seen. What did you do after that?"

"I intended to leave the governor's suite." She looked quizzically at Stretch. "You know how the wall at the entry to the suite has a darkened window on each side of the door?"

"Yes, ma'am. It has."

"Just as I reached for the door handle, a flicker of motion coming through the window caught my eye. I stepped back away from the door into the gloomy part of the entryway, hoping that the person on the other side hadn't seen me." Ms. Partington turned to face the jurors. "But my curiosity was too great. It made me sneak up to the window and take a peek."

She glanced back at Stretch and then turned to the jurors. "The man from the balcony was in the corridor right outside the door. He was shining a large flashlight on the floor like he was looking for something."

"What did you do?"

"I just watched. After a minute or so, he apparently found what he was looking for and dropped to his knees to scrub on the floor with a colored cloth."

"Can you describe the cloth? What color was it?"

"Objection." Bradley was showing that he knew what to do in court. "Multiple questions."

Stretch looked at the youthful deputy county attorney and then at the judge. "Of course, Your Honor. Mr. Bradley is correct. I asked two questions. Let me try again." Facing Sylvia Partington, he asked, "What color was the cloth?

"It was dark and hard to see. But the cloth appeared to be a kind of purple color."

Stretch glanced at Audrey. She was wide-eyed and sitting erect. He scanned the faces of the jurors before walking to the clerk's desk and picking up the scarf that Hogan had offered into evidence. Turning to the witness, he said, "I'm showing you what has been marked as State's Exhibit 9. Does this cloth resemble the one you saw being used to scrub the floor that night?"

Bradley was up again. "Objection, Your Honor. The witness has already testified that it was dark in the corridor. She also said that the color only *appeared* to be purple. That being the case, Mr. Bruce is asking for speculation on the part of Ms. Partington."

"I'm not asking her to speculate, Your Honor. I've simply

asked her if this exhibit resembles the cloth she saw the night Gloria Angel was killed. That's a yes or no question. She can answer it without speculation."

Judge Hastings nodded. "Objection is overruled."

Stretch turned his attention back to the witness. "You may answer the question, Ms. Partington. Does this cloth resemble the one you saw that night?"

Sylvia Partington pulled the plastic exhibit bag close. She smoothed a wrinkle from the plastic for a clear look at its contents. After turning the bag over twice, she looked up at Stretch. "The color appears to be similar. It could be the cloth I saw that night."

"But you're not certain?"

"No, Mr. Bruce. I'm sorry. I'm not certain it's the same."

Stretch returned the exhibit to the clerk's table. Back before the witness, he smiled and said, "Thank you for your candor. We don't want to give the members of the jury any misinformation." He folded his arms and returned to questioning the witness in the way Ambrose Swan had suggested. "What did you do after that?"

Ms. Partington dropped her eyes to her hands, which were clenched tightly together in her lap. "I continued to watch. The man turned as he rose from the floor so that some light fell on his face. I recognized him." She squeezed her eyes closed and shuddered. "God! I was terrified. That man had just killed a woman, right there in the capitol. He had influence and political power—the power to find me if he knew what I had seen. And I knew if he found me, he'd kill me just as surely as he killed Gloria." She looked up again at Stretch. "But, Mr. Bruce, it kept getting worse. When I read that Senator Welter was charged with the killing, I thought I had to do something. So I sent her an anonymous email saying I knew she didn't do it. But then I read about the flashlight, and all I could think about was that great big man battering Gloria with it." She turned to the jurors. "Please understand. I've been terrified ever since that night." Turning back to Stretch, she explained, "I finally decided that if I told my story here in court, he wouldn't be able to do anything to hurt me. So I went to Ambrose Swan to arrange it."

Stretch's head swiveled quickly to determine if the jurors heard her soft voice. Each one was leaning forward so as not to miss a word. So he asked the question that everyone in the room had waited for. "Who was the man?"

Ms. Partington seemed to recover, sat erect, and with a jab of a finger, pointed in the direction of Ellis Bradley. "He was sitting there—at that table—when I first came into this room." Looking back at Bruce, she added, "I recognized him from pictures on the television. He's the county attorney. His name is Hefty Hogan."

Absolute silence had permeated the room as every person strained to hear her quiet voice. When the crowd saw her point and heard the name, a rumble of conversation began and grew quickly to a roar. One reporter jumped from his seat and fled out the door, apparently in a rush to be first with the news.

Judge Hastings pounded repeatedly with the gavel, first while sitting and then after rising to his feet, all the while shouting for quiet. At length the banging of his gavel and his shouting seemed to penetrate the consciousness of those in the audience, and a semblance of quiet returned. When he next spoke, still on his feet, the judge's voice reflected his anger at the breach of courtroom decorum. Pointing with the handle of the gavel, he fumed, "I expect everyone who attends court to observe the rules. That includes the spectators." He scanned the entire courtroom to make certain each person got the message. In a calmer voice, he looked toward the lawyers and added, "It's near the end of the day. I think it would be wise to break at this time." Speaking again to the jurors, he added, "We'll recess until nine o'clock in the morning. Remember my admonition. Do not discuss with one another anything about the testimony that you've heard so far in this trial. And don't discuss it with anyone else either. I'll tell you when you're free to do so." The judge then turned his attention to Miss Partington. "You are still a witness, so please be here in the courtroom tomorrow morning." He gave the gavel one final smart rap and mumbled, "Gentlemen, my office."

Stretch turned to look at Audrey. Her hand covered her mouth, and the look in her wide eyes was one of surprise and sudden understanding. Logan, with a broad grin, was on his feet and reaching over the railing to squeeze her shoulders.

Cynthia was gently patting her arm. As Stretch watched his client, her body slowly seemed to collapse until she slumped over the table, arms crossed. Her head dropped onto her arms, great sobs shook her body.

47

Stretch and Ellis stopped near the doorway and heard the judge barking to his clerk, "Get the sheriff in here. I need to know what's happened to Hogan."

Judge Hastings turned and walked slowly to his chair where he seemed to fall into it—robe still in place. The scowl that had darkened his face began to relax. He gestured for the two lawyers to sit. When each was settled, he asked of Stretch Bruce, "I asked before, but I'll ask again. How long have you known what that young woman would say?"

"I heard it at the same time you did, Your Honor. As I told you, Ambrose Swan brought her to me and told me to put her on the witness stand."

The judge then turned to Ellis Bradley. "I don't suppose you had any prior inkling about the testimony we just heard?"

Bradley seemed shell-shocked. It took him a second to focus and respond. "No, sir." He began to recover his presence of mind to add, "And I don't believe that Mr. Hogan was the one that woman saw—*if* she really was in the capitol and *if* she saw anyone do what she described."

The judge's eyebrows went up. "You think she lied, just now?"

"Your Honor, I've worked for Mr. Hogan for more than a year. I don't believe he would hurt a woman. It just isn't his nature."

Turning to Stretch, the judge asked, "If he did it, what would be the motive? No man commits murder without a reason—

especially a lawyer who is a county attorney. Do you know of anything that would lead Hefty to bludgeon Gloria Angel?"

"Nothing of which I'm certain." Thoughts flew through Stretch's mind. Should he say more? Perhaps. "The sheriff told me about Ms. Angel's appointment book. It showed that she had dined with the county attorney several times and always at out-of-the-way places. Hefty may have had a romantic interest and discovered it wasn't reciprocated."

Fire crackled in Bradley's voice. "Speculation of the worst kind."

Stretch nodded. "I agree. It's nothing but speculation. And I won't voice it anywhere but in this room."

The judge leaned forward with his elbows on the desk. "Please don't, Mr. Bruce." He looked upward at the clock on the wall. "Well, we can't let this trial go any further without the county attorney." He turned to stare at Bradley as though in thought. "I suggest that you convene all of the lawyers in your office to discuss what has happened. You and the chief deputy may have a decision to make before tomorrow morning." Turning in his chair, he gestured toward the door. "You can go, gentlemen. Someone will let you know when the Sheriff finds Mr. Hogan."

The moment the judge left the courtroom, five reporters rushed forward to yell their questions at Audrey. Logan stepped aggressively in front of the nearest one, dropped his head into a fighter's stance, fists balled at his side, and growled, "Get the hell out of here, and leave my mother alone!"

That man backed away, but the obnoxious blogger tried to push past while yelling at Audrey, "How much did you pay that woman to lie?" It was a mistake. Logan grabbed the smaller man by the neck of his jacket and the seat of his pants and frog-marched him out the door—to the amusement of all of the other news people. Outside the courtroom, Logan gave one final heave that sent the obnoxious one sprawling near the top of the stairway. He lay there screaming, "I'll sue you!" After watching that spectacle, the more reasonable reporters decided they really didn't need a quote from Audrey after all. They had the testimony of Sylvia Partington. It would be good press to include a description of Logan's handling of the blogger in the report on the day's happening.

Stretch returned from the judge's office to find Audrey, Logan, and Cynthia waiting in the nearly empty courtroom. Without speaking, he grabbed Audrey's arm, waved for the others to follow, and led the small parade through the remainder of the crowd, down the stairway, and out of the courthouse. On the sidewalk, he took Audrey's other arm and said, "They haven't found Hefty Hogan. He isn't in his office, and he isn't at home. The judge gave the sheriff orders to scatter his men and search until they find him."

Audrey's tears had dried, and she seemed almost giddy. She reached for his lapel and said, "She saw him, Stretch. That woman saw Hefty Hogan kill Gloria Angel." She jerked on the lapel. "Don't you realize what that means? It's over for me, Stretch! It's over! I'm off the hook. The sheriff knows who the real killer is." She reached for the other lapel and pulled. "They'll have to dismiss the charges against me. Isn't that correct?"

Stretch looked down at her upturned face and smiled. "God, I hope so." Then the smile faded. "But Audrey, we won't be certain until we hear what Hogan has to say. He may have a perfect alibi for the time when Gloria was killed."

Audrey dropped her hand from his coat, her face crumpled. Logan reached around her shoulder. "Mr. Bruce must be realistic and so must we. But I'm going to assume that Hogan is the murderer until something proves otherwise." After a second of thought, he continued, "The evidence showed some large man killed Gloria Angel, not a tiny woman. Sure could have been Hogan. Could have been the governor."

Audrey appeared to recover and smiled at her son. "You're right, Logan. We'll assume it's over for me."

Stretch hated himself for bursting her balloon. "The judge said he'd let me know when they find Hefty. Let's go to the hotel so I can be near the phone. That's where they'll call me."

Turning to Stretch, Audrey said, "Okay, Counselor, to the phone. We'll hope the call, when it comes, will be good news."

It was a long wait. After half an hour Stretch suggested that the others go to the dining room for the evening meal. He wanted to stay near the phone. Audrey would have none of it. She wasn't leaving the room until they received some information.

Logan spoke up. "Come with me, Cynthia. We'll eat and leave these two to wait for the call." Turning to Audrey, he ordered, "Ring room service, Mom, and get some food delivered. It won't help anything to starve."

Stretch and Audrey sat in uncomfortable silence until the food arrived. Audrey arranged the two plates on the small table. When they were seated, she dropped her eyes, took one breath, and looked at Stretch to ask. "Would you be offended if I pray?"

Stretch shook his head as he clasped his hands. "Of course not. Please do."

Audrey lowered her eyes again and murmured, "Blessed Lord, we thank you for this food and for all of our blessings. I thank you for giving me my son who means the entire world to me. And, Lord, I especially thank you for sending Mr. Lynn Bruce to care for me when I've needed his care so desperately. And please, if I'm not asking too much, Lord, let this horrible burden that I have had to bear come to an end tonight." She paused and then whispered, "Amen."

Stretch echoed, "Amen." Raising his eyes, he allowed his lips to turn up in a faint smile. "Thank you for allowing me to try to care for you. I hope you realize that you've become precious to me—much more than any client—more than a fellow senator."

A touch of pink crept slowly up Audrey's neck. She reached across the table and covered his hand with one of hers. "That's awfully nice to hear, Mr. Bruce. And I've become very fond of you." To cover her embarrassment, she pointed at the food and said, "Eat up, Senator, before it's all cold." The blush made her even more attractive to Stretch.

It was almost nine o'clock when the young people returned. Before either Audrey or Stretch could comment, Logan grinned at his mother. "I was certain you would want me to treat this lovely lady properly. So we had a before-dinner nudge, a leisurely meal and then returned to the lounge to listen to some old-time cocktail music played by a really good pianist." He nodded at Cynthia. "She even tried to teach me to dance."

Cynthia was glowing as she looked up at her companion. "He dances skillfully. It was fun." She turned to Stretch. "I hope you don't mind, Mr. Bruce."

"Of course not. We've just been sitting here looking at the telephone. There's no need for four of us doing the same thing. Go on back down and dance some more."

Audrey looked at Logan and ordered. "Do as you're told. Show Cynthia a good time. We both owe her."

At last, the call came from Sheriff Mendenhall. "We finally found Hogan. He wasn't in his office or at home. No one seemed to know where he went. I remembered he once told me he liked to drive to a spot north of town where he could park and look out over the valley. He said it was a place to go when he needed uninterrupted time to think. I drove out there and found him."

After a long pause, the sheriff continued. "He was dead. In his car. Used a pistol to do it."

"Jesus, Sheriff!" Stretch looked at Audrey and mouthed, "Hogan's dead."

"Exactly my feeling when I found him" Mendenhall said. "The forensic people are there now. They'll bring the body in when they're finished."

"Was Sylvia Partington correct? Is that why he did it? Because he killed Gloria Angel?"

"That's my guess, but I don't have any way to know right now."

Stretch asked, "Have you told the judge?"

"First thing. And Ellis Bradley. The judge said you're to show up at the courthouse at eight thirty in the morning so we can sort it all out."

"We'll be there. And thanks, Sheriff, for the call."

When he finished repeating the things the sheriff said, Audrey asked the rhetorical question. "Why else would he have killed himself?" And then she smiled. For the first time since her ordeal began, the smile was the carefree one that Stretch had found enchanting the first time he saw her. "I'm certain of it now. I will no longer have to awaken in the night, terrified. No more nightmares and horrible visions of life in the penitentiary."

48

The group listened attentively as Sheriff Brent Mendenhall explained. "I found the hand-held voice recorder beside him on the seat of his Tahoe." The sheriff pushed the "play" button. A rambling voice, recognizable as Hefty Hogan's, began a monologue.

"That woman was a witch. When she'd get me in the bedroom, she could make me believe anything. I really thought she cared for me. I believed we'd soon be married. But she always had a reason why we had to wait. That very evening, I told my wife I wanted a divorce. When Gloria called and told me to meet her in the capitol building, I thought she was ready to set a date. How dumb could I be? She let me in the east door on the south side of the building at about eleven o'clock. It was a black night so I used the flashlight to follow the sidewalk to that door. She met me there, near the door to the governor's suite. Then she told me she was going to marry Henry Sawyer. I couldn't believe it. I told her I'd asked my wife for a divorce. She threw back her head and laughed at me. When she stopped laughing, she told me she'd never marry someone like me—someone who'd never be anything more than an insignificant county official. She said she was going to take Sawyer to the governor's office and then to the United States Senate. He had the makings of a great man, she said. And I did not!"

There was a long period when only the sound of heavy breathing could be heard. When Hogan's voice returned it seemed to carry a hint of a plea for understanding. *"I just lost it.*

I couldn't help myself. I hit her hard with the flashlight. The minute I did it, I was sorry. I wanted to take it back. God! All of a sudden she was no longer a beautiful woman, just a lifeless, crumpled body lying on the floor. Blood ran from the corner of her mouth. I knew she was dead before I even touched her."

After another silence, Hefty's voice continued, faster. *"I panicked. All I could think of was some way to hide what I'd done. And then I thought of the balcony over the rotunda. If I dumped her body over the railing, it would look like she fell and that the fall killed her. I had a hell of a time picking her up—her body just kept sliding out of my arms. I had the damn flashlight that I didn't dare leave behind. Once I dropped it in the blood from Gloria's mouth or nose or ear. Blood was coming from all of them. I finally got her draped over my shoulder and climbed the back stairs to the fourth floor. I thought I'd have a heart attack before I got there. It took all my strength, but I managed to push her over the railing."*

When his voice was heard again, it carried a sense of resignation. *"I watched her land, then I looked around to make sure no one saw me. How was I to know the Partington woman was lurking out there somewhere?"*

A long time passed with no sound. The listeners began to think that was the end, but then Hogan's voice continued. *"I may as well tell it all. Before I pushed her over the edge, I took the scarf from her neck and dabbed at the blood from her nose and mouth. Have no idea why I did that. The blood outside the governor's suite had to be cleaned up, so I ran down the stairs, used the flashlight to find the blood spots, and scrubbed at them with the scarf. When I'd done as good a job as I could, I thought I heard someone. I panicked. I ducked into the stairwell and hurried back up to the third floor. Once there, I just opened a door at random, pulled out a desk drawer, and hid the cloth under a big pile of paper. And then I got the hell out of there.* The voice stopped, but leaning closer, the group could hear sounds that seemed to be the shifting of Hogan's body before his voice continued.

"Once I got outside, I couldn't believe I'd been so dumb. As soon as someone found it, they'd know the fall wasn't an accident. They'd start looking for the killer. I didn't sleep a wink that night. But I didn't dare go back to get it." There was a short pause. His voice when it came back sounded weary.

"I thought luck was with me when Stretch Bruce and Senator Welter came to my office the next day. She told me that Gloria had been in her office earlier the night before. Right after that, I learned that it was Welter's office that I'd left the scarf in. I was ecstatic! I had a way to shift the blame—to get out of it. When the scarf wasn't found on the first search, I drove to the library in Bozeman and borrowed a computer. Then using a fake name, I sent myself the email about the scarf. My good luck seemed to hold when Senator Welter let the sheriff look for it in her desk without a warrant. How could I be so lucky!"

The tape was silent except for a soft sniffling sound. Then the voice continued. "I still had the flashlight and realized it could be the clincher. I thought I'd have to force my way into her car sometime in the night. But I was lucky again. The next day, when the Senate was in session and lots people were coming and going, I stopped by her car in the capitol parking lot and checked the door. It was unlocked. No one noticed that I opened the hatch and dropped in the flashlight. Then I sent the second email. The judge issued the warrant to search her car. With all that luck on my side, I was sure I could convict her."

There was a sound that could have been a bitter laugh or a sob, and then, "I'm sorry as hell for all the problems I created for Audrey Welter. And for Sheriff Mendenhall. Maybe I always knew I wouldn't get away with it. And I can't face my wife." There was a period of silence followed by a rustling sound. "There's no other *way out now…so this is it."* After those last words there was no more background noise—no sound at all It was apparent that Hogan had shut off the machine.

Wrapped in silence, Judge Hastings, Brent Mendenhall, Stretch Bruce, and Ellis Bradley reflected on Hefty Hogan's last words— each of them caught up in his own musings. How did it all go so wrong for the man? What kind of woman would take pleasure in causing so much heartache? What of the governor and the attorney general? The press had already spread the news of the "insurance" memo. Their careers were likely at an end.

The judge finally broke the silence and turned to look at the deputy county attorney. "Have you discussed the situation with others in your office?"

Bradley had been sitting with his elbows on his knees and with his head hanging down. Now he looked up at the judge. "Yes, Your Honor. We talked it over last night and again this morning. We agree there's nothing to do but dismiss the charges against Audrey Welter. The chief deputy asked me to handle it." He turned to direct his next remark at Stretch. "And we all regret the ordeal she's had to endure. Please convey that message to her, will you?"

Stretch nodded, appreciating the gesture. "Of course I'll tell her." Then he turned to the judge. "How do you want to handle it? Should it be done in open court?"

The judge rubbed the knuckles of one hand with the palm of other. "Mr. Bradley could prepare the motion for dismissal, and I could sign it here in the office." After a pause, he continued. "But we have to let the members of the jury know what happened, so let's call the jury and reconvene. Mr. Bradley, you can then make the motion for dismissal, perhaps with an explanation of the reason. I'll grant it, as part of the court record." Leaning

The Body on the Floor of the Rotunda

toward Bradley, he added, "It might be a good idea to tell the jurors about this recording so they understand that there is no question that Mr. Hogan committed the crime—not Audrey Welter. Once that's done, I can dismiss the jurors." Turning to Stretch, he asked, "Is that acceptable, sir?"

"It certainly is, Your Honor."

"Where is your client now?"

"She's waiting in the courtroom. And she's anxious to know what is to be done. May I go and tell her?"

"You may." Leaning back in his chair, the judge swiveled toward Mendenhall. "Good work, Sheriff. Not the most pleasant job, I'm certain, but good work, nevertheless. Now please ask the bailiff to fetch the jury." He pushed the chair back and added, "I'll see you all in the courtroom shortly."

Stretch smiled when he reached his client. "It's over, Audrey. And it will be official in a few minutes." In an instant she was on her feet. Ignoring both the jurors and the anxious crowd, she reached to put her arms around his neck. When he put his hands on her shoulders to stop her, she seemed to remember they were in a very public place. Audrey stepped away from Stretch, turned to her son, and pulled him close for a warm embrace with her face pressed against his chest. At last she released Logan from her grasp and turned again to Stretch. "Thank you Stretch Bruce. Thank you more than you can ever understand."

Stretch placed his hands on her shoulders and whispered, "It's finished. You can go on with your life."

The bailiff called, "All rise. Court's in session."

Judge Hastings climbed the two steps slowly, straightened his robe, and sank into his chair. He scanned the jury box before turning to Ellis Bradley with a nod, "Mr. County Attorney, you may proceed."

Bradley stood, took a deep breath, and announced. "The

state moves to dismiss the charges heretofore filed against Audrey Welter—with prejudice." He turned to the judge. "May I explain, Your Honor?"

"Please do, sir."

Turning to the jurors he continued, "Members of the jury, after we adjourned yesterday it was learned that County Attorney Hugh "Hefty" Hogan committed suicide. Sheriff Brent Mendenhall retrieved a voice recording of Mr. Hogan's last words. On it he admitted killing Gloria Angel and explained the reasons why he did it." The sound of muttering and shuffling came from the audience, but the jurors, without exception, remained erect, attentive, and sober-faced. "That being the case, the State is required to dismiss the charges against Ms. Welter, and it is only proper to do so."

Bradley shifted his attention to Audrey. "Ms. Welter, you cannot know how much I regret the ordeal you've suffered because we charged you with a crime you didn't commit. All I can do is apologize for each and every one of us in law enforcement." He bobbed his head in her direction, in a kind of abbreviated bow. Then turning again to the judge, he said, "I have nothing further, Your Honor."

A couple of reporters scrambled from the courtroom as Judge Hastings looked at the jurors and intoned. "Let the record show that the charge of deliberate homicide and all other criminal charges, if any there be, heretofore lodged against Audrey Welter, are dismissed with prejudice." Directing his full attention to the jurors, he added, "Your duties as members of the jury in this case are at an end and you're free to leave. The clerk of court will ensure that you receive pay for your service." He added, "I want to thank you for serving as jurors. And, frankly, I'm glad you didn't have to decide the fate of Senator Audrey Welter."

Shifting toward Audrey, the deep lines on his face formed

into a smile. "You are released from all the restrictions I imposed upon you, ma'am. And I join with Mr. Bradley in expressing regrets for the burden you had to bear." He nodded at Stretch "Fortunately, you found an excellent lawyer to represent you." Judge Hastings reached for his gavel. "I wish you well from this time forward." With that final statement, he rapped the gavel and rose to his feet. "Court's adjourned."

Logan was through the gate and hugging his mother before the judge was out of the room. Then he turned and grasped Stretch's hand with both of his. "The judge is right, Mr. Bruce. Thank God my mom found you."

He got no further. Two reporters, one from the local paper and one Stretch didn't know, arrived and began asking questions, each interrupting the other. Stretch stepped between them and Audrey with his arms outstretched and said, "No questions of Senator Welter right now. If you wish to wait in the anteroom, I'll take your questions in a few minutes." He pointed at the doorway for emphasis.

Stretch noted with some surprise that Ambrose Swan didn't approach to ask questions. He wasn't even in the room.

He couldn't help but smile when he turned again toward his client, to see Logan and Cynthia locked in a tight embrace.

Audrey and the others waited in the courtroom while Stretch dealt with the news folks. A television camera from a local station was set up in the lobby. The crew from the television station and four print reporters were standing by. He was surprised by the first question. "Why did that girl, Sylvia Partington, wait until the last minute to tell her story?"

"It's my understanding that she was afraid to talk about it for fear Mr. Hogan would hunt her down and do to her what he did to Gloria Angel."

"But why did she go to Ambrose Swan?"

"She said she felt she could trust him." He didn't add that Ambrose was not like most reporters who want to splash anything they learn across the front page of the paper as soon as possible.

"Where is Ambrose?"

"I've wondered the same thing myself. But I'm sure he's still with us and will turn up when there's real and interesting news to print."

The rest of the questions had to do with Audrey's reaction to Hogan's death and confession. Stretch answered them for a time, then stuck up his hands and said, "That's all. I have things to do, and you need to go get the whole story on newsprint and on the airways."

They trudged back down the hill from the courthouse toward the hotel, lugging bags of trial material. Logan was ecstatic, and Cynthia reflected his mood. "This calls for a celebration!" They said it almost in unison.

The little group reached the entry to the hotel. Logan grabbed Cynthia's hand and headed for the saloon, whooping over his shoulder, "Come on, Mom. And you too, Mr. Bruce. I'll buy the first round."

Audrey shook her head. "I need time to recover, but you two go ahead." She glanced at Stretch. "Besides, my attorney and I have some things to discuss."

Cynthia gave Stretch a questioning look. He reached for the trial briefcases that Logan had been carrying and smiled over his shoulder at her. "Be gone, Ms. Weaver. And toast Audrey's release from purgatory."

Cynthia's smile, when she grabbed Logan's hand, was so bright it sparkled. She teased, "Will you buy the second drink, too?" They dashed for the door.

Carefree youth, Stretch thought, smiling.

In Stretch's room, he and Audrey dropped the trial cases

onto the floor. As Audrey straightened, she found herself face to face with her former Senate colleague. With eyes locked, neither of them said a word for a full minute. Then Stretch reached with one hand and pulled her to him. With the knuckle of his finger under her chin, he raised her head and leaned down to kiss her. Audrey didn't respond for an eye blink. Then, as though allowing her emotions to take control, she raised herself up on tiptoes, wrapped her arms around his neck, pressed her body to his, and returned the kiss with passion.

But it didn't last. She pushed herself away, looking down and then back up. On her face was a wan smile. "It wouldn't work, Stretch. No matter how much I may wish, it just wouldn't work."

"Why not? God knows how much I care for you."

"And I care for you. And I wish it could work." Audrey sighed a long sigh. "Think about it, Stretch. I'm a creature who's grown comfortable in a university atmosphere. I just couldn't live in a town as small as Roundup." As he started to respond, she put her finger to his lips. "And you wouldn't even think of moving to Missoula where you'd have to start a law practice all over again. And even if you're willing to do that, you'd never be satisfied in the company of the university people I associate with." Another sigh. "It just wouldn't work."

"But you just said you wished it could work."

"I do, Stretch, I do. You're the finest, nicest, most lovable man I've ever known." She dropped her eyes and nearly giggled. "Once I told you of my fantasy that you sneaked into my bed." Eyes upward once more. "The truth is that I've done it over and over again." She reached to stroke her hand down his cheek. "I could love you, Stretch Bruce, like no man has ever been loved." She shook her head. "But we're not children anymore, we're middle-age people. We've lived in two different worlds, and those worlds have shaped us beyond change at this point in our lives.

Neither of us would be happy in the world of the other."

"How do you know I'd be unhappy in your world?"

"While we've struggled together with the Gloria Angel affair, I've really come to know you. You like the place where you live. You like the clients and the law practice that you have. All your real friends are in Roundup. And you like being the senator from Musselshell County." She smiled upward at him. "You're a small town guy, Stretch. There's no use in denying it."

Stretch Bruce's long body seemed to slump in sad acquiescence. He took a deep breath and blew out a huge sigh. "I suppose you're right." He reached for her upper arms. "You aren't the only one with fantasies." With a sad shake of his head, he mumbled, "Maybe those fantasies will have to be enough for both of us."

She stroked his cheek again. "You'll find someone. You're a catch, sir. Half the women who work at the legislature wish you'd at least give them a chance."

Stretch had to laugh in turn. "All the women who work in the legislature look at me and see a boring old man."

She gave his cheek one final pat and changed the subject. "You may lose your favorite paralegal. Do you realize that?"

"Who? Cynthia?"

"Who else? You haven't seen it? Logan hasn't said a word to me about it, but I know my son. He's in love—seriously in love."

Stretch rubbed his brow. "What about Cynthia? Does she love him?"

"We'll see. But I'll bet he asks her to marry him before you and Cynthia leave this town. And I'm just as certain that she'll say yes."

Stretch jammed his hands in his pockets, and his shoulders slumped in resignation to the inevitable. "And he won't want to live in Roundup either."

"Not a chance. She's going to leave you. You'll have to find someone else to take her place."

With a look of gloom, he said, "I'll never find someone to take her place. She's irreplaceable." The gloom changed to a wan smile. "But I hope you're right. They really are an attractive couple. And I'm certain Logan would treat her the way that she deserves. And she deserves the best." A brief look of concern crossed his face. "But she has a son. What about that?"

"Logan's ready. He's ready to take the package. And so am I."

Stretch stood for a long time staring at his client. The look on his face was one of sadness when he said, "I wish it could be a double wedding. But you're probably right. I guess it wouldn't work."

Audrey reached for his neck again, stood on tiptoes, and kissed him gently on the lips. "Thanks for all you've done for me, Senator Bruce." She stepped back and hesitated before turning away. "I need to rest a bit before I start for Missoula. And you need some time alone." At the door she added, "We will always be friends, Stretch." Audrey Welter stepped through the door and pulled it closed, leaving Senator Bruce forlorn and alone in the room.

Afterword

Logan asked, and Cynthia accepted. She would leave in two weeks. Mary was expecting another child and told him she planned to be a stay-at-home mom when the baby arrived. Of the three legal assistants upon whom he had relied so heavily, only Myrtle would remain. It was close to six o'clock in the afternoon. Stretch slumped at the desk, contemplating another lonely evening in the large house east of Roundup. Uttering an enormous sigh, he stood, shrugged into his sport jacket, and turned to see Myrtle, the probate paralegal, standing next to the jamb of the open door. Without preamble she said, "We need to talk."

"Myrtle, please come in and have a seat." Stretch returned to his chair.

The slender woman sat primly, took a deep breath, and spoke in a rush. "Mr. Bruce, I've never stuck my nose in your personal business before, but now I feel I must."

"What do you mean?"

"You've done nothing but mope since you got back from the Welter trial. It's obvious that you have fallen in love with Ms. Welter, and it's foolish of you not to do something about it."

Stretch stared in silence at the woman with whom he'd spent so many days, weeks, months, and years. Never had she mentioned anything so personal to him. At last he mumbled, "I didn't realize that my feelings for Audrey were obvious. But what can I do about it? She doesn't want to live in Roundup. I'd have a hard time accustoming myself to life in a university atmosphere. And I'd have to start a new law practice from nothing."

Myrtle scooted the chair closer to the desk. "Mr. Bruce, those of us who work for lawyers visit with one another. I talked on the phone with the probate paralegal for the Sullivan Law Firm in Helena—you know—Sullivan, Lawrence, and Wallace. They're looking for an attorney who has experience in agricultural law. She heard the senior lawyer say that if they could entice you to move to Helena, they'd bring you in as a full partner right from the start."

"That's interesting and even flattering. But why would I want to go to Helena? My life is here and Audrey would still be in Missoula." He paused and smiled. "And what would I do without you?"

"Mr. Bruce, I'm getting older." She waved a hand. "Shucks, I'm old. And I'm ready to take some time to smell the roses." She leaned forward with her hands on her knees. "Think about it, sir. You're losing Cynthia and Mary. They'll be difficult to replace. I really want to have some time to relax—maybe travel—before I die. If you are ever to make a move, now is the time to do it."

Stretch nodded his head without much enthusiasm. "I guess I can think about it."

"Do more than think about it. Get on the telephone and ask Audrey Welter if she could live in Helena." Myrtle rose from the chair. "Now, I've done what I said I would never do. I've butted into your affairs." She stood with her hands on her hips and looked down at him for a second. "Mr. Bruce, you are dying of the lonesomes. And from all I can learn, that lady is worth pursuing. Don't let her get away. You can handle any legal work for your Musselshell County clients from an office in Helena if necessary. And, if you ever really needed me, I could still help with any estate administration that may come your way from old friends in this town." With a frown she pointed. "There's the phone. Call her." Myrtle disappeared out the door.

Stretch sat for a long time wondering if there was any chance at all that Audrey would consider a move to Helena. Finally, he decided the only way to find out was to ask. Just as he reached for the phone, he heard it ring in the outer office. Mary was gone so he picked up the receiver and muttered, "Law office of Lynn Bruce."

"Stretch? This is Audrey." Before he could respond, she added, "I've been offered an administrative position at Carroll College in Helena." As Stretch inhaled to speak, she continued in a rush. "Would you consider moving there?"

"If you were there, Audrey? I surely would."

"Then meet me at the Colonial tomorrow, Senator. We'll begin to turn those fantasies into reality." Warmth flowed through him at the sound of her throaty laugh. "And I can hardly wait!"

Acknowledgments

This is a much better book because of
the contributions of others.

Thanks to everyone who read the manuscript
and offered advice and encouragement.
Special thanks to:

Sheriff Jim Cashell for reviewing the manuscript
and making helpful suggestions about law enforcement,

Deputy County Attorney Eric Kitzmiller,
who spent time on the manuscript and corrected
my criminal procedure mistakes,

Florence Ore, who spent many hours with
the manuscript and gave constructive suggestions,

Kathleen Mohn for her editorial expertise
and professional comments and suggestions,

and—as always—thanks beyond measure to Janet Muirhead
Hill for turning a long unwieldy narrative into
a readable story and publishing it.